HOUSE OF TRIBES

Also by Garry Kilworth

GARRY KILWORTH
HOUSE OF TRIBES

BANTAM PRESS

LONDON · NEW YORK · TORONTO · SYDNEY · AUCKLAND

TRANSWORLD PUBLISHERS LTD
61–63 Uxbridge Road, London W5 5SA

TRANSWORLD PUBLISHERS (AUSTRALIA) PTY LTD
15–25 Helles Avenue, Moorebank, NSW 2170

TRANSWORLD PUBLISHERS (NZ) LTD
3 William Pickering Drive, Albany, Auckland

Published 1995 by Bantam Press
a division of Transworld Publishers Ltd
Copyright © Garry Kilworth 1995
Illustrations © Paul Robinson

A catalogue record for this book is available
from the British Library.
ISBN 0593 033760

Typeset in 10/13pt New Baskerville by
Falcon Graphic Art Ltd,
Wallington, Surrey
Printed in Great Britain by
Mackays of Chatham plc, Chatham, Kent.

This book is for Suzi Sutherland,
a singer of songs.

ACKNOWLEDGEMENTS

My grateful thanks go: to Bernard Hall and Reg Mason for the superb plan of the 1930s style house, providing me with a map of mouse country; to Barbara Faithfull for the excellent key to the map; as always, to Andrew, for sparking off ideas during our regular Friday-night Indian take-away meals; to my agent, Maggie Noach, and to Patrick Janson-Smith, whose encouragement during this project was invaluable, even to a seasoned writer; and finally to my beloved Annette, who has had to put up with talk of mice during breakfast, lunch and dinner for over a year without complaint, and indeed offered much helpful advice on various aspects of the story.

TO A NUDNIK

Great, grabbin', snatchin', greedy beastie,
'O what a gob wi' which tae feastie!
Thou need na guzzle awa sae hasty
  Wi' slobbering jaws!
I canna scoff as snell as thee can
  Wi' these sma' paws!

A sudden oral outburst from
Snurb-the-rhymer (Bookeater Tribe),
after gnawing on a book of Scottish poems

Cheese rhymes with *greed*, almost.

Old House Mouse saying

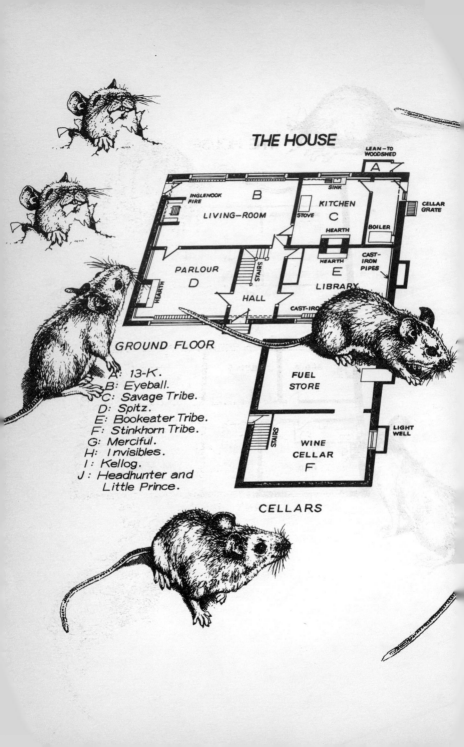

THE HOUSE

GROUND FLOOR

LEAN-TO WOODSHED

A

SINK

KITCHEN

C

STOVE

HEARTH

BOILER

INGLENOOK FIRE

LIVING-ROOM

B

HEARTH

CAST-IRON PIPES

PARLOUR

D

HEARTH

STAIRS

HEARTH

LIBRARY

E

HALL

CAST-IRON

CELLAR GRATE

A: 13-K.
B: Eyeball.
C: Savage Tribe.
D: Spitz.
E: Bookeater Tribe.
F: Stinkhorn Tribe.
G: Merciful.
H: Invisibles.
I: Kellog.
J: Headhunter and
   Little Prince.

FUEL STORE

STAIRS

WINE CELLAR

F

LIGHT WELL

CELLARS

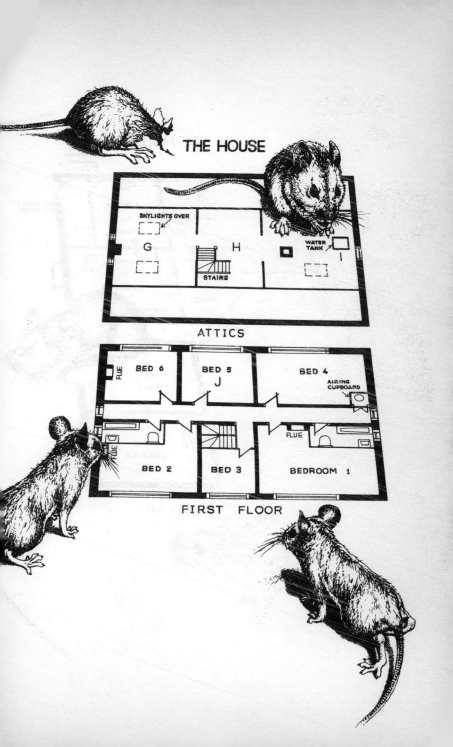

THE HOUSE

ATTICS

SKYLIGHTS OVER

G   H   I

WATER TANK

STAIRS

FIRST FLOOR

FLUE

BED 6   BED 5   BED 4

J

AIRING CUPBOARD

FLUE

FLUE

BED 2   BED 3   BEDROOM 1

LIST OF PRINCIPAL CHARACTERS

OUTSIDERS

PEDLAR   Yellow-necked hedgerow mouse, hero of the novel, a wandering mouse.

TINKER   Pedlar's cousin in the Hedgerow.

DIDDYCOY   Old yellow-necked Hedgerow sage.

STONE   Dormouse, lives by the garden privy, a Green who advocates getting-back-to-nature.

TUNNELLER   Common shrew who lives in a maze of tunnels underneath the house, bad-tempered and a ruthless fighter.

ULUG BEG   Ancient unknown species of mouse, hermit who lives in an abandoned tree-house in the garden.

SAVAGE TRIBE (KITCHEN MICE)

GORM-THE-OLD — House mouse, chieftain of the Savage Tribe, barbarian and thug.

ASTRID — House mouse, high priestess of Savage Tribe, talker to shadows.

HAKON — House mouse, Gorm's brother and principal double.

TOSTIG — House mouse, Gorm's brother and secondary double.

THORKILS THREELEGS — House mouse, foul-tempered invalid.

GUNHILD — House mouse, fond of military discipline, eventually defects to the 13-K Gang.

JARL FORKWHISKERS — House mouse, self-trained assassin.

Other members of Savage Tribe include: Gytha Finewhiskers, Skuli, Ketil, Elfwin.

BOOKEATER TRIBE (LIBRARY MICE)

FRYCH-THE-FRECKLED — House mouse, leader of the Bookeater Tribe, into witchcraft and black magic.

IAGO — House mouse, book gourmet, expert on paper eating.

GRUFFYDD GREENTOOTH — House mouse, self-claimed sorcerer and magician.

ELISEDD   House mouse, the youngster who dis-
                        covers Little Prince.

Other members of the Bookeater Tribe include: Owain,
Hywel-the-bad, Ethil-the-bald, Cadwallon, Mefyn, Rhodri,
Marredud, Nesta.

DEATHSHEAD (SPIRITUAL WARRIORS)

I-KUCHENG   Yellow-necked   mouse,   wandering
                        judge to whom the Goddess Unn has
                        given special duties.

SKRANG   Yellow-necked mouse, protector of I-
                        kucheng.

IBAN   Yellow-necked mouse, follows Yo and
                        the path of chastity, forever failing.

THE INVISIBLES (ATTIC MICE)

WHISPERSOFT   Wood mouse, brash and noisy leader of
                        his tribe.

TREADLIGHTLY   Yellow-necked mouse, heavy-footed
                        doe who becomes involved with Pedlar.

GOINGDOWNFAST Wood   mouse,   excellent   swimmer,
                        deadly enemy of Kellog the roof rat.

FALLINGOFF-
THINGS   Wood mouse, excellent balancer, can
                        walk a tightrope in a high wind.

NONSENSICAL   Wood mouse, mate of Goingdownfast.

FEROCIOUS   Wood mouse, meek and mild character
                        and friend to Pedlar.

TIMOROUS	Wood mouse, rival and political foe of Goingdownfast.
HEARALLTHINGS	Wood mouse, deaf, friends with the grandfather clock, pianist.
MISERABLE	Wood mouse, brother of Goingdownfast.

STINKHORN TRIBE (CELLAR MICE)

| PHART | House mouse, so-called chieftain of his tribe of two, flea-infested habitual drunk, reprobate and rogue. |
| FLEGM | House mouse, side-kick of Phart with all Phart's vices. |

13-K GANG (LEAN-TO WOODSHED REBELS)

ULF	House mouse, son of Gorm-the-old, dedicated terrorist and dissident, leader of the 13-K Gang.
DRENCHIE	House mouse, Ulf's female companion, complainer and unhappy soul.
HIGHSTANDER	Wood mouse, hates heights, rival to Ulf.

OTHER HOUSEHOLD MEMBERS

| NUDNIKS | Human beings, large useless creatures who eat enormous quantities of food. |
| HEADHUNTER | Small deadly nudnik forever torturing and murdering mice. |

EYEBALL	Burmese blue female cat, hides in the shadows, incredibly fast.
SPITZ	Old ginger tom cat, slower than Eyeball.
WITLESS	Senile old spaniel.
MERCIFUL	Cold and deadly little owl, lives in the attics, named by the Invisibles.
KELLOG	Old ship (or roof) rat, lives on the other side of the water tank, deadly enemy of Goingdownfast.
LITTLE PRINCE	White mouse, pet of the Headhunter, cannibal.
THE SHADOWS	Astrid's friends and confidants.

PART ONE
From Hedgerow to Hallway

STILTON

LIKE THEIR AGE-OLD ENEMIES, MICE TOO CAN BE CON-
sumed by curiosity.

Pedlar had heard about the House, ever since his
birth. It stood three fields away – too far away to be able to
see it from his Hedgerow – but stories about the House had
travelled with the travellers. Wandering rodents had enter-
tained the hedges and ditches with tales about the House.

It was a place where mice lived in comfort, they said,
warm all the year round. It was a place where food was in
plenty, whatever the season, whatever the weather. It was a
place where a variety of different species of mice made nests
above ground, yet still remained out of the rain, out of the
wind, out of reach of the fox and weasel, the stoat and hawk.

However, when Pedlar asked his older cousin, Tinker,
about the House, he received the reply, 'You don't want
to go near there – place is crawling with nudniks, so I hear.

Dirty creatures. Never wash themselves, so I'm told. They don't bend in the middle very well and their tongues are too short. I never heard of a nudnik even licking between its toes . . . must be covered in lice, they must. Fancy not being able to nip the fleas on your own belly – it doesn't bear thinking about, does it?'

'I wasn't thinking about the nudniks – everyone knows what bumbling oafs they are. No, I was just wondering about the House itself. You know, what it's like *inside*. Here, do you want to change that piece of beet for a haw?'

Tinker absently swopped bits of food with his cousin, as he considered the question of the House.

'What would any place be like, full of greasy nudniks? I hear they have swilling contests – that's how stupid they are – they try to guzzle as much coloured water as they can in one standing and they eat like – like *nudniks*.'

Nudniks were an endless source of speculation to Tinker, who said he despised them, but never stopped talking about them.

'I don't understand how they can stand up on their hind legs all that time,' he said, 'and not fall over. It's not as if they're the right shape for such a position, is it? You would think they would crash down on their poky-out noses, wouldn't you? I hear they only have a small clutch of fur – long stuff sticking up on their heads like a tuft of grass. Where's the rest of it gone? Maybe they had feathers and got plucked? Maybe they're supposed to be frogs, or something, but can't find a pond big enough . . .'

But Pedlar was bored with talk about nudniks. It was the House he was interested in. He let Tinker waffle on about his favourite subject and continued to ponder about the House in silence. He had heard that houses were the empty shells of extinct giant snails and there was no reason

4

to disbelieve it. Certainly, from the descriptions Pedlar had heard, they sounded like tough, hollow carapaces.

It was probably the contrast between the description of the House, and the Hedgerow, which consumed Pedlar's interest. Although in many ways the House was the opposite of the world he knew, he had a strong feeling that if he ever entered it he would be drawn into it and held, just as he was locked to the Hedgerow now. In one sense Pedlar was rooted to the hedge as surely as the hawthorn was to the Earth: it was part of him, he was part of it. The Hedgerow was magnetic, never letting its creatures stray far out into the wilderness that surrounded it, pulling them back in with fast-beating hearts and a discovery of a fear of open spaces. Yet Pedlar knew that if one hour he could break away, by sheer strength of will, he would experience something which would awaken his soul and open his mind to new light.

His mother had told him as a very young mouse, 'In the Hedgerow the spirits of mice and owls are able to touch each other, just fleetingly, for an instant in time. The weasels and stoats, they are our enemies – their language is terrible to our ears, their feeding habits are horrifying to our thoughts, their forms are monstrous – yet the Hedgerow binds us to them, because this is our common home.

'The Hedgerow is thick with the souls of animals dead and gone, and with birds that have flown out their time, their spirits all tangled in the networks of the blackthorn. It unites us, adds some harmony to a savage world, as much as anything is able to do so . . .'

The Hedgerow was Pedlar's birthplace: or at least the ground beneath it. Though he spent as much time up amongst the twigs and thorns as he did on the Earth, his mother actually gave birth to him in a clay chamber below the grassy bank of the ditch. There was a network of tunnels there, with chambers off them, which wood mice and yellow-necked mice shared.

It was here in the warm security of a hay-carpeted nest, held tightly in the great paw that was the Earth, where Pedlar and his brothers and sisters first breathed air. It was here that Pedlar's mother said of him to a neighbour, 'The moment *that* mouse was born a cockchafer came to the entrance of my nest and fluttered its wings.'

'So what?' said the neighbour, whose own offspring were, in her opinion, far more special than those of any other mouse.

'*So what?*' cried Pedlar's mother. 'Don't you know the cockchafer is the harbinger of greatness? A wandering vole told me that Frych-the-freckled, the great sorceress from the big House, has said so herself. I've been given a sign. That one's bound for greatness, you mark my words.'

'Cockchafers? – *beetle-brains*. Frych-the-freckled indeed!' sniffed the neighbour and went back to her own very precious brood.

'You watch out,' yelled Pedlar's mother. 'You might be changed into a cockchafer yourself if you take a witch's name in vain!'

Pedlar grew up in the Hedgerow, hour by hour, until he was a mature yellow-neck, the largest breed of mouse in the countryside. He was so named because he often traded one kind of food for another, first with his brothers and sisters, then with other mice. In this he was unusual, since most mice just ate what they had, there and then. They thought Pedlar was funny, wanting to swop a berry for a nut, but they often went along with the trade, enjoying the novelty.

6

The Hedgerow itself was the whole world for many of the animals and birds that lived there. Pedlar had been to the crest of the hedge several times in his life, dangerous though it was with kestrels and harriers abroad, and marvelled at its great length. One way it dipped and rose like a shoulder of the Earth following the gentle curves of the brown and green fields; the other way it disappeared along the steep bank of a chalk down, like an adder going into a hole.

Pedlar's eyesight was not good, mice rely more on touch and smell, but he could sense the permanence of the Hedgerow. It was *there*. It had been there since the coming of trees and it would always be there.

It was in the sanctuary of the Hedgerow, no stem of which was thicker than a cow's tongue, where Pedlar's great-great-grandparents had lived and died, and their ancestors before them, back to the time when all the world was grass and only mice inhabited the many-seeded Earth. Theirs were the ancient smells, the bits of fur caught on twigs and thorns, the old, old murmurs in the grasses.

The thorned Hedgerow was a castle too, with its spiked ramparts and palisades, keeping safe its many inhabitants from raptors and four-footed predators.

Even the predators used it for protection, when they were being chased by nudniks and their dogs.

It was the nudniks though, who trimmed and kept the Hedgerow healthy, squaring its broad shoulder in the spring, clearing its ditch of old leaves, twisting and twining its ethers to give it the strength to withstand winds and storms. Nudniks, guided by the great Creator, had their several uses, helping to protect the fabric of Pedlar's world.

In this way the Hedgerow survived as a community. It did not matter that many of its creatures, from butterfly to

7

hedgehog, from spider to stoat, spoke in different tongues. There was a second universal language – a language consisting of alarm sounds and movements, and of odours – which served the whole population of the Hedgerow in emergencies. So that when a storm was brewing, the creatures announced its arrival to each other.

'A storm's coming, a storm's coming,' the blackbirds would cry in their own peculiar speech, but the meaning would be understood by all, including Pedlar, who had heard the cry many times before.

'Let's get below,' his cousin Tinker would say.

On one occasion, however, a determined Pedlar replied, 'No, I want to see what happens. I'm staying up here, tucked in the fork of this blackthorn.'

'You're mad,' muttered Tinker. 'Dizzy as a nudnik.'

It was just that Pedlar wanted to hear the voices of heaven in full note, not deadened by the thickness of the turf and clay above his nest. He wanted to hear the archaic, clamouring tongues of bad weather, telling tales of bygone rains. The Hedgerow was always whispering to him, trying to tell him its primeval secrets, trying to pass on the lessons of his forebears with each rustling leaf, each creaking branch. Now he wanted to witness the sky giving birth to thunder and lightning. He wanted to hear the gales screaming through the whin, and the rain rattling on the old hollow oak.

'Tinker will be jealous that I've managed to stay outside,' muttered Pedlar, hopefully, to himself. 'He'll be sorry that I've managed to experience the great as well as the small.'

The scent of the storm came closer as the distant line of rain drove into the ground and new Earth-odours were awakened, rushing like river currents over the landscape towards the notch where he sat and waited.

Then came the wind, whipping through the tall stinging nettles, tearing at the Hedgerow garlic and bindweed. A mason wasp was ripped from its perch on a thorn and carried away into Infinity in an instant. Pedlar gulped and grasped the blackthorn more tightly. Hart's-tongue fern and broadleafed docks lashed the ground under duress: primroses closed, returning to buds. The wind screamed through the Hedgerow, reshaping it by the moment, sending great ripples along its broad flank. The Hedgerow became an excited animate creature, straining to run off somewhere, over the hills and valleys.

'So much for the wind,' said Pedlar, impressed but not overwhelmed by its power. He wondered what it would have been like in the mystical nights of long ago, when there were no Hedgerows or trees, when the wind tore through the long grasses to which Pedlar's ancestors must have clung like harvest mice.

Next came the rain wearing a cloak of darkness, hissing out of the sky.

A youthful vole which had ventured out of its hole below Pedlar, thinking the storm was over, shouted, 'Heck!' and went hurtling back down its hole again.

Pedlar gasped under the onslaught of the flood, hardly able to take a breath without taking in water. Then came the thunder and lightning, which almost blew him out of the Hedgerow and made his eyes bulge.

'All right, that's it!' Pedlar said. 'I'm scared.'

When the next lull arrived, he scrambled down the blackthorn and into the hole in the bank. The tunnel sloped upwards at first, which kept out the water, then dipped down to a number of chambers, one of which was Pedlar's nest.

* * *

The labyrinth of tunnels had been dug directly below a twisty-looped hazel branch – a *curlie-wurlie* – a powerful symbol in mouselore. A curlie-wurlie could be good or evil, had the properties of both: those who deserved good received it, and those who deserved bad, likewise. It protected the nests below from weasels and stoats, who were loath to pass under the shadow of such a significant emblem.

As Pedlar passed by Tinker's nest, his cousin called, 'Had enough, eh?'

'For now,' sniffed Pedlar.

Crossing his own odour-line he found his small nest and settled down on the warm hay, now safely closeted by the comfortable feeling of having earthen walls around him and an earthen roof above. A wych-hazel root looped out of one wall of his nest, which Pedlar often gnawed in times of boredom. It was something to do, something to keep his teeth in trim. He did it now, while listening to the distant thunder, now muted to a far-off pounding.

Curled into a spiral, his tail over his eyes, it was not long before Pedlar was dozing, and for the first time, he dreamed the Dream. In the Dream his ancestors came to him and urged him to go to the House, telling him that his destiny lay within its walls. 'History and mythology will become entwined,' they told him, 'as the columbine and ivy entwine.' His ancestors came to him as wisps of marsh mist, speaking with tongues of rustling leaves, but their meaning was plain. He was to leave the Hedgerow and go to the House: there to seek his part in the events that were to befall that great country, there to become the One who will walk with the many, they said.

When he woke, with a start and a shiver, Pedlar went immediately to a very old mouse, a sage, named Diddycoy.

The wizened old fellow was over four hundred nights and his grisly appearance frightened many of the younger mice. Diddycoy lived right at the back of the colony, in a large chamber, with a few of the older does and bucks, where he was not likely to be disturbed by the frantic energy of the young.

When Pedlar timidly entered his chamber, Diddycoy said gruffly, 'I've no food to swop, young mouse, nothing at all, so you can go and peddle elsewhere.'

'I don't want to swop anything, I've come to ask a question,' said the nervous Pedlar.

He was allowed to stay and he told Diddycoy his dream, asking the old sage whether it was true.

'What do you mean, *true*?' said Diddycoy.

'Well, do you think I must embark on a journey to the House?'

'Of course you must,' instructed Diddycoy knowingly. 'What do you think the damn dream was for? Heed the call of your ancestors, young 'un, or you'll regret it to the end of your nights.' The sage gave Pedlar a curious look, as if seeing him with new eyes.

'You think I must go *now*?'

'If this is a call, it means you've been given a great purpose and you'll dream the Dream again,' replied Diddycoy, 'and your ancestors will tell you when the time has come for you to leave home. Now, be off, my own time is past and my nap is overdue.'

Pedlar left Diddycoy's place, feeling awed that a humble mouse such as himself had been chosen to receive the wisdom of his ancestors. Yet once he was back amongst his own crowd, with excitable mice like the youngsters Totter and Pikey running around like mad creatures, it was hard to believe that he had been singled out in any way.

11

But he was visited by the Dream again, several more times, and the call became more urgent with each visitation. '*You are the One who will walk with the many*.' Only then did Pedlar begin to understand that he might be destined to tread a path different from that of other mice . . .

When deep spring came, Pedlar began wandering further and further away from the Hedgerow, out into the fields. He kept testing himself, seeing how far he could go away from familiar smells, sounds and sights, before he got worried. One night he went so far the Hedgerow's perfumes were lost to him and in the moon's bright glow its silent line became another curve of the Earth.

He knew that out in the open fields there were few animals, but in the shelter he had left there were hundreds, thousands of creatures. Yet for the first time in his life he could not smell them, nor could he hear them. They were closeted and contained in a world apart.

It was only out there in the fields that Pedlar really became aware of the rhythm of life in the Hedgerow, which in turn was in tune with the rhythms of the Earth. Only now that he was out of its immediate influence, did he see how important that rhythm was in creating harmony. This did not mean that there were no conflicts in the Hedgerow, no desperate lives, no terrible deaths, but that the harmony of the whole was safe and well. The Hedgerow was locked neatly and securely to the Earth and the vibrations of the Earth flowed through the Hedgerow.

Pedlar was a little frightened by this revelation. It made him feel like an exile in the making, looking at his own land from afar. But there was excitement too mingled with his fear, and he felt this was rewarding.

He also felt the Hedgerow drawing him back, very

12

strongly, but he was able to resist for as long as it took to satisfy his hunger.

'The beets are much nicer out there in the middle,' he told Tinker casually, when he returned.

The bees and wasps were buzzing in the Hedgerow, creating quite a racket, and Tinker shook his head sharply as if he couldn't believe his ears.

'You've been out *there*?' cried Tinker. 'You're crazy. Don't you know a kestrel can see you from – from as high as a cloud in open country?'

Pedlar thought his cousin was exaggerating. 'It's not exactly open country – there's lots of beet leaves to hide under.' He paused and spoke thoughtfully, 'You feel the Hedgerow pulling you back,' he said. 'It's strange. I wonder if you can get right outside that feeling – *right* away from its influence?'

When Pedlar reached the age of 142 nights his Dream told him he must say his farewells and set off on his journey to the House. It was time to turn his back on the ditch and Hedgerow on the edge of the fields, which had been his life since birth, and venture out to seek the mysterious 'many' with whom he must walk in order to satisfy the demands of his ancestors. Hours of chaff falling like golden rain were upon him, the dock leaves hung like limp, dried tongues in the heat of the summer, and yet his feet were itching to carry him away.

There were rituals to perform before the leave-taking, both secret and public. The secret ritual was done during the day, when everyone was asleep. It meant burying a wild rosehip under a primrose root. This had three-fold significance. It was to ensure he returned to eat the fruit of the Earth. It was an offering to the one Creator:

a gesture that the would-be traveller hoped might be returned by the Creator if the traveller became hungry on his journey. And finally, the wild rosehip was symbolic of a mouse's heart, which he left in his homeland of the Hedgerow.

The next step involved water, the life-blood of the mouse, which Pedlar took from the ditch, carried in his mouth, and deposited on the spot where he had buried the wild rosehip.

The public ritual took place at the time he was to leave. He broadcast his intentions of going by carrying pieces of his nest back to the surface and leaving it for the winds to strew, until his chamber was bare. Then he slept one hour in his bare chamber, on the naked Earth. This was noticed by other mice and a gathering took place at the entrance to the chambers. When he was ready, Pedlar left the hole without a word and travelled a way down the Hedgerow. He returned, then left again and went a little further along the ditch. Finally, he returned for the last time to say his goodbyes to the band that had gathered, for on his third departure he would not return again, unless it was for good.

There were many to see him off, including the elderly Diddycoy.

'It's not poor circumstances which drive me from the Hedgerow,' he told his friends and relatives, in a formal farewell speech. 'Now spring is here, food is plentiful on the edge of beet and corn country. It's not loneliness, though I'm considered a solitary animal and prefer my own company much of the time.

'Nor,' he said positively, 'is it any death-wish, for as a yellow-necked mouse you know I can be expected to live for five hundred long, long nights – half a millennium! –

and like most mice I consider myself fortunate in being a creature blessed with longevity. The mayfly comes and goes, a brief, burning life often lasting only a single day – but a mouse is almost for ever.'

There were murmurs of, 'True, true . . .'

'No, it is none of these. I have heard the call of my ancestors. They have bid me travel to the land of the House where a great multitude awaits me, and so I must leave you and my beloved Hedgerow. It may be that I shall return one night, to be back amongst you . . .'

'My own dear coz,' sniffed Tinker.

'. . . but by then I may be as old as Diddycoy here, not as *wise* of course, for he is unique—'

'Don't try to bamboozle me with your flattery,' grumbled Diddycoy, clearly pleased.

'—but until then, my friends, goodbye – and keep you safe from stoats, barn owls, weasels and their kind.'

And so he set forth, bravely, with heart beating fast and a kind of terror in his breast.

'You show those house mice,' shouted the young Pikey after him. 'You show 'em!'

This was a bit tactless, since there were many house mice living in the Hedgerow, one or two of whom had come to see Pedlar off, but those who heard decided to let it go, willing to accept that the youngster meant House mice, rather than house mice.

Pedlar acknowledged the yell with a wave of his tail.

As for his dangerous journey, Pedlar told himself if you had good ears, a good nose, and were quick, you stood as much chance as any other creature of not being eaten alive. And, after all, he could jump as high as hogweed in the air; dart as swiftly as an adder bites; balance with the aid of his tail on an out-of-reach twig; magically blend with

15

his surroundings. His ears were sharp, his senses keen, his whiskers fine.

There was not much that troubled Pedlar about going out into the great world, except meeting with a scarcity of food. No, his greatest burden lay in fulfilling the expectations of his ancestors, and perhaps gaining his own place in mouse history. But like all mice he *did* like to eat well.

And he could always come back, couldn't he?

RIBBLESDALE

Once in the thick jungle of the ditch-bank, Pedlar tunnelled through the grasses and weeds, trusting he would not meet a predator. The territorial urine markings he found along the way were many and varied, but so long as he did not pause he was in no immediate danger.

Some of his journey followed the Hedgerow itself, so he did not feel too alienated from his surroundings, but eventually he had to make the break and set off through a field of corn. He did so by urging himself, 'You-can-do-it-you-can-do-it-you-can-do-it.' And to his surprise, he did it.

What met him was a crop of oats and only yet in its infancy: still half-green. The ears hung sorrowfully, drooping high above him, forming a double-thick canopy to his forest of stalks. All the while he had to keep stopping and climbing an individual stalk to ask directions of both friendly and unfriendly mice, some yellow-necks like himself, some wood mice (known as long-tailed fieldmice out in the jungles of corn) and harvest mice.

Sometimes he was told to push off, sometimes he was ignored, sometimes he would be given a direction.

"Scuse me,' he would say, 'which way is the House?'

'Keep the sun over your left shoulder,' he might be told, 'and you'll come to a wide ditch. Ask again there.'

It was all very well to say 'Keep the sun over your left shoulder', but what about when he was at the bottom of a dense forest of corn, and later kale, and couldn't see the sun at all! After two days and nights, he began to feel like a veteran campaigner. But all the while he travelled Pedlar knew he had to beware of predators, especially stoats during the day and owls at night. With this in mind he tried to keep to the furrows, or ditches with plenty of bolt holes, or tree roots. When he needed to rest, he would find soft mosses to burrow in, this being the quickest and most efficient way of providing himself with cover for a short period of time.

Once, he saw a badger – a great giant of a fellow snuffling around amongst some acorns at the foot of an oak – and the sight almost made his heart stop. Badgers were not above snapping up a mouse if one wandered within reach. Even as Pedlar stared, the badger pulled a long earthworm out of its hole and chomped it down with great relish.

Finally, weary and travel-worn, feeling as if he had crossed the world and back again, Pedlar arrived in a strange land on the far side of a wide disused road. The smooth hard surface beneath his feet signalled to Pedlar that he was now in new territory and he knew that from now on new rules would apply. It took him some time to get the tar from between his toes, but once he was satisfied with the state of his paws, he looked up and around him.

It was dawn and the sky was almost obscured by the high, curving grasses which rose five times his own length above his head. However, towering even above this forest, as tall as a live oak, was an enormous square object which

17

filled him with feelings of relief and foreboding in equal parts. There could be no doubt that this was his destination. It was the House to which the voices of his ancestors had directed him.

Something stirred in Pedlar's racial memory. Some of his ancestors had lived in massive structures of stone, with thick walls and straw on the flagstoned floors, and crenellated walls and towers. Magnificent places of many chambers, many tunnels. Every so often the nudniks in these great buildings had put on suits of iron, grabbed iron sticks, and gone to confront other nudniks knocking on their door with treetrunks. All these images were transmitted to Pedlar as he drew on his empathy with the past and tried to use it to help him understand the present.

The big House before him threw a phantom shadow over the whole region. There were many mysterious square eyes in its surface, which shone blindingly down on the yellow-necked mouse. The House looked a sinister and wicked place, with a life of its own.

Another mouse might have turned back at this point, but Pedlar kept telling himself that he was the one and that inside were the many whom he must meet. The inhabitants, he knew, would be mainly house mice. These were savage little creatures who bit first and asked you your business afterwards. They would know the nooks of their homeland and any stranger entering from the Outside would automatically be at a great disadvantage.

Pedlar could hear some harvest mice in the tall grasses of the jungled plain before the House. He found their tracks, followed one, and found its maker, dangling from a stalk by its useful tail. Pedlar spoke in his bluff, Hedgerow dialect.

'Who lives in that great country standing above the grasses?' he asked, without preamble.

18

The harvest mouse looked up, a little startled since she had obviously not heard anyone enter the clearing. She dropped from the stalk and sat up on her haunches with a seed in her foreclaws – the 'high-nose' position mice call it – eating the kernel of the grass seed. Once she had eaten she dropped immediately to low-nose position, four feet on the ground, she sniffed and shuffled around a little, assessing whether this meeting was to be friendly or not, and finally decided the much bigger yellow-neck meant her no harm.

'Country?' she replied with her mouth full. 'Oh, the House? You want to stay away from there. It's full of barbarous tribes. You'd be killed. Anyway,' she continued, going high-nose and munching away on a new seed, 'there's only one way to enter the House and that's through the maze under the floor. The maze is guarded by a vicious shrew, called Tunneller. She'd bite your head off and spit it between your legs before your body hits the ground, believe me.'

Pedlar had met shrews before and knew them to be, in general, bad-tempered and violent creatures.

'And she won't let me past without a fight?'

'You have to give her a piece of cheese to get past, and you don't look as if you've got any.'

Pedlar certainly wasn't carrying cheese to pay any toll. He wasn't even sure what cheese was, exactly, and he didn't want to appear even more ignorant than he had already. There was a plant called 'bread and cheese' but it was nothing special, so he was pretty sure they weren't talking about that.

He turned again and used the high-nose position to look up and around him. The House was an imposing presence. Pedlar had never seen anything so enormous before. It reached up and touched the sky on two corners and its walls were vertical. Its roof was surely a perch for the highest-flying falcons: those that lived in the clouds. Looking up at the sheer front-face of the House, Pedlar felt very small. No wonder this mountainous place was so famous in the Hedgerow.

There was an upper storey that jutted out over the lower floor. It had windows with diamond-shaped panes. Dark timbers, great beams, were visibly locking the whole structure together, making triangular and square patterns on the plasterwork. Then there was a huge nail-studded door hiding shyly under the dark overhang of the porch. Climbing roses and ivy filled the gaps between the timbers and the windows, and embraced over the roof of this porch. There was a woodstore attached to the side of the building.

The influence of the House over its natural surrounds seemed to be tidal, reaching out unevenly in all directions, then gradually giving way to raw Nature. The garden's pale was indefinable, as short lawn washed into long twitch grass, and cultivated flowers linked roots with thistles, cow parsley and campion along an irregular frontier. To the approaching mouse, it was hard to tell whether the wilderness was creeping forward and would soon overflow the House, or whether the garden was gaining ground, gradually moving outwards and paring away at the wilderness.

Pedlar had an unerring feeling that whatever lay behind the walls of the House was in some way connected with his own destiny. He was drawn to those walls. He was curious about the creatures that lived in the limited space within the House and puzzled over their apparent brutal ways. He was an inquisitive creature, who once roused to interest followed his wonder to the dregs.

The yellow-neck preened his precious whiskers as he

studied the massive country before him, seeking an entrance to its inner world. He could see none, though he intended to investigate at the point where soil met wall rendering.

He went back to low-nose and told the harvest mouse, 'I think I'll have to try the maze, cheese or no cheese.'

She nodded. 'Yes, if you're really decided on going in, you might find a way through. Once upon a time there was an entrance through the lean-to woodshed, where the 13-K now live, but that was long ago, when it was made of wood. It's brick and concrete now, so the only way is past Tunneller.'

'The 13-K?'

'A bunch of no-good youngsters led by Ulf, son of Gorm-the-old, made up of riffraff from all the House tribes.'

This information was virtually incomprehensible to Pedlar and he decided to pursue it no further, though he found the names wildly exotic and exciting. *Ulf, son of Gorm-the-old!* A woodstore which was the hide-out of a bloodthirsty gang of thugs and a maze of passageways guarded by an uncivilized shrew . . . Pedlar enquired after the location of the latter entrance and then bid the harvest mouse good eating, before leaving her.

When he checked all around the base of the building, he found the mouse's information to be correct. There was only one small entrance hole, disappearing down below the foundations of the old building, near the cellar well light. He might not even run into the dreaded Tunneller; but if he did, he might be able to reason with her. Pedlar knew that a shrew's sight and sense of smell are poor. He knew also that its normal activity is feverish and full of nervous energy, obliging it to stop in its tracks and take frequent naps, even while it is out hunting beetles and earthworms.

21

He might have a chance to sneak by Tunneller while she slept.

Pedlar took one last look at the outside world, at its vastness. The sky was now a soft, pale blue, falling down to the Earth. He could only see those fields which rose up behind the high garden grasses in the background. There was an orchard to one side of the garden and an open view on the other. Through this window in trees and grass, he could see the hazy form of the Hedgerow, his former home.

He flicked his tail. His heart yearned to be back amongst the thorns at that moment, or down in his safe and warm chamber in the burrow. What was he doing, entering an unknown place full of such dangers, when he could be lazing around in the fork of a hazel branch, eating haws and drinking dew? He was going to miss the Hedgerow. But then, life could not be all comfort and no excitement, for how dull it would be if it were. There were challenges to face, adventures to experience, new worlds to explore. And he, Pedlar, was answering the call!

He slipped down the hole behind the rain barrel.

At once he found himself in a labyrinth of tunnels, running in all directions. Some were shrew tunnels, being oval in shape, while others were vole tunnels, being round. There were also wood-mouse tunnels, such as the kind Pedlar would dig himself, being a close cousin to wood mice. His sensitive whiskers just brushed the sides of the passage he had entered by, so he knew he was safe and would not get stuck. The darkness was a little bewildering, but he soon got a sense of his surroundings, using his nose and whiskers, as well as his instinct.

The pungency of the Earth was strong in his sensitive nostrils as Pedlar scurried along the tunnels. As he went, he marked his trail with his own scent, and soon found that he was backtracking on himself and became thoroughly lost. Sometimes he would be in a tunnel with fresh earth and the next moment his own scent would tickle his nose, and he would know he was travelling one way or the other down a passage along which he had already been. Mixed with his own scent, impregnated within the walls of the tunnels, was the smell of another creature, a shrew. Pedlar guessed this was Tunneller's odour. He entered a wider part of the tunnel system.

Suddenly, Pedlar stopped dead, as if he had come up against a brick wall. In the pitch blackness ahead, he sensed a form, and then he smelled the strong odour of a shrew. A voice came out of the darkness, confirming his suspicions. The tone was sharp and testy, and full of menace.

'Who's there? Speak up, before I kill you.'

Pedlar deliberately kept his own voice calm.

'A yellow-neck, Pedlar by name, on my way into the country of the House.'

'A yellow-necked mouse?' the shrew screamed in fury. 'What are you doing in my maze? Get out! Get out!'

Pedlar felt fear rising within him. A shrew was no mean opponent in battle. However, he had always been too stubborn for his own good, and alongside that fear was a growing anger. Did this female shrew think the whole world belonged to her? He had as much right as she did to travel through the tunnels. The network of passageways could not possibly have been dug by this creature alone: it must have taken an army of mammals to fashion the labyrinth. He supposed that Tunneller had simply taken the area over when the wood mice and voles had had no more use for it.

'Let me pass,' growled Pedlar at this gatekeeper between two worlds. 'I've got no quarrel with you . . .'

Tunneller cried, 'The toll! Give me some food!'

The harvest mouse had specifically mentioned something called *cheese*, otherwise Pedlar would have brought a nut, or a piece of fruit. He then spoke the fatal words.

'I have no food.'

There came a single shriek from Tunneller, then she launched herself at him. Pedlar felt a sharp pain on his ear and knew that she had buried her teeth in it. Fortunately, in her short-sightedness, she had only caught the rim and he shook her furiously until the edge of his ear tore and she went flying off somewhere.

Ignoring the pain in his ear, Pedlar located the shrew by her various odours. He could smell her shape in the darkness. There was always an olfactory map of his surroundings in his head. Tunneller's poor sense of smell did not allow her the same benefits. Pedlar knew she had to rely on her sense of touch. She had to feel her way through life. It gave him a small advantage. He remained absolutely still at first.

Tunneller then began to throw herself this way and that in an attempt to locate her enemy. The energy and speed with which she scrambled and jumped around was terrifying. Pedlar desperately tried to stay out of the way of her snapping jaws. Twice she almost had him by the throat. He could tell that she was not going to settle for an ear again, because she caught his flanks a number of times, letting go when she knew she had not got a vital part of him.

Pedlar did not let her attack him unscathed. He administered one or two nips himself. At one point he had a good hold of her jowl and tried to scratch her underside with his powerful back legs. They rolled backwards and forwards as she struggled like a maniac and he found it impossible to hold on to her. Finally he released her and she bit him on the nose as she retreated. A nose is a sensitive organ. The wound was agony and Pedlar's eyes watered furiously.

Finally, the pair of them, mouse and shrew, ran forwards both at once, and locked jaws.

They held each other with determination. Neither was prepared to let go. The hold was not painful for either creature, but it was a stalemate. They could only let go by common agreement. Neither could retreat without the consent of the other. No matter how much each one rattled and shook, it soon became obvious that they were locked together until they let go both at once.

After a long struggle both creatures settled with their bellies against the Earth, prepared to remain that way. Animal combatants have been found dead in such positions. If both are too full of pride, too stubborn, to acknowledge even a draw, then they stay locked and die of thirst or starvation.

Pedlar and Tunneller remained in the same position until, finally, Pedlar became bored and exasperated with his silly combatant. He slackened his grip ever so slightly. There was a response from Tunneller, who did the same. By degrees and mutual consent they gradually opened their jaws and released one another. This took a great deal of trust on both sides, for after a certain time, one could have lunged for the throat of the other, ripped it open, and let the blood flow forth. It would have been all over. There would have been a live winner and a dead loser.

Neither of them did this, however. Pedlar was a mouse with honour and pride. He would have died before carrying out such a dastardly act. He discovered, to his amazement, that the shrew had the same principles. She too, by her physical response to his suggestion, had given her silent word not to attack during the separation. She kept this unspoken promise.

When they had separated, they parted by a few lengths, to recover their strength. Pedlar heard Tunneller's breathing increase in strength and he knew she was having a nap. He could not pass her and he was not going to return to the outside world, so he lay on his belly and recuperated himself. They remained there resting for a long while.

Just when Pedlar was wondering if he was going to have to wake this shrew for a renewed fight, she suddenly leapt up and dashed forwards. He was caught unawares by this sudden attack.

The shrew stopped a half a length from him and snapped something from the ground. There was a fluttering of crispy wings, a crackling. Pedlar's heart was racing as these sounds were followed by a definite and final crunch. Then all was still again, except for a regular masticating noise.

'What's that?' he asked. 'What are you doing?'

There was a loud belch from his opponent, a smacking of the lips, then she replied, 'Nice fat beetle.'

'But you weren't even awake?' said the astounded Pedlar. 'Were you?'

'I'm aware of beetles in my sleep. Couldn't let a delicious one like that go by.'

They remained as they were for a few moments, then Pedlar said, 'Are you going to let me pass, or do we have to carry on fighting?'

'You could have left,' she said, 'while I was napping.'

'Backwards yes, but I want to go on. I'm *pledged* to go on.'

There was another long pause, then, 'Well, you'd better go on then. I don't want to fight someone as obstinate as you are to leave the real world and enter bedlam. What do you want to go into the House *for*? It's full of wild tribes of mice – House mice, wood mice and yellow-necks like yourself. They all have so much, yet they all want more. Crazy House.'

'I *have* to go,' explained Pedlar. 'My ancestors have told me my destiny lies in the House. I had a vision in a dream . . .'

'Oh, a *visionary*,' said Tunneller in a scathing tone. 'Well, you'll be all right with the Bookeater Tribe then. They'll take to you, if you're a mystic.'

Pedlar shook his head. 'No, I'm not a visionary as such, or a mystic. I didn't get any blinding flashes of light, or pictures in my head – nothing like that. It was a very clear message in a dream and the old wood mouse, Diddycoy, told me I must obey it. So here I am. I've travelled many fields to get here and I'm not turning back now . . . Anyway, who are the Bookeater Tribe?'

Tunneller said in a drowsy voice, 'Look, I need another nap. You're the first person who's beaten me in a fight . . .'

'A draw,' corrected Pedlar. 'It was a draw.'

'All right, a *draw* then,' yawned Tunneller. 'I don't want to argue about it. Whatever it is, you're walking away – well, not *unscathed*, but with your honour intact. No-one's ever done that before. I *always* win. I don't want you bragging too much about this. You must simply say "Tunneller and I fought to a standstill and parted enemies." '

'Enemies?'

'You don't expect me to call you a friend, do you? Of course, enemies. Enemies who admire one another. Enemies who respect each other. But *enemies* just the same. I don't have any friends. Even when I'm tender towards another shrew, I'm *aggressively* tender – I am passionate but not affectionate. I don't have fondness for another fellow creature. Not one in the whole world. I *like* it that way.'

27

While this speech was in progress, Tunneller's voice became fainter and fainter, and at the last word she fell asleep. Luckily she was in a wide part of the chamber and Pedlar was able to creep past her. He brushed against her smaller form as he passed and marvelled at her soft velvety touch. It made him wonder about all that hostility she had inside her. She felt so warm and inviting he wanted to snuggle up beside her. But then he knew that she was actually a creature capable of incredible ferocity – and he hurried on, following a draught to an exit that lay in the far distance.

There was an odour on the draught, of body fluid. It was quite a strong one, and he knew from this that he was coming to the boundary of another mouse's territory. The smell was there to warn strangers to turn back, but Pedlar bravely walked on.

ROQUEFORT

PEDLAR AT LAST CAME TO A CROSSROADS WHERE A GREAT many holes from the House side met those of the maze.

He chose to enter a hole from which he felt a strong draught, guessing it to be one of the shorter tunnels. Ignoring the deliberate odour-line of mouse urine, he went through into a large open area with stone walls and floor and a wooden ceiling supported by thick beams. He took careful note of his surroundings, always making sure to remain within instant reach of the exit hole in case flight was necessary.

Not for the first time he wondered why he had left his Hedgerow to journey out into the unknown. His longing to be back was like a lump inside him. He already missed the fragrant wild flowers, the dark smell of ditch clods, the green scent of clover leaves in the noonday sun. He missed the rough touch of bark and the taste of sap, the hawthorn blossom petals falling like soft gentle rain on his coat. The warm Earth called him to its womb. His fellow hedge-creatures, their sounds and smells, were running memory claws gently through his mind. It was hard not to answer this call, but a greater one urged him on.

There was a set of wooden steps on the far side of the great chamber, leading up to a door, around which light entered. It was this thin oblong of light which enabled Pedlar to see in the near darkness and take stock.

I must finally be in the House! he told himself.

It seemed an immense place to him: over ten thousand times larger than a chamber in a mouse warren. Perhaps bigger? Pedlar had never thought to experience anything like it. And almost everywhere was lined with stone: the walls, the floor. The ceiling, dizzily high, was of wood, far, far above him. The floor was vast and a feeling of fear came over him as he stared at the lone and level plain that stretched before him.

Yet, he told himself, *this is but one chamber in a hugeness of many chambers*. Above this chamber were more vast chambers, and above those even more, and above *them* were yet other great open spaces, unknown spaces.

His mind had difficulty grappling with the immensity of the whole House. It was a place of great valleys, echoing caverns and mountains, the sheer faces of which made him giddy to behold them. He was a mouse in another world: a world into which surely the whole mouse nation could fit and still find room to wander? It was as if the one Creator had said to Pedlar: 'Behold, here is the box in which the universe came!'

He remained by the hole, conquering his fear of the majestic scene before him, not wishing to move until he had ascertained that it was safe to venture out into the chamber. There could be anything waiting to pounce out there, from cats to weasels to stoats. Pedlar was aware that he was in a foreign land and if he was to survive he had to expect the unexpected. He swished his tail in the dust, to see if it attracted attention from anywhere in the room, and remained ready to bolt through the hole at the first sign of danger.

In the vast chamber were various items, some of which he recognized, others he did not. There were two huge racks of bottles, full of liquid, up against one wall. He had seen bottles before during his life in the ditch. There were also crates and boxes, both of which nudniks had dumped in the ditch at various times. Then there were what looked like two small rainbarrels, lying horizontally on some kind of support. These rainbarrels dripped a liquid which smelt like fermenting fruits of the autumn. It was near to these items that Pedlar noticed two living creatures. They appeared to be mice, one smaller than the other. It seemed to Pedlar he had disturbed their rest. They in turn were staring at Pedlar, who immediately became wary. One of the mice suddenly lurched towards him, walking unsteadily.

'Stay where you are,' snapped Pedlar, when the mouse was two lengths from him. 'State your business.'

The mouse stopped and blinked, before picking its teeth with one of its claws.

'No need for that, yer honour,' said the creature in a slurred tone, going high-nose. 'We're all friendly like, down 'ere, ain't we Flegm?' he called over his shoulder.

'Yeah, that we are, Phart,' came the reply from the mouse's companion, followed by a loud belch and an apologetic, ''Scuse my guts.'

Pedlar studied the mouse whom the other had called

Phart. Though it was difficult to determine just what he was, he seemed to be a house mouse. Phart's coat was matted and decorated with bald patches covered in eczema. What remained of his fur stuck up, ragged and unkempt, like clumps of grass on a frosty morning. The end of his tail was missing, his left ear was torn and three of his whiskers were bent. His eyes were red-veined and watery, above a puffy-looking nose and flaccid cheeks. Though he was running to fat, the muscles of his body looked worn and wasted, and great folds of skin hung from his belly. What was worse, Phart stank of something rotten, though it was difficult to conclude just what was the source – his breath or his body odour – or both.

'Might I arsk,' said Phart, suddenly taking the initiative with a haughty tone, 'what you might be doing in Stinkhorn territory? Just arsken, you understand.'

'Stinkhorn?'

'That's the name of this 'ere tribe, of what I'm proud to be known as chief.' Phart drew himself up as best he could under the circumstances, though Pedlar was a good deal taller and had considerably better poise.

Pedlar went high-nose and looked around him. 'How many in this tribe of yours?' he asked.

'That's a leadin' question, that is,' sneered Phart. 'But since you arsk, not a lot. Just Flegm 'ere, and yours truly. Used to be more, but our numbers is somewhat depleted. But me an' Flegm, we fights like maniacs, don't we Flegm?'

'Yeah,' came the reply, separated by slurps. 'Maniacs.'

'We fights anybody what comes in 'ere, looking for trouble, and sends 'em back where they come from. 'Ow did you come 'ere, by the way? We didn't see you come in.'

'Through the hole at the back of this chamber.'

32

'*Cellar*. Cellar is what this is. From the 'ole in the back you say? Out of the maze then?'

'That's correct.'

'Then,' said Phart, picking his teeth again, 'you didn't run into Tunneller?'

Pedlar said, 'You mean the shrew? Oh, yes, we met each other.'

'And?'

'And we fought to a standstill.'

Phart swayed a little, moving insidiously closer. 'You – fought – Tunneller?' he whispered, hoarsely.

'To a standstill. We parted enemies.'

'Strewth!' said Flegm from his position under the barrels. The scruffy little mouse let out a hacking cough before spitting something indescribable on to the floor. Once he'd divested himself of this unwelcome blob, he said to his chief, 'He gave Tunneller a smacking, did he? Well, he's likely to give you a walloping too then, ain't he Phart?'

'You keep your rotten tongue knotted,' shouted Phart over his shoulder.

Then suddenly, Phart was right up next to Pedlar, invading his body space, breathing foul fumes into his nostrils as he pushed his disgusting nose amongst Pedlar's whiskers.

'Look, yer honour,' he said in a conspiratorial whisper, 'we didn't mean no harm, you understand? We got to protect our property, ain't we. We got a right to do that. But you're very welcome, very welcome indeed, yer honour. I couldn't say how welcome you are. Our cellar is at your disposal. Would you care to partake in some liquid refreshment? We got plenty of red wine. We've already been indulgin' somewhat, ourselves, so you're very at liberty to join us for a few swigs.'

'Red wine?' said Pedlar, suddenly feeling quite thirsty.

'I don't think I know what that is.'

Phart laughed over his shoulder. 'You 'ear that, Flegm?'

'Why don't you find out then, yer honour?' called Flegm.

So Pedlar followed Phart over to the pool of red fluid lying on the floor of the cellar. There he bent his head and drank what tasted like heavy berry juice. The taste was good and he was soon lapping away with the other two mice. At first he remained wary of them and his surroundings, keeping a cool head and a sharp eye out. However, after a time, it didn't seem to matter.

While they were still lapping the wine Flegm said to Phart, 'Go on then. He's from the Outside. Arsk 'im.'

Phart looked at Pedlar and cleared his throat. 'You're from the Outside, yer honour?'

'I said I was,' replied Pedlar.

'That's what I thort,' said Phart. 'Y'see, what me an' Flegm 'ere want to know is, have you ever come across a sort of purple mushroom with red spots?'

'What?' said Pedlar, puzzled.

'Simple question, ain't it?' snapped Flegm. 'What're you deaf or somethin'?'

'Now, now, Flegm,' said Phart, 'his honour didn't quite understand what I was talkin' about.' He turned back again to Pedlar. 'See, it's like this, yer honour. I had an uncle – the Great Bile 'is name was – what once went Outside and found these mushrooms. When he ate 'em, he saw beautiful visions and such. Made 'im feel like he was walkin' on clouds of flour. Know what I mean?'

Pedlar was beginning to feel a bit like that himself. 'I think so,' he said.

'Well then, can you take us – me an' Flegm that is – to some mushrooms like them? We could – we could make you a honorary Stinkhorn if you did.'

'Don't know any such mushrooms,' said Pedlar. 'Sorry. Much as I would love the honour.'

Flegm tutted and said, 'Bleedin' useless,' and Phart glared at Pedlar for a very long time.

Phart finally said, 'You sure you're not keepin' these mushrooms to yourself?'

Pedlar said very emphatically. 'I don't know what you're talking about. And if you keep looking at me like that I'll bite your nose off.'

'Sorry for breathin',' said Phart, and went back to his puddle of wine.

Pedlar realized that previously he had been too cautious about the wine, now he relaxed and let himself enjoy his drink. Then, not so many laps after that, there wasn't any need to worry because he felt he could take on an army of weasels without any problems whatsoever. He felt careless and bold.

'Thisss-is good,' he said to the Stinkhorns. 'You get musch of this stuff here?'

'Oh, we gets the lot, in 'ere. Reds, whites, fizzies. You name it. There's always a leak or two, somewheres about, an' if there ain't, we soon make one,' Phart guffawed.

Said the flea-bitten Flegm, 'Bottled stuff's the best, but you don't often get bottles broke, more's the pity.' He nudged Pedlar in a friendly fashion.

Pedlar suddenly felt inexplicably angry at being jostled in such a familiar fashion.

'Don't push me,' he growled, giving Flegm his most menacing stare.

'What?' said Flegm, surprised. Then looking into Pedlar's face, he cried, 'Oh, strewth, we got one 'ere!'

'One what?' asked Phart, licking the drips off his whiskers and lifting his head.

'One of them what gets stroppy with a bit of booze.'

Phart turned to stare at Pedlar, who was rocking back and forth on his feet now, and glaring at the other two.

'Just don't push me, thass all,' he snarled.

'Oh dear,' said Phart. 'I think you're right, Flegm. I think we've got one and a 'alf.'

'Just don't push me,' growled Pedlar, wondering why the floor seemed to be slipping away from under his feet.

'Eloquent bozo, ain't he?' said Flegm. 'Sort of plays fascinatin' games with the language, don't he? A vocabulary that takes yer breath away.'

The two house mice continued to sip at the wine, while keeping an eye on their new companion, who was now looking up at the ceiling. They watched, interested, as Pedlar's head started swivelling slowly, as if he were trying to keep up with the turning of some unseen object. Then gradually, ever so gradually, Pedlar leaned over to one side, until he fell. He lay there in the dust of the cellar floor, panting heavily, his eyes wide with bewilderment. After a while they closed.

Pedlar woke some time later, with the sun directly in his eyes. His head was hurting and his stomach felt strange. Looking around, he saw the two mice he had met earlier hunched against the back wall of the cellar. Next moment, there was the sound of heavy footsteps on the stairs and then the sun went out with a quick snap.

Phart and Flegm soon returned to his side.

'You nearly got trod on by a nudnik,' Flegm told him, not without some satisfaction in his tone. 'Flippin' great feet missed you by a whisker, mate. Good job it was the one with white head and face fur. Blind as a worm, that one.'

Pedlar sat high-nose and rubbed his eyes with his paws, causing jagged pains to pass across his brow.

'You poisoned me,' he croaked. 'You've made me ill.'

'*We* poisoned you,' cried Phart. 'That's a joke! You poisoned yerself, more like. Nobody said you 'ad to guzzle our wine. You did that yourself, didn't you? Admit it.'

'You led me to the poison,' Pedlar accused him.

Flegm cried, 'It ain't poison, it's wine. If you can't take it, you should stick to beer.'

'Beer?' groaned Pedlar.

'Never mind,' Phart told him. 'In future, you should lay off all the good stuff. You threatened us with our lives, you did, tellin' us not to push you. I knew you thought you was a hard nut, when you bragged about beating up Tunneller.'

'I didn't brag – and I didn't beat her. I told you, we fought to—'

'—a standstill. Yeah, yeah. We 'eard all that, pal. But nobody has got past Tunneller before now, so it's just as good as beatin' her, ain't it?'

Pedlar did not feel inclined to argue with the two mice and crawled away to another part of the cellar.

'Gone off to puke,' he heard Flegm announce.

Pedlar stayed in the corner on a cool stone for some time, until he felt sufficiently recovered. He watched the other two go back to the wine puddle and start drinking again. It was strange how they weren't affected by the poison, but Pedlar decided their bodies must be used to it. They had grown immune to a liquid that was obviously toxic to visiting mice.

Pedlar was wondering about the sunlight he had seen. One minute the sun had been at high noon, then next moment it was dark. And what was the sun doing *inside* the House in the first place? He went to Phart and asked him for an explanation.

'Lights, that's what it is. Ain't you never seen lights before?'

'You mean, like stars?'

'Nah,' snorted Phart, contemptuously. 'Look, I know you come from the outside world, but I used to talk to Great Uncle Bile and I know about it too. I know there's street-lights and whatnot. What about the travelling boxes the nudniks use? You must 'ave seen them with their lights on at night, shooting down the road?'

Pedlar recalled the farm track near the Hedgerow and made the connection. 'Yes, are they the same sort of thing?'

'Lights is lights. You got 'em all over the House. Some-times they're on, and sometimes not. Usually if a nudnik's in the room, they're on, unless it's daytime, or a bedroom of course, then the nudnik could be sleeping, in which case they'd be off, if you see what I mean?'

'I think so,' said Pedlar. 'Can you predict them?'

'Sometimes,' said Flegm. 'Down 'ere in the cellar they're never on until a nudnik comes. When you hear the door open, the light goes on the next second. Unless it's the nudnik we call the Headhunter – sometimes that one comes down in the dark.'

'Why? Who's the Headhunter?' asked Pedlar, alarmed.

'Half-sized nudnik,' stated Phart. Then blowing off and belching at the same time, he added proudly, 'How about that then, Flegm? Both ends simultaneous.'

Pedlar ignored this crass show of vulgarity and enquired further after the Headhunter.

'Why would it want to come down here in the dark?'

'To catch us,' nodded Flegm, darkly, 'or any other live creature it can lay its hands on. It's a demon, that

38

one. Got Skabb last week. Skabb was another member of our tribe, until the Headhunter got him. Probably boiled poor old Skabb alive.'

'This Headhunter nudnik? It likes to torture us?'

'Us, cats, dogs, whatever. You should see its eyes. Straight out of hell, they are. I've seen the Headhunter pullin' the legs off a spider, then squeezin' the bulby body till it pops. The Headhunter wears a mouse's skull on 'ere,' Flegm pointed to a spot on his collarbone where a nudnik's lapel would be, 'like it was some sort of badge or somethink.'

'Cats play with mouse bodies,' said Pedlar. 'I've seen them do it in the Hedgerow ditch.'

'True,' Phart admitted, 'but cats haven't got the devious nature what this small nudnik's got. It's clever, this one. Very, very clever. It's shrewd, cunning and ten times more brainy than any cat.'

Pedlar decided the two Stinkhorns were probably exaggerating in order to impress him. The important thing was that he now understood the nature of house lights. They came on and went off without warning, but occasionally their state could be foreseen according to the movement of nudniks. Pedlar had not actually seen or encountered a nudnik. He was looking forward to the experience, because apparently they were not like any other animal. They stood high-nose the whole time, never going down to low-nose, except to sleep. Tinker had told him that when they slept they stretched their great galumphing bodies out full length and took up more flat space than a dozen cats.

'I should like to see one of these nudnik creatures,' he said to the Stinkhorn Tribe. 'Could you arrange a sighting?'

'We could, or we couldn't, yer honour,' replied Phart, after a long look at Flegm, 'dependin' on how much you can contribute to the tribe's larder, eh?'

'How do I do that? You mean I should go out and forage for food, to give to you?'

'That's about the size of it,' said Phart, 'though I'm not sure about the word "forage". *Fight* is more the word I'd use in that context. 'Ow about you, Flegm?'

'Fight,' confirmed his lieutenant. 'Definitely.'

'I have to fight for food? Who do I fight for it?'

Phart went high-nose and scratched his belly fleas. 'Well, less see now,' he said. 'You could start with the Bookeater Tribe . . . but then they ain't got no cheese, so that's no good. They're the weakest ones though.'

'Nex' to us,' interrupted Flegm proudly, but he was given a glaring down by his chief, who otherwise ignored the remark.

'. . . Then there's the Invisibles,' said Phart, 'but you got to travel all the way to the attic to find them. They ain't got no cheese either. You might have a go at the 13-K.'

'I've heard about them,' said Pedlar.

'And finally, there's the Savage Tribe. I wouldn't go near the Savage Tribe unless you can kill a cat with one set of claws – that's my advice. Easier to kill a cat than take on the Savage Tribe and walk away alive. Gorm would rip your 'eart out and feed it to his infants, soon as look at you.'

'Why are they called the Savage Tribe?' asked Pedlar. 'I know it's because they're savage, but *why* are they so fierce?'

'They got a lot to protect,' sighed Phart. 'They got the celestial larder in their territory. A larder is a food store what's always full, see, and it's got cheese in it. It never runs out. It's like . . . I dunno, to someone like you, comin' from the Outside, it's like there was a harvest all year round.' He moved in close to Pedlar, his breath going up Pedlar's nostrils. 'You don't want to have no truck with the Savage Tribe, yer honour. I'd stay away from them, if I was you. You can sometimes get a nice bit of cake, or bread, or even cheese and biscuit in the sittin'-room, or the library when one of the nudniks has been in there.'

'Speaking of food,' said Pedlar, looking round, 'is there anything to eat around here?'

Phart stepped backwards quickly.

'Oh, so you wants some of *our* grub now? I knew you was a scrounger, soon as I seen you. Comin' in here, drinking our booze, arskin for grub? Whatsay, Flegm?'

'Bleeding scrounger, that's what he is,' answered the faithful lieutenant.

Pedlar shook himself from head to toe. He was fed up with arguing with these two despicable creatures and decided to go off and look for food. There had to be something to eat in the cellar, even if it was a few seeds of something. He went nosing around, sniffing trails across the floor, until he picked up something which looked fairly promising. It was the odour of a root vegetable. He followed his nose, which led him to a sack in the corner. There was a hole in the sacking and he entered this to find himself amongst some potatoes. This was more like it! Potatoes were reasonable fare for a country mouse.

He ate his fill, feeling much better once there was something in his stomach. Then he left the sack by the hole he had entered, to find Phart and Flegm waiting for him with hurt expressions on their faces.

'Don't you feel any shame?' asked Phart. 'Stealin' the food out of our mouths?'

'What are you talking about? There's enough potatoes here to feed an army of fieldmice for months,' said Pedlar. 'You won't miss a few mouthfuls. In any case, where I come from, food doesn't belong to you unless you've got it between your paws. First come, first eat.'

'Down here it's different,' said Phart, 'as you'll soon learn. Down here supplies belong to whatever tribe whose territory it is. This is Stinkhorn country, and you've just pinched Stinkhorn grub.'

'So take it back or punish me,' said Pedlar, getting tired of all this ownership.

'We could make him a Stinkhorn,' suggested Flegm. 'That'd make it legal, wouldn't it?'

'I don't *want* to be a Stinkhorn!' said Pedlar. 'I'd rather throw myself into the mouth of a fox than be a rotten Stinkhorn.'

At that moment there was a thunderous roar from the room next to the cellar. Pedlar leapt about a metre in the air and landed ready for flight. The terrible noise continued for a few moments as he looked around for an escape route, then it stopped. Black dust came from under the door to the adjoining room in billowing clouds.

Still jittery, Pedlar wondered whether to run or stand. His heart was pounding in his chest. His legs were twitching with indecision.

Phart and Flegm were still standing, nonchalantly observing Pedlar's nervous antics.

'Cor,' sniggered Flegm, 'look at 'im. He's about ready to stain the floor, he is.'

Pedlar blinked in frustration, wondering what was going on. Suddenly, the thunder was back, even louder than before. He jumped again, this time not quite so high.

'Whey-hey!' yelled Phart, laughing. 'He'll be bashing

the ceiling light next time.'

The roaring stopped, the black clouds came again.

'What is it?' snarled Pedlar.

Phart grinned. 'Coal, comin' down the chute next door. The nudniks are fillin' up the fuel store, ready for next winter. Frighten you, did it, squire?'

'And I thought he was tough, din't you, Phart?' Flegm said. 'I thought he was quite a little hard case. But it seems he's scared of a bit o' coal . . .'

Pedlar made a move towards the other two mice, who turned and ran. Pedlar chased them across the cellar floor and up the steps. The three of them were about halfway up when the door to the cellar opened and the light went on. Pedlar saw two enormous feet descending the cellar steps. He did not look up. Instead he kept running, sweeping the other two mice before him, up to the top step and through the door.

The next moment the door had been closed behind them. Pedlar found himself in a long room with a shiny floor on which his claws kept skidding. Instead of chasing the two house mice now, he found himself following them, as they seemed to be seeking a dark corner. They found it around the hall corner, hunched in the shadows against the skirting, and were joined by Pedlar, who swallowed his fastidiousness and cuddled up against their flea-bitten pelts.

All three mice fought to get their breath back, especially the two Stinkhorns, who were gasping with bulging eyes, and looked as if they were each ready to burst a lung. When they had all settled down to a regular breathing pattern once again, Flegm said to Pedlar, 'Now you've done it! We're out in the hallway, with the Gwenllian Hole too far off.' He stared about him frantically. 'Any

43

minute we're goin' to see a cat come round that corner, or a bunch of Savages, or even the bleedin' Headhunter with one of his diabolical traps. All thanks to you, you rotten bleeder!'

CHEDDAR

IN THE SKIRTING-BOARD BEHIND THE WARDROBE OF THE sixth bedroom was the Rajang Hole, named after its architect, Rajang-the-peaceful, a long-dead Deathshead spiritual warrior. The Rajang Hole, like several others in the House, was known only to the Deathshead. The Rajang Hole was so intricately designed, the use of light and shadow so cunning, that it could not be seen from either side of the wardrobe. Only when a mouse was directly in front of the hole, could it be discerned. Otherwise, it remained a mere shady area on the skirting-board, below a cleverly marked nick in the dado to pinpoint its actual position in relation to the wardrobe itself.

From within the hole, which was a mere recess in the wainscot, emerged a mouse by the name of Skrang. She was a Deathshead who followed the teachings of Unn, a yellow-neck by species, and the dedicated protector of I-kucheng, the oldest member of the Deathshead. In any arbitration there is always a party more dissatisfied than pleased and I-kucheng had upset so many mice by his judgements that he was the target of numerous assassination attempts. Skrang had saved his life, often without him knowing, countless times.

Naturally any mouse that attacked I-kucheng from the front was swiftly dealt with by the old mouse himself, using a martial art known only to Deathshead, called *Ik-to*. However, I-kucheng in his later nights was partially deaf, and often failed to hear an attacker coming from his rear. Skrang, a relatively young Deathshead at 370 nights, had appointed herself his unknown guardian. I-kucheng was at present safely resting behind the Rajang Hole, and Skrang felt like stretching her legs and enjoying a little freedom.

When she reached the corner of the great, towering wardrobe, Skrang peered round to survey the room. The heavy curtains were drawn and the bedroom was in semi-darkness. The nudnik who used this room was an old female, who rose late. She was at this minute fast asleep in the bed. Curled at her feet lay a large, very old cat with a pugnacious face. One of its paws was as large as Skrang herself.

The cat was a ginger tom, known to the mice as Spitz, because of his habit of spitting at everything that moved. Normally, Spitz liked to roam the garden at night, but occasionally he stayed in, just to be unpredictable. Not nearly as dangerous as Eyeball, the Burmese blue, Spitz was nonetheless still formidable even in his old age. It did not do to turn one's back on the great beast.

Skrang listened carefully for the sounds of regular breathing, both from the cat and from the nudnik. When she was certain they were both fast asleep, she skipped up on to the skirting board and ran around the room to the partially open door. Then she was out on the landing and clear of any immediate danger.

Running along the polished wood on the side of the landing, Skrang had to pass an open door, behind which was bedroom number five, the haunt of the dreaded Head-hunter. Her heart beating a little faster, though Deathshead are supposed to be fearless, Skrang crept to the edge of the open door and stood there in a slice of shadow. When she had been there a few moments, she heard the voice of Little Prince. It froze her blood in her veins, as she listened to the horrible mocking tones.

'I can smell you, sweet mouse, delicious mouse, dirty *mean* little mouse. I know you're there.'

It was a dulcet voice, a syrupy voice, and its owner sounded pleased with himself.

'You think you can fool Little Prince? Not by a long shot you can't, you dirty house mouse, with such delectable, savoury flesh. Little Prince can smell a nasty house mouse from two rooms away. Dirty house mouse, I can smell you now. I bet you have nice crunchy ears.'

Yellow-neck, not house mouse, you little cannibal, thought Skrang. She knew that if there was a nudnik in the room with Little Prince, it would not understand his twitterings, and therefore Little Prince could only taunt. She gathered her courage in her breast and then made a quick dash across the doorway, glancing in to see the white mouse with the pink-rimmed eyes, pink lips and pink tail, who was watching intently from within a silver cage.

'Ha!' Little Prince cried, his soft, fat body clinging to the silver bars. 'I knew it! I knew it! You can't fool Little Prince. I grow fat on your flesh. I eat the luscious livers of micey mice after my master has boiled them alive. I'll pop your eyeballs between my teeth. Mousey mouse, I love the

47

taste of your honeydew tongue. Come back to me. Come back to Little Prince . . .'

Thankfully the voice faded away as Skrang got further and further along the landing and eventually reached the stairs.

All the mice in the House had their own favourite way of ascending and descending the staircase. Some went down the banisters, some used the banister support strip below the rail itself, and some used the dado down the wall. Skrang was one of the latter. She climbed the flock wallpaper to the dado, then ran down this strip to the ground floor.

Once downstairs she paused by the front door. She remembered she had not visited Stone in a great many hours. Stone, an old dormouse, lived near the ancient wooden privy at the bottom of the garden. Since the toilet was only used in an emergency, Stone was left in peace most of the time. The garden to this House had been allowed to grow wild. Stone was passionately in favour of allowing things to grow wild. Stone hated the way some nudniks cut, pruned and reshaped Nature.

Stone wanted all the mice in the House, in *all* houses, to return to their natural habitat: the fields, the woods, the ditches and Hedgerows. Stone believed that mice should not live in houses. Houses, as all mice knew, he said, had once been the homes of giant prehistoric snails, now extinct. Mice had gradually moved into the dead shells, along with rats, bats and other creatures – and lately of course, the nudniks had arrived too – but houses were not the natural homes of any of these creatures.

'Mice are meant to be out in the open, amongst the grasses, in the banks of cow parsley, under the woodlands. They're meant to drink fresh water from cuckoo pints, to eat crab apples and woodlice, and to sleep in beds of hay.'

Stone was quite fervent when it came to such things.

While Skrang was considering whether or not to go outside and call on Stone, the hall Clock chimed seven and jerked her out of her thoughts. Her decision had been made for her. Seven o'clock? Night was running into day.

Instinct, a tiny feeling at the base of her tail, made Skrang suddenly turn and look up the stairs. Staring at her from about halfway down the staircase, moving ever so, ever so slowly, was Spitz. His eyes were narrowed and intent: they glinted like polished brass. His tread purposeful. His face was set as hard as brick.

When he saw that he had been noticed, he sprang down the rest of the flight.

Skrang was fast away, much too fast for the old cat. She shot left along the hallway and ran towards the living-room. Even as she ran, she cursed her luck. The escape route known as the Gwenllian Hole was at the other end of the hallway, straight on from the stairs. Spitz would have caught her though, had she gone straight. The momentum from his leap carried him directly towards the hole.

Skrang made for the shadow in the corner below the stairs, and almost collided with three other mice. A moment later, Spitz turned and came in the same direction, looking around him wildly. Neither the cat's sense of smell, nor his sight, were good and he spat and hissed in annoyance as he tried to ascertain the whereabouts of his prey.

Until the appearance of Skrang, Phart had been patiently explaining to an hysterical Flegm (who had never before been out of the cellar) that all they had to do was run to the Gwenllian Hole at the other end of the hall. Now their only escape route was blocked by a monstrous ginger tom, who seemed intent on catching at least *one* mouse.

'Oh my,' whispered Flegm. 'Oh my, oh my, oh my . . .'

'*Shut up*,' hissed Skrang.

Spitz paced up and down, staring intently into corners and cavities, occasionally spitting like a frying pan of fat on a red-hot range. It seemed that he was not going to leave without having investigated every nook and cranny. He knew there was a mouse about somewhere and he was set on finding it.

The letter-box lid suddenly opened and mail dropped on to the mat. The lid closed with a loud *clack*. Unseen by the mice, around the corner an old dog came out of the parlour, scooped up the letters with his mouth, and trotted back into the parlour.

Spitz paid absolutely no attention to this diversion, intent on catching the mouse he had seen.

Pedlar, who had witnessed Skrang's narrow escape with some admiration, felt they were doomed. He had more than enough imagination to see himself slammed flat by a heavy pawful of claws, and his innards spilled on the hallway floor. It was this image, of his intestines draped over his own feet, which locked his mind shut against any hope, any possible thought that he might escape, even though the cat could obviously only catch two mice at the very most.

At that moment Pedlar would rather have been back in the aromatic Hedgerow than anywhere else in the universe.

Spitz continued to pace, muttering to himself, sweeping the hallway with his swishing ginger tail.

Suddenly, at the partially opened living-room doorway, appeared the second and most deadly cat in the House. At that precise moment all four mice not only believed, but *knew* they were about to die. Eyeball, smaller, quicker and more athletic than Spitz, came padding into the hallway.

Miraculously, she already had something in her mouth. When she was fully in the light, her blue fur dancing with electric shadows, they could see that the *something* was another mouse. It hung limply from her jaws, its eyes glazed, its limbs drooping, but it was clearly still alive. Some foolish house mouse had dared to venture into Eyeball's domain, the living-room, and had paid the price for its recklessness.

Spitz was taking a keen interest in this catch. There was a look of indignation on his face.

Skrang knew what the ginger tom was thinking: he believed that Eyeball had caught the very mouse *he* had been chasing just a few moments previously. *His* mouse was in the mouth of his rival and he didn't like it one bit. His fur went up and he began spitting and whining in a very low voice.

Eyeball did not look at the other cat, nor did she even acknowledge its existence. She simply dropped the mouse on to the hall rug, where it instantly came to life and tried to run. She waited for a second, then flipped it through the air in a double somersault. It landed, rolled over, ran again in another direction. Eyeball carelessly watched it for a few moments, then leapt on it, tossed it backwards and forwards between her front paws several times like a ball, then suddenly bit it hard with a horrible *crunch*.

She flopped sideways, and continued to play. She tossed the now dead creature against the wall, batted it from paw to paw a few times, before flipping the corpse high into the air and catching it deftly in her mouth. Finally, she dropped it between her front paws and lay there on her side with it, as if defying someone to take it from her.

Pedlar, sick with terror, watched this harrowing display with a feeling of disgust. To think that the mouse he had seen somersaulting through the air had been alive just a few moments ago made him wonder what it was all about. One moment you were a happy soul, considering what to eat for your next meal, the next you *were* a meal – for some creature with a pawful of weapons and a mouthful of sharp fangs.

He had no time to ponder this further, however, for something interesting was happening in the hallway. The ginger tom had obviously decided that the young female cat with whom he had to share the House, had robbed him of his rightful quarry. The old cat was now approaching Eyeball, spitting and hissing in a very hostile fashion.

Eyeball, extremely fast, was up on her feet in an instant, the dead mouse between her jaws. From her throat issued a low warning sound not so very different from that of a dog's growl. Spitz rushed forward, his hair on end, his face fearsome with its lips curled back revealing a show of spikes. Eyeball lashed out with a lightning-fast bunch of claws, catching the attacker behind the ear, pulling fur and drawing blood. There was a flurry of legs, a twisting of bodies, during which the older cat seemed to come off the worst, then the pair parted again. Spitz wisely retreated out of range of the faster cat's claws. Red beads decorated the side of the tom cat's left ear. There was more spitting and snarling, more low growling sounds, as the pair backed away from one another, assessing the situation.

'*Que tu es une voleuse!*' the ginger tom spat in anguish at the she-cat he believed to have stolen his mouse.

Eyeball dropped the corpse between her paws. '*Moi?*' she screamed back. '*Pah! Menteur que tu es! Espèce d'imbécile!*'

To the four mice, not more than a few feet away, it was

52

like witnessing single combat between the gods. Cats were invincible, completely devoid of fear, the absolute masters of the universe. There was *nothing* as cold-blooded, as inevitable, as determined as a cat. To see this clash of such creatures was like witnessing the impact of two mighty suns hurtling into each other from opposite sides of the galaxy.

Looking at Phart, Pedlar could see the mouse's eyes were round with fear. His lower jaw was hanging open, giving him a wooden appearance. His body looked stiff.

In contrast, Skrang seemed calm. She had chosen the deepest part of the shadow on the wall, but she appeared cool and thoughtful, concentrating on the situation out in the hall. There was a time for freezing and a time for running: it was knowing what to do when which saved lives. Skrang was not going to die because she was frozen with fear when she should be running. Equally, she would not be killed in flight, when she should be tucked up against the skirting-board.

Flegm looked as if he might start running at any moment. His muscles were standing proud, his tendons taut, his whole body quivering with tension. Pedlar found himself ready to pounce on Flegm, in case he did try to break, and give them all away.

'*Tu n'es qu'un clochard,*' screamed Eyeball at the ginger tom.

'*Et toi, tu es une prostituée,*' snarled the old cat, who had been called worse than a tramp in his time.

These final insults having been traded, the two cats went their different ways, leaving the corpse of the mouse lying on the hall rug. To Pedlar this was the worst show of contempt for his kind he had ever witnessed. The fight then, had not been about a dead mouse, but simply a power struggle. The supposed cause of the fracas had been left disdainfully behind, not really wanted by either of the two feline monsters.

As soon as the cats had gone, the two Stinkhorns bolted, running for the Gwenllian Hole at the other end of the hallway.

Pedlar and Skrang were left alone. Pedlar felt drained. Out in the Hedgerow he could have bolted into a hole, in amongst some thorns, up a hazel branch. He had never been so close to cats before and the stink of their coats made him want to be ill. The relief that he was still alive, still whole, was enormous, though his heart wouldn't stop thumping against his ribs. He huddled against the wall, getting his composure back, swallowing hard to get rid of the taste of fear.

'I haven't seen you before,' said Skrang.

'I'm new to the House,' admitted Pedlar, reluctantly leaving the comfort of the wall, 'and so far I'm not much impressed by the mice I've met here. Not you of course — you seem to be reasonably sane. I ran into those two in the cellar, on my way into the place. Are the rest of the mice here like them, or more like you?'

Skrang shrugged. 'Neither, really. What did you come here for, anyway?'

'Ancestral voices told me to come. I had to obey their call and leave the Hedgerow. Then I found the House sort of pulled me towards it.' Pedlar deemed it wise to keep to himself exactly what the voices had said.

Skrang nodded. 'Ancestral voices? You must have been chosen for something important. I wonder what? So, now you're here you might as well make the best of it. You need to find a tribe to take you in. You're a yellow-neck, like me, so you won't find it easy to fit in with the house mice.

You look a bit too old to begin Deathshead training, but I expect the Bookeater Tribe would take you in. They're not a prejudiced bunch, though a bit woolly-headed. If you don't mind a crowd of fuzzy-brains, you might well do all right with the Bookeaters.'

Pedlar considered this and then said, 'Can't I just be on my own, like you are?'

'I'm not on my own, I'm a member of the Deathshead. We're a semi-religious sect. It would take too long to explain what and why we are, but you wouldn't survive very long as a solitary mouse. You need the protection of a tribe. The only thing is, the Bookeaters don't often get cheese.'

Pedlar shrugged and sighed. 'I don't know much about cheese – I seem to remember now that there were myths about it in the Hedgerow – but apart from that . . . Anyway, the Bookeaters sound as good as any I suppose. Can you speak to them for me?'

'I'll do better than that. I'll take you to them,' said the spiritual warrior. 'And you don't need to thank me for it. It's what I'm trained for, to help other mice. How did you get into the House by the way. Did you pay the gate-keeper?'

'I came through the maze without any food. I had to fight Tunneller.'

'And you won?' said Skrang, her eyes widening.

'We fought each other to a standstill.'

'Now that *is* impressive,' the Deathshead said. 'Follow me.'

Skrang led the way along the hall, to a place where there was a knot missing from one of the floorboards. She slipped down this hole, which was partially obscured by the edge of a thick rug, and motioned Pedlar to follow her. Once inside, in the cavity between the cellar ceiling and the ground, Skrang explained the hole to Pedlar.

'That missing knot is known as the Gwenllian Hole, after a priestess of the Bookeater Tribe. Throughout the House there are mouse holes named after dead mice, some of them secret, some of them for public use. All rooms have one single passage leading to Tunneller's maze, in case of emergencies. The Gwenllian Hole is public too, anyone can use it, and it will get us to the library eventually.'

'The library?'

'A place full of books, where the Bookeater Tribe hold sway.'

'I don't know what books are, but I suppose I'll soon find out. What about the Savage Tribe? Are they near-by?'

Skrang said, 'Not too far away. They live in the kitchen. They rule the divine never-empty larder.'

'Why are they so feared?'

'Because they're strong fat warriors. They have to be strong fat warriors to protect their great wealth. And while they have the copious larder, they'll always have the food to help them become strong fat warriors. It's self-fulfilling.' Her voice suddenly softened. 'Just a moment . . .'

Skrang stopped dead, in a place where electrical wiring ran in bunches alongside a beam. Pedlar followed suit and stayed absolutely still, looking at Skrang for some indication as to why she had halted so abruptly. He soon got it. A shadowy figure glided in front of them, along a narrow passageway of flooring timbers, which crossed their own channel. It was big – much bigger than the two mice – and Pedlar felt a chill run down his spine. Then the shape was gone, in amongst the dusty timbers, vanishing in the jungle of beams.

When he felt it was safe to breathe again, Pedlar said, 'What was that?'

'That was Kellog,' replied Skrang, moving on.

'Sorry to be stupid, but who's Kellog?' asked Pedlar, feeling that the longer he stayed in the House, the more of its dark secrets arose to trouble him.

Skrang said, 'Oh, sorry, I was forgetting you're new. Kellog is a roof rat. He's probably on his way to collect tribute from the Savage Tribe. They're the only ones rich enough to pay him. His nest is in the second attic. The Invisibles – they're wood mice in the first attic – they have all sorts of trouble with Kellog. You won't see much of him in the library – he never goes into the rooms – always stays within the walls and between the floors, in case he's seen by nudniks.'

'I don't think I've ever heard of a *roof* rat,' said Pedlar, hurrying to keep up with his companion. 'We used to have common rats and coypus, in the ditches where I lived, but not roof rats.'

'Another name for them is ship rats: they sometimes call themselves that.'

'What's a ship?'

'I don't know. You ask a lot of questions, country mouse. I don't know the answer to everything. From what I've been told, a ship is something like a nudnik travelling box, only it goes on water. Don't ask me *why*, because I've no idea. Ah, here we are at the entrance to the library. Look, I'm going to have to introduce you to the leader of the Bookeaters, then leave you, because my friend I-kucheng will be waking up soon and I want to be around when he does. If he starts wandering I'll never be able to find him.'

'He sounds a bit senile,' said Pedlar.

Skrang stopped and looked at Pedlar, before saying sharply, 'He's a fine old mouse, and he knows more than you and I and a dozen other mice put together. There's nothing wrong with I-kucheng's mind, believe me. His eyes and ears, yes, but not his brain.'

'Sorry,' Pedlar apologized. 'I didn't mean anything by it. I was just making an observation.'

They came to a vertical area and began to climb after that, using sloping props and struts to ascend the timber-framed cavity wall enclosed on either side by plaster. There seemed to be a vast array of crosspieces, braces and girders to climb, with Skrang navigating through this forest of lumber, until finally they reached an exit hole.

Instead of going through the hole, Skrang called out.

'Hello there!'

'Who's that?' cried a voice. 'State your name and your business.'

'It's the guard,' whispered Skrang to Pedlar. Then she called, 'It's Skrang, the Deathshead. I have brought someone to see Frych-the-freckled.'

'Who? Who have you brought? How many?'

'One. A yellow-neck by the name of Pedlar. A mouse from the Outside.'

There was a grumbling from the sentry, then she said, 'You'd better come on in then, I suppose.'

Only then did Skrang go through the hole and Pedlar followed her.

Pedlar found himself in a very strange country. He was high up, standing on some blocks, looking down into an oak-panelled room with a dusty-topped walnut desk below. In front of the desk was a large creature, half as high as a doorway, with a loose skin. It had white hair on its head and face. It seemed engrossed in one of the oblong blocks.

Pedlar had no doubt this was a nudnik. He was a little disappointed in it, and certainly not impressed. The nudnik looked like a great stupid beast. There were mice playing not three limbs length away from where it sat, and it was obvious that they had not been noticed.

'It's not as big as I expected it to be,' whispered Pedlar.

'What?' asked the guard, a house mouse with a disdainful expression on her face.

'The nudnik.'

Skrang explained. 'Perhaps it's because it's folded up at the moment. That's how they sit, sort of bent in two places: at the legs and in the middle. When they stand up and walk they're twice as tall.'

'Oh,' said Pedlar, not convinced. 'Still, it's not as striking as I thought it would be.'

'Can't pander to your expectations,' said the guard, sniffing. 'Fact is, nudniks can be quite aggressive sometimes, if you catch them in the right mood. I take it you haven't seen one before?'

'Not as such,' said Pedlar, still staring at the frumpy-looking creature in its creased skin. 'This is my first sighting of one, though I've heard them, and very recently ran through the legs of one. I didn't look up because it was expedient not to, at the time. That one looks a bit pale around the head and paws, doesn't it? I mean, it looks like it's already dead.'

'No,' the guard confirmed. 'It's alive all right, even though it isn't moving. Watch — see? See? It moved, ever so slightly. That skin it's got on its back isn't its own — they steal them from somewhere. We know they put on stuff made out of sheep's wool, and some of them wear fox furs — all sorts of other animal coats. Its *real* skin is that whitey-grey stuff on its face and neck. You get white ones

59

like that, and some of the senior Bookeaters say there are black ones sometimes. Then there are all sorts of shades in between. The size varies a bit too.'

'I've heard there's a shrunk one around, called Head-hunter.'

'No, Headhunter's a juvenile. That's different again,' said the guard, knowledgeably. 'Headhunter will be as big as that one down there, one hour.'

'Heaven forbid,' muttered Skrang.

Pedlar lost interest in the nudnik and glanced around the rest of the library, letting his gaze fall briefly on an object below a chair which looked remarkably like a sleeping hound, then let it travel over the whole scene. It was an extraordinary place, full of interesting items.

There was little furniture, but what there was consisted of highly polished hardwood. Pedlar had learned about furniture from travellers, so he knew the common stuff like chairs and tables, and carpets, curtains and beds, things like that. Some items he did not recognize. There were strange things like giant flowers, sprouting from small tables, which the guard explained were called lamps. They provided artificial light, such as that which had appeared suddenly in the cellar.

All around the walls, hiding the panels in many instances, were these blocks, just like the one on which Pedlar was standing. The outsides of these blocks were of many different colours, though mostly of sombre hue, and they varied in size a great deal. They smelled musty and leathery. Pedlar could sense the spirits of the forest were amongst them, but in a slow and lugubrious form.

'Books,' said Skrang and, being asked, 'That's why they're called the Bookeater Tribe. Books are made of paper, thin sheets which taste a bit woody, and these sheets are covered in things like dead insects, all laid out in rows. The nudniks often come in the library to look at the books for some reason. It doesn't seem to excite them at all, so it's got nothing to do with sex. And they don't eat the books, like we do, so it's nothing to do with food either. They seem to get some sort of mystical benefit from staring at the dead insects on the page. Sometimes you see their lips moving and sounds come out. Quite eerie.'

Pedlar looked about him in wonder. Everything in the room was covered in a thin layer of dust and there were marks in the dust where mice had run. Even the shaft of sunlight from the smeared window-glass was full of dancing dust motes. It was a quiet place too, the sort of place where a mouse could fall off to sleep.

A second Bookeater mouse arrived to escort him down from the high place. During their descent the lump under the chair moved and Pedlar was horrified to see that it really was a dog.

'There's a hound down there,' he warned the other two.

The escort looked at him in disdain and Skrang said, 'He hasn't been here long.'

Skrang then explained to Pedlar, 'That's Witless, a spaniel. In all the nights he's been around the House, he's never managed to catch a single mouse. Insects are more his mark. He's all right at snapping wasps and flies out of the air, but when it comes to chasing us, he's hopeless. He doesn't even bother to try these hours.'

'So I see,' said Pedlar, as below them a mouse sauntered past the floppy-looking dog, with hardly a glance towards it.

When they were halfway down the shelves of books, they dropped down between the wallpaper and the back of a row of thick volumes. It was this space, between the books and the walls, that the tribe used as their hidden territory. There were droppings everywhere. Out in the wild Pedlar was used to having some droppings near his nest, but this place was covered with them. He also passed several nests, made of paper, in which mothers were suckling their young. On the whole, the Bookeater Tribe looked a thin, emaciated bunch, and Pedlar wondered whether this was really the right home for him. He wondered, too, whether these Bookeaters were the 'many' referred to in the dream message from his ancestors.

Finally, they came to another nest where a female was feeding her young ones. Skrang introduced the mother to Pedlar.

'This is Frych-the-freckled,' said Skrang, 'leader of the Bookeater Tribe, and one of the most feared mice in the House. Even Gorm-the-old is scared of her.'

The mother twitched her whiskers and stared at Pedlar without speaking. She seemed to float on a boiling mass of pink bodies, squirming beneath and around her. She seemed unperturbed by their strugglings, moving this way and that to let them get at her milk.

'I've heard of you,' said Pedlar, excitedly. 'My mother told me about Frych-the-freckled. Aren't you a famous sorceress or something? You must be *ancient*.'

Frych, Skrang explained, was a highly respected witch as her mother and grandmother had been before her. Their sorcery was legendary. They had terrible magic at their clawtips.

'Who is this yellow-neck?' said Frych. 'Give me his name that I may know the secrets of his heart.'

The enchantress looked down on Pedlar with piercing eyes. Pedlar shuddered, noting that Frych's head-fur was covered in whitish spots, the residue of some conquered disease, and this probably accounted for the additional part of her name. He was impressed by her presence, her charisma. He didn't doubt she could turn him into a gnat with a flick of her tail.

'My name is Pedlar,' he croaked.

'Ped-lar,' she seemed to savour the syllables, rolling them around in her mouth as if she meant to swallow them immediately afterwards. 'A strange name – a *Hedge-row* name.'

'Yes, yes. That's where I come from.'

'Pedlar,' she said slowly, staring deep into his eyes and nodding her head. 'You are bound for greatness.'

'That's what my mother said,' cried Pedlar, 'when the cockchafer flapped its wings over me.'

'Ah, the crispy cockchafer's wings?' said the visionary. 'Then you are surely ordained for some mighty achievement.'

'Frych,' said Skrang, interrupting this exchange, 'I can't stay long, because I have to get back to I-kucheng Pedlar's from the Outside and as you can see by his yellow collar he's one of my own species, but he wants to live with your tribe. *He fought Tunneller to a standstill.* Can you take him in?'

Frych shifted a little to allow her six offspring to get a better grip on her, then turned to Pedlar with narrowed eyes.

'You bested *Tunneller?*'

Pedlar was beginning to wish he had laid Tunneller out cold. It would have saved a lot of explanations.

'Not bested, just equalled.'

'Well, that's enough, isn't it? A hero's a hero. If you walk away from Tunneller with all your parts still attached, you must indubitably be a hero. Welcome, *Apodemus flavicollis* to

63

the humble residential halls of the *Mus musculus*, the mice amongst the tomes. You have the appearance of a robust and zealous warrior. Such creatures as you, displaying the banner of friendship, are eternally desirable and I offer salutations with agreeable zest.'

'What?' said Pedlar, blinking.

Skrang whispered aside, 'It's the books she eats. Fills her with these long words. Doesn't know what half of them mean, herself. All the Bookeater elders are the same. Basically, she likes you and wants you to stay.'

'Oh,' said Pedlar, wondering in panic whether he was going to have to make a reply in the same vein. 'Er, a great many thank yous, Frych-the-freckled.'

'You are most exceptionally acceptable – such aristocratic address and manners. Skrang, deposit the *flavicollis* with us and ascend the shelves. Our felicitations to your friend, the estimable I-kucheng.'

After which, Skrang said goodbye to Pedlar and left him with the Bookeater Tribe.

First, Pedlar found a place to sleep out the day, behind some books bound in hide. He was very weary from his journeys and adventures. The smell of the books reminded him of cows.

Later, when he woke, Pedlar began by getting to know his environment. He ran around the backs of the shelves, noting escape holes and retreats, just in case they became necessary. He met a great many mice, some of whom spoke in the same lofty tones as Frych-the-freckled, though the younger mice were less pedantic.

There was Gruffydd Greentooth, Owain, Mefyn, Hywel-the-bad, Ethil-the-bald, Rhodri, Marredud, Nesta, Cadwallon and a dozen or so others. The two he took to instantly were Ethil-the-bald and Rhodri, two mice about his own age, not yet walking around with their mouths full of pretentious words, though they did come out with the occasional longy which often stunned themselves as much as it did the listeners.

That hour Pedlar had his first taste of a book.

'Which ones are the best to nibble at?' he asked Ethil and Rhodri.

'Well,' replied Ethil, 'the old ones are obviously softer and easier to masticate – sorry, to *chew* – but the newer ones have more goodness in them. It's up to you. If you've got a good strong mandible, then I'd go for the new books.'

'Show me where,' he said.

'This way,' Rhodri said. 'Glossy or plain?'

'Plain I think, to start with,' replied Pedlar. 'Maybe I'll try glossy later.'

Thus he was led to a shelf where the books smelled of fresh printer's ink and crisp paper. He began to nibble at the pages with some suspicion, but after a while found that they were quite palatable. True, it was not a wholly satisfying meal, but it was as good as chewing on seeds. It filled his stomach and took away the hunger that pinched him inside.

While he was eating, the nudnik who had been there in the morning came into the library carrying a glass of milk and some biscuits. Then it seemed to become too absorbed in its book to eat, though it did drink some of the milk. Rhodri said that they would go down and eat the biscuits once the nudnik had left the room.

'It's every mouse for him or herself I'm afraid,' said Ethil, 'so you have to keep a sharp eye out. No-one's going to save you any crumbs. We get so little *suitable* provender in here and books become excruciatingly boring after a while. Sometimes we even manage to get a piece of cheese – though,' she added wistfully, 'it's not very often, I have to admit.'

'This cheese business makes me curious,' replied Pedlar. 'Why are you all so dead set on *cheese?*'

'Oh, lordy, don't you know it's the food of the gods – listen while I tell you a story . . .'

HERVÉ

The Quest for the Hallowed Cheese

There was once a great chieftain who lived in a house near to a nudnik docks. The chieftain's name was Rigolet and he was served by many Companions. The Companions were encouraged by Rigolet to consider themselves equal to each other in debate and thus the council meetings or Allthings were circular affairs, with no mouse setting itself up above his or her fellows. Rigolet, however, always placed himself in the centre of the circle, for he was the lord.

The House was a fortress against cats, who were unable to penetrate its interior. Rigolet's tribe grew strong and fat and was considered the most powerful in the area. It was Rigolet's intention to unite all the mouse tribes into one huge nation. Rigolet's sorcerer, Frolics-with-fleas had prophesied that Rigolet would one hour be transformed into a deity, a living god. Thus the great ruler would become unimpeachable, a divinity who could not be approached by mortals without they trembled in awe.

Frolics-with-fleas told him, *There is only one way for you to become a living god and that is to taste of the hallowed cheese, the cheese of cheeses.*

What, asked Rigolet of his sorcerer, is the name of

this wonderful cheese?

It has no name, replied Frolics-with-fleas, *but it is twice as rotten as blue vein, three times as runny as Brie, and seven times as smelly as the most terrible stink you've ever had the fortune to sniff.*

As good as that? cried Rigolet. Then I must send out my Companions to search the docks for this cheese.

So Rigolet's Companions went forth, each on his own separate mission, to seek the hallowed cheese. They went with the promise that whoever returned with the cheese of cheeses would share in ruling the great mouse nation. They went south and north, east and west, and various other fragments of the compass. The tales of their adventures are too many to recount in this story, for they fought with rats and snakes, weasels and stoats, hawks and eagles. They forged rivers, climbed mountains, explored new valleys, new jungles. They crossed lakes and oceans, deserts and badlands, swamps and concrete wastelands.

One by one they returned, disheartened and dishevelled, their failure a burden hardly bearable.

Only one Companion, Desirée, the most trusted of all Rigolet's Companions and his right-hand mouse, continued undaunted to seek the cheese of cheeses.

One hour, when the owl was still and the weasel slept, Desirée came upon a great building, a warehouse, where cheeses wrapped in damp muslin were stacked high and wide in vast numbers, too many to count, as far as the eye could see and further. Desirée squeezed through a small hole and walked among the high columns and mounds of cheese, her nose overwhelmed by the multifarious aromas exuded by these wonders.

Surely here must be stored the cheese of cheeses?

There were indeed many great cheeses stacked in the

warehouse, from Pont l'Évêque to Sage Derby to Pfeffer Kranz, and Desirée tasted of them all. Seventy nights the mouse stayed in that warehouse and in that time tasted of seventy cheeses. Finally Desirée came upon a tiny fragment of cheese set on a cool platter of slate. The mouse knew instantly by its smell and texture that this was the heavenly cheese of the gods which she had been sent to find.

Now, this Companion to Rigolet knew that she had grown too fat to squeeze through the exit hole, so she had to starve herself for the next seven nights in order to be lean enough to escape from the warehouse. During that time she just sat by the precious cheese of cheeses and drank in its deep redolence.

When the mouse was finally slim enough to get through the hole she took the piece of cheese gently between her jaws, to take it back to the chieftain Rigolet. She went through the hole and out into the night, set on a course for the House wherein Rigolet and the other Companions eagerly awaited the return of the most honourable and courageous of their number. It is true that Desirée had no wish to become a living god, for the Companions had their chieftain's promise that whoever returned with the hallowed cheese would share in ruling the land. However, after having starved herself for so long, and with the wonderful cheese only a swallow away from her craving stomach, Desirée's journey was a most harrowing one fraught with the possibility that the fragment might *accidentally* slip down her throat.

Eventually and without mishap however, Desirée reached the House and entered, requesting an audience with Rigolet. The chieftain eagerly went to greet his long-lost friend, and heaped praises on the head of his most faithful Companion.

The hallowed cheese was presented to the lord, who ate it with relish.

Rigolet was instantly transformed into a cat.

Desirée was caught and devoured, while the rest of the tribe scattered throughout the House, the sorcerer among them.

Thus did the prophecy come true. Rigolet was indeed a living god and for ever more his tribe went in awe of him. Desirée shared in the cat's rule of the House, for that loyal mouse was indeed part of the cat. There was no mouse nation however, nor would there ever be, for it is not the natural state of mice to grow into a nation, but to work in small tribes, for that is what makes them a successful and prolific group of mammals.

BRIE

E THIL WAS RIGHT, WHEN THE TIME CAME FOR THE
white-whiskered nudnik to leave it was every mouse
for itself. As the great old creature stood up from its
desk, stretched and yawned, and left the library there was
literally a riot. Young were abandoned on their nest, the
nipples of their mothers torn from their mouths in mid-
suck. The chewing of midnight snacks ceased abruptly and
the pulp of half-gnawed books was spat across space with
contempt. Scrapping stopped immediately, along with arguments and disagreements, even among those at the height
of a quarrel. Mating couples parted instantly, leaving their
passion floating somewhere in the air above the dust.

Dozens of house mice scrambled, jumped, clawed, raced
and pushed, to get to the milk and biscuits, hoping against
hope that they were cheese biscuits, or that a cheese sand-
wich had been prepared on the same plate, leaving tiny

traces of the precious food. Open hostilities began on the desk between families and individuals, all determined to get some of the food. Mice were tossed and knocked bodily to the floor from the desk top, only to scramble up the drawers of the desk again, to throw themselves into the fray. Frych-the-freckled was in there, battling with Gruffydd Green-tooth for a bite of biscuit. Mefyn and Nesta fought off Hywel-the-bad when he tried to force his body between them, to steal a crumb from under their noses. Even Ethil and Rhodri were in the struggling horde somewhere. The whole writhing mass of bodies around the food made Pedlar wary. He had never seen such lack of restraint in mice before, and he did not want to get involved in the furore, for fear of injury.

A reckless mouse called Cadwallon jumped from a top shelf directly into the nudnik's abandoned milk, causing a mighty splash to shower those on the outside. There were yells of alarm as the glass rocked under the impact. Then there were a few moments when Cadwallon was in serious danger of drowning, but luckily the great seething and surging finally knocked over the glass. Cadwallon spilled out, along with the milk, and was washed over the edge of the desk. Pedlar saw him regain his feet in an instant and begin lapping the white fluid that dripped from the edge of the desk.

Such a riot for such a small amount of food was outside Pedlar's experience and he could only look on in disbelief.

When the food had all gone and calm had been restored once more, Pedlar spoke to Ethil again.

'That was a strange display,' Pedlar told her, not wishing to antagonize his new friends by saying what he really thought: that it was a disgusting exhibition of greed.

'Oh,' said Ethil, proudly, 'that's nothing. You should be

here when the cream cakes are going. It's a fundamental *massacre.*'

'Does that go on every time there's a bit of food going?' asked Pedlar.

Ethil stared him in the eyes.

'Listen, my yellow-necked friend, when you've been masticating tomes here as long as we have, you'll realize that book-chewing can become very, very boring.'

For the moment, this statement meant nothing to Pedlar, but he would come to remember it once he had been in the library for a few hours. In the meantime, he found a nice thick stack of ledgers on a corner shelf, and he began to nibble at their pages to satisfy his hunger. However, the second and third experience of eating books was not as satisfying as the first had been. It seemed that even though his stomach felt full afterwards, he was left with a feeling of hunger.

On the whole, the Bookeater Tribe was a peaceful group, only brought to violence when attacked by another tribe, or when there was real food to fight for. They tended to be very grand mice, parading about a lot, promenading along the bookshelves, gesturing and speaking in lofty tones, but Pedlar was never accosted in any way. In fact he found them quite a likeable bunch. When night came they were inclined to partake in some unusual ceremonies.

He discovered this when he had a little nap after his snack on the ledgers and woke to find the room in near darkness. It was the evening hours. The sound that had woken him – a kind of low chanting – seemed to be coming from the side of the library where the French doors were situated. Pedlar made his way along the shelves and found half a dozen mice engaged in a peculiar dance in the moonlight that streamed through the glass. As they moved back and forth, swaying in tune to some inaudible rhythm, their eyeballs swivelled up into their skulls revealing just the blind whites. Pedlar saw Ethil on the edge of the group, not participating, but transfixed by the weird ceremony.

Pedlar went to her and said, 'What's going on?'

'Shhsssh!' said a mouse, standing next to Ethil. 'You'll interrupt the magic rituals.'

Ethil whispered very quietly into his ear.

'They're trying to invoke the spirit of Megator-Megator, the giant mouse who roamed the House before the nudniks came.'

Pedlar had never heard of Megator-Megator.

'Why?' he asked quietly. 'What for?'

'*Umm, umm, umm, umm, umm, umm, umm,*' chanted the dancers, as they weaved their mystical patterns on the library floor.

'So that he can annihilate the Savage Tribe for us – then we can move into the kitchen.'

Pedlar was disturbed by this. 'But if he's a giant mouse, why would he want to help mice decimate other mice?'

Rhodri, overhearing this question, looked at Pedlar and said, '*Decimate?* What book have you been gnawing at recently? Decimate doesn't mean annihilate – it means to kill every tenth mouse . . .'

Pedlar hadn't known the meaning of *decimate* anyway – it just came out – and he had surprised himself by using it.

'*Umm, umm, umm, umm,*' went the dancers.

Ethil said, 'To answer your question, it's because we're good at magic, that's why. Even if Megator-Megator doesn't want to destroy other mice, he will do so because we'll make him into a zombie. His spirit will be our slave. We can do that, you know. This is a den of sorcery and witchcraft. The

Savage Tribe have strength and fierceness, but we have our magic.'

One of the chanting dancers broke away from the main group, her eyeballs swivelling violently. She held her ears in her paws, staggered three paces into a convenient shaft of moonlight, and then stood stock still. The other dancers ceased their swaying and chanting, and turned their attention to the deserter from their number.

When she was sure she had her audience's undiluted attention, the solitary mouse opened her eyes, and shrieked, 'THE HOUSE WILL COME TO AN END IN THE HOUR FIVE MILLION AND TEN!'

'A prophecy! A prophecy!' screamed the others.

Ethil, however, groaned. 'Not again. That's the seventh end-of-the-House prediction we've had in eighteen hours. You'd think they'd know better. They go into a trance, you see,' she explained to Pedlar, 'and while they're in the catalepsy they see visions. I just wish they'd see something a little more original than the end-of-the-House.'

To Pedlar, who had never heard a prophecy before, it was quite a dramatic moment. It chilled him right down his spine to the end of his tail. He wondered if it might have something to do with his own role as the one who was destined to walk with the many. The prophetess had sounded quite genuine and he was willing to believe that something was going to happen in the hour 5,000,010. He said as much to Ethil.

She grimaced and shook her head.

'For a start, no one knows when the hour five million and ten will be reached, since the age of the House is questionable. If nothing happens, then they just shift the timing, and say, "Oh, the House must be younger than we thought it was", or something like that. You wait and see.'

74

Pedlar still thought the scene very moving. He had never really come across magic before and it seemed to exert a powerful influence over the Bookeater Tribe, although there was nothing *actually* there, little tangible evidence, little proof of sorcery. Except . . . was it simply an atmosphere, which pervaded the whole library, and made it seem a place that was dormant in some way? Hidden knowledge, *forbidden* knowledge, lurked in the corners of the room, amongst the dusty books, between the yellowed pages of the leatherbound volumes. There were strange words in the air; dark, unfathomable words which sounded like no foreign tongue Pedlar had ever heard.

He was not sure whether he liked books: neither the eating of them nor their contents. Around the library were several volumes which had been picked up and opened by nudniks, then put down and forgotten. Mostly these books just contained the usual strange symbols, like clawmarks in the dust, but occasionally there were pictures. In one of the open books Pedlar had been shocked to see a picture of two mice dressed in nudnik clothes. Were they – Pedlar thought, horrified – mice trying to look like, trying to *become* nudniks, or nudniks who had somehow changed themselves into mice? Looking at this bizarre picture sent more shivers down Pedlar's back, making his fur stand on end. This was the most potent evidence he had seen of magic, this picture in the open book. Something ugly and disturbing was going on here.

After the dance ceremony, which had its impressive finale in some poor demented mouse working herself up into a frenzy and then falling on the floor, gibbering in an unrecognizable language, Pedlar left to look for some food. It seemed he was always hungry in the library. Being a yellow-neck, he was a bigger mouse than the house mice that made up the Bookeater Tribe, with a much longer (and of course, more elegant) tail. He needed richer sustenance than the pages of books had to offer. It seemed he was going to have to leave the sanctuary of the library, to seek out better nourishment elsewhere in the House.

Pedlar left the library through one of the guarded holes in the wall. He told the sentry he would be back within an hour and the sentry looked as if he couldn't care less. Then Pedlar went between the walls and under the floorboards, to come out at the Gwenllian Hole and into the hallway.

He was beginning to understand the geography of the House now, and he stayed well clear of the living-room, where the cats were most likely to be found. He also kept away from the kitchen door, knowing that a meeting with the Savage Tribe was almost as dangerous as coming up against a cat. Instead, he decided to look upstairs, in the bedrooms. He had heard that nudniks often left scraps of food in the places where they slept.

Pedlar ran up the skirting-board alongside the stairs, to the landing above. Not knowing what to expect from any of the rooms, he entered the first one with an open door. Inside, he stopped and sniffed. It smelled musty. The light was poor too, but he went across some rugs to where the legs of the great nudnik nest seemed to grow from the floor. Here Pedlar found some small crumbs, barely digestible, scattered on the floorboards. He ate them quickly, keeping a fearful watch on the doorway at all times. They did not satisfy completely.

He went under the bed-nest itself, to search amongst the fluff and dust underneath, finding only a dead spider. The corpse was so old it was crumbling. Then Pedlar emerged on the far side. Evening light, soft and roseate, was coming through the leaded window. He climbed up on to a carved wooden chest, to look at the world outside, needing its familiar perspectives.

Once on the windowsill, he stared out through the panes. The sun was going down in a cardinal pond. House martins were slicing through the air outside, weaving bladed patterns around the eves. The unkempt garden seemed quite small now. Beyond it lay the fields, some brown, some green, falling away to a distant haziness where trees rose and shook their heads.

Out there the world abounded with chattering, field-happy life, whether predator or prey. In this musty, dusty inside world, where there was no fresh wind, no sweet rain, no bright warm sun on his fur, the heart was rarely light and life was too deadly serious all the time.

Pedlar sighed heavily, thinking of his old nest, with its warm hay and dry blackthorn leaves. Its hollow was made to fit his body exactly. Every strand smelled of *Pedlar*: every leaf too.

'I hope you're right, Diddycoy,' he said. 'I hope you're right.'

Then came memories of dear old Tinker in the next chamber, always worried about Pedlar's ancestral voices. Well, look where those voices had got him now! And he still had not found 'the many' who needed him.

'Never mind, yer honour,' said a rasping voice from behind the curtain. 'You can go back, one hour.'

Pedlar almost jumped out of his skin. Then he smelled the sour breath, the odour of the wine, and the rankness of unlicked fur. His whiskers twitched with distaste. He nosed aside the left-hand curtain, and there, nibbling between his paws, was Phart.

'Nice to see you, yer honour,' said Phart, his red-rimmed

and vein-crazed eyes blinking rapidly. 'I heard you was now livin' with the Bookeaters. Strange lot of coves, them. Start burbling them weird words at you, don't they?' He gave a little shiver. 'Bet they'd turn you into cat's leavin's, soon as look at you, eh?'

'They've been very kind to me,' said Pedlar, 'so don't you go running them down, Phart.'

Phart went high-nose and looked haughty. 'Well, I bet you miss some of our grub, don't you? Them books is all right in an emergency, but it's like eatin' bleedin' dust after a while, ain't it?'

Pedlar nodded. 'I can't argue with you there.'

'I was thinkin',' said Phart, getting a distant look. 'How would you like some nice cheese. Have you ever ate cheese? Sort of yellow stuff, made out of milk?'

'I'm told it's very nutritious,' said Pedlar.

'Nu . . . *nutritious*?' cried Phart, going low-nose again in his astonishment at this understatement. 'Why, it's the very life-blood of the mouse nation! Cheese is, sort of crumbly and yet smooth at the same time. Cheese has got this pungency what'll make your senses reel. Cheese is . . . is *cheese*.'

'You – you wouldn't happen to know where we could get some?' said Pedlar, salivating at this description.

'Me? I know where everythink is. I'm the source of all information, me. You must've heard that Outside?'

'No, I haven't, but what about it? Can you take me to some of this – cheese?'

Phart nodded conspiratorially, his moth-eaten face going very close to Pedlar's precious whiskers and breathing fumes into his sensitive nostrils.

'Just follow Phart, yer honour. He'll find you enough cheese to fill yer belly for a couple of hours.'

Phart led the way back through Claude's Hole, under the floorboards, between the walls. The leader of the Stinkhorn tribe moved very carefully, now that he was outside his own territory, the cellar. At times Pedlar almost became exasperated at his caution, thinking they would not reach the cheese this side of noon. Finally they reached a dark open area with soft felt underfoot. It was a place of rafters and floorbeams and it struck cool on the fur.

Phart's teeth were chattering when he finally stopped.

'What's the matter?' asked Pedlar. 'Are you cold?'

'Cold? Yeah, that's what I am, cold. Never mind there's a bleedin' owl up here somewhere. Never mind Kellog's got his nest here too!'

'Oh, you mean you're *scared*,' said Pedlar. 'Where are we then?'

'We're in the land of the Invisibles, that's where. They're a wood-mice tribe of the attic. You won't see 'em though. Not unless they want you to. Come on. The cheese ain't far from here.'

Still quivering with fright, Phart led the way. Pedlar decided that cheese really must be a wonderful food, if Phart was prepared to go through this kind of terror to get some. Of course, Pedlar himself was none too keen on owls. Out in the wilds of the Hedgerow they were the most feared of the flying predators. Tawny owls, barn owls, the murderous short-eared owl and the deadly little owl. They were the silent killers, the great grey faces of the night. Mercifully, he supposed, you wouldn't really know what had hit you if an owl snatched you from life.

When Pedlar peered into the dim distance, he could ascertain vague shapes of all kinds: rounded, sharp cornered, angular, smooth. There was a mysterious mountainous country beyond, where the light was ancient and soft dust had settled like a sheet over the whole region.

Pedlar swished his long tail nervously as he crept after Phart. There was also the famous Kellog to consider. Rats were known throughout the mouse world as being vicious creatures. Common rats were bad enough, but Pedlar had been told a roof rat would bite your head off as soon as tread on your tail. He considered what he was doing: following an unreliable creature like Phart into the unknown, into a place where owls and roof rats ruled. It was rather foolish.

Suddenly something in the darkness made Pedlar stop in his tracks. He sniffed the air, his whiskers twitching.

What was that absolutely *delicious* aroma of something that had gone off?

Phart, aware that Pedlar had halted, turned in the deep gloom and regarded his face.

'Ah, smelt it have you? Nice ain't it? Sort of sets you tingling from whiskers to tail, don't it?'

'Is that the *cheese*?' whispered Pedlar, awed.

'That's the stuff. Nice bit of blue-vein by the smell of it. You get all different sorts. This kind is sort of oldish and a bit more moist than most. Not like the runny stuff, of course, but softer than the solid yellow cheese. Makes your toes quiver, this one.'

Phart continued to lead the way through the cobwebs and dust and fluff of the attic, until they came near to some boxes. Pedlar could see a square of light lying flat on the floor, and guessed there was some kind of trap door there. Near to the trap door was a flat wooden object with a wire contraption on it. It was on this object that the piece of cheese stood.

Pedlar moved a little closer to the piece of flat wood and Phart suddenly stepped back a couple of paces.

'What's the matter?' asked Pedlar. 'Don't you want any cheese?'

'Eh?' said Phart, sounding nervous and picking at his nose with a claw. 'Oh, yeah, yeah. In a sec. You – er – you go first. I'll – I'll have a bit when you're finished. After all, ha, ha, you ain't tasted it before, eh? New experiences ought to be witnessed, didn't they?'

'You still seem very nervous,' said Pedlar, wondering exactly what was the matter with the house mouse. 'Is the owl around?'

'Well, yes and no – look, why don't you just grab the cheese and we'll get out of here pronto?'

Pedlar went over to the little wooden board and stared at the cheese in the middle. It seemed to be sitting on a spike or something, but it didn't look too difficult to pull off. The wood had a nudnikky smell about it, but then so did a lot of the things in the House: books, furniture, carpets. Everything smelled of nudnik. Phart was right. It was best just to grab the cheese and get away from rat-owl country.

'Go on, go on, *get* it!' cried Phart in a shrill voice. 'What are you waiting for? Get the bleedin' cheese, you country nit . . .'

Pedlar turned and glared at Phart. 'Don't call me names, cellar mouse. You'll find I have a nasty bite if I'm called to use it.'

'Sorry, sorry,' said Phart, his breath coming out in a whistle. 'I'm just sort of – sort of sweaty at the moment. Probably comin' down with something. Don't take any notice of me.'

Phart was looking around him the whole time, his eyes round and white. He was high-nose, as if he wanted to look over the beams around them, for any approaching enemy.

Pedlar decided it was now or never. He moved forward for the cheese.

'Good, good,' murmured Phart. 'Lovely . . .'

Pedlar stepped cautiously on to the wooden platter. It seemed all right. Nothing untoward happened. He moved to the middle of the board and sniffed the cheese. Good heavens, he thought, this is succulent food! He licked it with his long red tongue. Delicious!

Phart was running backwards and forwards now, his eyes on Pedlar and the cheese. He was muttering to himself, but the words were too soft for Pedlar to understand. Pedlar turned again and prepared to snatch the cheese.

A voice from the rafters shouted: 'Look out, you fool. JUMP!'

Pedlar instinctively leapt sideways.

There was a tremendous SNAP! and the board flipped high in the air. Pedlar blinked, not knowing what had happened. He felt a slight nip at the end of his body. When he looked he saw that the tip, just a fraction, of his tail had gone. He was bewildered. What on earth had happened? Where was Phart? Who was it that had shouted?

'Who's there?' asked Pedlar, looking up. 'Who called?'

A voice close by, from the shadows, responded.

'My name is Whispersoft,' said the voice, loudly. 'What were you playing around that snap-trap for? You could have been killed. Are you *that* hungry?'

'Snap-trap?' said Pedlar, feeling foolish at talking to the shadows. 'I've never heard of snap-traps.'

'Where have you been living? They're set by nudniks,' cried the voice. 'They put a bit of cheese on the trap to tempt you, then when you bite – BANG – the wire guillotine breaks your neck, or your back. Or traps you by the leg so you have to gnaw through it to escape. Nasty

82

things, snap-traps. Lucky I came along, or your carotid artery would be squashed against a lump of wood right at this moment . . .'

'Yes, I have to thank you for that,' said Pedlar, trying to peer into the gloom. 'Phart probably wasn't aware that the trap was ready to go off . . .'

'Phart?' exploded the voice in the shadows. 'Phart, damn his name to hell. That flea-bitten excuse for a house mouse brought you here did he? You're more naïve than I thought you were. Phart, my friend, was after the cheese. He couldn't get it until the trap had been sprung – they're *always* ready to go off by the way – and you were the idiot he chose to spring it for him. He would have walked over your twitching body to get the bounty and then left you for dead.'

Pedlar was at first astounded by the unseen mouse's words, then incensed.

'You mean that swill would have had me killed for a lump of rotten cheese?'

'Phart would poison his own babies for a lump of rotten cheese,' cried the voice. 'Phart would eat his own grand-mother if she was made of cheese.'

'I'll kill him,' snarled Pedlar. 'I'll bite his blasted head off!'

'If you can catch him,' shouted the mystery voice. 'He's probably halfway to the cellar by now, and still running. He won't hang around now his plan's been discovered.'

'Why are you shouting?' said Pedlar, looking around the attic nervously. 'Won't you attract attention to us?'

'Can't help it,' cried the mouse. 'That's why they call me Whispersoft. Well, can't stand here chatting all night either. I'm off. Good luck, yellow-neck.'

'Pedlar,' said Pedlar.

There was no reply. Pedlar thought he saw a ripple in

the grey shades amongst the warp and weave of the shadows, but he couldn't be sure. He heard nothing either. Whispersoft's voice might be loud, but his tread was light. Not even a swishing of a tail in the dust. Not even the brushing of whiskers against wood. Simply an acute awareness of the settling of fine dust on rafters and the sense that the air was now less dense in a certain corner of the world.

Pedlar turned his attention back to the cheese. Now that the trap had been sprung, he saw no reason not to eat the bait. He went back to the board and forced himself to step on it once again. It was not easy, not after he had witnessed the vicious springing of the wire. Instinct told him to stay away from such traps, never to set paw on one again. However the cheese *was* delicious. It was absolutely scrumptious.

When he had eaten his fill, Pedlar took some of the cheese in his cheeks, hoping to carry it back to Ethil and Rhodri in the library. However, before he had scrambled a few paces, the light changed dramatically. He looked up, to see a huge feathered shape flying across the attic, towards a hole at the end of the House. It landed on a beam and stared around it, obviously preparing to go out hunting, but cautious.

The owl!

He swallowed in fright, and the cheese went down.

Pedlar had lost many brothers, sisters and cousins to owls. They had such an array of weapons on their face and feet, such a swift silent glide, such a keen eyesight in dim light, that once they had you marked for prey there was nothing left to do but rub noses with your loved ones, wish them all they wished for themselves, and then bid the world *adieu*.

Pedlar stopped, his heart beating fast.

The owl inched its way along a rafter, its eyes glowing orange in the thin shafts of light coming from its entrance hole. It was a little owl, the characteristic white spots on its neck forming a 'V'. Squat, with a large head, it bobbed a little as it shuffled along its perch.

It was truly a monster.

Pedlar-remained-ab-solutely-still-not-even-breath-ing.

Then when the creature finally took off and flew out of the hole, he crept away, staying low and near to a floor-beam, slipping over, under and between a row of rusted nails that projected from the beam, as if he were winding soft wool around them. Only when he was through the hole and between the walls did he allow himself to expel the shallow air in his chest and breathe deeply. Only then did he allow himself to be angry with Phart again.

So angry was he that he couldn't help himself savaging an innocent old matchbox that some nudnik had left to gather dust between the walls. He leapt on it and ripped the box to shreds in fury, scattering the pieces over the long narrow cavity. Just the right proportions – that is, Phart-sized – the box made a good inanimate substitute for the missing chief of the Stinkhorn Tribe. The action helped to relieve Pedlar's feelings a little. Once that was over, he went on his way, finding his path through the maze of walls back to the library again.

When he arrived back amongst the books, he was amazed to see that the world was just the same. Activity in the library had carried on as normal while he had twice been within a whisker of death. It was as if the House had its own rhythm and this had not been altered by Pedlar's presence among its occupants. In fact Ethil passed him by with a cheery greeting, as if he had not left the library at all!

Rhodri, however, stared at Pedlar's tail.

'What has occurred?' asked the library mouse. 'You look as though you've been in a fracas.'

'Not a fight exactly,' said Pedlar, remembering the missing tip of his beautiful long tail with dismay. 'But something of the sort. Will it grow again do you think?'

Rhodri was unfortunately a very honest mouse.

'Sometimes they do, and sometimes they don't. More often than not, they don't.'

'Thanks, you're a great comfort,' said Pedlar.

'If I were you,' said Rhodri, 'I'd hie along to Frych-the-freckled and get her to magic it for you. She's a very good shaman, you know. She can cultivate a really good spell sometimes that will leave your eyes watering.'

'I don't want my eyes watering, I want my tail back,' complained Pedlar.

Nevertheless, he did go along to Frych later in the hour and asked her if she could do anything about the tip of his tail. She told him she could, but he had to believe she could. There followed a strange ceremony in which an ancient language was used and a lot of weaving and dancing was done around Pedlar's inert body. He felt acutely embarrassed when Frych chanted poems at his tail. It was all he could do to prevent himself from bursting out laughing. That would never have done, though, for Frych-the-freckled was deadly serious about her sorcery.

When it was all over, Pedlar asked Frych what he could do in return.

'You will discover opportunities to facilitate Frych before the epoch has incinerated itself.'

'Will I?' said Pedlar. 'All right then. Thanks.'

For the next few hours he inspected his tail-tip, hoping for some sign of change, but eventually he forgot all about it and only remembered when someone else mentioned it.

CAERPHILLY

'ASSUNDOON! ASSUNDOON!' THE BATTLE CRY OF THE Savage Tribe sounded shrilly over the kitchen floor tiles as house mice came hurtling out of their holes. Although it was night, moonlight streamed through the large windows, illuminating the racks of pots and pans, knives, the fine china in the Welsh dresser and the every-day crockery on the shelves.

'Smash their nests!' came back the answering cry from the invaders, the 13-K Gang. 'Steal their young!'

This raid, this battle, *all* battles in the House, had as their root cause one thing, one single nutritious delicacy – cheese, oh cheese of inestimable worth! – which could always be found in the kitchen. Cheese was the salt, the truffles, the roasted humming-birds' wings dipped in honey, the sheep's eyeballs, the ducks' tongues, the blow-fish, the caviar of the mouse world. Its aroma was more mystical, more wonderful, than myrrh or frankincense. Its taste was sublime. Its many textures could be discussed by mice, young and old, for hours on end. A mouse would argue the merits of one cheese over another until old age crept upon him. A mouse would hold open debate on the best of the best cheeses. Heaven, they would proclaim from the corners of the skirting-board, was fields fashioned of hard cheese, with runny cheese fountains. Hell was a cheeseless land where only the occasional tantalizing whiff of a rotten cheese might drift around to torment its denizens. A mouse would die for cheese. A mouse would kill for cheese. Cheese was the ultimate food. The many-textured, many-coloured cheeses of the Earth were unequalled, with their multiple flavours, soft or hard, their characters, their personalities, their blue veins, their red rinds, their deeply pungent odours, their glorious, glorious differences.

It was for cheese that mice fought to the death.

One or two skirmishes began around the entrance to the kitchen from the woodshed on this account, but the main objective of the raiders was of course the pantry. It was to this point that defenders of the Savage Tribe rushed. Gorm-the-old, with a snarl on his terrible visage, went immediately to the forefront of the battle and sank his teeth into the flank of a 13-K warrior, causing that creature to scream in agony.

At Gorm's right shoulder was Hakon, Gorm's principal double, whose job it was to confuse the enemy simply by acting and looking like the great chieftain himself. Hakon was echoing Gorm's words, copying his actions, and it was as if a looking-glass image was working alongside the chief. Those of the enemy who had the misfortune to be confronted by this duo were thrown into a state of panic and disorientation. Most turned and ran, not bothering to work out who was whom. Those brave enough to remain despite their bewilderment, suffered the full onslaught of twin pairs of incisors biting their flesh.

A 13-K *berserker* who ran full tilt at Gorm was picked up and thrown bodily across the tiles by the quicker-moving Hakon. Hakon, and his twin brother Tostig, always fought like crazy to protect their lord from harm. There was a good, practical reason for this. Any wounds Gorm collected would be visited on his doubles after the battle. On the other hand, they had to be mighty careful not to receive any wounds themselves: Gorm was none too happy when *he* had to receive purposely duplicated wounds.

Gorm's second double, Tostig, was at that moment leading a foray against some invaders who were attempting to reach the cooking pot hanging over the kitchen range.

Drenchie of the 13-K was spearheading this diversionary attack on the range and one of her warriors managed to run up the cold spit and leap on to the handle of the cooking pot. The idea was to dash around the lip and gather any pieces of stew stuck to the edge of the pot. Unfortunately for the poor creature the handle was greasy and the athletic warrior slipped and fell into the stew. There was one brief cry of terror followed by a sludgy *plop*. Then silence from the pot. Even though the range fire was out, and the pot's contents cold, death by drowning in stew was an unpleasant end.

'Bite their eyes out!' came the rallying cry from Ulf, rebel leader and estranged son of Gorm, now youthful chieftain of the 13-K. 'Tear their throats!' he screamed.

Ulf was surrounded by his protectors, the Chosen Ones, the most loyal and favoured of his gang, who repulsed any attempt by the Savage Tribe warriors at reaching their beloved and handsome chief. 13-K's experience in battle was limited, but they had great enthusiasm and energy, and they fought with the valour of youth. Ulf steered his warriors with determination towards the open pantry door and managed to break through the defenders with some of his warriors, to enter the bounteous never-empty larder of the Savage Tribe. The 13-K who were able to stay with Ulf had the contents of the hallowed ever-full larder at their disposal, though they did have to fight and eat alternately.

Gorm-the-old was furious at the breakthrough by the enemy and though his own personal bodyguards, the Immortals, had formed a semicircle around him and Hakon, Gorm could not manage to fight his way through the intruders to get to his alienated son.

'My own flesh and blood!' Gorm bellowed. 'Robbed by my own son. I'll rip his spleen out. I'll strip his belly of skin and fur. I'll have his gore!'

Drenchie by this time had managed to counterattack Tostig's forces, driving the defending mice back to the kitchen table. Two or three of her number scrambled up one of the legs and yelled in triumph when they found the surface laden with bread, cheese and vegetables. They sent pieces of food raining down on Drenchie's warriors, who snatched them up eagerly and ran towards the kitchen door. Highstander, another 13-K captain, helped to force a passage for these warriors retreating with spoils.

A milk bottle had fallen over in the corner of the kitchen and a pregnant 13-K warrior squeezed through the neck opening to get at an egg-cupful of milk inside. She drank the rich full cream until her belly was pendulous, then panicked when she found she couldn't force her body out of the bottle again.

'Roll in the milk,' yelled one of her friends on the outside. 'Get your coat wet and slippery.'

The frantic doe did as she was bid and managed, with great effort, to squeeze through the neck with a *plop*.

She hurried back to the woodshed, thoroughly frightened by her experience.

'Assundoon! Assundoon!' raged the leader of the Savage Tribe, rushing foolishly ahead of the Immortals that guarded his rear, as he chased after the 13-K brigands raping and pillaging his beloved larder.

Seeing Gorm without protection, some of the 13-K turned to face him, hoping for a moment of glory in overcoming the chieftain of the fiercest tribe the world had ever known. Hakon rushed to his lord's aid, hoping to reach him before he was overwhelmed by sheer numbers. Captain Gunhild of the Immortals, too, ran towards the isolated Gorm. There was already a yell of triumph from the 13-K warriors as they swarmed towards the solitary magnificent figure.

Suddenly, just when it seemed that Gorm would be overcome, the world was instantly bathed in blinding light and the battleground became a frozen tableau. A nudnik had come down from its sleep and had entered the kitchen. Mice scattered in all directions, heading for the nearest cover. Nudniks were stupid creatures, but they could also be very dangerous. No sensible mouse wanted a direct confrontation with a nudnik.

The raid was over. 13-K members scrambled through holes in the skirting and made their way through passages in the walls. Savage Tribe mice retreated to their nests in various hidden areas of the kitchen. The flight from the battleground had been so swift that it was doubtful the sleepy-eyed nudnik had even noticed any mice at all.

Later, once the intruder had gone, Gorm-the-old called a tribal Allthing, a meeting of the principal members of the clan, including Gytha Finewhiskers, Gunhild, Elfwin, Ketil, Skuli, Astrid and Thorkils Threelegs, as well as his trusted brother-doubles, Hakon and Tostig.

First, Astrid the High Priestess gave thanks to the Lord of the Shadows for a timely intervention by the gods of Assundoon, in order to save their leader from injury or death. Then Gorm had his usual debriefing exercise, which the others all hated.

'I want to know what happened tonight,' growled Gorm, 'and why the sentries weren't alert. The 13-K should never have got past our odour-line. There *were* proper marks at the edges of the kitchen, I hope?'

Gorm was referring to the method all mouse tribes, all mice anywhere, used to warn others that they were approaching occupied territory. This was the odour-line, where they marked their boundary with urine.

He received some nods.

'Then someone was asleep.'

Elfwin studied the face of her chief, with his nose scarred from a hundred battles, his ear torn in single combat with the previous chief, his left jowl sagging lower than the right where it had been punctured by incisors. That Gorm was ugly, was a known fact. That Gorm had a foul temper, could not be contested. (Only Thorkils Three-legs, with the evil disposition that substituted for his missing front limb, had a worse choler.) That Gorm was clever and fearless in battle, was known throughout the House. Gorm was 400 nights old, but his strength and brilliance were undiminished. And, of course, all his battle scars were echoed by his doubles, Hakon and Tostig, who bore the marks of identical wounds.

Elfwin asked, 'Who posted the sentries tonight? Who was the captain of the guard?'

There was a shuffling from the other members at the meeting and finally Ketil spoke.

'I am the captain of the guard tonight. It must have been my warriors who were less than alert . . .'

'Less than alert?' thundered Gorm. 'They were low-nose and in dreamland, that's what they were! Were they, or were they not, your responsibility?'

'They were my responsibility,' murmured Ketil, realizing that someone was going to have to suffer for the attack tonight and, yes, it was going to be him.

Gorm came right up to Ketil's face and pushed his nose amongst the captain's whiskers. 'I ought to rip out your liver,' he growled.

'Yes,' said Ketil, flinching.

There was a long silence during which Ketil simply stood and shook with terror, the fur rippling down his back. Then someone spoke.

'*Three* extra guard duties, no food for two hours and a loss of captain's privileges for seven hours, ought to do it Gorm,' said Astrid quietly.

Astrid was one of Gorm's favourites, who had borne him several young (his hated and rebellious son Ulf not being among these particular offspring of his loins). She was now unable to have babies, but Gorm still called her to his nest. Astrid sometimes intervened on behalf of the other captains, when they had incurred the displeasure of their chieftain and stood in danger of being executed on the spot.

Gorm continued to glare directly into Ketil's eyes, making the poor captain's legs shake with fear. Then finally the old chieftain said, 'Think yourself lucky you have someone to speak up for you. The punishment stands. Thorkils, you will time the period by the chimes of the Great Clock in the hall. No food for two hours and seven — no, *eight* hours,' he snarled, stamping his own authority on the punitive arrangements, 'loss of privileges.'

Ketil gulped, 'Thank you. I shall see that the sentries are suitably punished.'

'Nip their whiskers off,' growled Gorm, but he showed by a brief curl of the lower lip that he wasn't altogether serious about this ghastly punishment. Then the great chief turned to his doubles. He showed Hakon and Tostig a new cut on his body, where he had been bitten in the recent battle. It was a bloody rip on the right foreleg. Hakon and Tostig looked upset to see this mark. Nevertheless they inspected the wound closely, noting how it twisted in the middle and then forked at the end.

'How do you want to do it?' asked Gorm, not totally insensitive to their feelings.

'We'll do it to each other,' Tostig replied in a despondent voice.

'Just so long as the scars are identical to this one,' Gorm told them. 'The next time I see you both, I shall expect it to be like staring into a brace of mirrors.'

The pair nodded unhappily. It was ever thus after battle had taken place. Hakon and Tostig were forever trying to persuade Gorm that his place in battle was at the rear of the field, conducting his forces from a place of safety. 'You're too precious to us, to risk on the front line,' they told him hopefully. But Savage Tribe chieftains had always been by nature bad-tempered and fierce creatures who loved fighting and wanted to be up where the killing and maiming was to be had. Having such a disposition was, after all, how they came to be chief in the first place. Hakon's and Tostig's flattery fell on deaf ears.

When the Allthing was proclaimed over, and everyone

stood while kings and captains went their various ways, Thorkils Threelegs followed the unhappy Ketil to ensure that punishment was carried out.

'If I had my way,' grumbled Thorkils, 'I'd have bitten your leg off and have done with it.'

'If you had your way,' said Ketil, 'you'd bite *everybody*'s leg off. You want everyone to suffer the way you do, you foul-tempered old rotbag.'

'Watch your language, convict,' snapped Thorkils, limping along with surprisingly deft grace. 'I might have to sort you out myself after all.'

'You and whose band of hopefuls?' jeered Ketil.

'Don't push it, or I might just miscount the chimes, and it won't be in your favour.'

Ketil shut up after this threat, which had not occurred to him before now. Thorkils had real power over his immediate future, especially since he, Ketil, did not know how to count. He wondered whether he had ever told Thorkils this fact. It was a worrying thought . . .

FOURME D'AMBERT

Astrid, the visionary and prophetess of the Savage Tribe, went away to commune with the Shadows. Unable to make any sort of relationship with other mice, except for her almost furtive liaisons with Gorm, Astrid had formed a strange and exotic affinity with the Shadows around her. She talked to them, and they answered her. No other mice could hear these replies of course, which far from giving her concern, made her feel special and chosen by the gods.

'Shadows,' she said, her voice echoing amongst the pots

and pans, 'why didn't you warn me of the attack that's just taken place?'

Her tone was censorious, for she was not afraid of the dark nebulous shapes with whom she conferred. Astrid felt she should have been given some sign to indicate that the 13-K would attack the opulent ever-full larder, so that she could have forewarned her tribe. It would have brought her great honour, if she had been able to raise the alarm prior to the incursion.

The Shadows were quiet, not willing to communicate.

'Well?' she demanded.

Finally the reply came, *You have been neglecting us*.

'No I haven't. I spoke to you not three hours ago.'

But your mind was on other things. You were thinking of Gorm, not of us. You were savouring your last meeting with him, behind the vegetable rack. A priestess should not enjoy carnal encounters, she should be chaste.

'It's different for me. I'm now barren. I can no longer have any young.'

We're talking about the way you enjoy the company of this brute of a mouse. He has no sensitive feelings for you. He simply uses you for his own pleasure.

'And I use *him*. I can't help it. Anyway Gorm is the only one who wants me.'

Astrid was close to tears now. The shadows were always chiding her for her liaisons with Gorm. They seemed jealous of him – of the fact that he could give her something which they could not. Yet she needed such meetings, otherwise she had nothing at all to look forward to in life.

'It's all right for you, you Shadows. You don't have these – these *feelings*. You're just envious because you don't know how to be emotional with one another . . .'

'Of course they're envious.'

Astrid blinked, staring into the copper-bottomed pots and pans that gleamed in the moonlight. She could see nothing but her Shadows. Yet the last voice was surely not that of her critical friends? It had sounded more like another mouse. Someone had been eavesdropping, listening to her talking to her Shadows. This was sacrilege! Gorm would be informed.

'Who's there?' she demanded to know.

'It is I, Iban!' and a mouse stepped from behind a kettle, into a moonbeam. It was a yellow-neck, larger than Astrid who was a house mouse. The intruder however had a humble bearing and manner.

'I know you,' said Astrid, 'you're a Deathshead.'

'I am called such,' sighed Iban. 'But I am an unworthy follower of the god Yo, the Dark One. As his disciple I must eradicate *memory* as well as self, but try as I might I am unable to forget who and what I am. I have immense difficulty in shedding knowledge and achieving Great Ignorance. Even at this moment the musk of your perfume threatens to overthrow my vows.'

'What a shame,' said Astrid, rather flattered by his confession. 'But what did you mean when you said of course my Shadows are envious?'

'I meant this – the gods, and their Shadow messengers, do not approve of you finding ecstasy with Gorm because it is *they* who promise ecstasy – in the Otherworld, in Assundoon, in the afterlife. It is *their* territory. It is the only thing they have to offer. So naturally they discourage the ecstasy that exists when bucks and does have feelings for each other.'

'You seem to know a lot about ecstasy?'

'I am of course chaste, being a Deathshead.'

97

'So, you think my Shadows are just jealous?'

'I know they are. Anyone would be, of course. You are so beautiful.'

'Me?' she said, astonished. 'I'm always called *plain*.'

'Those who do so cannot see into your soul, as I can. It is a most wondrous place. A place of – of beauty. The thought of sharing a nest with you . . . ahh – I told you.' Iban looked miserable. 'I am unworthy of being called a Deathshead. You see, I still have wild, untamable thoughts. I must whip myself with my tail, to cleanse my mind, my spirit—'

'Oh, I wouldn't do that,' said Astrid, quickly.

'I must, I must! I am so unworthy. I must go now before my vows are shattered beyond repair.'

'Yes, you must go,' Astrid whispered, half turning her back on him, a gesture which any other male would have recognized as an offer.

A dry croak came from Iban's throat.

The scent of her wafted through the air, a fragrance too overwhelming to ignore. It caused Iban to choke his words back. He felt a deep tenderness towards her, even though such feelings were to him forbidden fruit. A great shudder went through his body. He could see her trembling, vulnerable, and he wanted to protect her. He wanted her to be his, to have and to hold. He wanted to watch over her.

'You-are-so-lovely,' he gasped.

It was the first time Iban had ever been so close to a doe – he was a mouse of nearly 400 nights – and this fact alone made the experience celestial for him. There were bright lights in his head, flashes before his eyes. There were odours the chemistry of which caused his brain to reel with astonishment and delight. He loved the look of her soft pelt and the way her silken whiskers brushed his face.

For Astrid it was like a dream, to be engulfed like this in someone else's passion. When Gorm was with her it was always as if he was thinking about which guards to post on watch that night. Now, here she was, being *adored*, but by a mouse who had sworn to be celibate.

Finally, Iban sat high-nose and stared down at her. 'Perhaps – perhaps we shall meet again some hour?'

'I would like that,' said Astrid, noting how firm Iban's muscles looked in the moonlight. 'Are you quite sure you can't stay for a while longer?'

'Farewell, priestess.'

'Farewell, Deathshead.'

As Iban disappeared behind the utensils, Astrid whispered to his shadow, 'Bring your master back again.' Then she went to her bed, ready to dream delicious dreams.

ROULÉ

In the 13-K camp there was both rejoicing and sorrow. Everyone had made it back inside the woodshed except for the mouse who had drowned in the stew. There was sadness at this death, but mice do not mourn. In fact one or two thought it would have been fun to watch the nudniks dish up their dinner tomorrow night, but since the 13-K were more or less confined to the brick-built woodshed attached to the kitchen, there wasn't much chance of that.

The food snatched during the raid was handed out, not always fairly but with some effort to ensure that everyone got *something*. There was a nice soft-textured piece of cheese amongst the spoils, of which Ulf and Drenchie received the first bites. They feasted and toasted their missing comrade at the same time. They sprawled amongst the woodpiles, languishing, enjoying being idle after the exercise.

Ulf was standing high-nose on the topmost log, saying, 'So, my fine band of outlaws, you did extremely well tonight. We can eat well instead of crunching on dry old spiders' legs and dead woodlice. 'Tis cheese, for the palates of the victors!'

He was cheered by his youthful followers. The 13-K consisted entirely of runaway adolescents from all the other tribes in the House. Ulf was from the Savage Tribe of course, Drenchie from the Bookeater Tribe, Highstander from the Invisibles who lived high up in the attic – and so on, and so on. They were eager creatures, full of righteous wisdom about how the world *should* be run. Theirs was the philosophy of discontented, disillusioned youth. Once they ruled the whole House, it would be a much better place to live in.

'The old leaders should make way for *us*,' Ulf was fond of saying. 'Their ideas are outmoded. They've got cobwebs for brains. We – *we* are a shining example of mice who know what is right and good for the world.'

The 13-K loved sitting around in groups, putting things to rights, discussing spiritual enlightenment. They said they wanted a world where there was only peace; where everyone loved each other, where there were no tyrants, no despots, only mice who ruled justly and wisely, first among equals. Learning, following in the oral tradition, was to be of the highest importance in their world. A storyteller was to be a valued tribe member. The historians, the mathematicians, the philosophers – those clever mice who carried knowledge in their heads and could impart it to others by word of mouth – these were to be amongst the most revered.

In order to get such a peaceful world of light and love, the 13-K had to fight and kill for it of course.

Ulf, like many others in the 13-K, would dearly have loved to be a Deathshead, one of the House's wandering, holy spiritual warriors who eschewed all material wants, all worldly desires, and gave themselves to Unn, the goddess of Light and Wisdom. (Though occasionally an unusual Deathshead, such as Iban, might dedicate him or herself to Yo, the god of Darkness and Ignorance). They drank only rainwater and ate iron-hard crumbs that had lain amongst the dust for centuries of nights. Followers of Unn were intent on the eradication of *self*: followers of Yo were expected to obliterate *memory*. The Deathshead were necessarily very few in number, due to their high suicide rate.

Purity of body and soul were the prime objectives of these spiritual warriors, the foremost of whom was known as I-kucheng – mediator, arbitrator, or (by those who disliked him) 'that infernal meddling judge'.

Ulf had often told Drenchie that he wanted one night to be a Deathshead. But the physical and mental training, the mastering of skills, before spiritual enlightenment and physical superiority were achieved, was both arduous and long. There were nights of meditation to pass through; hours of renunciation; vigils to undergo; chants and verses to memorize; martial arts to master; fear of personal isolation to overcome. Furthermore, one had to come to enjoy asceticism, celibacy and seclusion. This was not an easy task for creatures whose greatest delights were food, wanton games and the riotous company of their fellow mice.

Finally, it took 350 nights to make a Deathshead and

to most of the 13-K this was a lifetime. If they were going to be chaste and humble, they wanted to be so *now*, not when they were too ancient to be able to flaunt such virtues and bask in the admiration of others. Ulf was just as impatient as the rest of his gang, but continually voiced his intention to begin training for Deathshead 'any hour now'.

Typically, Ulf was speaking to a group of his followers even as he ate his share of the spoils from the raid.

'A Deathshead knows the way to *Truth* through the teachings of Unn,' he stated. 'You can only find that path when you eradicate *Self*. The true Deathshead doesn't know who or what he is – he's in a state of complete ignorance.'

Drenchie, lying limply over a piece of kindling, remarked sourly, 'I thought the way to Ignorance was through Yo, not through Unn.'

Ulf glared at his constant companion and occasional mate. 'Yes, well, that's true of course,' he said, 'but it's a different *kind* of ignorance. With the god of Darkness you don't know anything, but with Unn you've deliberately taught yourself to *forget* everything.'

'Sounds the same thing to me,' sniffed Drenchie, getting the attention of the crowd once more. 'If your head's empty, it's empty, isn't it?'

Ulf ground his teeth as he chewed on some slivers of pork.

'It's the *way* to that emptiness that's important – for the sake of purity of soul. You see, Drenchie, you're just looking at the mental state, but you have to take into account the spiritual state too. You can be ignorant and have a soul black with sin, or you can be ignorant and be pure.' Ulf felt very pleased with himself at having reached

102

this conclusion, simply by making it up as he went along. 'You do see what I mean?'

'Yes,' said Drenchie, 'you've got a skull full of mouse droppings.'

Ulf put on the air of condescension which he knew infuriated his mate. 'That's hardly a reasoned argument,' he said.

'I don't give a vole's orphan whether it's reasoned or not,' snapped Drenchie. 'I know *you*, and I know when your jaws are just rattling for the sake of hearing your own voice. If you want to be a Deathshead, just go away and be one, don't go on and on talking about it.'

Ulf showed her his haughty expression. 'I shall do, one of these hours, but my gang needs me at the moment, to lead them.'

'Huh!' was the short answer his mate gave to this statement.

Ulf, irritated as usual by this female runaway from the Bookeater Tribe, turned his back on her and began to wander amongst the other members of the gang, lounging amongst the logs and kindling. Most of the time the 13-K did not even bother to post sentries around the woodshed. They had nothing that the rest of the house mice would want. The woodshed was a relatively safe place for mice. Nudniks came occasionally, for fuel for their fires, but Eyeball had only managed to enter the woodshed once, many, many nights past.

There were two entrances to the woodshed, one from the kitchen, the other from Tunneller's maze. It follows then, that there were only two exits. One way led to battle, the other way to a bad-tempered gatekeeper who demanded food in exchange for right of passage. The 13-K situation was not ideal, but they were close to the kitchen and the bounteous larder, and that made the difference between life and death. If a cat did get in, then the chances of escape were very limited.

It was true that Eyeball had killed four 13-K in as many seconds during her visit, but Ulf was aware that you couldn't be on high alert twenty-four hours a day, every day, simply because a deadly cat managed to get inside once in a blue moon. Eyeball was an act of god, like a plague. You couldn't sit around worrying whether the plague would come or not, could you? You simply forgot about it until it happened, *then* you worried about it. There was no answer to Eyeball anyway. She was the fastest thing on four legs the world had ever seen. A Burmese blue, she was fond of hiding in the shadows, and the last thing you saw, before death, was her eyes widening as she struck.

As Ulf strolled among his wassailing warriors, the satisfying smell of drying applewood logs in his nostrils, he recalled that there was something which had to be done in the near future. It was time to send an expedition to secure the second cupboard on the landing. This particular cupboard belonged to the 13-K by right of conquest. All the cupboards and drawers in the House belonged to different tribes, whether they were in a particular tribe's territory or not. Expeditions had to be sent to make sure such outposts of empire had not been used by rival tribes. Any trespassers had to be punished by a raid on the tribe responsible.

There was usually nothing in these cupboards and drawers of any interest to mice, but it was necessary to have safe havens available when out on forays in a foreign part of the House. The 13-K knew that if they needed sudden refuge from Eyeball, or a loose nudnik, they could nip into a cupboard or drawer owned by their tribe. Likewise with the Savages, the Invisibles, the Stink-horns and the Bookeaters, who all had their safe havens, while the Deathshead went where they pleased.

Ulf called two new young mice, recent runaways from the long-tailed harvest mice in the grasses outside the wood-shed, and explained all this to them – before presenting them with the startling news that they were to form the next expedition.

'B-b-but,' stammered one of the terrified duo, 'we don't know the way to the cupboard.'

'Oh, I'm not going to send you alone,' laughed Ulf. 'You'll have a guide. Miskie will go with you as far as the top of the stairs. She'll point out which cupboard is which and then all you have to do is scuttle along the landing and squeeze under the cupboard door. Nothing to it.'

'Nothing to it,' echoed the second harvest mouse, hollowly.

'Oh, and one more thing,' said Ulf thoughtfully. 'If you should meet Eyeball – no, on second thoughts, never mind.'

'Oh, oh, what, what? Tell us!' cried the first mouse, going high-nose.

'No, it doesn't matter,' said Ulf, strolling away. 'Good luck, both of you. We'll hope to see you back in an hour or two. I'll get Miskie to come to you right away.'

He left the two harvest mice looking as if the death sentence had just been passed on them. They were certainly regretting ever entering the House. As things stood, there didn't seem the slightest chance of them getting out again, since they had nothing with which to bribe Tunneller, and anything they did get they would have to eat, or they would starve.

Now, harvest mice are not blessed with the most gigantic

of brains. They're seed and insect eaters and fairly simple creatures really, but with a special place in mouse mythology. It is said that in prehistory, before the coming of trees, when the grass used to grow taller than the highest oak today, a harvest mouse one day climbed to the top of the tallest corn stalk and inspected the sun at close quarters.

Then, climbing down again, she gathered together the golden stems of wheat, barley and oats, and wound them into a semblance of the sun, leaving a small hole to enter by. This today is the harvest mouse's home, a golden ball, an exact replica of the great golden ball that hangs in the sky above the fields.

The harvest mouse then, is a landscape artist, not a great thinker. These two particular individuals had got themselves into the House, but had no idea how to get themselves out again. They needed a miracle in order to escape.

A short while later, just as dawn was breaking, the two harvest mice were sneaking with Miskie across the recent battlefield, the kitchen floor. It was their only access to the rest of the House. At any moment the two newcomers expected the alarm to go up and a dozen or more of the Savage Tribe to fall on them and tear them to pieces.

One of the harvest mice was shaking so badly he could hardly stand. It was one thing for a harvest mouse to enter the woodshed, but quite another to go into the House proper. He darted from the deep shadow of table leg to chair leg to Welsh dresser with his heart pounding in his chest and his eyes starting from his head.

Finally, after an age, they reached the hallway and ran up the banister alongside the stairs. This was all supposedly neutral territory, though the two house cats and the resident dog were not in the habit of observing any rules of this kind. The Great Clock sounded the half hour as they ascended and the more timid of the two harvest mice was so startled he slipped off the banister and landed on the stairs. Then there was the chink of bottles outside the front door as the milk nudnik came and went, which worried the fallen mouse even further.

It took him all of two minutes to gather his wits and scramble up one of the rails again, to rejoin his companions.

When the band of three reached the top of the stairs they ran down the post to the floor.

'This is as far as I go,' said Miskie. 'There's our cupboard over there.'

The two harvest mice looked along the landing, which seemed to stretch into Infinity, to find the door indicated.

'What do we do when we get inside?' asked one of them.

'You have to inspect it for droppings,' explained Miskie. 'If you find any, first see how fresh they are, then look for signs of who left them there. Traces of paper in the droppings shows that mice from the Bookeater Tribe have been encroaching on our territory. Richness of colour and smell means the Savage Tribe have been there – they often eat fruitcake, you know.'

'I see,' said the second mouse. 'And if we find you've, I mean *we've*, had trespassers, what happens then?'

'Then we make a raid on the tribe responsible, to punish them. Look,' Miskie said, glancing around nervously, 'I've got to go now. I'll see you back in the woodshed.'

The two newcomers were left on their own in the grey light of the approaching day. They remained for a long time hunched against the corner post of the banisters, looking through the gloom along the skirting-board to where the door to the cupboard stood. Every small sound, every creak and groan of the old House, had them pressing tighter against the post.

A voice in the distance sang out softly, '*Nice* honey-tasting mice – come to Little Prince.'

At that moment there was a loud *clack* from the front door, which made them both jump in terror. The daily newspaper had been pushed through the letter box and had got stuck halfway. A fresh draught from the outside world came up the stairs and ruffled the fur on their backs. The marauders could smell the grass and trees, the scent of flowers, the odour of the soil. It reminded them of the natural world of the garden beyond the front door. They were, after all, mice from the *Outside*. Out there were other mice who made golden sun-nests in the high grasses and romped on the mossy patches of the great plains.

It was a miracle!

The letter box was on a heavy spring and almost always snapped shut again, the newspaper or mail falling to the floor, to be picked up by Witless. Their escape was obviously meant to be. It was as if the god of harvest mice, the golden grain god, had poked his finger through the great door of the House, creating a hole through which the two mice could leave.

One of them turned to the other and spoke. 'Do you think our clan would have us back again, if we went home now?'

'I don't really care, I'm going anyway. You coming?'

There was a short nod from his companion and then the pair went racing up the post, down the banisters, up the door panelling and through the gap made by the paper in the letter box. Once out in the morning air, with faint stars shining in the grey above them, they paused to gather their breath on the door mat. They were still shaking. There and then the two youngsters made a vow that they would never enter the House again, unless they were dragged in, kicking and screaming.

'They're all crazy in there,' said one.

'It's a crazy house all right,' replied the other, 'and we're well out of it.'

The two harvest mice believed themselves to be fortunate in escaping the House, but Astrid's shadows could have told them that the House did not take harvest mice to its bosom, nor had any wish to keep them within its walls. The House decided who lived within its boundaries and who did not.

Recently the House had invited one outsider, a newcomer to the region, inside its walls. However, it had done so for reasons long preordained. The newcomer's name was Pedlar and the House was preparing itself for what would follow Pedlar's arrival.

EDAM

THE RAID BY THE 13-K GANG ON THE KITCHEN HAD to be punished by the Savage Tribe. Gorm-the-old led the retaliatory raid on the woodshed, accompanied of course by his doubles Hakon and Tostig, sporting their new scars. Captain Gunhild with her band of Immortals endeavoured as usual to protect Gorm's flanks and rear.

'Assundoon! Assundoon!'

The cry went up from the Savage Tribe, invoking the gods of the Otherworld to which all warriors went, provided they died with their teeth buried in the flesh of an enemy.

At one point Gorm's Immortals clashed with Ulf's Chosen Ones and when the two leaders' personal bodyguards realized they were attacking each other, they quickly parted and sought battle elsewhere. It did not do for two bands of élite warriors to be wasting their superior skills in an evenly matched fight.

Visiting the woodshed at the time of the raid, was Iban, the Deathshead spiritual warrior-priest. Deathshead were permitted by all tribes to wander amongst them at will, since they didn't eat anything except hard, stale crumbs, and they had no designs on territory. The Deathshead were responsible for the spiritual needs of the whole community. They were the conscience of the mouse nation as a whole.

Iban had been quietly attempting to endarken some 13-K members with the teachings of Yo. He had been explaining to them that though Yo was the Dark One, and the opposite of Unn the Light One, he was not a *bad* god. On the contrary, Iban explained, the goddess Unn regarded Yo not as a contrast but as a complement. Yo was her mate.

However, when Gorm and his vanguard broke through the outer sentries, instead of standing still and proclaiming his neutrality, Iban tried to hurry away through an exit hole. The truth was he did not want to run into Astrid again, since he was still in a state of sin after the last time they had been together. Then of course there was Gorm himself, for though Astrid was only one member of a vast harem, Gorm would not take kindly to a warrior-priest who was servicing one of his favourite females.

Iban made his way quickly towards Tunneller's Hole, occasionally having to pause to administer an Ik-to bite on some *berserker* too blind with battle-lust to notice whom he or she was attacking. Suddenly, Iban was confronted by Astrid.

Astrid's 'battle-face' was not pretty. She was most artistic at twisting her features into a mask of fury, which was intended to frighten her opponents. It did. It was the most terrifying vision Iban had ever witnessed. Her teeth were bared to the gums, her eyes were narrow slits of hatred, her nostrils were red and flared.

111

'A – Astrid . . . I . . .' he faltered.

Instantly the mask was replaced by a look of adoration. 'Iban! Oh, Iban.' She looked around her quickly, and then hissed fiercely, 'Meet me on the pan shelf at midnight.'

Then she was gone before he could explain that Yo did not wish him to rediscover that enlightenment he had undergone the last time they had been together.

Iban hurried outside into the garden, where the harvest mice were hanging by their prehensile tails from bendy stalks of grass, dangling in front of the cracks in the woodshed wall. They were watching the battle going on inside. Iban could hear the shrill squeaking of Drenchie, the 13-K sidekick of Ulf, calling more warriors to her side to help her with the ferocious Thorkils Threelegs.

'Bloodthirsty bunch,' snapped Iban, jostling a grass stalk so that the resident harvest mouse had to grab at it with his claws to hang on.

Iban made his way cautiously through the jungle that was the back garden to the House. There were giant thistles on all sides, great purple-headed things covered in spikes, reaching up into the clouds. Iban was not used to the outdoors, though like all the Deathshead, he made this occasional pilgrimage to the home of Stone, the dormouse. The outdoors worried him. He liked the tight dark corners of small rooms. This world of blazing light was not to Iban's liking at all.

He finally reached the hazel dormouse's nest under the privy, knowing when he had come to the boundary of Stone's territory by the fresh odour-line. He found Stone busying around, marking the extent of his territory with his urine.

'Set yourself down, set yourself down,' called the dormouse. 'I'll be with you in a moment.'

112

Iban found a spot in the shade of the privy where he felt relatively safe from whatever might swoop out of the sky and carry him off to kingdom come. Stone joined him a little while later, settling down beside him, curling his fluffy tail beneath his neat body.

Stone sighed, looking about him with a happy expression on his face. 'Wonderful world isn't it? Course, you house mice don't know you're living . . .'

'I'm a yellow-neck,' corrected Iban.

'Yellow-neck, house mouse, what's the difference when you're stuck in that dusty old box? You should be out here, in the wild, eating proper food. Not that junk you get in there. *Proper* food. Fruit of the guelder rose, hawthorn, hazel and wild rose! That's the stuff.'

'If you say so,' said Iban, unconvinced. 'Personally, Stone, I think the outdoors is a pretty scary place. It makes me anxious. The stress would kill me within an hour.'

'Nonsense, nonsense,' said his larger companion. 'You should try it before you make judgements. You'd soon get used to it. We have to get back to Nature, us mice. Show the rest of the creatures in this world what to do and where to go. Get some bark between your claws! Get some real soil in your creases! Thousands of nights ago, before the nudniks came to lead us astray, mice lived in unending grasslands . . . why they just stretched out for ever.' His eyes became distant. 'You wouldn't have seen anything else, just waving grasses. And many different kinds. Dozens of varieties. Not just one or two, such as we get now. Dozens and dozens. *Old* grasslands. All sorts of seeds there were then. Gone now.'

'Well, I suppose it's sad that all those grasses have gone, but . . .' All Iban knew was that he had been born and raised in the House. The House was all he had known, until he had decided to become a Deathshead. It was required of all Deathshead, even the followers of Yo, that they first learn everything there is to know, experience all things (the company of the opposite gender excluded); then, and only then – if they were followers of the god of Darkness and Ignorance – to try to forget it all.

One type of experience essential to a Deathshead was visits to the outside world. Iban had faithfully carried out this exercise, but he was not happy with what he had found. Whereas mice like Stone had quite the opposite view. Stone had visited the House once, and had announced his intention never to enter again.

'Breathe that clean atmosphere!' said the dormouse, filling his lungs with the garden's air.

Iban, acutely aware of the proximity of the privy, thought the atmosphere anything but clean; especially since the privy was not emptied as often as it should have been, since it tended to be forgotten now that it was not the major bolt hole for nudniks in distress.

'What about the pong?' he said to Stone.

'Country smells, country smells,' said Stone in a satisfied sort of way. 'Can't live outdoors without a few whiffs of this and that.'

Iban let the subject drop. 'The reason I came to see you,' he said, 'concerns a private matter. I need your advice.'

The dormouse wiped his whiskers with his paws. 'Really? A spiritual warrior asking my opinion?'

Iban was very embarrassed. 'Well, this is a *worldly* matter, you understand.'

'Oh, well, speak on, speak on. Worldly matters are my *forté*. I know little about *housely* matters, you understand, but in worldly matters you are speaking to the expert.'

'Well,' continued Iban, 'the thing is this – you know I'm

114

dedicated to Yo and the path of darkness and ignorance?'

Even as he spoke, Iban distractedly bit into a stalk of something next to his ear.

The dormouse looked suitably sad. 'Alas, yes, and you are unable – excuse me, please don't chew on that campion, there are so few of them in the garden – if you're hungry there's plenty of herb robert over there. We've got herb robert growing out of our ears at present. Now, where was I? Oh, yes, you're unable to forget all you know, who you are, and what you're here for? Well, don't worry Iban, these things will sort themselves out. I'm sure old Yo knows you're trying very hard.'

Iban sighed and then blurted, 'I've been affectionate with another mouse. I can't say who.'

Stone blinked and shrugged. 'All perfectly normal,' he said in his old-mouse scholarly tone. 'Nothing to be ashamed of. Don't need a female myself, of course, but can't see any objection to other mice cuddling in the privacy of their own nests. Certainly as far as the environment is concerned, one should procreate when the urge is felt. The earth is a creative entity – it thrives on the production of new life, provided that life is organic, natural.'

Iban cried, 'No, no, you don't understand, because I'm a Deathshead I took vows of chastity.'

The dormouse nodded. 'Ah, umm. See the point now. And I suppose you can't stay away from the little temptress. Is that it?'

'Exactly,' sighed Iban. 'My immortal soul is in agony.'

'Mmmm,' Stone considered. 'In my experience the only way to get rid of one obsession is to find another that's not quite as harmful.'

'Like what?' asked Iban.

Stone said, 'To my mind, the one you already have

115

is probably the least harmful. I mean, you could become obsessed with illness and death. Or with food and drink, like those ghastly cellar mice.' He placed his fluffy tail over Iban's back in a gesture of friendship. 'Forget the state of your soul for a while. From what I know of Deathshead, a few smirches won't do you much harm. There's such a thing as too much purity, you know . . . you off then?' called Stone, as Iban wandered away, back towards the House. 'Be careful not to wade through any stitchwort, if you come across it. It's becoming quite an unusual sight these hours . . .'

That night Iban fought a tremendous battle with himself – and lost. On the stroke of twelve, by the Great Clock in the hallway, he found himself amongst the copper-bottomed pans, waiting for Astrid to appear in the moonlight.

BOURSIN

The old and venerable I-kucheng, who might have been acknowledged as leader of the Deathshead, were they a hierarchical tribe, shuffled along the hallway past the Great Clock. Had he looked up at the Clock-face he might have recognized the eye of a female mouse of the Invisible Tribe, Hearallthings, peering out of the wind-up keyhole. Hearallthings, though she heard nothing, saw much, and was often a silent witness to events that occurred in the hallway. What she was witnessing now was the start of a peace mission.

Some few lengths behind I-kucheng came Skrang, her eyes on every nook and cranny they passed.

Suddenly a figure came dashing out of a niche in the woodwork below the stairs. Skrang darted forward, was on the intruder in a second, and had spun the creature off its feet with an Ik-to butt to the flank. Then, as the other mouse was lying on its back, legs in the air, she was instantly at its throat, threatening the exposed area with her bared teeth.

'Don't – don't bite me,' whispered the defeated mouse.

I-kucheng shuffled on, as usual unaware of the danger he had been in, saying over his shoulder, 'Come, Skrang, we must speak to Gorm before the next hour . . .'

'Why are you attacking my comrade?' hissed Skrang to the supine figure on the floor.

'That damned meddling judge,' said the mouse. 'He ruined my relationship with my family.'

'His judgement is always wise, taking into consideration all aspects of any dispute.'

'He's a doddering old fool,' snarled the mouse, 'and he ought to be locked up somewhere.'

Skrang, having had this conversation many times before, and now weary of such exchanges, did not feel inclined to argue.

'The next time I see you,' she said, 'I'll tear your throat out, you hear me?'

'I hear you,' said the mouse sullenly.

'Dear me, dear me, we are going to be late,' called I-kucheng over his shoulder. 'Do hurry Skrang.'

Skrang let the mouse go and it dashed into the shadows of the hallway.

'I'm coming,' she said, wearily. 'I'm following behind you, as always.'

'Such an unsociable mouse,' grumbled I-kucheng. 'Never keeps me company properly. Always dawdling on behind . . .'

'Stop muttering to yourself,' said Skrang. 'Mice will think you're going senile.'

To get to the kitchen, their destination, they had to make a quick dash across a short corner of Eyeball's living-room. Skrang had seen the cat being taken away in a carrying basket that morning, and knew she would return smelling like the medicine cupboard in the bathroom. She would be back — she *always* came back — but in the meantime the living-room was relatively safe. Spitz was in the parlour dozing and would not dare to enter Eyeball's territory even during her absence. It was more than his life was worth to leave his ginger hairs on her cushions.

There were just two nudniks sitting drinking coffee, clinking their cups. They were chattering loudly, clacking their teeth together, making gestures with their free hands. There was a pink cloud of pong around them, sweet-smelling, flowery, but not at all to the taste of Skrang. One of them had something that looked like a squashed wastebin on its head. The other had a circle of coloured bones around its throat. Both were draped in bright curtains.

The two Deathshead squeezed under the kitchen door. A nudnik with thick-glassed spectacles was working at the kitchen sink. Occasionally it chased mice, when it saw them, so the two ambassadors of peace didn't hang about. They quickly slipped behind the stove, where it was warm. Several Savage Tribe guards at once came running, ready to protect their territory.

'It is I, I-kucheng, and my companion, Skrang.'

A sentry stared at them in the dim light and then waved his paws at the running guards.

'False alarm. All's well. Deathshead.'

Grumbling, the guards stopped in their tracks, then turned and went back to their warm nests. I-kucheng and Skrang were permitted to enter the kitchen. They headed straight for the nest of Gorm-the-old, who had heard the sentry's shout. And by the time they had trekked behind the sink unit and dashed through the door to the boiler room, Gorm had roused his officers and called an Allthing.

'To what do we owe this delightful visit?' snarled Gorm. 'The respected I-kucheng come to praise us for winning our most recent battle, has he?'

'Certainly not,' said I-kucheng, settling down before the council. 'I don't approve of war.'

'I was being sarcastic,' Gorm snapped.

'Oh,' said I-kucheng. 'Wasted on me, Gorm. I should save it for those who can return it in kind.'

Gorm suggested, 'Why don't you just tell us why you're here? We're all waiting with bated breath.'

Ignoring the continued sarcasm, I-kucheng said in his infuriatingly calm voice, 'The reason I'm here is because of the recent hostilities between the Savage Tribe and the 13-K. It's got to stop, you know. There's too much violence in the House. We're just destroying each other. It's bad enough that we have the two cats, an owl, a despotic rat and the nudnik Headhunter.'

Gorm shrugged his back. 'We've always lived like that. We have to protect our own, or we'll all starve.'

On his leader's left, Elfwin said, 'Gorm's right. *We* have the bounteous larder. Everyone else in the House wants the larder. They can't have it, so they send parties to raid it. We have to send out punitive retaliatory raids, or we'd be looked on as weak, and there would be more raids against us. It's a vicious circle, I grant you I-kucheng, but I don't see any solution. We have to remain at a constant state of war.'

Skrang drummed her tail angrily on the floor and stamped her feet. 'You could decide to *share* what you have in the ever-full larder with the rest of the House,

119

then everyone would be happy.'

Thorkils Threelegs snorted. He never sat high-nose when there were outsiders around, because he felt it emphasized the fact that he had a missing forelimb. It was his habit instead to crouch in a fighting position. This intimidated a lot of mice, but not Skrang.

'What does that snort mean?' she said. 'You don't approve of sharing?'

'Damn stupid idea,' said Thorkils. 'Bloody idiotic.'

'What he means,' Gorm said, 'is that there isn't enough in the larder at any one time to go round. We know it looks a lot, and the divine larder's never empty, but the fact is the nudniks eat most of what's there. Then what they don't eat, they give to the blasted cats and the dog. We do get a lot to eat in here, but it's not enough to share around the House, and that's a blasted fact – like it or lump it.'

Ketil, not regarded as one of the brightest of mice – even amongst the Savage Tribe who were renowned for fighting, but were considered a little short of the grey matter – sighed and said, 'Yes, if we could get rid of the nudniks, the cats and dog would have to go too, and we'd have the measureless larder all to ourselves.'

Every eye in the Allthing swivelled round and stared at Ketil.

The little house mouse stared back at each one in turn and then said, '*What?* What did I say?'

'You said,' replied Gorm, '*if we could get rid of the nudniks, the cats and dog would have to go too.*'

'So?' squeaked Ketil, wondering if he had said something really moronic this time and would have to do extra guard duties. 'So?'

Elfwin cried, 'That's *brilliant!*'

'Is it?' said the stunned Ketil, wondering whether or not

he was being made fun of.

Gytha Finewhiskers added in an awed voice, 'Not only the cats and the dog, but Little Prince and his master, the Headhunter. They'd all have to go, if the big nudniks went.'

Gorm took a deep breath. 'What are we talking about here? I mean, let's look at facts and figures. There's five permanent nudniks in the House, right? Then the one with glass on its face that comes into the kitchen during the day . . .'

'And don't forget that every few days one more comes to use the sucking machine and wipe the shelves and stuff,' said Skuli.

'That's seven all together, isn't it?' said Gorm. 'Astrid, is that seven . . .?'

'Astrid's not here,' Elfwin interrupted. 'I saw her near the pots-and-pans shelf earlier.'

Gorm muttered, 'Never around when you want her these hours, that priestess. Doesn't she know I called a tribal Allthing? Everyone's supposed to be here.' While the mental arithmetic was going on behind it, Gorm's face was screwed up in concentration. 'Well, I *think* that's seven. Close enough, anyway.'

I-kucheng shook his head. 'But this is unheard of. Never in all my hours have I heard of any house tribe managing to get rid of nudniks. They're too *big*. They're too stupid. I mean, they're just like walking vegetables. What can you do with something of that size, which hasn't the brain of a Brussels sprout? They just . . . *are*.'

'The Headhunter isn't stupid,' said Thorkils, 'that little maniac knows what he's doing all right.'

'The small ones do,' replied Skrang, 'but they seem to grow out of their brains.'

'I've never heard of it happening,' repeated I-kucheng.

'Never in all my born hours. The nudniks have always been here, like great lumps of walking furniture. They fall and rise in numbers, even though they don't ever seem to breed, but they're always here.'

Skrang said, 'I-kucheng is right. How would we get rid of the nudniks? It's a dream.'

'Damn pests, they are,' growled Gorm, frustrated. '*Pests!* They don't do anything except eat great dollops of food – masses of it in one swallow – and then lie around belching for the next hour.'

'Sometimes they light up weeds and make smoke,' suggested Ketil. 'I made a nice nest out of one of the empty weed packets.'

'Yes, we know all that,' agreed Gorm with an impatient edge to his voice, 'but do they ever do anything useful? Anything *sensible*? They don't behave like proper animals at all. Not one of them marks its territory in any way, that's how intelligent they are. They go into that little room near the big bedroom to urinate. What a waste of marking odour! Fancy chucking all that good wee down a white bowl . . .'

Elfwin sighed. 'Well, that's nudniks for you. They'll slosh water all over the kitchen floor, washing away precious crumbs, but they don't *add* anything. They're vermin, plain and simple.'

Gorm's eyes were alight with passion now. 'But,' he said, 'wouldn't it be glorious if we *could* drive them out of the House? If we concentrated all our efforts on harassing the nudniks, instead of fighting each other? We'll have to think about it, hard. There must be a way of doing it.'

'I thought of it!' cried Ketil enthusiastically.

'By accident,' muttered Elfwin.

'Yes, but I still thought of it.'

'You get extra rations for that,' said Gorm generously. 'I'll see to it myself. A mouse gets punished for his misdeeds, even when he doesn't do them deliberately, so there's no reason why he shouldn't be rewarded when he does something good by accident, is there?'

The Allthing agreed unanimously.

I-kucheng spoke next. He'd come on a mission to establish peace and seemed instead to have bred revolution. All in the space of a few minutes. But if out of revolution came peace, he would have fulfilled his aim. His main concern now was that the energy which his peace initiative seemed to have unleashed should be controlled and channelled. 'What you must do next, Gorm, is call an inter-tribal Allthing with your son, Ulf. And Frych-the-freckled. And perhaps also Whispersoft of the Invisibles. There must be a truce amongst the tribes, while these talks are going on.'

'A truce, yes,' growled Gorm, 'but if any tribe starts any funny business, we'll bite their . . .'

'Think *positive*,' hissed Skrang. 'You must start out with a positive attitude.'

'Oh, all right,' grumbled Gorm. 'You make the arrangements, I-kucheng.'

At that moment Astrid the high priestess came wandering in with a silly smirk on her face. This expression was instantly wiped clean when she saw the place behind the boiler was full of mice.

Gorm growled at her, 'Didn't you hear me call the Allthing? Where have you been?'

'I, er, just . . . around.'

'Around where?'

'I was on the pan shelf,' Astrid explained. 'Communing with my Shadows.'

'You're always on the pan shelf,' snarled Gorm. 'What's

the fascination with a few pots and pans these hours? Can't you talk to your blasted Shadows somewhere else? If you start leaving droppings up there during the night, the nudniks will start putting poisoned powder down again. Do you want all our youngsters to be put in danger?'

Astrid shook her head violently and waved her tail around in an embarrassed fashion. 'Of course not, I wasn't thinking. I'm sorry.'

'So you damn well should be,' admonished Gorm. 'Especially as you've missed something unique. We've been talking about getting rid of the pests in the House. What do you think of that?'

'Pests?' asked Astrid helplessly.

'The nudniks,' snapped Thorkils. 'What else?'

'Get rid of the nudniks?' said Astrid. 'I have to meditate.'

She went into a trance immediately, there before their eyes. Unlike most of the library mice, Astrid was a genuine mystic, with real psychic powers. She could foresee – though not with any real clarity or depth – certain aspects of the future. Her vagueness was often unsatisfactory to Gorm, who liked his pictures to be absolutely clear and precise. Gorm was not good at interpreting things, especially prophecies.

'Well?' he yelled, breaking Astrid's trance.

'Don't do it,' she said, her eyes hollow and dark. 'Don't drive out the nudniks. Disaster will follow.'

'Nonsense,' cried Gorm. This was not the answer he wanted to hear at all.

'There will be a great famine,' whispered Astrid. 'A plague will sweep through the House.'

'Balderdash and poppycock!' shouted Gorm.

'Many will die, few will survive,' finished Astrid.

'What a load of codswallop,' bawled Gorm. 'You employ

124

these people to give you a sensible forecast of the future and all they give you is doom and gloom. We're going ahead with the plan, whatever this religious nut predicts.'

Skrang said, 'Do you really think we should? Remember the legend of the hallowed cheese? Astrid may be right. She usually is.'

'Not this time,' Gorm growled. 'And that myth thing is daft – whoever heard of a mouse changing into a cat?'

'I don't like it,' said I-kucheng. 'Did you see her eyes?' Once again he was wondering what he had spawned.

'You don't have to like it,' said Thorkils rudely. 'It's up to Gorm.'

Gorm set his expression into hard determination. 'We're going ahead,' he said firmly.

Gorm-the-old was a legend in his own time and the story of his rise to power was told to every new infant of the Savage Tribe, whether they wanted to hear it or not. Now he was placing that legend on the line.

GIETOST

Gorm had been born one of a litter of seven, but his appetite for his mother's milk soon whittled that down to three. His brothers Hakon and Tostig were the only survivors in the battle for the teats. Though the three brothers started more or less equal in weight and size, by the time they were ready to go on to solid foods, Gorm was easily the most vicious, brutal and ruthless member of the trio. The other two simply followed his lead and where he went they went too.

Gorm had two main concerns in life: his own unlimited

ambition and the welfare of his mother. He had killed his own father while still a growing mouse because his father had dared to fight with his mother over a piece of cheese. Gorm ripped him open and left him dead in the dust, while his brothers looked on. Such an act of barbarism was unusual even amongst the Savages.

'Nobody hurts my mother,' Gorm had said.

Thereafter the mild but doting mother of this terrible mouse encouraged Gorm in his dreams of leading the tribe, even though Gorm's father had been a lowly warrior mouse with no rank. When Gorm openly confessed his aspirations to the tribe's chieftain at the time, Olaf-the-ugly, that mouse laughed and called Gorm 'old before his time'. Thereafter Gorm became known as Gorm-the-old, a title of which he was proud.

Gorm-the-old was rapidly promoted as his prowess in battle became a byword in the Savage Tribe. He seemed invincible. Always at the forefront of any fighting, he lay about him with skilful and fierce abandon, so that very soon even the sound of his name was feared. In this way he made himself the natural successor to Olaf-the-ugly when that old chieftain was found dead. There were those among Olaf's kin who perpetrated the rumour that he had been assassinated by Gorm's henchmen as they sought to live under the rule of Olaf's son — Harald-the-less-ugly. But Gorm had his warriors suppress most of this camp. He himself dispatched Harald in a bloody claw-to-claw combat. The remaining dissenters joined Gorm's own army, but forever afterwards there was a certain brooding rebel element in the Savage Tribe, which was only kept down by Gorm's reign of terror.

The new chieftain set about consolidating his position by raising his mother to the position of most-high-priestess, and his brothers to senior ranks in the army. When his mother died, Gorm abolished the post of most-high-priestess and the position below that, high priestess, became the most senior post in the spiritual temple of the great god Assundoon. This was Astrid's role.

Thus did Gorm-the-old's rise to power go from fact to legend in his own lifetime. And it was later writ within mouse history that this empowerment must have been destined to take place when it did, because it coincided with the arrival of the Outsider who was to lead them all to the Hour of Change. With new blood reigning in the Savage Tribe, the old traditions of these kitchen dwellers no longer held sway, and everything was in place for the coming of a new era.

WENSLEYDALE

OUT IN THE HEDGEROW THE RHYTHMS OF LIFE HAD been in tune with the Earth, but the rhythms of life in the House were independent of the Earth, separated from it. The House had its own pulse, which beat out of time with the Earth. Pedlar sensed this, during his periods of meditation in the library, and it concerned him. Anything out of tune with the rest of the planet had nothing greater than itself to help regulate its rhythms, or realign itself when disharmony threatened.

It was a dangerous isolation.

Pedlar was not altogether happy in the library. One couldn't survive properly on a diet of books. He had held long conversations about this with Iago, the gourmet of the Bookeater Tribe. Iago had patiently explained to Pedlar which were the tastiest, the best, the most nutritious books.

'Remain suspicious of glossy paper. Colourful though it

might appear to the uninformed eye, it has a tendency to clog the intestines. Treat with wary regard crisp paper with strong black lines of insects – many a mouse has been poisoned by unsavoury paper. Stay clear of books with pictures of cheeses in them. I've known mice driven crazy by such pictures. It usually results in eating too much paper, in the hope that the pictures might contain some of the qualities of real cheese, and then in the death of the mouse. If you find a book like that, it's best not to look.

'Now, a nice leather cover is so much more satisfying than a cardboard one. Remember my maxim: "Old and soft, rather than stiff and fresh." Pages with the consistency of blotting paper are by far the most agreeable, but failing that look for books with these dead earwigs on the front or spine . . .'

And Iago drew these marks in the dust with his claw: CLASSICS.

'Books which have the following squashed spiders on the front are easily digestible, but have little nutritious value and are prone to give one dysentery . . .'

And Iago drew these marks in the dust with his claw: BESTSELLER.

'If quantity is what you want, rather than quality, then books with these symbols should be sought, but beware of serious after-effects in the form of constipation.'

And he drew these marks in the dust with his claw: NON-FICTION.

'There are those too, with spiky insects that stick in your throat, groups of insects of inconsiderate length that give you worms, great rounded spiders without anything inside, obscure small ants with too much acid – all thrown together in a recipe which turns out to be disappointing once on the tongue and amongst the taste buds. Such works bear these particular combinations somewhere on their tasteless dust jackets.'

And he drew these marks in the dust with his claw: LITERARY NOVEL.

'What one would really like,' said Iago, 'is *fully formed* insects, insects with all their legs, insects that seem recently squashed yet taste as if they have matured between the covers as long as a good cheese. I dream of a book containing combinations of these insects on nice digestible unpretentious paper, making no claims to being anything but an amusing meal with a mild aftertaste – but alas,' he finished with a sigh, 'I haven't yet found it.'

So Pedlar was left unsatisfied, whichever paper he ate.

It was true that occasionally a nudnik came into the library with food, but there was such a battle for the scraps afterwards it was a wonder there weren't more injuries. The whole colony lived on the edge of existence.

The Bookeaters also appeared to live on the edge of madness. Being so close to starvation all the time, they tended to get hallucinations and feverish dreams, which they called magic. Half the time they were out of their heads, chanting and moaning strange litanies the meanings of which were obscure to say the least. Several times Pedlar had been roused from a deep sleep by a blood-curdling scream, and had rushed to the edge of his shelf expecting to witness some horrible disembowelling, only to find a mouse wandering around with its eyes glazed, crying, 'A vision! A vision!'

And every so often, Frych-the-freckled would address her tribe on momentous matters, sometimes while still suckling her babies.

'Bookeaters,' she had said that very morning, 'I've assembled you *en masse* because of what is about to transpire.

130

Gorm-the-old has transmitted a desire to parlay with your nominative leader. Now we all perceive the lack of couth in the Savage Tribe, especially in its chieftain whose stumbling methods of communication are inordinately unrefined. However, my sensitive social filters are very adept at devulgarizing the crude and so I shall meet with Gorm and listen to his proposals, for at the very heart of his recommendations is the possibility of unlimited cheese.'

An excited murmur went round the room as soon as the word most likely to stir mice had been mentioned.

'What's all this about?' whispered Pedlar to Owain and Mefyn who were sitting high-nose, next to him on the shelf.

Owain frowned, as if to silence Pedlar, but Mefyn replied, 'Gorm-the-old has asked to speak with Frych.'

Pedlar was surprised. 'That's all?'

'Well, it might not sound like much to an Outsider,' sniffed Owain, getting in on the conversation now that his leader had finished her address, 'but to *us* it's a very consequential thing for the leaders of two different tribes to visit each other.'

'I didn't mean that exactly,' said Pedlar, 'though what you say is interesting. What I actually meant was, is that *all* Frych said? She used so many long words and went on for so long I felt she must have conveyed – you've got me at it now – she must have meant a great deal more than just that.'

'No,' said Mefyn. 'That was the gist.'

'Oh. Anyway, the Savage Tribe and the Bookeaters are going to discuss something, is that it?'

'That's it.'

'I wonder what?' asked Pedlar.

Owain sniffed. 'I expect they'll tell us when they feel we ought to know.'

'You trust these leaders do you?' Pedlar said, failing to disguise the scepticism in his tone.

Mefyn looked shocked. 'Of course we do! The reason they're leaders is because of their intellectual superiority, isn't it? They comprehend what we ordinary mice are unable to grasp, until of course it is simplified and put into our sort of language.'

Owain added, 'Our leaders have a spiritual depth to them which is far greater than ours. They can interpret the intricate pathways of mouse logic. That's why they're in charge.'

Pedlar wondered if he should keep quiet, but found himself quite unable to do so.

'Well, I've only been here a short while, you understand, but I rather thought that Gorm got to be leader of the Savage Tribe because he's a ruthless, greedy, power-loving tyrant . . .'

'He does have a certain lack of ruth, I'll grant you,' agreed Mefyn.

'. . . and Frych-the-freckled is leader of the Bookeaters because she threatens to dissolve any opposition with dark and deadly magic?'

'Frych can sizzle a mouse at fifty feet with just a look, that's perfectly true,' agreed Owain.

'So,' said Pedlar, 'where does all this intellectual superiority, spiritual depth and inner knowledge of the workings of the universe stuff come into it?'

Mefyn looked unhappy. 'You have to believe they're better than the average mouse, don't you? Otherwise, well, it would be Brute Force and Ignorance leading us to our destiny.'

Pedlar said no more in reply to this. He could see how upset the other two mice were getting. They were not willing to have the whole fabric of their political system unpicked in front of them. Mefyn was right, thought Pedlar, you have to believe you're being guided by the Good and Honest, the Intelligent and Wise, or you get the sensation that the world is not founded on order after all, but on chaos. Once you come to that conclusion, with the added knowledge that you can't influence it at all, there's nothing much to hold it all together.

Out in the Hedgerow, Pedlar had lived pretty much by his own wits. Now he was having to live by other mice's wits. Not only that: the other mice in question were themselves following mice who — it seemed to Pedlar — hadn't got an inkling of what was going on or what to do themselves. The noseless leading the noseless. It seemed to Pedlar — though he would be the first to admit that he was new to it all — that the very *worst* people were running the show. There were bright mice around. There were Cadwallon and Ethil, both quite capable mice, with a lot of common sense. But it seemed you never got a Cadwallon or an Ethil as chief of a tribe, because they hadn't got the ambition, the arrogance, the ruthlessness actually required to drive them to the top positions.

It seemed you had to be dense and callous to make it to the highest positions of mousedom.

Pedlar sighed. It was all beyond him. He was as useless as the rest of them when it came down to it, when it came to changing things. The only difference between him and Mefyn or Owain, was that he *knew* it was all a mess, and they believed that everything was under control.

He spent a desultory hour wandering the shelves of the library, tasting this and that book, even trying a cover or two here and there. Nothing really pared away the hunger which gnawed his insides. His stomach was a hollow place with an animal inside it, trying to get out.

Iago stopped him again, on the third shelf, and made a few more suggestions. But Pedlar was rapidly coming to the conclusion that Iago was full of technical jargon and professional mystique, but no genuine information. He continued to roam over the tops of the books, traversing the hills and valleys created by the rise and fall of different spines. The ink insects on them were of interest to him only when they looked fresh and tasty.

Halfway through the next hour a nudnik came into the library and the whole colony waited patiently to see if any food would follow this creature. However, it just sat and turned the pages of its book, staring into the insect markings.

After a while, Pedlar confessed, 'I'm so hungry this hour, I could eat a dog.'

A mouse called Gwladys, sitting high-nose beside him, said, 'It would taste awful.'

'Yes, it would, wouldn't it? Look at that great lump of a nudnik, sitting all folded up. Strange creatures, aren't they?'

'They're just so *dense*,' said Gwladys. 'I mean, they've got a lot of flesh and bone, but their brain is the size of a dust mote. It's a wonder they haven't become extinct.'

'What's *extinct*?'

'Died out. You know, the species disappeared, like wolves have become extinct.'

'Wolves?'

'Great big wild canines. They used to be around, so the legends go, but not any more. You come from the Outside. Did you see any huge canines?'

Pedlar thought very hard. 'Not as such. Cows and horses. They're pretty big.'

'Yes,' agreed Gwladys, 'but they're not canines. Canines are the dog family.'

'I know that,' said Pedlar, getting huffy.

Pedlar went back to his new nest which he had made in the spine of a huge book with a leather jacket which lay on its side at the end of the highest shelf. He had chosen the height for safety reasons, but the spinal tunnel between the cover and the pages of the great book had been picked because it vaguely reminded him of his old nest below the Hedgerow.

He had lined the dark tunnel with soft chewed bits of paper and some cotton wool he had found under the nudniks' chair. These were unnecessary comforts in the warmth of the library, but they were extra reminders of his old nest. He entered the spinal tunnel from the wall side, squeezing between the plaster and the entrance, so that he was facing the opening which looked on to the library. All he could see were the far bookshelves, but he felt easier in his mind, looking in the direction from which danger, if it came, would surely appear. It would be difficult to attack him from behind, because he would hear any intruder scrabbling to get into the narrow entrance.

He would lie in this nice, comfortable passage, with a little to spare either side of his whiskers, and dream of the summer with its golden chaff and cornseed, its fields of ripe vegetables, its nuts and nibbles. Oh, yes, there was comfort in the House, but there was also comfort in the wild. There was moss and lichen. Nothing was softer than a bed of star moss on a sunny day. Nothing was scratchier than lichen baked under a hot sun.

Oh yes, he still missed his old home. Strangely enough

135

he also missed the ancestral voices which had spoken to him in his Hedgerow nights. It was those voices which had led him here, and now they seemed to be leaving the next step to Pedlar himself. Well, here he was. He was the one. Where were the many who he imagined would be waiting for him? With this thought, Pedlar shuffled out of his nest.

The last straw was when he passed two mice who were having a discussion which neither of them understood, since they were in an after-book-meal trance, and just letting the words flow.

'Accelerator cable, shoe-brake linings, gear stick, differential, spark plugs, distributor cap, exhaust manifold and piston rings with cam-rod alternator,' said one.

'Add a pinch of salt, some thyme and rosemary,' said the other, 'after letting it boil for two minutes. Then strain through a colander and use the liquid for stock. This will help retain the flavour of the vegetables.'

After staring at the two mice, who had obviously been gorging on quite separate and entirely different books, Pedlar decided it was time to go off again, into other parts of the House, with all its inherent dangers.

He left the library by going into the hearth and climbing up the chimney. There was no fire in the fireplace of course, it being summer, but the flue was full of soot. The other mice had told him that the fire was only lit in the coldest weather because of the hot iron radiators and pipes all round the House in the winter. The big boiler in the boiler-room at the back of the kitchen was lit late into the season and after that the radiators and pipes became almost too hot to walk on.

Pedlar found nothing at all in the chimney and emerged, a dusty black, on another level of the House. Sure enough, he found himself trailing soot under a bed and across a room which sported a pink carpet. He found a hole in the skirting board, which he went through and then discovered a cold and chilling place which he recognized from descriptions. It was one of the two toilets and bathrooms. There didn't seem to be anything at all worth investigating, so he slipped under the door and out on to the landing. There he struck lucky.

In one of the darkest corners of the landing he found food. It was cheese again – that delicious aroma – but this time it wasn't on one of those snap-trap boards. It was inside a sort of wire box.

Pedlar went all round the outside of the wire box, sniffing at this and that, making absolutely sure there were no tightly wound springs, or guillotines made of stiff wire. He could see nothing that resembled the neck-breaking wire on the trap in the attic. This box looked perfectly innocent.

He had been in boxes before and nothing untoward had happened to him. In the library there was a cardboard box in which young mice played. Mothers sometimes went there, out of the way, to give birth. There'd also been a wooden box in the cellar, when Pedlar had first arrived, which Phart and Flegm had used as a place in which to sleep off their binges. Boxes seemed to be quite harmless objects, which the nudniks left lying around the house.

Still, Pedlar was not sure of this particular box, and he wanted to check everything before going inside it. The smell of the cheese was making him salivate profusely, but still he was not going to be caught off guard. That had happened once, and he was determined it should not happen again. He was not going to let the redolence of the deliciously pungent cheese lure him into difficulties.

137

He wanted to be sure he could escape from the box if a cat or nudnik appeared on the landing.

The door to the wire box was wide open. If he could march in and take the cheese, then presumably he could march right out again, without any trouble whatsoever? It would be absolute madness to let that aromatic food go to some other mouth.

Finally he took his courage in his paws and entered the wire box.

A step inside. Nothing happened. A further step. Still there were no spikes threatening to impale him, no nooses waiting to strangle him, no expectant steel jaws ready to spring shut. Only the open box and the cheese in the middle.

He reached the cheese, licked it, and dashed backwards.

Everything remained as it was.

The taste of the cheese was wonderful! He went back to it and nibbled it a bit, glancing round nervously, looking for the deadly guillotine.

Nothing. All was well.

The best thing to do was pull the cheese off its stand and run with it back to his nest in the library.

Pedlar snatched at the cheese.

There was a loud *thwack* which made him jump so high he hit his head on the top of the box. Startled though he was, he was still alive. He ran towards the opening of the box, hit something, and bounced backwards.

Panic-stricken, he tried again, only to do the same thing.

After he had done this twice more, he realized what was happening. A wire door had closed the exit. Pedlar was trapped inside the box. Frantically he gnawed at the door, at the hinges, at the little catch. It failed to open. He found he was getting nowhere.

The next thing he did was try all the other corners of the box, to see if there was a second way out. There was not. The whole creation was a tight little world from which there was no escape, except through the doorway, which had now been closed off by the wire door.

Disaster.

Pedlar crouched low-nose in the middle of the box, wondering what his fate was to be. How could he even begin to perform the will of his ancestors now? He was terrified. What if Spitz or Eyeball should come along? Would they be able to get to him? He wasn't sure of anything now. What was the box here for anyway? It was a strange place to leave such a thing, where mice could accidentally become locked inside.

While he was thus engaged in thought, a creature came cautiously out of the shadows and approached the box. It was another mouse! Pedlar recognized him before he even saw him, by his body odour. It was Phart.

The chief of the Stinkhorns sat high-nose, scratched his fleas and picked at his scabs, while he contemplated Pedlar's position.

'That's some fix you've got yerself into there, yer honour,' said Phart. 'How'd you get stuck in that cage?'

'Cage?' cried Pedlar gripping the wire mesh. 'Is this a cage?'

'Course it's a cage, dumbo,' sneered the cellar mouse, throwing politeness to the landing draughts. 'Where've you bin? My grandfather, the Great and Honourable Snott got trapped in one of them. Nat'rully, he should have known better, but then he was tipsy on wine at the time. Mice do

139

a lot of things when they're under the affluence of incohol. You got *no* excuse.'

Pedlar gripped the wire and rattled it, hoping for something to give. When nothing looked like happening, he began to gnaw at it frantically. Phart just shook his head in disgust.

'You won't get out that way, mate. What do you think it's made of? Paper? Bloody tensile steel wire, that is pal. You couldn't bite through it if you was Eyeball. If I was you I'd just give it up.'

'Phart, I have to escape, otherwise I'll be here for ever. I – I have *things to do*—' He stopped helplessly – how could he hope to make this cellar mouse understand that he, Pedlar, was a mouse of destiny?

'Not for ever, yer honour,' smirked Phart. 'The Head-hunter lays these things. He'll be along any moment to see if he's caught anything.'

Pedlar went berserk at these words and began running round and round the cage, throwing himself at the wire, scrabbling, biting, pulling and pushing. All he did was wear himself out and fall exhausted on the floor. Phart watched this great burst of wasted energy with interest.

'Cheez, you country mice are really fit, ain't you? I never seen such a display of acrobatics. I often wisht I was an athlete sometimes. Don't do you no good in there though, does it?'

Pedlar lay panting, 'You really are a rotten swine, Phart,' he said. 'One of these days you're going to get your come-uppance. It's just a pity I shan't be around to see it happen.'

Phart came right up to the wire and pressed his nose against it, breathing foul breath into Pedlar's gulping lungs.

'Ah, but you could be, yer honour,' said Phart, returning

140

to his former sycophantic civility. 'You could live hand-somely to see me boiled in bacon fat. You could live long enough to see your beautiful little 'uns grow to fat round yellow-necks, and maybe even long enough to watch Eye-ball carried out of the house as stiff as a bleedin' log of wood one mornin'. If you was very clever, that is, which I know you can be, yer honour – otherwise I wouldn't be teasin' you, would I?'

Hope sprang into Pedlar's chest. He pulled himself to his feet and crouched low-nose opposite the foul Stinkhorn, ignoring the halitosis and the stench of damp fur.

'What do I have to do, Phart? Just tell me. I'll forgive you for leading me into that snap-trap. Just tell me how I can be clever. Tell me, Phart.'

'The first thing you have to do, yer honour, is fetch me a piece of that there cheese . . .'

Pedlar glanced behind him and for the first time since the door had closed on him he remembered the cheese. The bait. It was why he was in the cage. He had let his eyes, nose and stomach rule his head. The cheese.

'What do you want to do with it?' Pedlar asked.

'Do with it? Eat the bleedin' stuff, what else?'

'Phart,' snarled Pedlar, 'you get me out of here or . . .'

'Now, now, yer honour,' clucked Phart infuriatingly. 'You get me the cheese first, push it in bits through the mesh, and *then* I'll get you out. That's fair, ain't it? I mean, I've got to put a lot of brain power to this. I needs the cheese to feed me head.'

Pedlar saw that he was not going to get anywhere with the other mouse until he did as he was told.

'How do I know you'll get me out?' he said.

'You don't. You got to trust me, yer honour. That's all it takes. After all, I let out me grandfather—'

141

'. . . the Great and Honourable Snott,' finished Pedlar.

' 'Xactly!' smirked Phart.

Pedlar realized that time was running out. Whoever laid the cage – heaven forbid it was the Headhunter, for the thought made him swoon – would be along soon. Yes, he had to trust Phart.

Crossing the cage, Pedlar began to ferry little crumbs of cheese to the mesh walls and push them through to Phart on the other side. Phart ate greedily, his eyes on the landing behind. Pedlar had never seen food disappear so quickly. When the feverish fetching and carrying reached its pitch, there was a sound further down the landing, a shuffling noise of scraping feet.

Phart almost choked as he tried to swallow a huge lump of cheese in one go.

'Quick,' hissed Pedlar. 'Let me out now!'

'Can't,' coughed Phart, spraying Pedlar in the face with fragments of cheese. 'Dunno how to.'

Pedlar's hopes went screaming down the landing.

'But you said you let your grandfather out—'

A door to a bedroom opened and there was the clump of nudnik boots on the floor.

'I lied,' Phart said simply. And then the Stinkhorn was gone, melting back into the shadows around the edge of the landing, down one of the holes to the gap between the ground-floor ceiling and the floorboards of the landing.

'You – you – you – rotten . . .' gasped Pedlar, too late.

A great shadow fell over the cage. Pedlar looked up to see a chunky nudnik leaning over, looking down on him. There was an evil row of teeth visible across the nudnik's face. A clumpy shock of dark hair stuck up from the top of its head. Its eyes were like burning ice. Its nostrils were like twin deep mouse-holes in a bank of mud. While it stared down at Pedlar, it scratched its nose with a fat finger and let out a horrible grunt of what sounded like joyous satisfaction.

Then it folded in the middle and reached out with an arm to grab the cage. Pedlar felt himself lifted up swiftly, his stomach turning inside out with the motion. Then he was but a length away from that horrible mouth. He could see the fat tongue inside, sort of lolling redly in the huge cavity of a mouth, like some monster worm. Sweetly smelling breath, carrying jam and beef broth, engulfed Pedlar, making him gag. He rushed over to the far side of the cage.

From there he could see the whole horrible head of the nudnik who had him in captivity. It was the Headhunter! There was no reason to doubt Phart's words now. He was in the hands of the most notorious mouse-killer, mouse-torturer, in the House. These were his last moments, he was sure. And the role for which he had been marked out would now fall to some other mouse from Outside, some other mouse who had yet to hear the ancestral call.

The nudnik, who wore the mouse-skull badge that Flegm had once mentioned, made a roaring sound. Then Pedlar was carried, swinging, along the landing and into the bedroom. The cage was plonked heavily on to a table, shaking Pedlar off his feet. When he looked up he wished he hadn't. A macabre sight was before him. On a shelf not far away, almost level with Pedlar's eyes, was a row of grisly skulls and bones, all neatly arranged.

They were the skeletal remains of dead mice.

Pedlar almost swallowed his teeth in fear. Not only was he looking at the skulls of mice, but of birds too. Wing bones were spread like pictures and pinned to the wall, beetles were impaled on pins on a board of cork. A rabbit's skull, a squirrel's tail, a weasel's ribcage . . . The shelves and boards were a graveyard of bleached bones. Pieces of fur and individual feathers were in evidence here and there.

On another shelf, above the skulls and bones, was a cluster of sealed jars with liquids in them. There were objects floating in the liquids. Some of these objects were unidentifiable, being greyish-red nebulous lumps, but one or two were definitely recognizable as whole mice. To Pedlar, they looked peaceful floating inside the jars, with their eyes closed tight. Peaceful – and very dead.

'Pretty, pretty mouse. Nice fleshy mouse. Let me see your plump little body . . .'

Pedlar spun round to see himself being studied by a pair of glittering eyes rimmed with pink. A fat white mouse in a silver cage shared the table-top with him. It had a short pink tail and a pink nose. It sat high-nose and regarded him with a strange expression on its face.

'Did you get captured too?' asked Pedlar, in an attempt to shatter that peculiar stare.

The mouse simpered. 'Haven't you heard of Little Prince?'

A vague memory of a conversation passed through Pedlar's mind. The trouble with being in a new place, learning a new geography, new faces, was that the things you were told went in one ear and out of the other. There was so much to learn that your brain became saturated and no more would go in. You discarded what you felt was unimportant.

'Yes, I have heard of you,' said Pedlar, 'but I'm not sure in what connection.'

'Let me refresh your memory,' said Little Prince in his sing-song voice. 'How about – cannibalism? That ring a bell my lowly little yellow-neck? Did they tell you I like *eating* other mice?'

A shiver rippled along Pedlar's fur. 'You're – you're joking of course.'

A sickening tinkly sound came from between the teeth of the Little Prince.

'I do like to joke of course, you sweetmeat you, but not about eating. I never joke about eating.'

Pedlar swallowed hard and stared around wildly.

The nudnik was busy fiddling with something on one of his shelves. Then he turned to stare once at Pedlar in his cage, before turning and leaving the room, slamming the door behind him. Pedlar was left in the dubious company of the creature who liked the flesh of his fellow mice.

'Where do you come from?' asked Pedlar. 'Why are you that funny colour?'

'Funny colour?' sang Little Prince. '*You're* the one that's a funny colour. I'm a perfect tame mouse, perfectly bred for my perfect coat. I am well beloved of nudniks. My master likes to stroke me with his finger. He croons to me in the accents of nightingales. I am his pet, his beautiful Little Prince, and he treats me with great tenderness and understanding.'

'But not other mice?'

'Not dirty, mean little house mice and yellow-necks, with their grubby coats and sordid ways . . .'

'We're not grubby or sordid,' gasped Pedlar.

'Slovenly and shabby, grimy and unkempt – nasty little creatures you are, but with candied flesh – oh, yes – honeyed meat. I love your loins, your lungs, your liver, mouse. I adore your abdomen. I cherish your cheeks. I thrill to your throat. I hold your heart holy. Your spleen is special to me. Your brain is beautiful. Your—'

'SHUT UP!' shouted Pedlar.

Little Prince blinked with his pink-rimmed eyes and cried in his peculiar sing-song voice.

'Don't you like talking to me, mouse with the savoury flesh? Do I bother you, sweetheart? Can I suck the marrow from your broken bones, when you are dead and boiled in brine? Can I? Can I? Can I lick your skull clean of its brain, and pick with my teeth between your toes? Can I?'

'You're disgusting,' said Pedlar in contempt, and turned away from the white mouse to contemplate the wall.

The next time Little Prince spoke, his voice had a semblance of normality. 'I've been here a long time,' he said. 'All my life. I've lived in this cage since goodness knows when. Probably I was born here. My name is Little Prince but I'm an emperor of my domain. I rule over the captives in their cages. You have to obey me, you know. You have to be nice to me. My master won't kill you until he sees me looking at you and licking my pink lips with my pink little tongue. *Then* he'll stick pins through your eyes, into your brain, and boil you in brine. That's because he knows I want to eat you. He enjoys watching me gobble the flesh of my own kind. He's like that.'

Pedlar said wearily, 'Don't you ever get tired of listening to yourself?'

'Yes, all the time. That's why I want *you* to listen to me. I'll let you live a little longer if you'll do that.'

Pedlar sighed heavily, turning round, 'What is it you want to say?'

'Anything and everything,' cried the Little Prince brightly. 'Let's play a game. I'll think of something nice to eat and you have to guess what it is. All right? Go.'

'Cheese,' said Pedlar.

'Nooooo!' said Little Prince.

'Cake.'

'Noooooooo! I'll give you a clue. It's the nicest nicest sweetmeat in all the world.'

'A mouse,' growled Pedlar.

'Something *specific*.'

'A mouse's heart.'

'Yes, yes,' cried Little Prince, delighted. 'How did you guess so soon? You *are* a clever dirty little mouse. I like to save that bit for last, because it's so soft and sweet, isn't it? Shall we play another game?'

'No,' snapped Pedlar, 'the sooner I die the better for me. Anything, even a slow death, would be better than lying here listening to your drivel. It's the worst torture I've ever heard of in my life.'

'That's very hurtful,' said Little Prince in a chastising tone. 'Aren't you ashamed of yourself, you nasty creature? I would be. I think I have a lovely voice. I speak with the notes of a song thrush. You should be happy that I'm making your last moments so beautiful. How can you complain, you sweetmeaty little mouse, you?'

Pedlar groaned and turned again to the wall. *You are the One who will walk with the many*, he thought. Was this it, then? He was the One and the mice already eaten by Little Prince were the many whom he was about to join? For all their augury, for all their urgency, the ancestral voices had brought him to a dreadful end in a foreign place.

PFEFFER KRANZ

'**I** SEE A SMALL CHANGE IN THE PATTERNS OF LIGHT
by that rafter. Ferocious, is that you?' said a bodi-
less voice.

'Yes – who's that?'

'It's me, Fallingoffthings. I'm just on my way to the far
side of the attic.'

'Where are you, by the old stuffed chair?' asked
Ferocious.

'No, near the broken clock.'

'Still can't see you. Never mind, catch you later, Fallingoffthings. I'm off to look for food.'

'Good luck.'

The two mice, members of the Invisible Tribe, parted
silently, without actually seeing one another.

The Invisibles were actually wood mice, with large
rounded ears and large eyes. Bigger than a house mouse,

but smaller than a yellow-neck, the wood mice Invisibles lived most of their life in the dark. They *liked* the dark. The attics were ideal for their nocturnal style of existence. They used their smell and hearing far more than other senses, yet they were able to distinguish shapes in the darkness where other mice would have seen nothing. Their gift from the Creator was in the nature of evaporation. Even when they were known to be there, allowed themselves to be evident, they appeared to be insubstantial, a piece of visible darkness. They were the velvet phantoms of the House and respected even by Gorm for their evanescence.

Like Pedlar and his yellow-necked race, wood mice normally lived in woods and hedgerows, gardens and fields – they are also called long-tailed fieldmice – but sometimes they move into the giant snail shells alongside the nudniks. This is what had occurred with the original great-great-grandparents of the Invisibles, who came into the House to escape a particularly freezing winter – the worst for many nights – and founded their tribe. When spring came round again, many were reluctant to go back to the wild, since they had been born in the attic.

There were essentially three attics: a roofspace sectioned off into three areas. The mice stayed mainly in the middle attic, though they occasionally spilled over into Merciful's attic on one side, and Kellog's on the other, depending on their number.

The middle attic was a jungle of junk. There were trunks, boxes full of old clothes, artefacts ranging through a dress-maker's dummy, photograph albums, suitcases, discarded furniture to bottles and broken toys. The Invisibles loved it, for it enabled them to move around from one hiding place to another.

Mouselore said that the great Creator made junk first,

and then the nudniks gradually spoiled things by turning each bit into something useful. But the attic held pure, unadulterated junk, straight from the hands of the Maker. It was brilliant for nests.

Whispersoft had his in the bell of a battered trombone which hung from a nail in a rafter; Timorous's nest was deep in the heart of a sea chest; a lacrosse racquet made a swaying hammock for the nest of Miserable; the wonderful balancer Fallingoffthings went through the ear of a diver's helmet to reach the only mouse home with a picture window.

Yes, it was a wonderful varied landscape in which the tribe of the Invisibles lived and died.

Tribe it was, though not often called such: most mice simply referred to them as 'the Invisibles'. They followed cryptic ways, secret paths, and the mystic silence of their approach and departure was renowned throughout the House. In the whole history of their existence as a colony, not one had been caught by either Spitz or Eyeball. Only Merciful, the owl, had ever actually eaten any of the adult Invisibles, though Kellog often stole babies from their nests. Owls are known for their Silent Killing, so it was a case of Silence meets silence, with the former carrying deadly blades and hooks about its person.

Merciful swooped with never a whisper or a sigh, her thick, soft plumage ensuring a noiseless flight. She was an excellent and pitiless hunter, with a deadly accurate eye. Once marked, the prey was doomed, unless a place of safety was an instant away. Merciful's beak and talons could open up a mouse quicker than the time it took to blink. Even Kellog was frightened of Merciful. Fortunately Merciful did not rely on the attic for her source of food, but went out into the wilderness at night to do her hunting.

150

However, she was ever hungry and only the very cleverest of the Invisibles grew to adulthood in her domain.

It was the strange habit of the Invisibles – none knew why, nor cared much – to name creatures contrary to their natures. Thus the mouse that spoke loudly was called Whispersoft, the brilliant swimmer went by the name of Goingdownfast, the agile balancer answered to Fallingoffthings, the most timid of them was hailed by the name Ferocious, and the noisiest of the group (though quiet in comparison to the mice of other tribes) was a yellow-neck who had been given the title of Treadlightly.

Merciful had been named by the Invisibles on first entering the attic from the outside world. There had been strong lobbies for the names Compassionate and Kindly, but Merciful was the name which finally won over all others. Kellog, of course, was a rodent who spoke the language of all rodents and he was quick to inform everyone that he already had a name and wouldn't look kindly on any creature giving him another one. Kellog was certainly not one from whom individuals hoped for a kindly look.

Kellog's main opponent amongst the Invisibles was Goingdownfast. Kellog's nest bridged the gap between the outer wall and the water tank, and Goingdownfast liked to swim backwards and forwards across the tank when its custodian was absent. Kellog had sworn to kill this brave wood mouse, but had thus far been unable to catch him.

One of the reasons why Kellog made his nest on the edge of the tank was so that he could control the water supply for the whole attic. Those who wished to drink at the waterhole while Kellog was present had to fall under the eye of the rat. Those in his disfavour had to wait until he was out on one of his trips around the House, before they

151

quenched their thirst. Mice do not often need to drink, but it was galling to have to await someone else's pleasure when they did want to. Goingdownfast could never drink while Kellog was at home and this incensed the great swimmer beyond endurance.

At about the same time as Pedlar's ears were being assaulted by the syrupy-sick tones of Little Prince, Going-downfast was swimming across the water tank, his deter-mined eyes just above the waterline, his nose taking in quick breaths of air. Beneath the surface his legs were kicking furiously, driving him forward over the wide stretch of water.

Until now, Goingdownfast had been content to leave signs around Kellog's nest: signs that showed he had simply *been there*, to irritate the brute and let him know he wasn't invincible. A piece of cotton out of place – a button planted in the centre of the nest – things like that. However, Kellog had recently ravaged the nest of Goingdownfast and his mate, Nonsensical, and Goingdownfast wanted revenge. Goingdownfast knew he would have to keep the location of his own new nest a secret, for Kellog was going to be absolutely furious when he came home.

It was dark and still in the middle of the tank, and Goingdownfast made hardly a ripple on the dusty surface of the water. His large keen eyes took in any small move-ment around the edges: spiders, insects and even floating dust motes. He did not want to be caught on Kellog's terri-tory. Kellog, being a ship rat, was of course an excellent swimmer.

He reached the other side of the tank and climbed out. He could smell the offensive reek of Kellog's nest. It wafted down – a kind of stale musty odour – to assail the nostrils. He wrinkled his nose and twitched his whiskers as he shook off the droplets of water from his coat. Then he fastidiously wiped his face clear of water using his paws, before he regarded the target of his attack.

So! Kellog thought he could wreck the nest of an Invisible with impunity did he?

The rat's nest was fashioned along the same lines as a squirrel's drey: spherical in shape with a single entrance hole. It was a great hollow ball made of strips of cardboard, rubber, electrical wiring, string, old felt, paper, cloth and slivers of wood. Anything, in fact, that Kellog had been able to pick up or tear loose. Decorating the south-facing wall was a beautiful red silk ribbon, incongruous with the rest of the dark, foreboding fortress. Had Kellog been in the wild, the nest would have been made of twigs and grass, but there were no such building materials to be had in the attics.

Goingdownfast shivered as he stared at the black entrance hole, glad that he had observed Kellog leaving the nest that morning. It would have been fatal to have begun knocking the nest about, only to have its occupier emerge from that black hole. Just the thought made the mouse shiver.

'So – to work!'

He began pulling out the various strands of wire and string which held the nest together, getting them in his teeth and tugging hard until they came away from the main frame. It was hard work because Kellog was a good weaver and had entwined the strands very tightly in the construction of his home.

Soon, however, Goingdownfast was tearing bits of dry paper away from the edges. Cardboard strips came off with a few determined tugs. The nest began to sag in a very satisfactory fashion. Its rounded bulging shape started to look decidedly oval, then flattish, until finally it collapsed.

Goingdownfast, gulping for breath with the exertion of the task, stepped back and admired his destructive handiwork.

'Saboteur!' he congratulated himself.

His was the artistry of the guerrilla, the freedom fighter. He could hit and run as well as any roof rat! Sneak in, devastate, sneak out. That was the method. Do it quietly, but do it effectively.

His work done, Goingdownfast claimed the rat's red ribbon as his trophy, put it in his mouth and slipped back into the cool waters of the tank. He swam silently back across its dusty surface. The whisper of spiders was louder than his strokes. The murmur of beetles was noisy in comparison. He reached the other side and climbed, dripping, out on to the edge. A brief shake of his coat and he was gone, in amongst the shadows, moving like a black ghost along the floorbeams.

When he reached his brand new nest, tucked in the cab of a toy tin truck, he first of all quietly hid his silken trophy under its base. Then he went inside where his own Nonsensical was waiting to hear the news.

'Are you all right?' she asked him.

'Right as a joist,' he said, slipping his wet form in beside hers. 'You should have been there.'

'I would have been, if I could swim as well as you,' she said, 'but none of the Invisibles can do that.' She added proudly, 'You're the best swimmer in the tribe.'

'Oh, I'm just lucky to have the gift,' he said, modestly. The nest was warm and smelt good. A comfortable feeling came over him, of drowsiness mingled with satisfaction. It had been a good hour's work, one that would be remembered in tribal legends for some time to come. *'Did I ever tell you youngsters, about the time long ago, many, many hours in the past, when a brave mouse called Goingdownfast destroyed the evil roof rat's nest? Well this is how it happened . . .'*

MASCARPONE

Kellog crouched on a beam, his black back hunched almost in a perfect arch. He had just eaten of some apples stored in the garden shed. The tribute he collected from the Savage Tribe was not enough to satisfy his hunger fully, though he could have survived on it if the necessity arose.

Kellog and Tunneller had the House sandwiched between them, he at the top where he knew he belonged, and she at the very bottom. They both collected dues and therefore Kellog saw themselves as very much alike, though the mice would have pointed out that with Tunneller, you were getting a right of passage for your payment. Kellog would have countered with the argument that the mice *were* receiving something: the right to live.

The Savage Tribe were the ones to pay him the tribute simply because they were the only tribe that had food to give. The others were as poor as church mice and Kellog simply could not be bothered to collect their dried crusts or book chewings.

Thus, having travelled what was always a hazardous journey from the attics to the garden, using Merciful's hole to get out and descend down the rough-cast wall cladding, then returning by the same way, Kellog felt he was entitled to a rest.

He took a calculated risk using the owl's hole, even at a safe time of night: Merciful would have ripped his throat open if she had caught him at it. But Kellog was waxing arrogant in his later nights and the older he grew the more imperious he became. It was to do with his status in the House, as the unassailable one, whose great, dark nest was feared by every mouse in the House. In that motley collection of attic debris he lived as the dread lord whose shape was terror to everyone from the leaders of tribes down to every mother's smallest infant.

For himself, Kellog feared little. He was afraid of the owl, it was true, but as long as he was cautious at dusk and dawn, the unsafe twilights, he would never be caught out. He was *concerned* about the nudniks, but he was very careful never to be seen by them, remaining between walls, beneath floorboards. He was worried by the cats, whose territories he never entered.

The only thing he was really terrified of was being rhymed to death. All rats, everywhere, are fearful of being rhymed to death by a clever rhymer. Even a wheel rat — fashioned from a dozen ordinary rats who have knotted their tails to form an invincible ring — even the twelve-hearted, twelve-headed wheel rat feared the rhymer.

Kellog had heard, and knew it to be true, that a rat would stiffen to immobility, his mouth would fall wide open, his eyes would glaze over and his heart would stop, on hearing relentless rhymes of which the rat himself was the subject:

> *Fie, rat, fie*
> *Thou must die.*
> *Stiffen back,*
> *Jaws fall slack,*

Eyes do start,
Stop, thy heart.

Spoken aloud, in front of him, this kind of rhyme would kill Kellog stone dead. Yet he had little to fear because no mouse knew of this vulnerability in rats and in any case none of the attic mice were clever enough to make killer rhymes. They didn't have the ear for rhythm or rhyme. They knew nothing of metre and could not scan. They were poem deaf, so to speak, and unmelodic.

The library mice were capable, of course, but this was why Kellog stayed well clear of the library. They'd once had an ace versifier among their number – Snurb-the-rhymer – but one fine night he'd left their cosy quarters, succumbing to the urge to become a real poet that wanders lonely o'er hill and dale. Kellog had never stopped rejoicing.

One night, when the time came, Kellog would drive the Bookeaters from the House, in case his secret weakness was ever discovered. Until then, if ever he heard of another mouse who could rhyme, why, he told himself, he would rush upon the creature and kill it before it could speak a word.

In his wakeful fancy he saw himself doing this act of great courage, but he was sometimes aroused from a deep sleep by terror, soaked in sweat, having dreamed that the mouse kept on speaking, even with a broken neck, and rhyming its deadly rhymes so very, very cleverly.

The nudniks, towards whom Kellog showed a much greater respect than did the mice, were so far unaware of his presence. Once he was seen by one of them, all hell would be let loose: he had experienced their fear of his kind before. Once they knew he was there they would go to any lengths to kill him. Nudniks did not like mice, but they *hated* and *loathed* rats.

The mice believed nudniks to be stupid bovine creatures, but Kellog knew otherwise. When it came to rooting out and destroying rats, they could be incredibly inventive, as well as ruthless. As one of the library mice might say, where roof rats were concerned nudniks were completely without ruth.

Kellog was well at home amongst beams. He carried his ancestors' remembrances and dreams – vague shadowy racial memories – of the bellies of tossed wooden ships. The smell of caulking tar was buried deep in his brain. So too was odour of gunpowder and iron, hemp ropes and canvas sails; the sound of timber against timber; the taste of salt water in the cheese and flour, in the apple keg. In that hot rat brain of his, was the pattern of cross-spars on masts; the lacework of ropes running from cleats to booms; the matrix of rope shrouds to mizzen and main – all pathways, escape routes, for the running rat to follow.

Kellog was not a mariner himself, but his grandfather had travelled over the seas on a nudnik vessel. Ship rats hate the cold, unlike common rats who will happily live out in the orchard, and the colony had finally established themselves as roof rats in the House.

Immediately a war began between the nudniks and the rats, and Kellog's family were subjected to a brutal slaughter.

Most of the rats died in agony, kicking and jerking, and finally curling into a stiff ball. Poison was the cause of the deaths: powder left to be eaten in the most obvious areas of the House. By degrees the survivors became immune to the poison and could eat it with relish, without any ill effects. Kellog was one of those: one of the last three rats in the House. One of the three finally died from old age and the other was chopped in half with a meat cleaver on a sunny day in spring, by the kitchen nudnik who caught him stealing cake.

Kellog was now all on his own and his dark mind was well suited to his cloistered existence. Perhaps another rat, for they are social creatures, might have died from loneliness, but Kellog was Kellog and not another rat.

The roof rat stretched himself and yawned, revealing his formidable teeth. Then he dropped with a heavy *plop* from the beam to the floor proper and made his way back to his nest. Kellog was looking forward to crawling into his cosy home, where he intended to curl up and dream rat dreams.

He swam across the water tank, giving his fleas a soaking as well as himself. Then he pulled himself out by his nest.

His nest!

Kellog stared at the collapsed mess in front of him, first in bewilderment, and then in growing anger. Finally, a great sorrow came over him when he realized that his beautiful red silk ribbon had gone. It had been Kellog's one concession to the unnecessary, and he had treasured it like a talisman. So strong was his feeling of rage it made him feel sick and giddy. He swished his tail in the thick dust. A hot sickness was in his stomach, radiating throughout his whole body. His eyes blazed and his teeth clattered together as he tried to contain his wrath.

He said only one word.

'Goingdownfast!'

SAINT PAULIN

Whispersoft had called a council meeting and all the

Invisibles over the age of sixty nights were in attendance. Called to order, the Invisibles stepped forward into the grey light, murmured their own names, and then drifted back into the darkness again. Once he was sure they were all there, the loud-voiced leader spoke to his tribe.

'You will all be aware that Tostig, of the Savage Tribe paid us a visit yesterhour . . .'

'Couldn't very well miss him,' said Fallingoffthings. 'He tramped through here like a nudnik and tried to hold a conversation with a rag doll.'

Everyone laughed.

'Well,' agreed Whispersoft, 'Other mice do not quite have our skill for silent unseen passage. Never mind, I'm sure Tostig felt he was creeping ever-so-carefully.'

There was another laugh. If the Invisibles had a fault it was that they tended to be a *little* self-congratulatory where their own talents were concerned.

'Tostig brought a message from his chieftain, Gorm-the-old, who is anxious that I get together with him to discuss something of great matter which will affect all the mice in the House.'

Timorous, standing on the edge of the meeting under the shadow of a rafter, grunted audibly.

'You have something to say, Timorous?' asked Whispersoft of his eternal rival for leadership of the tribe. 'I didn't doubt that you would.'

'Look,' said Timorous, a brutish and violent wood mouse with a frosted eye. 'I know I argue with everything you say, Whispersoft. That's as it should be. You talk a lot of drivel most of the time. But this is going beyond the pale. Gorm is a barbaric mouse . . .'

'That's rich, coming from someone like you,' called Whispersoft, and those who were farthest away from

Timorous dared to laugh.

Timorous growled softly in the back of his throat. 'That's as maybe, Whispersoft, but what I'm trying to say is, you can't trust him. You can't trust any of those Savage mice. They're treacherous and sneaky. Come on – you know as well as I do what trouble we've had from them in the past.'

Whispersoft nodded slowly. 'I'll concede that. There have been problems with the Savage Tribe from time to time. However, I'm inclined to think that we should talk with them *this* time. One of our number has been invited to an inter-tribal Allthing. I'm told that there's some big idea of achieving Utopia by chasing the nudniks out of the House and us mice living in peace together. Without the nudniks around, there would be food in plenty, for all . . .'

'Oh, for . . . you don't believe all that claptrap, do you?' cried Timorous, unable to take in such a vision. 'The Invisible that attends that Allthing will never be seen again, I'll bet my tail on that. It's just a trick to get one of us down there in the kitchen, where some ritual murder will take place.'

'The Bookeaters will be there too,' yelled Whispersoft.

'Well that confirms what I'm saying,' said Timorous. 'Witchcraft. Sorcery. They need an Invisible to torture and then bite his or her throat open, so that they can use the blood for one of their foul ceremonies. Send along a thirty-night-old, why don't you? Let them have a nice *innocent* victim for their diabolical rites.'

Treadlightly cleared her throat and said, 'It is true, Whispersoft, that the Bookeaters slaughter healthy babies in moonlit hours, and lap the blood . . .'

Whispersoft stamped his foot and drummed his tail. 'So we've been told. So we've been *told*. But has anyone actually seen this happen?'

'An uncle of mine once heard . . .' began Treadlightly, but she was interrupted by Nonsensical.

'Prejudice and bigotry!' snapped Nonsensical. 'We don't know what goes on in the library – it's all hearsay – and until someone actually witnesses these deeds, we should ignore these childish tales. The Bookeaters probably tell their children similar stories about *us*. Ignorance like this has got to be stamped out.'

Timorous said, 'If they tell stories about us, then we're entitled to do the same.'

Nonsensical snapped again, 'Rubbish! It's up to us to set an example, not to follow after with tattle-tales, otherwise the cycle of mistrust and hate will never be ended. This is serious. It's our chance to get the tribes together, see for ourselves that the Savages are not all bloodthirsty destroyers with rape and pillage on their minds. It's our chance to discover that the Bookeaters are just like us really, only a bit more mystical, a bit more learned . . .'

Timorous said craftily, 'In that case, I think Nonsensical should be our envoy, since she's so keen on improving inter-tribal relationships. What do you think, Ferocious?'

The browbeaten little Ferocious, frightened of his own tail and certainly terrified of Timorous, whispered, 'Oh, quite. Quite.'

'No!' cried Goingdownfast, stepping out of his shadow. 'She's pregnant. She's not going anywhere.'

But it was Nonsensical who answered this. 'Yes, yes I am. I'm just the right mouse to send. Whether I'm pregnant or not . . . It's a dangerous journey, I know, but I'll be all right. I'd like the envoy to be me, Whispersoft.'

At this everyone seemed to add their own point of view at once.

'Nonsensical doesn't get too emotional about things.'

'She listens carefully to all the arguments and then uses her common sense to guide her to a conclusion. She's perfect.'

'That's settled then,' said Nonsensical. 'Now, you were telling us the reasons for this meeting, Whispersoft?'

'Yes, like I said, there's revolution in the air and we Invisibles don't want to be left out. It could mean goodbye to the nudniks! I'm told by Tostig that the Bookeaters are very excited by it and of course the Savage Tribe are for it.'

'What – what about Ulf and his 13-K?' asked Ferocious.

'Ahhh, there's the first difficulty so far, I gather. Ulf and Drenchie have categorically stated they will never join anything in which Gorm has a part. Still, you never know, they might be brought round in the end. Or we can manage without them. Just imagine living in the House without nudniks! Especially if the tribes are at peace. The nudniks would take the cats and the dog and we could wander where we wished, without fear . . .'

Many of the mice were overwhelmed into silence by the very idea of such anarchy.

Timorous said, 'You don't expect Kellog and Merciful to go too, do you?'

Whispersoft replied loudly, 'I have plans for dealing with Merciful.'

A gasp went through the Invisibles. A mouse? Taking on an owl? Was this possible?

'I can't reveal too much at the moment,' said Whispersoft importantly.

'My backside,' growled Timorous. 'You? Fight with Merciful? The idea is pathetic. When you come up with a plan to kill Merciful, I'll leave the House, I promise you. And what about Kellog? Have you got plans for him too?'

'Kellog is involved in my scheme for getting rid of Merciful,' replied Whispersoft smugly. 'I'll tell you *that* much even now.'

'I wonder if Kellog knows that?' muttered Timorous, but the meeting was beginning to break up in sheer excitement, and no-one was taking any notice of him except Ferocious, who kept nodding and saying quietly, 'I'm with you, Timorous.'

Timorous looked at him disgustedly. 'You'd better be, you little insect, or I'll bite your ears off.'

Suddenly, there was another shape alongside Timorous, and a voice hissed in his ear, 'If anything happens to my Nonsensical, I'll come looking for you, Timorous.'

Timorous remained unruffled by this threat. 'Well, I'll be here, Goingdownfast. Bring an extra set of teeth with you, because you'll need them.'

Goingdownfast glared at him. 'Just you remember what I'm saying. It'll be to the death. Only one of us will walk away afterwards.'

'Get lost, waterbaby,' snapped Timorous, rolling his frosted eye. 'I've no more time for you. Come back when you're ready to use teeth instead of words.'

'I will, you can be sure of that.'

Then Goingdownfast was gone, like mist in a draught, and Ferocious was left with chattering teeth, wondering if he was going to get caught up in the conflict between his friend Timorous and the determined Goingdownfast. He wanted nothing to do with such combat, which was against tribal laws and would surely result in the victor being banished. Anyway it sounded as if a greater conflict now lay ahead and they should all be concentrating on that.

Ferocious wandered away from the meeting with a troubled mind. This business about getting rid of the nudniks was frightening to him. It was true he was frightened by most things – he was a coward, that was a fact to him – but in this case it wasn't so much that he was concerned for himself, as for the whole nation, the several tribes. The existing order. He had the feeling that the whole House was heading towards a disaster. These feelings had come over him before and they had always turned out to be right.

But what could he do about it? Could he go up to Whispersoft and say, 'Look, Whispersoft old chap, I've got this sort of funny feeling about chasing out the nudniks. I don't think we ought to do it.'

Oh, sure, that would work all right, thought Ferocious. He'd only get swung round by his tail and thrown into the water tank to toughen him up. That was the trouble with being a sensitive creature like himself. No one took you seriously, no one thought you had the general good at heart. They all thought you were scared sick of something happening to *you*, which was also true, sad to say. They didn't realize that you could be worrying about *them*, as well as yourself.

He was too sensitive for his own good. All his life he had been teased and tormented for it. When he was a youngster the other mice would exclude him from their games, make fun of him with jibes and taunts, and generally make his life miserable. It was an old story, with an old result. Ferocious had withdrawn into himself, kept his own company, and consequently he thought about things far more deeply than other mice. He was also far more sensitive to possible threats to the environment in which they all lived.

He now saw that environment under threat, from these new plans of Gorm-the-old. He couldn't say anything

165

though. Gorm was about as sensitive as a house brick. It would be easier to reason with Eyeball, than get Gorm to understand how he felt. Anyway his main worry was bound to antagonize the Savage Tribe leader, so Ferocious had to voice it to himself. 'Where is there one among us,' he fretted, 'who would even be capable of leading us through revolt to freedom?'

Deep in thought, Ferocious wandered over the whole of the three attics, amongst cardboard boxes full of old nudnik junk. He moved like a phantom, using the deep shadows as camouflage. Coward he might be, but he was still an Invisible, and he had the power of cloaking himself with the darkness. When you lived under the eye of Merciful, you became as silent and indiscernible as a wraith, or you died a horrible death. Finally, he settled down to rest in a box of cotton wool, containing one or two cheap trinkets. The cotton wool was soft and reassuring, and he let himself drift away into sleep.

When he woke, he felt thirsty. There was only one place to get water, so he travelled across the floors to the water tank, hoping that Kellog was away. Kellog always made him very nervous, so that he bolted his water and often ended up choking. Not that Kellog had ever touched him, for the roof rat was very choosy about his enemies. It seemed that enemies were very special to Kellog. If you weren't an enemy, then you were nothing at all. It wasn't that he *liked* mice like Ferocious, he was simply indifferent to them.

Ferocious reached the water tank and was dismayed to see Kellog lying on the far edge of the tank. However, there was a raging thirst in the back of his throat and he knew he had to drink or die. Cautiously he crept up to the edge of the tank, only to find that the waterline was low and that he would have to drop into the tank to drink.

After hesitating for a long while, Ferocious finally fell into the water with a little *plop*. He came to the surface and trod water, looking anxiously towards Kellog. The big roof rat had not moved an eyelid. Ferocious drank quickly.

Once he had satisfied his thirst, he crawled out of the tank, on to the lip and shook himself. Still the dark shape of the rat had not changed a hair since Ferocious had first arrived on the scene. Then suddenly, Kellog turned his great head. The piercing eyes stared across the slate-black darkness of the water. Ferocious shivered violently as he felt those eyes boring into him. Yet could he turn himself away? He was transfixed to the spot, staring at the monster on the other side.

Monster was right. Kellog was immense. A solid plumb-bob shaped creature ridged with iron-hard muscles. His terrible jaws had been known to crack the bones of the strongest wood mouse. Kellog maimed and killed, not wantonly, but with individual intent. He did not eat adult mice, but he certainly had no compunction about attacking them.

Ferocious stood and trembled under the terrible gaze.

'What are you looking at, you ant?' the rat said harshly, in a tone that sounded as if his throat had been roughened by recently eating sandpaper.

The wood mouse's teeth clattered together. 'No-nothing, Kellog.'

'Then go, before I give you something to stare at. You want to be looking at your own spilled guts, do you?'

'N-n-no Kellog.'

Ferocious was still frozen to the spot with the horror of the situation and it seemed certain that at any moment Kellog was going to dive into the tank and chase him. Still, he could not move, his legs refused to obey the clanging commands of his brain, to *run, run, run, run, run*.

Kellog shifted slightly on his perch, then in a very ugly voice, said, 'And you can tell Goingdownfast from me that he's as good as dead. I'm going to kill him before the autumn. I'm going to tear his limbs off, rip his head off, and scatter the spare parts all over the attic. You tell him that from Kellog.'

At last movement came to Ferocious's extremities and he turned and scurried away over the floorbeams, wondering what his fellow wood mouse had done to Kellog the roof rat, and glad, just glad, that his own name was Ferocious, and not Goingdownfast.

CAMEMBERT

PHART AND FLEGM CONFRONTED TUNNELLER. FLEGM was gibbering with fright. Phart was made of sterner stuff than the other half of his tribe and was merely trembling. He was standing high-nose, holding some unidentifiable scrap in his claws. He could smell the arrowhead shape of the shrew in the darkness and his whiskers twitched with apprehension as he spoke.

'We've brought you some meat,' he said to Tunneller. 'You got to let us through.'

'Got to?' cried the little shrew, her deadly shape ready to leap one of her famous leaps. '*Got to?*'

'Well, that is,' smirked Phart, 'would you 'ave the kindness to let us through to the garden, eh?'

'Yes,' squeaked Flegm, shaking violently, 'the garding, please.'

Tunneller snorted her contempt of the two house mice

who were soiling her lovely labyrinth by their mere presence. They stank. They were dropping bits of themselves all over the place which she would have to clean up later. They had been down every blind alley and false trail in the maze before she'd had to go and find them. It was best, she decided, to accept the cooked meat and get them out of her beautiful network of tunnels as quickly as possible.

'Give me the toll,' she snapped.

Phart quickly dropped the piece he was carrying in front of her. Flegm also had a piece of meat, but they were keeping that for when they returned. They needed to pay the toll to re-enter the house once their mission was over.

'Now,' she snapped, 'take that passage over there and keep turning right. You do know which is your right I suppose?'

Flegm lifted his front left forepaw and said, 'Uhhh?'

'Your *other* right, stupid,' said Phart in a superior tone, and then led the way out of the maze.

'And if you get lost,' cried Tunneller after them, 'I'll leave you to starve and rot.'

'Yes, thank you ever so much,' called Flegm over his shoulder, without a trace of sarcasm. Then to himself he kept muttering, 'Turn right, turn right – me *other* right . . .'

Eventually, the two cellar mice managed to smell the outside air blowing through the tunnels and followed this welcome scent. Suddenly the darkness of the interior gave way to an early evening light. The pair of them had risen from their stale beds very early, in order to be out of the garden before Merciful and her fellow owls were gliding through the murk. There were some things which chilled any mouse into immobility and a meeting with Merciful was one of them. They stepped cautiously

170

from the maze exit into the grasses around the rain barrel.

They were on a great expedition, to meet Stone, the dormouse they had heard so much about. Stone, they had heard, knew all about the natural world. The countryside was in his care, he loved and cherished it as a mother her infant, and it was to Stone that Phart and Flegm wished to put the Great Question.

Flegm's teeth were chattering as he clung to Phart's tail. It was not a cold day. On the contrary, the sun was blazing down, the air was hot and still, and full of wasps, bees and other lazily-droning creatures. Flegm was scared.

'Can't we go back now?' he whined. 'I hate it out here. It's too bleedin' big for a start and ... WHAT'S THAT?'

Phart jumped about two lengths in the air and looked around him in a startled fashion.

In the shorter grasses, not far away, a long shape was slithering.

'I think it's a snake,' whispered Phart.

'A what? What d'they do?'

'They eat bleedin' mice,' said Phart, hurrying into the taller grasses.

Flegm raced after his friend and leader, his breath coming out in short sharp gasps.

On their expedition across the garden towards the tall privy, which never seemed to get any closer, they saw all manner of monsters, from terrifying magpies to an aggressive robin. Phart said he could definitely smell weasel on the track, though he'd never seen or smelt a weasel in his life, and only had a vague idea what one looked like. Flegm touched, actually touched, a 'whacking-great-toad-thing' which scared him half to death.

171

The two cellar mice were very, very shaken as they later emerged from some tall grass close to the privy.

At that point the nearby grasses parted and an untidy-looking creature appeared. From all the descriptions Phart had been given by his Uncle Bile, who had been Outside, it appeared to be some kind of pygmy squirrel.

Since the creature was no bigger than Phart, he challenged it immediately. 'What the bleedin' hell are you?'

The creature glared at him. 'I'm a dormouse, you ignorant mammal. Judging by your condition and smell, you two would be Phart and Flegm. Yecchhh! Disgusting.'

Phart's heart soared on realizing that he was in the presence of *the* keeper of the garden. He stepped forward out of the jungle and went high-nose. 'Dormouse Stone, I presume?' he said.

When Stone did not answer, Phart said, 'Sorry we mistook you for – well, I thought you was a squirrel or somethink, with that tail, you know?'

Stone regarded his shaggy tail and then nodded towards an oak not far away, which reached with its great knotted branches high up into the misty blue.

'That is a squirrel,' he informed Phart, who looked upwards to see a huge rusty giant sitting in the oak's branches.

'Blimey,' he said, swallowing. 'I'm glad you're not one of them, then, yer honour.'

'I shouldn't worry, to my knowledge squirrels don't eat mice. That one's eating oak mast, which it prefers to flesh . . .'

'Oak mast?' repeated Flegm, mystified.

'Nuts. Acorns, if you will,' said Stone.

'Oh.' Phart nodded. 'Nuts. They come in bags don't they? Sort of hard knobbly things.'

'They grow on trees,' growled Stone. 'And they have shells.'

'Well, ain't that a revulation?' Flegm said. 'I always thought like you, Phart. We never seen 'em come into the House except in bags, did we?'

'That's because you're a pair of ignorant house mice,' observed Stone.

'You what?' growled Phart, then remembering that he was on a quest for mushrooms, magic mushrooms what made a mouse go doolally, suddenly changed his tune to, 'Oh, *ignorant*. Oh yes, we're that all right. We ain't been given a proper education, that's why we come out here, to find you an' get one, so to speak. We don't know a gnat from a house martin, do we Flegm.'

'Naw,' confirmed his comrade. 'You know about mushrooms then?'

Phart gave Flegm a nudge. 'Not so fast,' he hissed. 'This one's a bit of a purist.'

'What I mean to say is,' amended Flegm, 'can we come back with you to your nest? We'd like to have a little talk, like, so's to be able to learn more about Nature and stuff like that.'

Stone frowned a little and then seemed to acquiesce. 'Follow me,' he said.

The two house mice trailed after the dormouse, following him back to the privy, where Stone said, 'This is my home. I've been told the smell from the privy is rather ripe, but I never notice it.'

'Can't smell nothin' out of the ordinary,' said Phart truthfully, as he sniffed a stench not very dissimilar from the odour of his own body.

'Not a bit,' confirmed his comrade.

'Well that's reassuring,' said the dormouse. 'You're the

first two who haven't complained.' He looked the two cellar mice up and down. 'I take it you've come out here to improve your condition? Don't worry, we'll soon have those coats looking glossy – can't do much about the bald bits, I suppose, but those sores will soon heal out here in the clean air . . .'

Phart decided it was time to interrupt. 'No, no, you old . . . yer honour. No. We've been sent on a mission, see. We've been asked, ahem, by the Bookeater Tribe if we can find this sort of special fungus, this mushroom. There's some sick youngsters in the library what need a mushroom cure.'

Stone looked grave. 'I see. Well, I have every admiration for Frych and her knowledge of natural medicine. Comes from eating all those books, I suppose. Of course, paper's not the best thing for one's digestion, which is probably why she's got an epidemic on her hands now. Paper must clog the bowels, surely? And there's no little green things in paper you know. None at all.'

'Little *green* things?' exclaimed Flegm.

'Little green things,' repeated Stone. He explained, 'You can't see them, but they're there all right. They put the sparkle into one's eyes, the spring into one's gait. You must have them in your diet or the physical condition starts to deteriorate and becomes . . . well, like *your* bodies, for example. Without the little green things, the body is vulnerable to all sorts of illnesses.'

Flegm looked at Phart and rolled his eyes.

'Little *green* things,' he mouthed, without sound.

Phart answered the eyeroll with his own and then turned to Stone and huffed a little, as if in agreement with what had been said, though under any other circumstances he might have taken umbrage at the slight against his own

174

physical appearance.

'Listen, yer honour,' he said. 'I'm sure there's a lot of good in fresh cabbage – a lot of good – but what we're after here is somethin' to make the youngsters better, see. We can give 'em the prevention later, but what we need now is the cure.'

'Right, right. Now what exactly . . .?'

Phart became more businesslike. 'It's like this, yer honour. What we need is this mushroom. It's a purple thing with spots. It cures, well, sick mice and such. We thought you'd know where to get some, you being into Nature and the like.'

Stone went into deep thought. 'Well – there's wood blewitt,' he murmured. 'That's a kind of bluey-mauve colour. No spots though. Or *deceiver*, perhaps? No. Elf cup? No, no. Wait a minute . . .!'

'Yes, yes?' cried Phart.

'I think I know the fungus you mean,' said Stone triumphantly. 'And there's quite a bit of it, so I don't think there would be any objection to you taking just a little.'

'Lead us to it, yer honour!' cried Flegm.

'That way,' said Stone, swishing his tail in the general direction of a copse. 'Come back in the autumn and I'll take you there.'

Flegm looked at Stone first, then at Phart, 'What's an autumn?'

'It's a season, you nit,' said Phart. Then turning angrily to Stone said, 'Are you trying to tell us that this mushroom only grows in autumn?'

'Exactly that,' said Stone.

'But what about all these library mice, lyin' sick to death in their nests?'

'My dear little cellar mouse,' said Stone, with a lofty

175

look, 'I can't *force* mushrooms to grow out of season. You come back in the autumn since you seem to need this fungus *very* badly, and I'll see what I can do. I'm sure you realize you have to be very careful with the fungus you're talking about. It stimulates the brain, you know – has a kind of intoxicating effect.'

'Really?' said Phart in a bitter tone. 'No, I didn't know that.' Autumn. Rotten-apple autumn. The Fall. Phart sighed.

The two cellar mice left the dormouse sitting high-nose, as they made their way back through the tall grasses.

'I'm sure he flippin' knew what we wanted the stuff for,' grumbled Flegm, when they were out of earshot.

'Course he blasted knew,' said the Stinkhorn chieftain resentfully, wishing he had never left his comfortable sack in the cellar, where there were potatoes in plenty and unlimited wine. Finally, to his relief, they reached the rain barrel and he turned to Flegm. 'Right, now where's the toll for Tunneller? We got to get back in before the twilight comes.'

'Toll?' said Flegm.

Phart looked at his tribe.

'Yes, the blasted toll. You're the one carryin' the toll to go in – I was carryin' the toll to go out. Do I have to think of everything?'

Flegm looked aghast, 'I've – I think I've gone an' et it by accident.'

'AAAAAAGGGGGHHHHH!' screeched Phart.

'We'll have to find another way in,' said Flegm meekly.

'There *ain't* any other way in,' shrieked Phart, losing all control. 'We're doomed to death, an' it's all your fault, you rotten gannet!'

When Phart had calmed down a little and informed

his miscreant tribe member that their only hope was to re-enter the House by going up the drainpipe and into the attic – realm of Merciful and Kellog – that miscreant wished he was already dead, so that he wouldn't have to go through the horrors that seemed to wait up the pipe.

GORGONZOLA

H IGH ABOVE THE SPOT WHERE PHART AND FLEGM
were gathering together their woolly courage to
enter the drainpipe, Pedlar was undergoing extreme mental torture. He had awoken from a fitful sleep to
find the Headhunter in the act of lighting a bunsen burner
with a match. A soft *pop* heralded the birth of a blue-hot
hissing flame. There was some liquid in a small pan by the
Headhunter's elbow and this was held over the flame.

Despite himself, Pedlar was fascinated by the blue flame.
It seemed eternal, yet from that side of eternity which
housed the damned. This demon's tongue licked away at
the bottom of the pan, and soon the water began to sizzle.

Little Prince was running up and down in his cage,
chortling with maniacal delight.

'Honey-flesh, jam-flesh, delectable sweet-sweet mousey
meat.'

Pedlar wrenched his eyes away from the infernal flame and turned in fury on the pet mouse. 'You're an abomination, you!'

The white mouse stopped running and his expression showed that he was hurt.

'How can you say that?' said Little Prince. 'Why, I'm a *beautiful* mouse. I'm so dazzlingly beautiful I hurt the eyes. I'm an Ooo-Aaah mouse, I am. Nudniks stroke little me with their fingers and ooo and aaah like anything. They cup me in their hands and make kissing noises!'

'Yeccchhh,' exclaimed Pedlar, much in the same tone as Stone had used when confronted with Phart and Flegm.

He turned away from the pet mouse again, and looked upwards to watch the Headhunter, who was now boiling a solid object in his little pan. When the small chunky nudnik finally lifted it out with tweezers, Pedlar could see it was the body of a vole. Pedlar's cage was directly below the nudnik's hands. Some of the boiling hot water dripped through the wire mesh of Pedlar's cage on to his back, and he jumped and yelled with the pain.

The Headhunter noticed this and showed Pedlar a row of even white teeth. Then he opened his mouth wide, as if he were going to roar as he had done earlier. The rows of hollow-eyed skulls on the shelves had that same look on their cadaverous faces: their jaws were wide open as if about to bite the head from a fellow creature. It was not a pleasant expression. It emphasized their needle-sharp fangs.

Just at that moment Little Prince began screaming. 'Master! Master! Master!'

Pedlar glanced at the white mouse to see that he was cowering in the corner of his cage, seemingly frantic about something. Pedlar looked in the same direction as the nudnik's pet, and realized that Eyeball was creeping into the room. At first the cat seemed intent on the boiled vole in the Headhunter's fingers. It must have been the odour of cooking that had attracted the feline monster. She inched her way into the room, only noticing the two cages containing the mice when Little Prince screamed again.

The Headhunter was paying no attention to Little Prince's cries. He now had the head of the cooked vole in a toy wooden vice and was using the instrument to squeeze open the jaws of the dead creature. When the jaws had locked in an unnaturally wide and silent roar, the Headhunter removed the vole's head from the vice and slit the underbelly from teeth to tail with a sharp penknife. Then he began to peel away the skin, revealing a soft pink and grey mass beneath. The smell of cooked flesh filled the whole room.

Eyeball had not advanced further than just inside the partly open door. She sat with narrowed eyes in the shadows below the bed. Being a Burmese blue, she was hardly discernible from the patches of light and dark which she used so effectively. There she sat, poised and patient.

'Oh lord, oh death, oh help!' cried Little Prince. 'Why doesn't my master see her? She'll have my nice little body in her mouth . . .'

'What are you whining about?' said Pedlar. 'She can't reach us inside these cages. Get a hold of yourself. Have you no control?'

'None at all,' confirmed Little Prince. 'I don't want to die. I'm too beautiful to die.'

The Headhunter, however, was engrossed in his task of stripping the skin from the vole. It seemed a very delicate and intricate operation. Bits of unidentifiable organs were beginning to plop and drip on to a piece of newspaper now, as the Headhunter poked around inside the belly of the vole with the penknife. There were grisly scraping sounds when the blade met bone and gristle.

Finally, the skin was off, still retaining the macabre head of the luckless vole. The Headhunter looked up and showed Pedlar his teeth again. Then he fitted the slimy voleskin over his forefinger, with his nail poking through the wide open mouth, and waggled it as if the creature were still alive. The finger-puppet vole was then used in a series of pretend attacks on Pedlar's cage, as the hand that carried it darted backwards and forwards, while the owner of the hand made noises.

This monstrous ritual unhinged Pedlar more than frightened him. It was indeed a weird and horrible experience, more nightmare than real. What the Headhunter got out of such display was impossible for the mouse to imagine, but there seemed a certain savage joy in the nudnik's expression as he rattled the bars of the cage with the vole's teeth. Under such atrocious mental torture, Pedlar was beginning to lose his reason a little, and he gibbered and jabbered nonsense at the attacking puppet, as if it were actually alive and attempting to get inside the cage.

Once the Headhunter had tired of his game, he went back to carving the flesh from the skinless corpse, and began feeding the bits to Little Prince through the bars.

Despite his fear of Eyeball, Little Prince gobbled down the slivers of cooked flesh with fanatical greed. He began crooning in between morsels, in a high unearthly voice, which only served to add to Pedlar's distress.

Suddenly, something landed on the sill just outside the leaded windows and distracted the Headhunter. The nudnik turned and stared through the bottle-thick glass at a robin sitting there, seemingly attracted by the spurting blue flame of the bunsen burner, still hissing away on the table.

At that moment, Eyeball sprang on to the table, snatched the remains of the cooked vole, and streaked away again. In a flash she was running through the doorway. The Headhunter let out a piercing yell. He grabbed a wooden bat and swung it at the retreating form of the cat. On its journey through the air the bat caught Pedlar's cage a blow and sent it crashing to the floor. The door to the cage sprang open on impact with the lino.

Despite the fact that he was shaken, Pedlar was through the open trapdoor in an instant, and under the bed. There he cowered in the comforting shadows, gathering his wits together. The next second the Headhunter's face was close to the floor, looking under the bed. Pedlar came to his senses and streaked past the face and through the open doorway, out on to the landing.

Had Pedlar been a long-time resident of the House, he would instinctively have headed for one of the holes on the landing. As it was, he was simply disorientated, and didn't know where to go. The Headhunter came crashing out of the bedroom, his boots thumping on the landing floor.

'Quickly, this way!'

Pedlar heard the shout, but didn't know which way to turn.

'*This* way, *this* way!' shouted the voice.

Finally, Pedlar located the owner of the voice, a wood mouse near a hole leading to the bathroom. Pedlar zipped towards the hole, just as a heavily booted foot smashed down on the spot where he had been sitting dithering. The next second, Pedlar was into the hole, and following the wood mouse.

When they were well into the intricate maze of the wallways, the wood mouse finally stopped. She turned to Pedlar and said, 'Are you all right? The Headhunter almost had you then.'

'Almost?' said Pedlar, gasping for breath. 'He *did* have me, but I escaped.'

The other mouse's eyes widened. 'He had you and you got away? That must be a first! How did you manage it?'

Pedlar sat high-nose, gathering himself together. 'Funnily enough,' he said, 'it was Eyeball who helped me get away. She snatched a . . . a *thing* the Headhunter was boiling in a pan, and he threw something at her. It struck my cage and knocked the door open. That's how I got out.'

'Well, you're very lucky, my friend. You should be Prince-meat by now.'

'Don't I know it,' sighed Pedlar. 'I must have some good spirit looking after me. I am *so* lucky.'

He shivered, the experience still having an effect on him. He doubted he would get over it for a long time to come. 'Nightmare' wasn't strong enough, he thought. There should be some word which adequately described the hell he had been through, but he couldn't think of one. Ordeal, suffering, atrocity – they just weren't accurate enough.

'You seem to be a bit shaken up,' said the other mouse. 'Do you have anywhere to go?'

Pedlar shook his head. 'I was living with the Bookeaters, but I've had enough of that life. I never got enough to eat there. Who are you? Where are you from? I haven't seen any other wood mice around.'

'My name is Nonsensical,' she said, 'I'm an Invisible. The Invisibles own the attics. You can come with me if you like, but first I've got to go to an Allthing – a meeting of all the tribes, in the cupboard under the stairs. I'm the Invisibles' representative.'

The last sentence was spoken with some pride.

'An Allthing? What's it about?' asked Pedlar.

Nonsensical became very excited. 'Apparently there's a plan to drive the nudniks out of the House, so that we have enough food to share between everyone. Representatives from nearly all the tribes will be there.' She meant all except the unmentionable and untouchable Stinkhorns, and the rebellious 13-K.

Something sparked inside Pedlar. He had a sudden flashback, of his younger self sitting in the hazel curlie-wurlie. It was as if he had heard all this before, somewhere long ago. As if it had always been destined that he, Pedlar, would be in this place at this time. In some way what the mice did next was going to involve him: he felt his life was about to turn a corner. How? Why? When? Pedlar had no idea. He just knew that he ought to find out as much as possible.

'Can I come with you?' he asked.

Nonsensical looked doubtful. 'It's for the tribes' representatives,' she said.

'My name's Pedlar,' he told her, 'I'm from the Outside. I could represent the Outsiders.'

'Weeelll . . .' she said, uncertainly.

'Thanks for saving my life by the way. If you hadn't been along . . .'

'Oh,' she replied, 'think nothing of it. And yes, you can come with me to the Allthing, but once we get there you'll have to persuade Gorm that you should be present. I hope you understand that? I can't really protect you.'

'Oh, don't worry about me,' he said, 'I'll be all right.'

He followed her along the mouse highways through the walls of the House and they came out at the Gwenllian Hole. From there they made a quick dash to the cupboard under the stairs, the mouse nerve-centre of the House, where inter-tribal Allthings took place. They squeezed through the gap beneath the door. It was dark inside, but Pedlar's senses soon adjusted, until he was completely aware of his surroundings and the mice around him.

There were tough-looking little house mice, one or two harvest mice and some yellow-necks like himself. Nonsensical seemed to be the only wood mouse present. She sat low-nose at first, on the edge of the circle, and Pedlar sat beside her in the same position.

'You're late, Invisible,' said a gruff house mouse, sitting up on top of the gas meter with his two doubles. 'Who's that you've brought with you?'

Pedlar shook his head, thinking he was seeing things, but the three identical mice were still there when he looked again. They were so alike even their scars were the same. It was as if the speaker was caught between two mirrors.

Nonsensical replied, 'This is Pedlar, he's an Outsider.'

'What's he doing in here then?' growled the belligerent house-mouse triplet. 'Haven't we got enough mice in the House without more coming in?'

Nonsensical ignored this question, saying instead, 'The reason I'm late was because of Pedlar. He escaped from the Headhunter and I had to show him the way to a hole. Being an Outsider, you see . . .'

'Escaped from the Headhunter?' exclaimed an elderly yellow-neck. 'Impossible, surely?'

'Not impossible,' said Pedlar, deciding it was time he spoke for himself, 'because, as you can see, here I am. Not so long ago I was in a cage that snapped shut on me.'

'One of the Headhunter's traps!' said a house mouse.

Pedlar continued. 'Yes, I suppose it was. Anyway . . .' he told them the story of his escape.

'Sounds a bit far-fetched to me,' growled the middle one of the triplets, which made Pedlar's yellow-neck hairs rise.

'Listen, you,' he said. 'I don't know who you are and I don't really care – you and your . . . brothers don't interest me a great deal – but I won't be called a liar.'

'My name is Gorm-the-old,' snarled the house mouse, 'and if you don't keep a civil tongue, I'll bite the damn thing out.'

Gorm! The leader of the Savage Tribe. Well, he would be a formidable opponent, thought Pedlar, but not an unbeatable one, not unless his bookends joined in the fight too.

'I'm from the Hedgerow,' said Pedlar, 'and we don't recognize tyrants there.'

'The *Hedgerow*,' sneered Gorm. 'Home of country bumpkins and rustics who eat damned hips and haws.'

'You watch what you say about my birthplace,' said Pedlar, his whiskers twitching. 'The Hedgerow is fine country, home to some of the greatest mice.'

'Turnip eaters,' smirked Gorm. 'Nut nibblers.'

'Now you listen to me . . .' began Pedlar, squaring up, but he felt Nonsensical's tail fall across his shoulder.

Just then another mouse spoke. Pedlar recognized her, by her quiet tones. It was Skrang, the Deathshead spiritual warrior-priestess. She said, 'Don't be too hasty, Gorm. Pedlar over there beat Tunneller the shrew to a standstill in single combat.'

This obviously impressed Gorm, who took another look at Pedlar and then grunted, 'Well, so he might have done. I heard something about that. It doesn't make any difference to me. If he wants a scrap, I'll give it to him, now if he likes. I've knocked down a few sloe gobblers in my time.'

'I don't want a fight,' said Pedlar, 'but I won't be spoken to as if I was some cellar mouse.'

' 'Ere, steady on,' muttered a joker, copying Phart's accent, and there was quiet laughter in the wings.

The mimic had broken the tension and things were left at that.

Pedlar said to Gorm, 'If you object to my being here because I don't belong, then perhaps you'll recognize me as representing the Outsiders?'

Skrang said quickly, 'That sounds fair – the Outsider Tribe?'

'Sounds daft to me,' grunted Gorm, 'but I haven't got the energy to argue. Let's get on with it.'

The meeting settled down into some kind of order, with Gorm doing most of the talking. The leader of the Savage Tribe seemed to like the sound of his own voice, and only rarely gave way for anyone else to get a word in edgeways.

'. . . so,' Gorm was saying, 'someone from every tribe is present. Even it seems,' he glared at Pedlar, 'the Outsiders are represented. Everyone but the 13-K are here.'

'What about the Stinkhorns?' questioned Pedlar. 'I don't see them.'

'The Stinkhorns?' snarled Gorm. 'They're not a *tribe*, they're degenerates.'

'True enough,' said Pedlar, 'but if you're going to form some kind of concerted attack on the nudniks, you'll need the co-operation of *all* the mice in the House – even *me* – so it doesn't make sense to leave out the Stinkhorns.'

I-kucheng piped up, 'What Pedlar says is true. It's foolish to leave anyone out, whatever their worth. I'll speak to the Stinkhorns myself, later.'

'If they're still alive,' sniggered Tostig.

'What do you mean by that?' asked I-kucheng.

'Well, the last I heard they visited Stone, out in the garden, and couldn't get back in again. Tunneller's probably bitten them both in half by now. Or they've been eaten in the wilderness Outside.'

I-kucheng gave Tostig a very serious look. 'You find that amusing, do you?'

Tostig withered under the glare of the elderly yellow-necked Deathshead.

At that moment there was a nudnik yell from the kitchen.

Gorm, Hakon and Tostig leapt off the gas meter with remarkable alacrity. The rest of the mice scattered to the far triangular corners of the cupboard-under, including Pedlar, whose instinct was to follow the crowd for once. Something had happened in the House and though he had no idea what it was, Pedlar knew that the other mice were expecting a knock-on development.

Sure enough, when they were all quietly crammed into the far reaches of the cupboard, the door opened and a bent nudnik shone a light inside, illuminating the gas meter. An arm came in, the hand clutching a round shiny object, which was pushed into a slot in the gas meter. A small handle was turned by the great fingers, then a click was heard, and there was another yell from the kitchen. The arm disappeared and the door to the cupboard-under was closed and latched.

Gorm resumed his stand on the gas meter and without further ado continued with the Allthing as if nothing had occurred.

'. . . so now we come to the next item.'

Pedlar wasn't listening. His heart was still hammering in his chest.

'What was that?' he asked Skrang quietly.

'What? Oh, *that*? It happens sometimes – not often, but you can't tell when it's going to. Something to do with the kitchen oven.'

'Oh,' replied Pedlar, none the wiser. Nothing like that ever happened in the Hedgerow. Yet he wondered if there *were* things that happened there, which would confuse the mice who lived in the House. They seemed so sophisticated, yet he would bet that the first time they saw a grass snake, they would be as confused as he was about the grey box. Wouldn't they?

Gorm then brought up the question of the 13-K, who were not represented at the Allthing.

'It seems that the 13-K do not want to join with us, in our great task of ridding our world of nudniks. They made my envoy eat dirt, when I sent him to them last night. I shall punish Ulf for that insult later, but in the meantime we're going to have to resign ourselves to going ahead without them.'

The Great Clock in the hall struck three, interrupting the conversation for a while. It was a beautiful set of notes that reverberated through the House as if through an empty temple, echoing. Everyone always stopped what they were doing if within earshot of the sounding cymbal of the Clock. There was always reverence for the passing of time, given numbers by the hidden bronze. The meeting let the last deep note die before carrying on with its business.

Skrang said, 'Why don't I have a word with them? I'm sure I can make them see reason. They wouldn't dare try to make *me* eat dirt.'

Gorm-the-old shrugged, his bent worn whiskers drooping. The cares of leading his tribe over the long hours were evident in the way his shoulders slumped when he spoke of his son and the breakaway youthful 13-K. It was his one great sorrow, that his son had not only rejected him, but had also actively set himself up against his father. Gorm had many, many sons and daughters of course, but Ulf was the one who had rebelled and consequently Ulf was the one Gorm wanted to return to the fold, repentant and father-loving. As Astrid had once said, Ulf would be a minor guard in an obscure squadron of the tribe's army if he hadn't turned his back on Gorm. His father would certainly not have been interested in him, if he hadn't run away. Gorm's ego was massive and all-embracing, and if your actions did not touch him personally, you did not exist.

Skrang then said, 'Do we want to consult Ulug Beg?'

'There's always a price to pay when consulting that old sage,' said I-kucheng. 'However, it might be best.'

Gorm shook his head. 'I would only want to consult him in an emergency. We don't even know if he's still alive.'

'He's always still alive,' murmured I-kucheng.

Pedlar had followed this mysterious conversation with some interest and was disappointed when it was dropped. He wanted to know more about Ulug Beg. However, it seemed that there was to be no more discussion about the 'old sage'.

Nonsensical the Invisible, Pedlar's new friend, spoke up now.

'I would like to ask the Allthing, or rather Gorm in particular, what Astrid thinks of this plan to rid the House of the nudniks.'

Gorm grimaced and looked testy. 'Astrid's not been herself lately,' he said. 'I think she's losing it.'

'By that answer, I take it she doesn't approve of the plan,' said Nonsensical.

190

Gorm looked uncomfortable. 'Well, not as such, but then I've noticed she's not the mystic she was once, you know. I think her visionary powers are wearing out.'

'Visionary powers don't wear out,' interrupted Skrang. 'You know as well as I do, Gorm, that Astrid is one in a million. She aids you quietly and firmly, without any wailing at the moon, or reliance on choral backdrops. And I've never known one of Astrid's prophecies not to come true. If Astrid is against it, it's because she's had a genuine vision.'

Skrang didn't add, *unlike the library mice, who are a load of fakes and frauds*, because Frych-the-freckled, Owain and Iago were all present at the meeting.

Nonsensical said, 'Until we find out what that reason is, I think the Invisibles will be very wary of joining the enterprise. We have a lot of respect for Astrid.'

Hakon said, 'Can I say something here? I've been observing Astrid lately. I think she has found, er, how shall I put it, a male companion. A buck.'

Gorm's head spun round and he stared at his principal double.

'What do you mean, a buck? *I'm* her buck.'

Hakon shifted uncomfortably and changed his sitting position, only to resume the old one almost immediately. Pedlar thought it strange that the two mice on either side of Gorm should even copy the way the old mouse sat. It really was like seeing triple.

Hakon said, 'Yes, we know that Gorm, but she has a secret mate – she meets him on the pan shelf.' Hakon cleared his throat. 'Everyone knows but you, I'm afraid.'

'Why wasn't I told this before?' roared Gorm. 'I'll tear someone's liver out! Who is he?'

'No one knows,' said Hakon, hoarsely. 'No one's actually

191

seen him, but you can tell by the way she acts . . .'

'I'll kill her! I'll kill him too, whoever he is!'

I-kucheng interrupted with a stern, 'This is neither the time nor the place to sort out your domestic quarrels, Gorm. You invited us here to discuss the Great Nudnik Drive. We're not here to waste our costly time listening to your private affairs.'

This was the first time the scheme had been called the 'Great Nudnik Drive', and because it sounded right this was the title under which it was subsequently known. This became its historical epithet. It was never called a 'war' because you can't have a war with dense creatures like nudniks. It would be like declaring war on cows or sheep. You *drove* them out, if and when they became a nuisance. The intention was to drive the nudniks out into the wilderness, ridding the House of these pests. Where they went to, once they were driven out, was of no interest. Perhaps they might graze in the fields beyond the House, or take to the woodlands, to live on mushrooms and moss. It didn't matter to the mice. Mice had wars with mice, but they drove away anything else.

Thus I-kucheng tried to get the Allthing back on track again, but Gorm was too incensed by this personal insult to his reputation to let it drop just like that. His own wounded ego was more important than a unique and unprecedented meeting of the tribes. His pride had been hurt and someone else was going to be hurt, physically, to balance the scales. Punishing the offenders was more important than House peace.

He said, 'This priestess has been disloyal to me! Does no one care about that? I'm the greatest chieftain the Savage Tribe has ever seen. I am glorious in battle. I'm courageous to the last drop of my blood. And I'm – I'm not *bad* looking. Why has she turned her face from her lord. Is loyalty to be cast aside as if it were nothing, these hours?'

'Let's not deviate, Gorm,' said Frych-the-freckled, getting in on the row. 'If Astrid has discovered a grand obsession for some other rodent, her judgement is not only impaired, it's probably non-existent for the duration. It's common knowledge that mice in the throes of new and pristine relationships have their craniums bursting with pyrotechnics. We can't expect Astrid to behave like a proper possessed-by-Shadows visionary if she's recently discovered some willing member of the *mus muridae* to expound on her virtues amongst the culinary implements, now can we?'

'Will someone please tell me what that gobbledegook means?' growled Gorm, looking at Tostig.

Tostig obliged. 'She says that if Astrid is spooning with somebody amongst the pots and pans, she's probably gone doolally.'

'Well, anyway,' growled Gorm. 'Her judgement's not the point here. It's her betrayal of me, I'm concerned about.'

Skrang said, 'You talk about faithfulness and loyalty as if it was coming out of your ears, Gorm. *You?* – you change your nest partners at a whim.'

Gorm went low-nose and stared around him dangerously. 'Right, that's *it*! I'm not taking these insults without a fight. Come on, Frych, let's have you! Come on Skrang! See if I care about your Ik-to bites. I won't be spoken to like this.'

Pedlar felt that a little calm ought to be injected into the proceedings, before the whole Allthing erupted into a battle which would go down in mouse history. This was why he addressed the meeting for the first time as a participator rather than an Outsider. 'Aren't we all supposed to be here under a truce?' he said. 'I mean, it's meant to be a discussion of common interests, isn't it?'

Gorm snapped, 'Don't you stick your whiskers in, yellow-neck, or you'll be sorry too.'

I-kucheng spoke then, in his usual composed manner. 'The Outsider is right. Let's have a few moments' silence to compose ourselves, and then continue without all this bickering.'

There was quiet for a time, then Gorm broke it.

'Well,' he grunted, nodding to Nonsensical, 'in the light of what's been said about Astrid, d'you still think your tribe will need her go-ahead?'

Nonsensical shook her head. 'No, I think probably Skrang is right. If Astrid has found a matching mate, then her judgement is to be suspected. Emotions can interfere with psychic powers. They're on the same sort of mystical level – they can get tangled with one another. I think we can say that the Invisibles won't take too much heed of a warning from Astrid in her present condition.'

'Good,' grunted the old warlord. 'Right, well the advantages are obvious. If the nudniks go, so do their creatures – cats, dogs and the Headhunter. The food will be all ours . . .'

'What about Kellog?' said Nonsensical. 'He's bound to realize the nudniks have gone.'

'Ah, yes, the roof rat,' muttered Gorm. 'Well, I think we can see he's so well fed that he won't bother any mice in the House. There'll be enough food for even that. There's not a lot we can do about the owl, except keep out of her way.'

'You don't think,' said Skrang, 'that Kellog might invite

194

other rats into the House, once he knows it's safe? He'll be out of control, you know, without nudniks here to keep him in the shadows. You give him tribute from the larder to keep him quiet at the moment, but he won't need that if there's been a Great Nudnik Drive. He'll be able to take what he wants, and bully us mercilessly. He'll be lord of all he surveys, with no constraints on him.'

Frych-the-freckled replied, 'Well, I suppose the Invisibles understand his foibles better than most ... but I would have imagined he was too ancient and inflexible to desire companionship. There's never been anything to stop him issuing invitations to a female *rattus muridae*, except that he probably doesn't wish to cohabit.'

'In any case,' added Nonsensical, 'the rat nation is not exactly extensive. How would he contact other rats? He's been on his own for so long.'

'There are some rats in the ditch at the bottom of the garden,' said Pedlar, 'because I smelt their markings on my way to the House – but they're common rats, not roof rats. Does that make a difference?'

'All the difference in the world,' said Gorm, though his voice had softened somewhat from the last time he spoke to Pedlar. 'They're not like us mice. Roof rats would rather die than live with common rats. The roof rats consider themselves above their cousins, and who can blame them? Common rats are pretty low creatures, after all.'

Nonsensical interrupted here, with a quiet statement. 'Though the Savage Tribe have always fed Kellog, by paying his tribute, since they are the richest tribe in the house, it has always befallen the Invisibles to keep a watch on his affairs. We will continue to make it our business to keep Kellog under control, after the nudniks have gone.'

'How do you propose to do that?' asked Gorm.

'We shall do it,' replied Nonsensical carefully, 'and there's nothing more to be said on that score at this meeting. You and I can speak later, Gorm.'

Gorm shrugged, hearing something in Nonsensical's tone which stopped his objections. 'On your heads be it,' he said. 'You can talk to me afterwards about the details. Now, we need a plan for the Great Nudnik Drive itself . . .'

There was a general blitz of ideas then, which were thrown into the arena, and which Skrang sorted through very carefully. It was decided that a campaign of wholesale sabotage was the best resource to see off the nudniks and that, initially, the tribes would each be responsible for one particular line. The Bookeaters would chew through electric cables, their teeth being sharper than most, having been honed on leather and paper. The Savage Tribe would attack sacks of flour, grain, and other kitchen goods. The Deathshead would try to bite into the gas main . . .

'And the Stinkhorns,' said Gorm in a very satisfied tone, 'can gnaw holes in the curtains and cushions, fittings and furnishings, in the living-room and parlour.'

'Isn't that a very dangerous job?' queried Pedlar. 'I mean, they're the domains of the two cats.'

'Yes,' said Gorm, smugly.

'What's the second plan, if the first fails?' asked the practical Skrang. 'We must have a back-up plan.'

Nonsensical suggested, 'If acts of sabotage fail to drive the nudniks out, then the Bookeaters must attempt to get them out by means of magic spells.'

Frych-the-freckled nodded. 'Magic is very unpredictable – often the results are not what one expects – so since it is an inexact science I see the need to keep it in abeyance, as a second line of attack.'

Not wishing to spend any more time on magic, Gorm

asked, 'What's the time in the outside world?'

I-kucheng looked at Skrang, who had recently been out to see Stone.

'Well, last time I was out,' she said, 'the Traveller's Joy had not yet turned to Old Man's Beard.'

Gorm said, 'When it does, I suggest we strike. It will be cold Outside then and the expelled nudniks will need to go far away, to find a new house – they won't hang around in a cold garden. Nudniks are always a lot slower when the weather turns cold.'

'So,' said Nonsensical, 'the end of summer then. In the House it's marked by the lighting of the boiler. We'll need to organize ourselves, make definite plans, but I suggest we strike on the night the boiler gets lit and the iron radiators come on for the first time. That'll be quite soon by my reckoning, so those of you with nests touching the radiators, and between the walls and pipes, had better move 'em soon. Pass that on to your tribes. The iron gets as hot as anything in the winter.'

'I distinctly remember the radiators,' said Frych. 'It seems like a millennium since they were functioning.'

'It's one hundred and eighty nights since the boiler was last alight,' confirmed Skrang.

'Is it really as long as that?' said Hakon to Tostig, across the front of Gorm. 'Doesn't time . . .?'

'Do you two mind,' growled Gorm. 'Save your chatter for when the Allthing is dismissed.'

'Yes, lord,' muttered Tostig and Hakon in unison. The truth was that each of them was shell-shocked by the idea of the coming Revolution, and resorting to common-or-garden trivialities was their way of absorbing its impact.

The historic Allthing then broke up, the mice leaving in ones and twos. The fact that many of them were unusually subdued was a measure of the import of what had just taken place. What lay ahead was a call to arms, and each individual mouse began to worry about his or her role in the Great Nudnik Drive.

Pedlar went with Nonsensical, saying, 'I'm impressed. Gorm has probably never been out of the House, yet he knows all about autumn. I don't remember autumn myself – I was born in the spring – but it seems remarkable that a house mouse has all this knowledge of the outside world.'

'He doesn't know *that* much about it,' said Nonsensical, hurrying towards the Gwenllian Hole. 'But even in here one picks up things. The Deathshead pay visits to Stone, in the garden, and they teach others what they know. It's only a matter of passing on knowledge. You don't have to actually experience it yourself, do you?'

'I suppose not,' said Pedlar. 'Look, are you sure your tribe won't mind you bringing me back with you? If it's any problem, I'll go and find somewhere else.'

'Of course they won't mind,' said Nonsensical. 'Why should they?'

POLDAR

Astrid had left Iban and was communing with her Shadows. It was a full moon and the light coming through the windows aroused her old friends from their sleep. They came out of the furniture, out of the banisters, out of the corners and landings. They gathered in an eerie silence which might have intimidated anyone but Astrid. They were soft Shadows, misty at the edges, unlike those brittle, sharp creatures who came out when the artificial lights were on. They were *her* Shadows.

'Shadows,' she said. 'You are my friends . . . and I have come to talk to you about a very serious subject.

'Gorm-the-old has suggested we chase the nudniks from the House, so that they will not be able to consume their usual vast quantities of food from the divine larder. He promises that there will be cheese enough for everyone once the House is under mouse rule, and I must admit that sounds attractive to most tribes. Once they hear the word *cheese*, their eyes glaze and they start to sway from side to side. To promise cheese is to promise untold wealth. What do you think of the plan, Shadows?'

It stinks.

'Why?'

Any plan of Gorm's has got to stink.

'But apart from that,' said Astrid, profoundly impressed by the keen insight of her Shadows.

Apart from that there's some strong connection between a full larder and the nudniks.

'Do you know what it is? Can you tell me?'

We can't – we just know there is.

Astrid sighed, even more impressed. 'Oh dear, well I'll just have to convince the other mice that Gorm is wrong, simply by relying on my mystique as a high priestess. That sometimes works. Anyway, I'd better be getting back to the kitchen. I'll be accused of meeting with someone on the pots-and-pans shelf if I stay away too long. They've got such nasty minds, those mice!'

But you do rendezvous on the pots and pans shelf.

'That's beside the point,' she grumbled. 'They've got no proof – and anyway, it's not all the time.'

Most of the time.
'*Some* of the time. Well, good night Shadows.'
Good night Astrid.

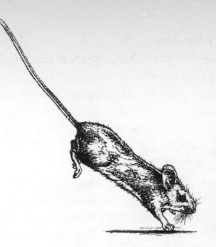

DOUBLE GLOUCESTER

NONSENSICAL WAS FAR LESS RESERVED REGARDING THE secrets of the House than any other mouse Pedlar had so far met. She was quite willing to disclose information on anything Pedlar cared to ask about, and even on anything which he did not. On the way to the attics, through the tunnels and spaces, she pointed out several more holes, naming them for him.

'Thyra's Hole – she made it so that she could visit a forbidden mate called Svyen Twistail. They were both caught one hour by Cynan-the-nasty, one of the Savage Tribe's old leaders. He bit Svyen so badly the wounded mouse ran from the House and was never seen again. Thyra spent the rest of her life sitting high-nose, waiting . . .

'Skuli's Hole . . . Idwallon's . . . now *this* is the Tangwystl Hole. Tangwystl was a swashbuckling kind of mouse, one

201

of the Bookeaters, but not at all stuffy like most of his tribe. Everybody liked him. A very fast runner too. Then one night he got it into his head that he could beat Eyeball over a long distance – well, the length of the landing, actually. He gnawed this hole ready for the end of the run. Never made it of course. Eyeball caught him halfway, and . . . well, the rest is too gory to go into. Ahhh, Llandud's Hole! Llandud was another Bookeater, but quite a different temperament from Tangwystl. He made this hole in order to become a recluse. It doesn't lead anywhere, except into a sort of cavity in the inner wall. We call them "hermit holes". There's quite a few of them scattered over the House, mostly made by the Deathshead, who keep the location of *their* holes secret . . .'

Pedlar was impressed by the holes and the histories behind them. There was nothing like this in the Hedgerow, no sense of providing against the future, only the present.

In the ditches a hole might be dug, but if neglected it would be reoccupied by another, perhaps different kind of creature altogether. Abandoned rabbit holes, for instance, were often taken up by ducks. Or the wind and the rain would fill such holes again, with loose dirt, twigs and old leaves. The Hedgerow was cut, the ditches dug, the fields ploughed. That was the cycle. Mutability was the way of the countryside. There were simply no markers on which to dwell, to throw the mind back to an earlier hour. The seasons ruled: grasses grew, hawthorn leaves withered and died, berries fell to the Earth and were consumed. New life came, old life left.

And the *future* in the wild was too uncertain to worry about. There were not only far more predators, with fewer escape routes – you couldn't just dash down a hole and hope to be safe in the ditch, for whatever was after you might well dig you out! – but there were also storms to contend with, fierce winters which might freeze your blood solid, poisons from the nudnik machines, a whole host of dangers.

Here in the House, time was revered, was somehow a more solid, established thing. It had majesty and grandeur. It was *told* by the voice of the Great Clock. It had a kind of formal structure to it. Just as the actual way in which the mice had gathered, sorted themselves out into tribes, and long maintained their lives. This too had a structure to it. Here in the House was a kind of *society*, not just an accidental collection of mice living in nests built at random. The realization made Pedlar feel in awe of the forces that had brought him here.

But it was the concern with the *passing* of time that impressed Pedlar the most. Hour by hour mice lived and died with the ghosts of their ancestors here. They also involved themselves with the future, as well as the past, by planning and bringing about what might be. Hence the scheme to drive the nudniks from the House. That sort of combined initiative towards a better future would never have happened in the Hedgerow.

'Such a lot of famous mice,' he said to Nonsensical. 'I've never known anyone famous before. Who's Ulug Beg, by the way? Everyone seemed impressed by him. Is it a secret?'

'No, not really. He's a very old mouse, some say he's almost six hundred nights old. He lives in the abandoned treehouse in the garden. I've never actually seen him, because the only way to reach him is by jumping from a sill at the back of the House, on to the washing line, the other end of which is tied to the tree.'

'Can't you just go out into the garden and climb the tree?'

'It's not as easy as that. The treehouse has been built

around the trunk, so when you reach it you have this flat surface going out – the underside, or the floor, of the treehouse – and it's like trying to walk across a ceiling upside down. No mouse can do that, not on a smooth surface.'

Pedlar nodded, 'So someone has to tightrope walk – but isn't that just as difficult?'

'It is for most of us, but we usually ask Fallingoffthings to do it. She's brilliant at balancing.'

'And Ulug Beg is pretty wise, is he?'

Nonsensical said, 'He knows everything.'

'Such famous mice, with such famous skills,' sighed Pedlar, feeling very inadequate.

'Where are you from, exactly?' asked Nonsensical, as they hurried along.

Pedlar shrugged. 'Oh, just a hedgerow, with a ditch running alongside it. It was a nice place, and I miss it. But—' Pedlar didn't feel able to talk about the ancestral voices that had guided him to the House and certainly not about his role as 'the One', '—I've always been one for variety, that's how I got my name. I would get fed up with eating haws and try to exchange them for blackberries with mice further along the ditch. So I was called "Pedlar".'

'That's rather a good story,' said Nonsensical. 'You see, you *do* know a famous mouse. You're one yourself. I don't know anyone who's been on an expedition into the Unknown, like you. You just gathered your tail and went. An adventurer. That's something to be proud of.'

'I suppose it is,' said Pedlar, impressed with himself for a moment. 'I don't know anyone else who's done it either.'

When they reached the attics, Pedlar was suddenly aware

of the strength of the darkness there. He could smell the urine markings put down by the Invisibles, but that was the only evidence of mice – that and the soft, musty smell of dried and drying droppings. There were no mouse sounds, no mice visible.

The only time he had been anywhere near the attics before was when he'd been taken there by Phart, and to his eternal shame, he had been more interested in the cheese than in his surroundings. The atmosphere of the attics was quite eerie and close. It was whispering country.

'That's the water tank over there,' murmured Nonsensical. 'Kellog the rat lives in a nest on the other side. He's sworn to kill my mate, Goingdownfast.'

Pedlar shivered. A rat was a formidable enemy.

Nonsensical seemed to glide like a shadow through the pathways of the attic over which they were crossing. Even though she was quite close to Pedlar, he had difficulty in making out her form. In darkness like this his senses were normally strong enough to distinguish objects around him, but Nonsensical seemed to drift like smoke, shifting her shape, re-forming somewhere else. There were no footfalls. Her paws were as soft as cherry-plum blossoms.

Pedlar tagged on behind her, following the paths she took as best he could. There was no way he could emulate her movements, so he didn't try, but she made him feel awkward and clumsy, like a nudnik blundering around.

Finally, they came to a nest, and Nonsensical called a name softly.

Then she entered, bidding Pedlar to follow.

Inside the nest was a male, who bristled instantly on seeing Pedlar.

'What's this?' said the buck of the nest. 'What's going on here?'

Nonsensical replied, 'This is Pedlar. He just escaped from the Headhunter. He's also beaten Tunneller to a standstill, so you can stop posing in that aggressive manner, Goingdownfast.'

'Oh, taking over my nest, is he? Well we'll see about that, even – even if he did beat Tunneller.'

'. . . *and* escape from the Headhunter,' added Nonsensical, 'but he doesn't want to fight you. He's not coming in here with me. He just wants to live in the attics. I want to ask Whispersoft if he will allow it, because I think Pedlar will be a valuable member to have up here.'

'He's not even a wood mouse,' cried the aggrieved Goingdownfast.

Pedlar could see why the other mouse was so upset. It was not usual for does, or their mates for that matter, to bring home other mice. Such a thing would have been unheard of in the Hedgerow and certainly, going by this mouse's manner, was not the done thing in the attics either.

'Look,' said Pedlar, 'I don't want to upset anyone. Perhaps I'll just—'

'You'll just *nothing*,' said Nonsensical severely. 'You'll be our guest, that's what you'll be. If Goingdownfast wants to be silly about this, he can be so by himself. There's far too much suspicion and distrust around here. It's time we were more open with one another, which we'll have to be if the tribes are to unite against the nudniks.'

Goingdownfast opened his eyes at this remark.

'It's going to happen then?'

His mate replied with the air of one delivering solemn news, 'The Great Nudnik Drive has been agreed upon in principle. I've got to talk to our tribe tonight, to get their reaction to what's been said.'

Pedlar said, 'She spoke very well at the Allthing, your mate. I'd be proud of her.'

'I am proud of her,' Goingdownfast said, whipping round so fast his tail lashed Pedlar's legs. 'I don't need *you* to tell me when to be proud of her.'

'I'm sure you don't,' said Pedlar in a conciliatory tone. 'I'm sorry I mentioned it. It was just that I was there and you were not, so I thought you'd like to know.'

'Well, now you've told me, haven't you?'

'And,' said Nonsensical sweetly, 'you don't have to kill Timorous now, do you, since I got back safely from the Allthing?'

'No I don't,' growled Goingdownfast.

He went off into a corner to sulk for a while, as if he actually would have liked an excuse to murder this member of his tribe and was annoyed to be thus thwarted. Pedlar realized there were tribal politics going on, about which he had no understanding, so he didn't enquire why Goingdownfast wanted to kill Timorous.

Nonsensical then left the nest, to report to Whispersoft on what was said at the Allthing.

While Nonsensical was away, Goingdownfast said nothing to Pedlar, and Pedlar did not feel inclined to open any conversation. Fortunately, she returned shortly with another mouse in tow: a nervous character who said to Pedlar, 'Look, er, Nonsensical said you wanted to share a nest with someone, so, er, would you – I mean, you can sleep in my nest if you, er, want.'

Nonsensical made the introductions, 'Pedlar, this is Ferocious. He's not got a mate and his nest is quite large, so he's willing to share it with you while you're here. *Some* of the

Invisibles can be quite understanding – quite hospitable,' she added, glaring in the direction of Goingdownfast, whose attention seemed to be taken up wholly with the inspection of his own toes.

'That's very kind of you, Ferocious.'

'Good, good,' muttered Ferocious. 'Well then – well then, come with me, I'll show you where to go.'

'Thanks for your help,' Pedlar said to Nonsensical.

'Think nothing of it,' she said.

Pedlar then followed Ferocious out into the attic again. Once more the yellow-neck was astounded at the natural camouflage adopted by a wood mouse. Ferocious was just as nebulous in the half-light of the attics as Nonsensical had been. It took all of Pedlar's concentration to keep up with the other mouse. Then, when they were crossing a rafter, something happened.

The light changed dramatically, as the attic suddenly became darker. A source of illumination had been blocked by the entrance of a foreign body. Ferocious stopped dead where he was, and seemed to melt into the roofwork of beams and sheets of tarpaper. Pedlar instinctively did the same, finding a deep shadow in which to drown himself for a few moments. A second later the attic returned to its former gloom, lit only by thin rays coming through pinholes in the tarpaper.

Pedlar was aware of a swift shape gliding through the atmosphere of the attic, cutting through the slim rays of sunshine. It was as if a slice of the darkness itself had been shaved away and silently skimmed by an unseen hand.

Then there was a brief flutter of soft-feathered wings and all was motionless again in the dust-moted air of the room in the roof.

When Pedlar felt able to speak, he whispered, 'What was that?'

'Merciful the owl,' said Ferocious. 'She's – she's still there, on her perch. Don't – don't move yet.'

Pedlar had no intention of moving until he saw some motion from his guide. The thought that there was a silent, deadly killer not far away was enough to make his blood run cold. It was one of those times when a mouse had to be patient and wait for his best opportunity before stirring.

After a very long while Pedlar became aware that Ferocious was moving ever-so-slowly, shadow by shadow, along the wooden beam. Pedlar followed the wood mouse, stepping into his vacated shadows while they were still warm. In this way they managed to reach a nest tucked in the bustle of an old dress on a dressmaker's dummy. Pedlar had never been so glad to see a safe haven.

'She can't get us in here,' said Ferocious. 'She flies over the junk jungle, and never creeps around inside it.

'Thank goodness,' breathed Pedlar, his legs shaking.

'We can get some rest now.'

But Pedlar needed no telling. He had immediately curled up, exhausted by all his adventures. Now that he was in a nest, not even his own, he felt safe from harm. It was the nice, tight feeling of being wrapped by the familiar scents of a fellow mouse; the security of the darkness; the lovely touch of the nest itself, which engendered this feeling. Outside the world was full of owls, rats and nudniks, but in here was shelter. Relaxed and assured he fell fast asleep.

In the woodshed, there was another council meeting going on, between the three mice at the head of the 13-K gang. They had been arguing for at least an hour. It was two against one. The three quarrelling mice were Ulf, Drenchie and Gunhild.

Gunhild had recently had enough of the Savage Tribe, and had run away to join the 13-K on the promise that she would be put in charge of discipline and drill, the two things she loved most in life. On learning of her defection Gorm had voiced an order to the effect that if 'that treacherous grunt was found', the finders were to tear off her legs and drag the limbless body into his presence, so that he could finish the job himself. Gorm hated traitors, almost as much as he hated his son.

Gunhild did not intend to go back, and was now in the same position as Ulf and his band.

Ulf was explaining his decision not to join the other mice tribes in uniting against the nudniks.

'It's not that I have any love for nudniks,' he said to his audience, draped as usual around the logs and kindling, 'but this Revolution is against everything we stand for.'

'What do we stand for?' asked his mate Drenchie, her low-nose stance suggesting she would rather bite his ears off than converse with him. 'If we're not in favour of revolution, just exactly what *do* we stand for?'

'We're *rebels*,' Ulf stated passionately. 'That's why the original thirteen of us, the founder knights of the gang, left the other tribes in the first place – because we don't agree with all those old greywhiskers. We left because we stand for New Ideas, New Thoughts, New Ways. If we join with them again, what will we be protesting against? How can we be revolutionaries if we join with the very society we hold in contempt?'

Drenchie snarled, 'But, you dumb-cluck, a Nudnik Drive *is* a New Idea. If we're for New Ideas, we ought to be able to recognize what they are and support them.'

Gunhild said, 'You're missing the point, Drenchie. It has to be *our* New Idea, not Gorm's. Gorm is the Old Guard, the epitome of outmoded tactics and strategies. It doesn't matter what he comes up with, *we* have to set our teeth against it.'

Gunhild saw everything in military terms. She had left the Savage Tribe because it was 'a mob, a horde' and not a well-organized army. Unfortunately, though the 13-K were not such barbarian fighters, they still lacked order themselves. They were full of the laziness, ineptness and thoughtlessness of youth. If she had her way, the 13-K would be arranged in regiments and battalions. They would sit to attention, unless *she* ordered them to sit at ease. She was a strict disciplinarian, and she detested the sloppiness of Drenchie, who was completely the opposite in nature. Drenchie was a loose, languid sort of creature, not even given to organizing herself personally, let alone the tribe.

Drenchie however had one thing going for her. She was bright. She knew how to string two ideas together and could be a parallel thinker when the situation called for it.

'There is a way we can be part of it all,' said Drenchie. 'We can suggest a New Idea to work within Gorm's plan. What I mean is, we can denounce his plan as an Old Idea, but when they begin searching for specific ways of driving out the nudniks, we can suggest a way and call it a New Idea. Instead of just being rebels, we'll be the counter-rebels.'

Ulf looked at his mate with admiration. 'That's excellent, Drenchie! I like that.'

Any plan that required no immediate attention or action was approved of by Ulf. Drenchie's scheme sounded just the right kind of thing for the 13-K to consider. It involved waiting until all the hard graft was over, until Gorm's plan reached a stumbling block, then stepping in with a quick, bright idea, saving the situation and grabbing all the glory.

'That's pretty damn good, Drenchie, you know you get flashes of genius sometimes . . .'

'Well,' said Gunhild stiffly. 'If you've no further use for me, my general?'

Ulf looked at Gunhild as if he had just realized she was still there.

'What? Oh, no. Thanks Gunhild. Oh, there is one thing by the way, I thought the Chosen Ones did pretty well in that last scrap we had with the Savages, didn't they? All down to you and your training, of course. Don't know what we'd do without someone like you − someone who takes their duties seriously. I've been thinking, you don't feel we ought to reorganize a few mice within the Chosen Ones? It's getting rather large and unwieldy as a personal bodyguard. What if we were to cut some of them out? The very best of them? I was thinking you might use, say six of them, as your personal guard. Give them a name − something like *The Companions*. I would still be protected by the Chosen Ones as a whole unit, but the six Companions would be responsible entirely to you. What do you think?'

Just when she was about to throw it all in, in disgust, Ulf said something like this and made Gunhild's eyes water with gratitude. She felt sniffly, which was more like Drenchie than her. This wonderful leader knew her heart and he was showing her that she was not a forgotten item, that she was useful and necessary to the 13-K Gang. *Gang*. How she hated that word. Perhaps she would suggest they change it when the mood was right, to something like *force* or *legion*? Not now though, while Drenchie was here, looking like a rag draped over the edge of a bucket. Some other time.

'Thank you, my general,' said Gunhild quietly. 'I shall carry out your orders.'

Once Gunhild had gone, Drenchie repeated in a high, whining voice, 'Thank you, my general. Would you set up nest with me, my general? I'd be a much better mate than Drenchie, sir. I'll march to your tune, sir.'

Ulf said, 'Don't be unfair, Drenchie. You know she's an odd sort, and it doesn't do any harm to please her.'

'I know what she wants, even if she doesn't herself!' snorted Drenchie. 'She wants to take you away from me. She wants to drag you off to her nest – no, not *drag* – *march* you off in fine military fashion, shouting "Charge!" when she reaches the entrance.'

'Now, now Drenchie, that's really not fair,' protested Ulf.

But the leader of the 13-K was thinking about what Drenchie had said. Did Gunhild really want him to set up nest with her? He hadn't thought about it before. Perhaps, one hour? But Drenchie would kill him, of course. She would take it as a personal insult. Any other doe in the gang, but not Gunhild. Now that he thought about it, Gunhild was the one female who really excited him. She was so – so *military*. Going with her would be something quite different.

No, Drenchie would never forgive him.

'Life's a bitch, and then you die,' Ulf sighed, rolling on to his back and staring at the uneven planks of the woodshed's ceiling-cum-roof.

'What's that about dogs?' asked Drenchie, who sounded

as if she were drifting into a lazy daze. 'You said something about dogs?'

'Nothing, nothing at all.'

FETA

PEDLAR WOKE IN A DARK CORNER OF THE NEST TO THE unpleasant sound of a loud belch. There was a putrid smell in the air, as if something had just wandered in from the cesspit. He could hear voices too, and found them vaguely familiar.

'Strewth,' said one of the voices, full of joyous relief. 'I thought we was goners, didn't you Phart? You should have seen us, Ferocious, climbin' up the inside of that rotten pipe! It was the worst journey of me life. Black as sin in there, it was—'

Pedlar's eyes opened slowly as he came to realize who was in the nest with him.

Phart was saying, '. . . too right. It was a tunnel to ruddy heaven, but you had to go through hell to get there – if you know what I mean, Ferocious. You've got no idea what's up them pipes. Muck, bugs, the lot. Then we got to the gutter,

215

ran along it, and just at that second this thing came out of the hole—'

Flegm's excited voice took over again. '*Thing* is right – *thing* it was. It was Merciful. I tell you I wet meself, Ferocious. I wet meself and I ain't ashamed to say it.'

At this point Flegm broke down and started sobbing.

'Anyways,' Phart continued the story, with a scowl at his weaker companion, 'we crouched at the end of the gutter, and she didn't see us. We had to wait there until she took off into the sky. Once we was sure she wasn't comin' back, we nipped through her hole!'

Pedlar stared hard in the direction of the creature who had caused him so much grief, knowing he had not yet been scented, probably because Phart's nostrils were still full of the odours from the drainpipe.

'So, we got here,' sobbed Flegm in relief. 'And I'm so hungry I could eat a dead spider.'

Phart looked about him. 'You haven't got nothing to eat, I suppose? No nice bit o' cheese for two brave adventurers what have just come back from the Unknown, 'ave you Ferocious? I haven't had a nice bit o' cheese since . . .' he stopped.

'Since when?' asked Ferocious.

Phart suddenly sniggered. 'Since I conned a bit from some stupid twit locked in a cage. Some mice,' he shook his head, laughing. 'Some mice ain't got the sense they was born with.'

'No, but they have got the *teeth*!' cried Pedlar, springing from his bed in the darkness. He nipped Phart sharply behind the ear – not a deep bite, but in a very tender spot.

Flegm had stopped sobbing, and probably thinking he was in for the next attack, rolled on his back and started kicking his legs in the air.

'Get away from me,' he shrieked. 'Get away!'

'I'm not coming anywhere near you,' Pedlar said in contempt.

Ferocious had watched all this activity in great alarm, and now it had settled, he said to Pedlar, 'That wasn't a nice thing to do. You're my guest, but so are Phart and Flegm. I won't – I won't have my guests attacked in this manner.'

'Phart deserved that – and a lot more,' said Pedlar, simply. 'I'm not easily roused, but he almost had me killed a little while ago, and even after that he took advantage of me while my life was in danger, simply to get some cheese. I'm afraid if *he* stays here, I must leave. I can't be responsible for my actions towards him.'

'Is – is this true Phart?' demanded Ferocious in an unsteady voice.

There was blood trickling from behind Phart's ear as he rubbed his head on the wall of the nest.

'Don't worry, I'm goin',' he sneered. 'I wouldn't stay in a nest with that maniac, even if you was to offer me some grub . . .'

'I was going to,' said Ferocious.

Phart stopped rubbing his head and looked solemn.

'What if I was to say "Sorry", Pedlar?'

Pedlar gritted his teeth. 'Get out of here, Phart, before I do something really awful to you. Get going quickly! Don't say another word, or it might be your last.'

Phart stared at Pedlar for a few more moments, before slipping out of the nest. When he was a few lengths away, he shouted something back, but it was too muffled for the mice in the nest to hear.

'I'll bet that wasn't complimentary,' muttered Pedlar.

There was a sniffling sound from the corner and Pedlar turned to see that Flegm was still there.

Flegm choked, 'I didn't do nothin'. I never even knew he'd done that about the cheese.'

'Done what – *did* what?' asked Pedlar, suspiciously.

'It wasn't my fault,' Flegm said. 'I never had nothin' to do with it. I just went for the magic mushrooms, then I had to climb up the drainpipe in that bleedin' awful dark and muck, and then I was attacked by Merciful—'

'You were no such thing,' Ferocious interrupted. 'If you'd been attacked, you wouldn't be here.'

'*Nearly* attacked,' corrected Flegm. 'It was whisker close, I can tell you. Maybe even closer. I—'

'Flegm?' came a voice out the depths of the attics. 'You comin' or what?'

Flegm went to the exit hole of the nest. 'Get lost, you rotten slug!' he shouted. Then he came back inside and said to the other two, 'You got to let me stay now – he'll beat the shades out of me if I go out there.'

So Flegm was allowed to remain with Ferocious and Pedlar, though the latter was not really happy at co-habiting with either of the cellar mice.

Pedlar was intrigued by Ferocious. The wood mouse had been worried by the commotion in his nest, but he had been firm and resolute about his rights as the owner. Pedlar was beginning to wonder whether Ferocious was as cowardly as he actually gave the impression he was. Moreover, it was unusual for a mouse to share his stored food. Most mice, Pedlar included, ate what they could find, without a thought for others – unless they were family of course – and hoarded food in secret places, with no intention of sharing.

Pedlar was beginning to suspect there was more to Ferocious than other mice believed.

While Flegm gobbled away at Ferocious's provisions, the

host asked Pedlar, 'What do you think about this business of driving out the nudniks? Do you think it's a good idea?'

Pedlar couldn't help being excited by the idea of mouse-rule but he tried to weigh up his response carefully. 'Well,' he said, 'there's all that food in the kitchen larder which would be ours. Some mice have reservations, I understand. There's a priestess or something, called Astrid, who fore-tells famine – and one or two others who are uneasy – but most mice think it's a good idea.'

'Yes, it does sound like the answer, doesn't it? I'm – I'm afraid I'm one of the uneasy ones though. Drastic change bothers me. You never know what's going to come after, do you?'

'Lots of ruddy grub, that's what,' Flegm interrupted, speaking with his mouth full and spraying the other two. 'I'm goin' to eat cheese till I'm sick.'

'What happens when the larder's empty?' asked Pedlar. 'Has anyone thought of that?'

'It never is,' replied Ferocious. 'It sort of keeps going, filling itself up as it goes on. I don't know how it works.'

'A bit like growing veg and stuff,' said Flegm. 'You know, cabbages, carrots and stuff comes every year, some-times twice, out in the gardin. That's what happens in the great larder – it grows itself all the time.'

Pedlar, used to the countryside producing food, except in certain seasons, said, 'What about the winter? I've only been here in the summer, but does the munificent larder stop growing food in the winter?'

'No, it still keeps growin' itself,' replied Flegm. 'That's cos it's warm in the House, what with the boiler and radiators and all. That's what stops the growin' Outside – the cold weather, the ice and whatnot. In the House it's warm as anythink.'

Ferocious said, 'I'm inclined to agree with Flegm. Conditions in the House are not like Outside during the winter. It is always warm in here. This would account for the lavish larder being full all the year round.'

'Well,' said Pedlar, 'it looks as if Gorm's plan is unstoppable now, so we'll find out in the end.'

When Flegm had finished stuffing himself, Ferocious sent him on his way. Then Ferocious and Pedlar went to an attic meeting to hear Nonsensical speak. She informed her tribe of what had taken place at the Allthing and opinions were sought.

While the tribe was deep into discussion, Pedlar took the opportunity of looking around and studying its members. There was Whispersoft, who was the leader: a very down-to-earth character, a bit like a male Nonsensical. Pedlar recognized Whispersoft as the mouse who had saved him from the mousetrap. Then there was Timorous, who seemed to be the main dissenter, and though he did not speak as loudly as Whispersoft, he certainly spoke at more length and with great passion. Goingdownfast was also much in evidence, usually arguing hotly with some other mouse.

There were also two does who seemed to be in each other's company: Ferocious had introduced them to him as Fallingoffthings and Treadlightly. Treadlightly was one of the few yellow-necks amongst the Invisibles. The two females were standing fairly close to Pedlar and Treadlightly kept looking across at the new yellow-neck, then turning away when he looked back. They were both acutely aware they were under observation by each other.

Skrang and I-kucheng were also present. The two Deathshead seemed to be quite deeply involved in the affair.

Having already borne the brunt of Goingdownfast's annoyance, Pedlar was not surprised to see this mouse constantly locked in loud conflict with another mouse, whose name appeared to be Timorous. The two Invisibles seemed to hate each other with venom and constantly attacked each other's suggestions, often rowing furiously over trivial matters. In fact several times the leader, Whispersoft, had to step between them to calm the scene. Other mice were obviously tired of the feud between the two males, especially Nonsensical, who kept trying to distract her mate to stop him from making a fool of himself.

It was an embarrassing situation, which Pedlar realized had been going on for some time. At one point, Timorous muttered, 'One of these hours I'll see you dead!' This caused a few shocked gasps amongst the listeners and earned the speaker a rebuke from his leader.

While the meeting was going on, Pedlar couldn't help wondering how mice like these would ever achieve revolution when they couldn't stop bickering among themselves for five minutes. He took the opportunity of washing himself down, licking his fur where he could reach, and generally cleaning himself up, which included nipping out a flea or two. This was in no way considered a breach of etiquette: a lot of the mice were doing the same. One could listen, take part, and still use the time usefully. And once the meeting was over, even with revolution in the air, there would still be nest-building and food-gathering to do. Where there was a family there would be young to suckle and much fetching and carrying. The hours were short and mice are busy creatures, always active in the pursuit of comfort.

'Shall I do the places you can't reach?' said a voice near

221

him, and Pedlar turned to see that it was Treadlightly who had spoken.

Fallingoffthings gasped, and said, 'Treadlightly! He's a stranger! How could you?'

Treadlightly took no notice of her friend, nor waited for any answer, but proceeded to lick and nip away at the fur which Pedlar could not reach with his own tongue and teeth.

She was quite efficient, there being no sense that she was acting too familiar, and when she had finished, she said, 'There, that's much better isn't it? What happened to your tail?'

Pedlar swished his tail and glanced behind him. 'Oh, that? Got caught in a mousetrap.'

'Such a beautiful tail too! Us yellow-necks have the best tails, next to harvest mice of course. You can't beat a harvest mouse's tail, can you?'

'No, you can't. The way they use them to hang on to things is quite remarkable,' agreed Pedlar.

They were being awfully polite to one another. Treadlightly kept getting nudges from Fallingoffthings, especially when Pedlar asked if he could return the favour, and clean her fur for her. Treadlightly declined with thanks, saying that her friend had already been of assistance earlier in the hour.

The meeting broke up after agreement was reached that the Invisibles would indeed go along with Gorm's plan. There was to be peace amongst the tribes for the first time in many nights. When the Traveller's Joy finally became Old Man's Beard and the boiler was lit behind the kitchen, then the Great Nudnik Drive would begin. Until that time they were to live their lives and not bother each other, each tribe preparing in its own way for the great freedom that lay ahead.

'It'll be strange not hearing "Assundoon" ringing about the House,' said Ferocious.

'What exactly is that?' asked Pedlar. 'What does it mean?'

'It's — it's the Otherworld of the Savage Tribe, the place they go to when they die. They use it as a battle cry. However, the rules about getting there are quite strict. You have to die with your teeth meeting through the flesh of an enemy.'

'Not many make it then?'

'You'd be surprised,' muttered Ferocious. 'They're — they're a barbaric lot. I'm amazed they've agreed to this peace, or truce, or whatever it is. Gorm and his tribe seem to like nothing better than sinking their teeth into other mice.'

The crowd broke up, Treadlightly going off with her friend, but giving Pedlar a last glance over her shoulder. Pedlar watched her go, while continuing his conversation with his host.

'What's the Deathshead's interest in all this? I thought they ate nothing but stale crumbs,' said Pedlar.

Ferocious said, 'That's true, but they go along with the general currents and tides of House affairs. They don't seek to control, only to be involved in the natural flow of life, so that they can guide us in our endeavours. I-kucheng would never say, "You must do this" or "You must do that", like Stone would, for example. But he would suggest that one path to the same goal might be better than another.

'The Deathshead are our spiritual navigators, our mentors, our advisors. They steer us gently down the rivers of morality: they direct us when we lose our way.'

Pedlar said dubiously, 'Sounds very much like control

to me, but then I'm not really one of you.'

'No,' agreed Ferocious kindly, 'you're an Outsider. It's hard for Outsiders to understand.'

'By the way,' said Pedlar casually. 'That doe, Treadlightly – does she – does she have a mate?'

Ferocious frowned. 'Our clumsy-footed Treadlightly? No, I don't think she does. She's a yellow-neck, of course. Didn't want to be a Deathshead, so she lives with us. Whispersoft is the one with the most mates, and it's he who takes his pick, being the leader of the tribe, but I don't think . . . why? What's the problem?'

'No problem, no problem. Just curious, that's all. I noticed her with that Fallingoffthings, and just wondered, that's all. The pair of them seemed to be quite close.'

'Oh, they are. Good friends. Do you – do you, er, want me to speak to Treadlightly about – er – anything?'

Pedlar snatched at his own tail and subjected it to close scrutiny, as if concerned about its condition.

'No, no. Just wondered, that was all. Just wondered. Just *curious*, nothing more. Just curious.'

'Well, that's all right then,' said Ferocious.

'Yes, just wondering. Just curious.'

'That's fine.'

After that Pedlar watched a mouse crawl down a glassless brass telescope, while another used a rafter to leap into a rusty coal-scuttle. There were nests in every hanging valley, on every hill. The attic was indeed a magic place, full of arcane landforms and contours, lanced by dusty spears of sunlight – a gloaming world – a high penumbral country with its one still lake.

TALEGGIO

Some hours after the meeting to discuss the Great Nudnik Drive, Kellog made his attack on his enemy. He had been waiting, biding his time, planning his plans, ever since he had sworn to kill Goingdownfast. A patient rat, but not willing to wait until doomsnight to obtain his revenge, Kellog had watched the activity amongst the Invisibles with curiosity tempered with caution. The roof rat had long since ceased to allow inquisitiveness to dominate his actions. Such behaviour could cause self-injury and death, and Kellog wanted to live for ever.

Kellog's body was nothing now but a lump of gristle and muscle held together by bones. Kellog's mind was nothing now but a corroded mentality held together by instinctive self-preservation. Kellog's soul was nothing now but a dry spirit held together by hot thoughts of reprisals.

Kellog was steeped in the bitter juices of his own hatred of arrogant mice.

'I will have him,' said the roof rat quietly to himself, several times a night. 'I will eat his brains.'

After the meeting had reached its historic decision and terminated, mice went out looking for food, and it was then that Kellog made his move. He picked his target and followed behind, cautiously, tracking more by instinct than by sight, smell or sound. The Invisibles were not easy to stalk, even if one had been marked out. Kellog had to watch for changing patterns of light, and catch the smell of stirred dust, to sense the direction of his prey.

The keeper of the lake came from a line of brilliant trackers, his ancestors having had to survive long sea voyages in overcrowded conditions. In those nights, aboard ship, his great-greats killed mice for food, rather than for revenge. Their skills had been passed down to him, through racial memory. The stalking rat was in his veins, and he used his intuitive talents to the full.

Moreover, he too could use light and shadow, mask his scent and tread with the softness of a spider running over a cobweb. He too was invisible and soundless.

Just when the unsuspecting mouse was entering a hole in the loft floor, Kellog leapt, and sank his teeth into the throat of his victim. Even though the neck was broken instantly, Kellog shook the corpse savagely, his blood-lust high and his mind a red haze of sweet revenge. The mouse's head lolled and the teeth rattled in the jaws, as Kellog allowed his delighted fury full rein.

Then he flung the body high in the air, to let it drop with a small thud on to the boards. Kellog stared triumphantly at his dead enemy, at the lifeless corpse of what used to be the arrogant and insolent Goingdownfast, now brought low in the dust.

Except that it was not, after all, Goingdownfast.

The mouse Kellog had killed indeed looked very much like Goingdownfast – in fact it was his brother, Miserable. Not only did they look like one another, their movements were also the same, their method of walking identical. Kellog had killed the wrong wood mouse.

The bitter disappointment rose like bile to the roof rat's throat as he turned the corpse over several times, hoping he was mistaken. But it was indeed, the body of Miserable. Kellog was so disgusted with the mouse, he bit it savagely on the breast, despite the fact that it was already dead. Then he slunk away, back to his nest, to plan fresh plans.

SAMSOE

The Invisibles survived in an attic which was home to an owl because they had unerring judgement, not of time, but of light and shadow. Merciful was a creature of habit, who rested during the days, and hunted during the nights. She came and went according to the light of the evenings, the greys of the mornings. A cloud-covered sky would have her leaving the attics earlier than normal, or arriving before her usual time. She flew according to the density of the gloaming.

The Invisibles could judge the flight-times of Merciful by the thickness of the shadows, the texture of the light. They were tuned and locked to the mind of Merciful. If they too had had wings, were predatory birds, they would have stirred their feathers at precisely the same time as Merciful.

They did indeed stir when she stirred, returned to their nests when she returned to the attics. They knew the cryptic ways of the owl as well as they knew their own hearts. They lived and survived under her cold stare.

The death of Miserable had come just before the return of Merciful. Consequently his body was not found until several hours later. The mouse who discovered the remains of Goingdownfast's brother did not need to be a detective to decide who had perpetrated the deed. There were thick, coarse, dark hairs on the corpse — rat hairs. And the punctures in Miserable's throat were too large to be those of a mouse.

Goingdownfast, on learning of his brother's death, knew that a mistake had occurred. His heart was heavy, since he knew it should be himself lying in the dust.

No one removed the body of course, for mice do not inter

their dead like some creatures. Once the spirit has gone, the corpse is left to dry to a husk, or be eaten by predators. The mouse itself lives on, in others, and is thus revered. 'Miserable used to say that,' it would be remarked upon, or, 'That's the way Miserable used to twitch his ears.'

'So, Kellog,' Goingdownfast said to himself. 'So. We'll see. Great Nudnik Drive or no Great Nudnik Drive, first there has to be a reckoning. There has to be a reckoning for all such deeds.'

And a reckoning there would be.

BÛCHE DE CHÈVRE

A DARK SHAPE SLIPPED ACROSS A BEAM IN THE ATTIC, making its way towards the water tank. Kellog caught a slight change in the consistency of the light, and knew something was out there, something was approaching his precious water. He stared out through the hole in his nest, watching and waiting. The Invisibles knew he was always home at this hour and it did not make sense that they should disturb him at his rest. They valued their lives.

Unless! Kellog peered, searching the darkness. Unless it was a mouse come to do him harm? Come to avenge the death of a brother? Kellog recalled his small error, still not amended, in killing Miserable when he had meant to kill Goingdownfast. Would that mouse dare attack him in his own nest?

The mouse who was approaching the water tank was

now in view. Kellog could see its shape, smell its scent, hear the scratching of its claws on wood. It was not Going-downfast. It was in fact Goingdownfast's enemy, Timorous. Kellog prepared to launch himself into the water at a moment's notice.

Kellog called softly, 'If you dare to drink while I am in residence, you do so at your peril, mouse.'

Timorous had paused on the edge of the water tank, on the far side of the reservoir. 'I didn't come to drink, I came to talk,' he replied, looking behind him nervously.

'Why do you look over your shoulder? Is someone with you?'

'No,' said Timorous. 'I want to make sure I wasn't followed.'

This promised to be an interesting meeting. Kellog did not normally live a very interesting life. He ate, he slept, he prowled the House, but rarely anything happened which was out of the ordinary, except that his nest got wrecked by cowardly mice while he was doing these ordinary things. A mouse who wished to speak to him in private, who was afraid of being overheard, now that was interesting.

'Swim over the tank,' Kellog said. 'I want you on this side.'

Timorous hesitated, seemingly afraid.

'Come on,' said the big roof rat. 'I won't hurt you.'

'Do you promise?' asked Timorous.

Kellog said, 'I promise,' then under his breath he added, 'for what it's worth.'

After another short period of indecision Timorous finally entered the water and swam across, his back and the top of his head shining with wetness. He climbed out the other side and approached Kellog.

The mouse stared at the rat, aware of the immensity of the beast: the great humped back, covered in coarse dark hair; the thick snaking tail; the great head embedded with piercing eyes, and the mouth with its large teeth. The mouse shuddered from head to foot, recalling the atrocities perpetrated by this giant.

'Hello Kellog,' Timorous said.

'What else do you have to say before I kill you,' snarled Kellog. 'Quickly now.'

'You – you promised!' said Timorous in dismay.

'Promised?' the rat's eyes glittered. 'Do you think I need to honour such a promise? I'm a roof rat, you're a wood mouse. Do roof rats take any note of wood mice?'

'Not as such,' breathed Timorous, 'but if they bring you something worthwhile, then they might.'

'What is it that you've brought?' asked Kellog. 'I can take it anyway, whatever it is.'

'Not this you can't,' replied Timorous quickly, 'because it's in my head.'

'I'll crack your skull open and suck it out!'

'It's a *plan*. By *in my head*, I mean in my thoughts. You can't learn a plan unless I tell it to you. Listen to this – "My enemy's enemy is my friend" – do you understand that? It's an old saying. *I'm* your enemy's enemy, therefore I must be your friend . . .'

That phrase Timorous had used sounded a bit too much like poetry for Kellog's liking but to his credit he didn't flinch. Poetry was a killer in the wrong mouth but this visiting mouse didn't look like he could trim his own coat, never mind rhyme a rat to death. So Kellog decided on the confrontational approach that came naturally to him.

'What is this? A lecture?

Timorous shifted his feet, going high-nose. 'No, no.

231

Not a lecture. A *gift*. The gift of a perfect plan for catching Goingdownfast.'

A plan for catching Goingdownfast? Now that was something quite different. Kellog became even more interested. His great head moved in the darkness of his nest.

'You mean you're turning traitor?' he said softly. 'Betraying your own kind?'

'Not turning traitor,' Timorous cried, vehemently. 'You can only betray your friends. This – this *creature* that I give you has humiliated me too many times, has stolen the mate I wished to have for myself, has usurped my position in the tribe. Goingdownfast is no friend of mine.'

'So I hear, so I hear. Go on.'

Timorous's voice became a little calmer. 'You hate Goingdownfast for your own reasons, as he hates you, but you can't catch him. I can give him to you. I can arrange to have him in a certain place, at a certain time, so that you can ambush and kill him. Let's get rid of him before it's too late. Then we can all enjoy our new freedom without troublemakers like him!'

The great rat thought about this as he studied the wood mouse before him. The situation was unusual enough to warrant caution. No mouse had ever come to him before, willing to betray a member of its own tribe. But then again, no mouse had ever hated another as much as this one seemed to hate Goingdownfast. It was the sort of hatred that could not be faked. The conflict between them was evidently deep.

'I will make sure you get him,' repeated Timorous, unable to keep the venom out of his tone.

'Good, good, so be it then, but if you fail me, you know I will eat your heart.'

Timorous said, 'I shall not fail, I will prevail.'

'What?' cried Kellog, recoiling.

'I said I won't let you down, I'll succeed.'

'Never mind – go,' the rat said quickly.

Timorous left and Kellog shuddered. The mouse had rhymed, but it had surely been an accidental coupling of sounds, not a planned intimation? A mouse's ear was not tuned finely enough for rhyme. It was made for picking up discordant sounds, to warn it of strangers, not harmonies. Kellog relaxed. Just an unhappy coincidence, a slip of the tongue, nothing more.

STRACCHINO

Phart had been summoned to the presence of the mighty Gorm and he was feeling very nervous.

The Stinkhorns, named after a fungus, had once been a much larger tribe than they were now, but the females had all upped and deserted the drunken males one hour, having had enough of revelries, wassails and lazy boisterous bucks who were never good for much but eating potatoes and drinking wine and beer.

So the tribe had gradually diminished in size, with the Stinkhorn females becoming integrated instead into the kitchen ranks of the Savage Tribe, until only Phart and Flegm were left. Phart assumed leadership and Flegm was quite happy for him to do so.

Now, as leader of the tribe, Phart had been summoned. He went to the appointed place with trepidation in his heart, going over in his mind all the things he had done in the past few hours, trying to figure out if Gorm might have taken offence at any of them. Try as he would, he couldn't find anything out of the ordinary. If he had done something wrong, it was not evident to him, especially in his state.

'You're *drunk*,' growled Gorm in disgust, when Phart met him behind the kitchen range.

Phart didn't argue with this observation. 'Sorry, yer honour,' he mumbled.

Gorm shook his great gnarled head and sighed, clearly giving up on this pathetic creature before him.

'Phart, I've called you here in your capacity as leader of the Stinkhorn Tribe, because we need you. Unfortunately, we need *all able living souls*, and it's been suggested to me that you're included in that group . . .'

Gorm really was in top form, but Phart was wise enough not to guffaw at the dry humour.

'. . . we're planning on driving the nudniks out of the House. You'll have a part to play in that, though I'm not sure what it is at the moment.'

The import of Gorm's statement sunk in.

'Drive out the nudniks, yer honour? Wass – what's that for? I mean, why?'

'That's not your concern,' said Gorm importantly. 'All you need to know is that you're required to help with it. You got any problem with that?'

'Not me, yer honour. I live to serve.'

'Good. Well, that's all then. Back to your cellar. Oh, by the way,' Gorm made his words sound like a casual afterthought, 'you know this yellow-neck, Pedlar?'

'Yes,' replied Phart warily.

'Hmmmm. What – er – what do you think of him?'

Phart shrugged, wondering what answer was required. Did Gorm *like* Pedlar, or dislike him? It was necessary to be noncommittal until the truth was known.

'He's an Outsider, ain't he? I mean, you know what Outsiders are like.'

'Impudent oafs,' nodded Gorm. 'Thieves and wasters. Into all sorts of thuggery – luring away innocent females, stealing food, insinuating themselves in the good graces of fellow mice.'

'Yeah, that's it,' replied Phart, getting his cue. 'Bloody uppity swines, if you ask me. This Pedlar's no different. One of the worst, I'd say.'

'That's what I thought,' nodded Gorm, seemingly satisfied. 'Well, that's it. Don't stand there gawking. I'll call you again when the plans have been finalized. And Phart?'

'Yes, yer honour.'

'Glad you're with us. Just wanted to round up the stragglers. We need every mouse we can get. Some of us may not survive this dangerous stroke, but the nation will go on to greater glory by our selfless actions.'

A trickle of pale fear went through Phart's frame. 'Dangerousss?' he murmured.

Gorm-the-old revealed his teeth in a nasty sneer. 'Your bit will be, if I have anything to do with it.'

Phart's heart shrank to the size of poppy seed. 'Yes, well, if I'm not fit enough meself, there's the rest of the Stinkhorn Tribe to help out. I'm sure they'll be ready to do their duty.'

'You'll be fit, don't worry,' confirmed Gorm, with a hard nod.

Phart left Gorm and went back to the cellar, his mind in a numbed condition. Yet it was not too numb to register that Gorm had used their tête-à-tête to mention only one mouse by name. That bleedin' Outsider what called himself Pedlar and liked to deprive other mice of their rightful cheese. By the end of his drunken musing, Phart had convinced himself that what had just taken place was a coded instruction from Gorm to the effect that this Outsider mouse had to be seen off the premises. And he, Phart, had been chosen for the deed. Or had he?

The Stinkhorn leader staggered off to find Flegm, his cohort, needing to consult him about what lay ahead for their illustrious tribe.

CHAUMES

Stone was lecturing some harvest mice out in the wilds of the garden, where the grasses grew unkempt and high, and the prehensile tails of the mice were of great use to them. Stone liked harvest mice, because they seldom entered houses. It was true that they did go in occasionally, some of them to live, but they were not like house mice, who preferred to be indoors, and they certainly didn't take up residence as often as yellow-necks and wood mice. Harvest mice liked to eat insects of an evening and they couldn't get enough of those inside the House.

Elegant at a distance, close to the harvest mice were sort of skeletal, big-footed and small-bodied. There were black guard hairs amongst their orange russet dorsal colours, the belly fur being white. They were good listeners. When you're the smallest rodent around, you tend to listen while a bigger mouse speaks. Stone thought of them as Nature's little favourites, decorating the grasses with their slight forms.

'The paths of mice and nudniks crossed thousands and thousands of nights ago, back in the mists of time, before the coming of trees,' he said to the dangling creatures

236

before him. 'Nudniks started harvesting the grasses, like corn, and mice sort of latched on to them. Now the whole world is full of corn and vegetables and we don't need nudniks any longer. It's time we turned our backs on them.'

One of the harvest mice swung back and forth from a campion stalk by her tail.

'*We* don't need them anyway,' she said smugly. 'We don't share food with the nudniks – not like the house mice.'

'Ah, but you do. I've seen you going to the dustbins. You're not averse to plundering them, are you?'

The harvest mouse inspected her toes, rather than compromise herself by answering this question.

'Anyway,' said another harvest mouse, 'I've heard that Gorm-the-old is raising a revolt against the nudniks. They're going to be driven out of the House.'

'Who said that?' asked Stone, looking around. He had no idea until now that the spirit of the times had caught up with his own feelings about the nudniks.

'I did,' said a mouse dangling from a cow-parsley stalk.

'No, no – I mean, where does the remark originate from? From whom did you obtain your information?'

'You sound like one of the Bookeaters I've heard about,' sniffed the harvest mouse. 'Anyway, it's common knowledge. Everybody knows *there's going to be a Great Nudnik Drive when Old Man's Beard is on the Hedgerow . . .*'

Having uttered those historic words, the very first time they had been spoken aloud by an Outsider, the harvest mouse felt quite faint and almost fell from his stalk. It was as if the words had been placed in his mouth by the gods, to be uttered for the benefit of history. Later, there would be mice who would try to recall that harvest mouse's name, but unfortunately for the oral storytellers, that name was never passed down the annals of mouse history. He or she remained anonymous thereafter, and mouse history was the less rich for it.

Stone's eyes were shining. 'That's what they're saying? Well, well, I knew that one hour the time would come for mice to assert themselves! So, at last we come to it – the nudniks will be vanquished, the House will return to its natural state, and mice will find their true destiny.'

'Eh?' said another harvest mouse. 'What natural state? What true destiny.'

Stone shook his head, having said enough. 'Never you mind, young whippersnapper,' he muttered. He felt he needed time to think about this wonderful news. 'All right, you're dismissed you lot.'

'Dismissed?' cried a mouse. 'Who do you think you are?'

But Stone wasn't listening. He was wandering back to the privy area where he could sit in the sun and think. Stone knew, if the mice in the House didn't, that all the nudniks in residence (except one) ranged between ancient and *very* ancient. He knew this because they all had white or grey hair on top of their heads – or in the case of one, no hair at all – and they walked stiffly and awkwardly. One could hardly walk at all. The furniture in the House, the mats and rugs, the beds, and the nudniks themselves – all smelled of life at the wrong end of the ageing process. The pets, the dog and the cats, were not groomed as often as they should be, and Witless was never given a bath. All these were signs of overripe nudnik bodies.

Finally, there was the biggest sign of all: the mere fact that the House was overrun with mice, had a rat and an owl in the attic, proved that the nudniks did not notice or were past caring about their surroundings.

There was the Headhunter of course, the half-grown nudnik. The reason he was out of control was because all the other nudniks were past the age where they were *able* to control one of their own young. The Headhunter had arrived last winter and was, as far as Stone was concerned, a temporary resident.

Since the Headhunter's parents were not with him, Stone deduced that something must have gone wrong with them. Perhaps they had been killed by nudnik predators? Stone didn't know whether any such predators existed, but he guessed there was something nudniks were afraid of, or why would they lock themselves inside the giant snail shells and only come out very occasionally?

And Gorm and his motley crew had decided to drive these old nudniks out of their shell? Stone had never heard of that happening before, and he had talked with all sorts of rodents, all kinds of rats, voles, shrews and even a wandering giant coypu once. Still, there was always a first time, and the fact that the nudniks were ancient creatures was in favour of the mice.

But there was the delicious thought, in Stone's mind ever since the harvest mouse's words had fallen on his ears, that the whole plan might backfire on the house mice. Stone didn't want any great harm to come to Gorm and company, but there was the chance that the forthcoming Revolution might see the mice themselves driven from the House, and back out into Nature where they belonged.

To Stone, that was a wonderful idea, and one that gave him his own reason to look forward to the Great Nudnik Drive.

GOUDA

In the attics it seemed strange to no one but Pedlar that Treadlightly was always in the same vicinity as himself. He did think it was a little *unusual*, but since he enjoyed her company, he didn't remark on it to her. They were both busy gnawing at individual crusts one hour, when the most extraordinary thing happened. An unknown house mouse was passing by when it suddenly leapt at Pedlar. If the Hedgerow yellow-neck hadn't been quick, the house mouse would have sunk its teeth into Pedlar's throat.

Pedlar managed to kick out with his hind legs and drive off the attacker, but he was left very shaken.

Treadlightly rushed over to him. 'I saw that!' she said in a shocked voice. 'What was it all about?'

'An assassin?'

These ominous words were spoken by Goingdownfast who had been nearby, digesting his own crust. 'Someone wants you out of the way, yellow-neck. Who have you upset recently? Or to be more specific, who in the *Savage Tribe* have you annoyed? For I know who that was. It was Jarl Forkwhiskers, one of Gorm's number.'

'They must really want rid of you, to send an assassin at a time like this, when they should be concentrating on finalizing plans for the Great Nudnik Drive.' This was Treadlightly's view.

'It's a pity,' said Goingdownfast, 'that you didn't hold on to him. We could have tortured him and got him to talk.'

Pedlar shuddered. He knew why he'd been targetted by Gorm and his gang. It was because he was 'the One'. Nevertheless he did the only thing he could. He took it upon himself to visit Gorm-the-old. Pedlar believed in direct confrontation and he wanted things settled, one way or the other, between the Savage Tribe chieftain and himself. He did not want assassins sneaking up on him at any given moment, leaping out of the shadows, jaws clashing, teeth gnashing. He could do without all that looking-over-the-shoulder stuff. So, after taking the sensible precaution of asking Skrang to accompany him, Pedlar went to meet with Gorm.

BEL PAESE

S KRANG, BEING A DEATHSHEAD, OPENED THE WAY FOR this meeting. She was well respected, an excellent travelling companion and was used to dealing with leaping assassins. Anyone coming at Pedlar out of the dark was likely to be given a sharp Ik-to bite on a painful part of the anatomy.

For reasons best known to himself Gorm had decided that the meeting should take place in the chimney of the inglenook fire in the living-room. It was to be at midnight, when Eyeball would be sleeping upstairs on the end of one of the nudnik's beds, well out of the way. Spitz always went out for the night and terrorized the garden. Much as Gorm might have wanted the conversation to end in a bloodbath, he didn't want it to be *his* blood, dripping from the jaws of a cold-eyed killer.

The chimney was warm, if a little sooty. The fire had

242

been lit during the day, but by midnight consisted of warm grey ashes. It was not difficult to skirt the grate where the logs had been burning, to scramble up the sooty brickwork, to the ledges above.

Skrang and Pedlar had travelled beneath the safety of the hot-water pipes leading to the radiators. From here they crossed the living-room floor, through the forest of tall furniture legs, using the canopy of the table-top and chair seats as cover.

They reached the ledge where Gorm was waiting just as the Great Clock was chiming the midnight hour.

Gorm sneered. 'I thought we agreed we would meet alone? I see you've brought a bodyguard with you. Please note that I kept my word and came without any escort. But then I'm no coward.'

Pedlar ignored this remark, coming to the point immediately. 'What's the problem? Why are you sending your assassin after me?'

'Why don't you just get right down to it? – no need to greet me or anything,' growled Gorm sarcastically.

'I haven't got the time for niceties Gorm. You're the aggressor here. Kindly tell me why.'

Gorm's eyes narrowed and he shuffled around in the soot. 'Because I've found out your little game, Outsider, that's why. I know that you've been having secret liaisons with the high priestess Astrid, and I'll see you dead for it.'

What followed was one of those rare moments when innocence communicates itself. Pedlar looked so genuinely puzzled that Gorm began to realize he was wide of the mark even before he'd finished speaking. As a result his accusation became more and more defensive. 'Well, she said she was going with a yellow-neck, one who could take care of himself in a fight . . . From what she told me, it sounded like a stranger. At least, she said I would never guess who it was, so I knew it must be a mouse she thought I didn't know.'

'Or who didn't normally share nests with other mice,' said Skrang, interrupting.

'What?' said Gorm. 'What do you know about this, Skrang?'

'Not a great deal. I have my suspicions, but I'm not going to pass them on to you. One thing I do know, and that is that Pedlar has had nothing to do with Astrid. I mentioned his name to her the other night and there was absolutely no reaction from her whatsoever. Instead she kept asking me whether it was too late for her to become a Deathshead.'

'Ha!' shouted Gorm. 'She was trying to put you off the scent!'

'I don't think so — in fact I'll go so far as to say I'm positive she was not. Being a spiritual warrior, I am adept at discovering whether someone is telling the truth or not, simply by studying their eyes. For instance, I know that you did not come here alone tonight, even though you say you did.'

'What?' cried Gorm. 'You call Gorm-the-old a *liar*?'

'Will you continue to deny it, or do I have to expose you in front of Pedlar here?'

Gorm shuffled around in the soot for a moment longer, his tail whipping this way and that, his brow lowered as if ready to charge. He must have had second thoughts, probably because he remembered he was dealing with a Deathshead, a warrior trained in the deadly martial arts. Skrang could deliver an Ik-to bite before Gorm was three paces into his famous charge. For a house mouse he was big and very fierce, but he relied on his bulk and ferociousness,

244

not his speed. Pedlar saw the chieftain gradually relax and the tension go out of his frame.

'Well,' said Gorm at last. 'I'm not going to stay around here to be insulted. But if you say the yellow-neck is innocent, Skrang, I'll have to accept that, even though you're a yellow-neck yourself. You Deathsheads are supposed to be impartial and completely unbiased. This yellow-neck here can leave us – *me*, that is – now.'

'And you'll call off your assassin?' said Skrang.

'I'll call off Jarl Forkwhiskers,' agreed Gorm with a growl.

Skrang turned to Pedlar and looked at him quizzically.

The Outsider had established his innocence by his silence and now it was time for him to speak: 'I'm satisfied, though it would be nice to get an apology for being attacked. I could have been killed.'

Gorm muttered, 'No-one gets apologies out of me. It was a mistake and that's that. If you want an apology, you'll have to take it out on this . . .' and Gorm thrust his grizzly face forward aggressively.

'Forget it,' said Pedlar. 'With the Great Nudnik Drive almost upon us, we all have more important things to think about now. No more petty personal battles! Speaking of which, haven't you settled your differences with your son yet?'

'The 13-K,' Gorm answered, 'have not settled their differences with *me*.'

'Well, someone ought to persuade them to join the Revolution.'

'How about *you*?' crowed Gorm, sensing a chance to trap this upstart Outsider at last, or reveal him as a coward.

Pedlar stared at the chieftain with unblinking eyes.

'All right,' he said carefully. 'I'll do it. I'll come to the kitchen soon and you can let me into the lean-to woodshed.'

'Right!' snapped Gorm, trying to grasp it as a victory, but finding his sense of conquest slipping away from him.

'Come,' said Skrang to Pedlar. 'It's time we left.'

Pedlar and Skrang left Gorm, who was muttering, 'If it wasn't the Outsider, *who* was it? Astrid is making me look a fool. She'll be sorry for this.'

'That was very brave of you,' said Skrang to Pedlar, when they were out of earshot. 'Are you sure you want to meet with Ulf and his motley crew? I've tried persuading them, you know, I got absolutely nowhere.'

'Someone's got to drag them into this thing. It's got to be unanimous,' replied Pedlar grimly. 'I'm determined they shall be with us when Old Man's Beard is on the Hedgerow.'

When the pair were a short way from the inglenook fire, but hidden from view behind the table leg, Skrang stopped and motioned for Pedlar to be quiet. A nudnik had dropped a cotton reel on the floor by a chair and Skrang motioned for Pedlar to creep up and hide behind it. 'Go up there, and watch,' she whispered. She nodded towards the fireplace. Pedlar did as he was told, lying flat on his body behind the cotton reel.

Peering around the side, Pedlar could see Gorm-the-old was standing there, staring out into the room. The chieftain of the Savage Tribe suddenly turned and called, 'You can all come out now. They've gone.'

From the walls of the chimney appeared several lumps of soot shaped like mice. They were coughing and spluttering, spitting out ash. Pedlar could see the whites of their eyes, and the pinks of their mouths as they blew down their noses and cleared their throats.

'Hakon, Tostig, Ketil and Skuli,' muttered Skrang, 'but I can't quite make out the fifth one, can you?'

The two hidden yellow-necks were soon rewarded as to the identity of the fifth mouse when this lump of soot spoke to Gorm in a high whining voice.

'Can I go home now, yer honour, please? I got soot in every orifice – up me nose, in me ears, in me mouth—' he shifted his hind legs uncomfortably and flicked his tail '—and in other places too . . .'

'Yes, yes,' growled Gorm, irritably. 'Get out of my sight, you slug.'

'I only come to visit,' cried Phart. 'An' I get dragged into taking a barf in soot. I mean, I'm not even a Savage, I'm a Stinkhorn.'

'You served the nation, you should be proud,' Skuli told him.

'I couldn't give a gnat's bum for the nation,' shouted Phart, already halfway across the living-room, trailing black pawprints across a white rug. Within a moment he was through the Miglan Hole and presumably on his way down to the cellar.

Pedlar watched all this activity, half tempted to shout out and reveal his presence, but he decided that it would be better not to antagonize the leader of the Savages any more than necessary. Gorm was incorrigible and was never going to change, so there was no point in provoking him. Instead, he sneaked back to where Skrang was waiting for him.

On the way back to the attics, Skrang collected I-kucheng from the Rajang Hole. Pedlar was not allowed to go with her and remained outside the nudnik bedroom, so that the hole would stay a secret of the Deathshead. When he finally saw the old mouse, being led by Skrang, Pedlar was shocked. I-kucheng had suddenly become very old and appeared to be almost blind. He hung on to the end of Skrang's tail, following her slowly and stiffly.

'Hello, I-kucheng,' said Pedlar. 'How are you?'

The old mouse turned his head towards the sound. 'Oh, quite well, quite well. Who is that?'

'It's Pedlar, the Outsider,' said Skrang.

'Oh, Pedlar. I see, yes, yes of course.' There was a short pause, then, 'Do I know a Pedlar? Never mind, I'm not too old to learn new faces, I hope. *Pedlar*. Strange name.'

Pedlar thought it was sad that the great brain of the old mouse was reduced to such a state and he mentioned this quietly to Skrang.

Skrang said, 'He's going deaf and blind, but his brain still has bursts of great energy. Don't worry about him. He'll last a lot longer than any of us, you wait and see.'

Pedlar did not pursue the matter further. He could tell that Skrang would not allow herself to believe that I-kucheng was going to die soon. She had invested her whole life in the old spiritual warrior and Pedlar was afraid that once I-kucheng had gone, Skrang would go into a decline herself.

There was one mouse, however, who wished he could do just that. Iban was just about as wretched as any mouse could be. He knew that Gorm was determined to find out who was stealing his high priestess, Astrid, and had threatened to kill the culprit. Now Iban was not personally afraid of Gorm: being a spiritual warrior he was not afraid of anyone. However, being in the wrong, he knew he might not defend himself if attacked by a self-righteous Gorm-the-old. He knew he would just stand and take the bites, without retaliating, because he was the sinner and deserved punishment.

Finally, Iban decided the only honourable way out was suicide. He had to kill himself. Since he was a Deathshead, it needed to be certain death. He didn't want to end up like Thorkils Threelegs for the rest of his life. So his decision was to seek death by the claws and teeth of Eyeball. Nothing was more certain than the weapons of the world's most efficient killer. If anyone could end his miserable life at a single stroke, it was the terrible queen of cats, Eyeball.

Iban entered the living-room through the open doorway. In a chair by the fire was a folded nudnik, peering at a magazine. Another nudnik was standing almost in the inglenook, poking the coals with an iron rod. A third was arranging flowers in a vase high up on the sideboard: she was humming to herself. There was soft music playing, coming from a wireless standing on the small table. It was a jigging type of tune, except that Iban did not feel like jigging, unless it was the kind one did when one's neck was caught under a snap-wire trap.

A fourth nudnik entered the room and slammed the door behind it. The massive oblong of timber crashed into its square hole causing an enormous wind to riffle Iban's fur. Iban shook his head. It always amazed him when nudniks displayed their tremendous strength with shows like shutting the door. It would have taken a hundred mice to move that massive piece of lumber just a few inches.

The new nudnik opened its mouth and boomed something, causing other nudniks to boom in response. They seemed to need to do this. It appeared to give them comfort.

Iban inspected the room further.

On the carpet by the first nudnik's feet was Witless, fast asleep and snoring. On the windowsill, lying on the bottom edge of the pretty lace curtain, was the terrible shape of Eyeball.

She too had her eyes closed and appeared to be sleeping, but Iban knew that cats never really slept. There could be a thousand discordant sounds in the air, all ignored, but the one sound in a thousand – the chink of a cat dish, the scratch of a mouse, the rustle of a flea-powder packet, the creak of a cat basket being carried into the room – any of these would have those eyes flying open, like shutters on strong springs, and the cat ready to run or pounce. Cats were instant creatures, their thoughts electric. They could seem, and probably were, totally relaxed one second, yet could become flashing, slashing, lithe and lissome creatures the next.

Iban ran boldly towards the windowsill and sat, high-nose, beneath it, studying his enemy.

Eyeball was not a large cat, but still she was awesome. Beneath that soft fur was a heart of thorns. There was not a seed of compassion in her breast. Iban watched the fur rising and falling gently and wondered that the great god Yo had ever thought to put such a cold nerveless mind in such fluffy wrappings.

Pulling all his courage together, Iban drew a claw across the lino, causing the faintest of scratching sounds.

The cat's eyes flew open.

She stared for the minutest part of a second, almost unable to believe what she saw: a mouse sitting high-nose, looking up at her as if waiting to be chastised for doing something naughty. Then she sprang, claws bristling, with but a single word escaping her lips.

'*Mourir!*'

For Iban, time slowed down to become almost motionless. The great shape of daggered fur seemed to part with the windowsill reluctantly. Iban waited for death to descend. He had made his peace with his god, and he was ready to depart this life.

Unfortunately for both creatures, for the one who wanted to die and the one who wanted to kill, chance intervened. As the cat's hind legs left the windowsill, they left with claws exposed: an array of terrifying weapons ready to plunge into Iban's breast. Several of these curved spikes snagged on the hem of the lace curtain.

When the cat was some way down, with the curtain stretched to its full limit, there was a ripping sound. Virtually the whole lace curtain tore away from the window and descended with the Burmese blue, trailing behind Eyeball like a ghost coming to the rescue of the sacrificial offering. This ghost seemed to wrap itself around the cat on landing, causing the creature to rip and tear at the netting with great ferocity and blinding speed. The more the feline creature struggled, spat and screamed, the tighter it became caught in the wispy folds of the curtain.

'*Un piège!*' shrieked the hapless animal. '*Un piège!*'

Iban, confused and frightened, attempted to decipher the cat's babblings about the trap she now found herself in.

Then from the other side of the room came pandemonium. The nudniks, bless their delayed-action brains, had suddenly realized something was happening. There were shouts and yells, screams and curses. Witless, seeing one of his two mortal enemies trapped and helpless, bounded across the room. For an old hound he moved remarkably swiftly. His slobbery old jaws opened wide and he bit the cat firmly on the rump, a look of sheer joy in his eyes. There were more cries from the nudniks. Eyeball screamed what must have been dire threats at

Witless, who made the most of the opportunity and bit her again.

One of the nudniks had grabbed a broom and started to beat Witless around the head with it. Iban felt the wind of the weapon as it swept past him to strike Witless. Witless wisely moved after the first stroke and the second and third strokes caught Eyeball across the back. The cat was incensed at this and gave out an ear-splitting yell.

'Assassiner!'

The second nudnik bent down and tried to release the cat from its entanglements, only to be bitten and scratched for its trouble. The nudnik retreated with a little cry, blood trickling from its hand. Witless, no doubt thinking that Eyeball had now turned her allies into enemies, crept forward for another bite, only to be whacked around the head again.

More nudniks entered the room from other parts of the House, among them the Headhunter. A distressing cacophony filled the air. The wounded nudnik was led away by bovine comforters: two fat nudniks from the kitchen. The Headhunter seemed very interested in the way the cat was bound and kept pushing to the front to study her. Iban could see in the Headhunter's eyes a definite desire to boil the cat and feed it to Little Prince.

Witless was still looking on in glee, making occasional forays to the front through the assorted legs, but was wise enough not to attack again.

It was plain that the chaos would continue for some time to come.

Iban crept away, mortified at the disorder he had caused, and slipped through the door unhindered.

He went straight from the living-room to the Gwenllian Hole and from there he made his way to a passage which would lead down to Tunneller's domain. He intended to go out into the garden and offer himself to a passing kestrel, or perhaps await the exit of Merciful from her hole in the eaves.

On the way, he passed the dark shape of Kellog, hurrying to pick up his daily tribute from the Savage Tribe.

'Kill me!' cried Iban, standing in the rat's way.

'Damn mice,' grumbled Kellog, barging Iban aside with his broad shoulder. 'I'm in no mood for jokes.'

Then the ship rat was gone, having melted into the black, dusty spaces beneath the floorboards. Iban picked himself up, covered in dust and cobwebs, and sighed. He continued his journey down to the maze.

Once in the maze he followed the route to the centre of the labyrinth, having been many times before. Suddenly he found his way barred by Tunneller.

'Where do you think you're going?' asked the gatekeeper.

'I - um - Outside,' said Iban.

'Not without paying *me* you don't,' said the terrible shrew.

Iban faltered. He had forgotten about the toll. Having no cheese on him he could not pass Tunneller. She had never been known to break her rule. *No cheese, no way*, she was fond of telling the mice.

Iban drew himself up. 'You'll have to kill me then.'

Tunneller narrowed her eyes. 'How about I just beat you black and blue and send you back inside with your tail between your legs?'

'That's no good,' sighed Iban. 'What about if I was to promise you a piece of cheese later?'

'What about if I was to bite your ear for you?'

'I'm good at Ik-to,' warned Iban.

253

'I'm willing to let you try,' snarled Tunneller, who never took kindly to threats.

Iban sighed again. He could smell the outside world from where he stood. Primroses and cherry-plum leaves. The fresh air with all its dangers was just a few snaky tunnels away, providing he didn't get lost down some of the blind alleys. Tunneller was like some rock blocking his right to suicide. It was always so difficult to get out of the House, if you weren't a kitchen mouse and very rich.

Eventually, he saw it was no use and turned around and went back up into the House, unhappily admitting defeat.

While he was emerging from the Gwenllian Hole, a nudnik came out of the living-room and strode down the hallway. Iban watched as the nudnik went to the front door of the House, opened it with one quick movement, stepped outside and shut the door behind it. It was done so easily, so effortlessly, it made Iban gasp with frustration. A journey to the outside world was made so hard for a mouse! It all seemed so unfair.

TOMME AU RAISIN

PEDLAR WAS OF COURSE ALLOWED FREE PASSAGE through the territory of the Savage Tribe, to the hole leading to the lean-to woodshed. Some of the kitchen mice stayed around, to watch him go through, certain he would not be making the return trip. Pedlar noticed how plump and well-fed they looked and thought to himself, *We'll all look like that soon.*

When he reached the hole there was a general forward surge from the crowd, which now gathered around his point of departure. There was an air of anticipation about the kitchen mice. Ulf had promised to attack in person any mouse not of the 13-K Gang who entered the woodshed uninvited. They would not be able to see such a show, but they might be able to hear it if they were close enough. *Ghoulish lot*, thought Pedlar, *waiting to hear my screams.*

255

Pedlar stopped at the entrance to the hole and called to the sentry on the other side.

'Hello in there! Pedlar the Hedgerow yellow-neck, here. I'm coming in.'

There was a commotion on the other side of the hole, then a voice cried out, 'How many of you?'

'Just one,' Pedlar replied.

'One will come in, but many will leave,' sniggered the same voice.

For a second Pedlar was reminded of the destiny forecast for him by the ancestral voices of his dreams. 'What does that mean?' he asked of the nearest kitchen mouse, who happened to be Elfwin.

'It means you'll come out in pieces,' Elfwin told him.

'Not a good start,' muttered Pedlar to himself. 'Well I'm coming in anyway,' he shouted.

He decided on a quick dash through the hole and found himself ringed by youthful mice on the other side. They were all crouched low-nose, ready to attack him. A quick glance around the woodshed told Pedlar there were others, lounging on the wood piles, in amongst the logs, watching the spectacle.

He did the only thing he could do – he introduced himself as, 'Pedlar the Outsider come to speak with Ulf the leader of the great 13-K Gang. Otherwise known, out in the far-off Hedgerow, as Ulf-the-cool.'

'Ulf-the-cool?' Ulf identified himself in a surprised but pleased tone. 'They've heard of me in the distant Hedgerow?

'That's what they call you. Your fame spreads even further than that. It goes way out into the wheatlands, amongst the fieldmice. "Ulf-the-cool", they say, "best guerrilla fighter this side of the main road".'

'Ulf-the-cool,' said Ulf. 'I like that. Better than Ulf-the-son-of-Gorm,' he added darkly. 'Maybe I've got out from under the shadow of my father at last?'

'I should say so,' said Pedlar, 'though unfortunately you've inherited his pathetic lack of brains along with his bigotry.'

'Eh?' cried Ulf, looking up.

'Well, what's the one thing on everyone's mind right now? The Great Nudnik Drive! Everyone knows it will benefit the whole of the mouse nation within the House, yet here you are, stubborn as hell, refusing to join anything which involves your father.'

'That's right,' growled Ulf.

'Let me ask you one thing,' said Pedlar. 'Do you want access to the great larder?'

'Of course we do!' chorused a background circle of mice, answering for their leader.

'Then why are you fighting Gorm? Why are you against the Great Nudnik Drive? The whole point of it is that we get rid of the nudniks and their pets, so that the contents of the celestial larder can be shared out amongst *all* mice in the House.'

Ulf shook his head slowly. 'Do you really believe Gorm is going to share the food with us? Do you think he would ever give us a single crumb of cheese – oh beloved cheese of inestimable worth! – do you? Once we get rid of the nudniks, he'll start up his old battles again. It's in his blood. He's a warmonger, and he'll never change. I *know* him. He's my father. If he doesn't die with his teeth sunk into an enemy's flesh, he'll never get to Assundoon, and believe me he's determined to go there.'

Pedlar nodded. 'From what I've seen of Gorm-the-old

I think there's something in what you say. However, this is the first time all the tribes have come together, as a house-mouse nation, and the nights when Gorm could count on divided interests are gone. Gorm's Savages could only survive while the tribes were all at war with one another. If you join us now he'll have the whole House of tribes to contend with – he won't be *able* to keep the larder to himself.'

Ulf turned to his captains, Drenchie and Gunhild, and said, 'Well?'

Drenchie answered, 'He's talking sense.'

Gunhild snapped, 'My troops are ready at any time – now or in the future. Yes, I think the yellow-neck has got a head on his shoulders.'

The leader of the 13-K Gang did not look entirely convinced.

'Look,' Pedlar tried, 'you've said that the reason you won't join the Great Nudnik Drive is because you don't trust Gorm. Well, I personally guarantee that Gorm will cause no trouble once the nudniks have gone. If he does, I'll fight him myself.'

'You'll fight Gorm?' Ulf said. 'You realize you'll have to fight his doubles too – Hakon and Tostig, his brothers?'

'I do realize that,' said Pedlar, his heart sinking a little, 'but I give you my word. I will battle Gorm to the death if necessary. Is that good enough?'

Ulf nudged him with his nose in a gesture of friendship.

'Good enough for me, friend. We'll join your Great Nudnik Drive as from tonight.'

The rest of the 13-K suddenly came to life and dropped from the wood pile, crowding around Pedlar

258

and Ulf, cheering. They had lived on the edge of starvation for so long, this was like a dream opening up before them. Whiskers were preened, tails were flicked, noses began twitching in expectation of the wonderful gorging which lay ahead.

When the clamour had subsided a little, Pedlar said to Ulf, 'Well, you'd better come and see Gorm . . .'

Suddenly Ulf's eyes narrowed in suspicion. 'You want me to come and see Gorm – alone?'

Pedlar nodded. 'Well, that's the whole idea, isn't it? That you make peace with the kitchen mice. Then we can forge ahead all together.'

'It's a trap,' snapped Gunhild. 'Send me instead, Ulf. I'll choose three good mice and go in—'

'No,' said Pedlar. 'It's got to be Ulf. Just me and Ulf. If you trust me, then you should have no fear. If not, then I go back and tell them I've failed.'

Ulf stared into Pedlar's eyes for a long time and then he let out a determined-sounding sigh. 'I don't know why, but I do trust you, yellow-neck. I just hope it's not going to be the death of me. Come on, let's go.' He gave the crowd a twisted expression. 'I'm dying to see their faces anyway, when we step through that hole together, into the kitchen.'

The 13-K Gang cheered again, as Pedlar and Ulf walked to the hole.

The Savage Tribe were still clustered around their side of the hole. They all moved back a little when the handsome young 13-K buck stepped out of it. Pedlar followed.

The two of them stood there, under the glare of the crowd, when suddenly a voice roared from the rear.

259

'Out of the way, out of the way,' and there stood Gorm, his gnarled features wearing a triumphant expression. He stared at his rebellious son with hard glinting eyes. There was the anticipation of revenge in that face.

Pedlar said, 'We have an agreement from the 13-K Gang – peace amongst the whole nation – Ulf is here to ratify the terms of the treaty.'

These words were ignored as Gorm rushed past Pedlar and confronted his son.

'At last!' snarled Gorm, baring his teeth at his son. 'Grab him. Grab the dissident! At last I've got you, you little runt!'

Some of the Savage Tribe warriors began to move forward, but Pedlar spoke. When he did so it was with an authority that was rare in a Hedgerow mouse and which reflected the great strides he had taken since being singled out by the spirits of his ancestors. 'Stop!' he shouted, 'I've given my word. If you do this Gorm, you'll have all the tribes of the House on your head. They all heard you tell me to negotiate a peace with your son.'

'If we kill you too, no one will know about it, will they?' said Gorm.

'We will,' cried a voice, 'and you can be sure, *very* sure Gorm, that you won't get away with a thing.'

All heads turned to see I-kucheng and Skrang standing together with Iban. Three Deathshead. One Deathshead alone could take on a dozen Savages. It would have to be brave kitchen warriors who would take on three of them.

Gorm scowled at the Deathshead and then turned to face Ulf. 'Well, what have you got to say for yourself . . . *son*?'

The last word was delivered with heavy sarcasm.

'What have I got to say? You offered me a truce and here I am. Of course, I knew you wouldn't keep your word – you never do. But Pedlar here persuaded me that you had somehow changed, that you were now a leader with a sense of honour. I was stupid to think he might be right, but then I take after you for brains . . .'

'Oh, stop your yattering,' growled Gorm, 'you're worse than a natterjack, you always were. A truce it is then.'

'Good,' said I-kucheng. 'It's what we've always hoped for, that the Savage Tribe and the 13-K Gang should come together—'

At that moment there was the sound of heavy footfalls and then the kitchen was flooded with light. Mice scattered in all directions. Ulf and Pedlar shot through a gap between the sink unit and the wall. Others found places of safety within a split second.

A nudnik in night attire padded across the kitchen floor, its cavernous mouth yawning. It reached the larder door and opened it, going inside. It emerged a few moments later with a huge slice of cake and a bottle of milk. The milk was guzzled down in hasty gulps – enough to satisfy two dozen mice – and then the cake was crammed into the enormous mouth.

There followed some shuffling around near the sink. From his hiding place Pedlar could see a massive bare foot not a couple of lengths away from his nose. It was an offensive object of hard cracked skin underneath, soft wrinkled skin on top, and carrying a peculiar odour. The tops of the toes were covered in coarse, curling hair, which gave them the appearance of being individual live creatures, captured and enslaved by the great ugly

261

foot itself. The nails were chipped and dirty and there were callouses and a huge bunion decorating the edges.

Pedlar had a strong urge to rush out and bite this monster, to drive it away. It offended him so much. As other mice had told him and he had subsequently discovered for himself, when a nudnik was so close it was difficult to think of it as a single creature. Its parts were so gross one thought of it as an amalgam of several grotesque creatures, who had got together for purposes known only to themselves, and merely *functioned* as one animal. This was the closest he had ever been to an adult nudnik. The whole thing was revolting!

The foot moved away after a while and then came the slapping sound of bare soles on tiles.

Finally the light went out again.

Mice emerged from their hiding places.

'Did you see that?' growled Gorm. 'It just ate enough for an army. We've *got* to get rid of them.'

Pedlar shuddered. 'That smell!'

'And that's just its feet,' remarked Hakon, who was standing near to Pedlar. 'You should whiff its breath. Why I was standing on a shelf once, and—'

Hakon never finished the sentence. He gave out a sudden strangled scream and was gone, whisked upwards by a mighty force that Pedlar could now smell, though he still couldn't see it. The grotesque had been replaced by the horrible. When the nudnik had left the kitchen and returned it to darkness, it had not closed the door behind it, and a blue-grey beast had entered swiftly and snatched Hakon from the floor in one lightning grab.

Mice scattered again, their ears ringing with Hakon's desperate screams of 'Help me! Somebody help me! Ahhhhgggggghhh!'

But Hakon was gone. He was still alive, still unbroken, but it was best to try to forget him. To shut one's ears to the terrible screams, close one's mind from the torture, the sound of pain. Some of the mice were now even talking about mundanities, albeit in strained voices, for nothing could be done to save Hakon.

Hakon was in the jaws of Eyeball, whose eyes could now be seen glittering, as she lay on the kitchen tiles with the wriggling mouse securely in her mouth, clasped lightly with her teeth. At some time, perhaps not too soon, those teeth would close and crush Hakon to death. Perhaps in a few moments she would toss him around, flick his terrified form with her paws, pin him to the ground with a pawful of needles. But for now she was happy to stare triumphantly into the darkness.

I am a killer of mice, her eyes seemed to be saying, *I am invincible, invulnerable, almighty.*

And so she was. There was no force greater in the world of a mouse. The cat was death itself, as sure as a heart attack or the severing of a head. She was descended from heaven, ascended from hell, and untouchable.

I am a terrible god, all powerful, without pity or favour. Look on my countenance ye puny rodents, and despair.

But they did not despair. They simply tuned out the cat from their thoughts, considered other things, discussed the coming Revolution, current intrigues, tribal affairs, but not the lack of compassion in a cat.

Some while later, they heard the crunching of bones and gave a blessed collective sigh. Hakon's worldly cares were over. Gorm was short of one brother, one double. When the commiserations came to him, he replied typically, 'Well, I have little need of doubles these nights, there being no wars, so it's no great loss – but thank you for the sentiments anyway.'

Life emerged once again, moved around, filled the rooms, and Hakon was now but a tragic blemish in the history of the House. Hakon was either amongst the cheeses of heaven, or the rotten whiffs of hell, and there was an end.

PART TWO
The Great Nudnik Drive

MOZZARELLA

THE BOILER WAS LIT IN THE KITCHEN AND IN THE outside world Old Man's Beard covered the Hedgerow: the word went from mouse to mouse that the season had changed. The Outsiders sent the message to the Insiders, and the Insiders sent the message to the Outsiders. It was time. The Revolution was ready to boil over and spill throughout the great House. The whisper went from mouth to mouth, from nest to nest, from tribe to tribe. And all the tribes rose up as one nation, joining together under a single cause, that cause being true and just. Mice came out of their holes, out of the darkness, into the light.

The Great Nudnik Drive began.

This necessitated a great deal of to-ing and fro-ing, exposing mice to more risk than normal. The cats were instinctively aware of the increased activity and they responded in like fashion. Spitz was less alert than Eyeball, but they both became intensely vigilant.

According to the particular role that had been allocated them, each tribe went into motion.

The Bookeaters began chewing the electric cables that ran below the floorboards and between the ceiling and the upper storey.

The Savages bit through sacks of flour, spilled bags of beans, opened up barrels of grain.

The Deathshead gnawed on gas pipes.

The 13-K, rebels that they were, created havoc in the neutral cupboards and drawers, gnawing clothes.

The Invisibles attacked the water pipes in the attics, hoping to cause a great flood.

The Stinkhorns were forced into the living-room and parlour by Gorm and there they hid, trembling, under a china cabinet until it was time to go back down to the cellar again.

Even Kellog fell in with the spirit of the thing, by poisoning the water tank with dead slugs, worms, snails, weeds, vomit, rodent droppings and unidentifiable slimy things. He liked putrefaction and stench. It gave him great satisfaction to make things start to rot and smell. He enjoyed watching the water turn an ugly yellowish colour and begin to grow grey things on the bottom of the tank. He liked stagnancy. This fitted in with the philosophy of his kind and with the places in which they chose to live: sewers and cesspits.

With the progress of the Great Nudnik Drive, Kellog's arrogance began to increase. He saw his future as being one of great power. Once the Revolution was over and the nudniks were gone, he would be the undisputed master of the House. Kellog began to fall under the influence of his own ego, believing himself to be chosen of the gods, the king of rats.

One night he broke his own rule by squeezing through Claude's Hole and going into the House proper. The beleaguered nudniks were all asleep and the cats, he knew from reports by the mice, were both out in the garden. The mice were all busy of course, nibbling away at this pipe, or gnawing away at that cable. Kellog strode along the landing as if he already owned it and the nudniks had all fled to the far side of nowhere.

'Nice sugar mice,' crooned a voice from one of the bedrooms. 'Little Prince can smell your fleshy-flesh. Sweet honey mice . . .'

Kellog went and hunched in the middle of the doorway, glaring at the cage containing the white mouse.

'. . . lovely – ulp – er – *rat*?'

Kellog flexed his broad back and showed his teeth.

The white mouse stared at him with wide eyes for a few moments then it said, 'Time for sleepy-byes, Little Prince,' and lay down on its sawdust nest and closed its eyes tightly.

Kellog stared for a while, then strode off along the landing. He plopped his way down the stairs to the hall below, intending to use the Gwenllian Hole to get back into the safety of the walls and between-floors. It was all very well being reckless, but there was a limit. He had made his point to himself: he was no longer worried about nudniks.

Suddenly, from the living-room, appeared a rheumy-eyed ancient spaniel. It stood in the doorway for a moment, blinking, regarding Kellog with amazement on its hairy face. Its floppy silken ears came forward and its grey-gold curls fluffed.

Kellog's instinct was to run. Then he remembered that this was Old Witless, about whom the mice talked. He had heard them say that Witless was the slowest creature on earth, that he had never in all his hours caught a mouse, and that the teeth in his mouth were probably blunt and useless.

'Go stick your head in a bucket, dog,' snarled Kellog.

Those few words seemed to be the only sounds necessary to put a tremendous amount of explosive power and energy behind the hound. Witless came off the hallway rug as if he had been fired from a gun. His mouth was open and there was a look of absolute delight on his face. His eyes were suddenly clear and sparkling. His joints were no longer arthritic. His nostrils flared wide with sheer joy. He was two years old again.

Kellog streaked up the stairs with Witless right behind him, snapping at his tail. The rat's heart was rattling away at a tremendous rate. Kellog's legs were a blur of movement as he flashed over each stair, hardly touching the carpet. His eyes were bugging out of his head. Kellog knew he had made a terrible error of judgement. The dog had a hidden reservoir of power which the mere sight of a rat had unleashed. The hound was like a thing from hell! Its eyes blazed, its jaws snapped, its legs were full of vigour. There was no thought process behind its pursuit: it moved on pure instinct, the edge of which had been honed by many years of ratting as a youngster.

Glorious past hours were responsible for Witless's litheness and vitality: hours in the ditches, his master urging him on, *kill, kill, kill*. In those times he had killed rats by the dozen. He was a brilliant ratter, a supreme champion ratter, and the mere word uttered into his ear still made him go berserk with excitement. A nudnik only had to breath the

270

sound for Witless to dash around sniffing in every corner of the room, overturning furniture in his eagerness.

Kellog flashed along the hall, found himself in a corner, panicked and dashed forward through the dog's legs. Witless did a beautiful somersault in mid-air, worthy of a puppy a tenth of his age. He gave an ecstatic yelp and continued the chase, his claws skidding on lino as he ran.

Witless was not especially interested in mice, as mice went, though he would put up a half-hearted chase. But tell him there were rats in the vicinity, *show* him a rat, and all his cares and aches were cast aside, and the dynamo of old spun to life within him.

Witless had been trained by being thrown into an empty barrel with a rat and the lid being jammed on. It was a case of either emerging the victor from that barrel, or being bitten to death by the rat. He had won that first battle and had never looked back since.

Gasping for breath, Kellog retraced his run to the stairs, with Witless still snapping at his back legs. He took the flight of stairs in one, landing at the bottom with a thud. Witless hurled himself down too, but Kellog managed to recover before dog hit mat. His hair on end with fear, Kellog flew along the hallway and into the Gwenllian Hole. He hardly touched the sides though anyone watching would have said he was much too big for such a small knothole.

Once down below the floorboards Kellog wheezed for breath, lying on his stomach listening to the dog scratching and whining at the Gwenllian Hole. A mouse came by and stared with enquiring eyes at Kellog's heaving body as it passed.

The mouse hurried on, wondering what kind of creature it could have been to cause Kellog such distress. One of the cats surely? Or a fox? For clearly the rat had undergone a very harrowing experience.

Kellog made his way slowly back to his nest, vowing to himself that he would *never*, ever again, leave the sanctuary of the walls and between-floors, until the nudniks were well out of the House and that hound from hell with them. The House proper had nearly done for him this time.

The House actually seemed very receptive to the efforts of the tribes to drive out the nudniks. Some of the mice were saying it was as if the House itself were on their side, allowing itself to be operated on by their surgery. It poured forth water from its wounds, it sparkled electricity from its cuts, it hissed gas from its holes. There were parts of the House that had rotted on their own, over the years, without any help from the mice, and these were now crumbling and sagging, making the place unsafe for anything heavier of foot than a medium-sized rodent. Slates began to slip on the roof, wastepipes clogged with hair, cisterns were bunged up with gunge.

'Predestination!' shrieked Frych-the-freckled. 'It was meant to be!'

In the first few hours of full-scale Revolution two mice were killed – one of them by Eyeball, who played with the body until the Headhunter stole it from her for his own nefarious purposes. The second was skewered by the kitchen nudnik with the breadknife. The nudnik threw the body in the wastebin, where Spitz found it. Much to the disgust and horror of hidden onlookers, the tom cat swallowed the still-contorting mouse whole, and was promptly sick on the kitchen floor. Witless came and sniffed the lump in the puddle with obvious interest until chased away.

'Nobody said it wouldn't be dangerous,' growled Gorm,

at an emergency Allthing in the cupboard-under. 'Nobody said it wouldn't involve a great deal of courage.'

'But,' whispered Tostig, 'two mice *already*.'

'You gutless lump of lard!' Gorm shouted at him. 'What are you? I won't have anybody in *my* tribe whining about numbers. One, two, three – what's that to the Savages? But I'm not going to browbeat you. I'll leave it to your conscience. We'll vote on whether to continue with the Drive. All those in favour of going on with the Drive, leave the Allthing now . . .'

There was a short pause, during which a scuffle ensued, and then silence.

Gorm screeched, 'What, you still here, Tostig? Get out, before I bite your backside.'

'But you said—'

'What I said and what I mean are two different things,' snarled Gorm. 'We're the only two left – I suppose you noticed how swiftly everyone else went through the exit hole? They got jammed in the opening before the sentence was even out of my mouth. Why was that, Tostig? Was it just because they were eager to continue with the Drive?'

'N-no Gorm – because they're scared of you.'

'Remarkably astute for a mouse with a brain the size of a mote. And you're *not* scared of me, I take it?'

'I'm leaving n-now, Gorm,' came the whimper.

Gorm grunted, 'I knew I could rely on you, *brother*.'

Scenes like these were quite usual for the first few hours of the assault, but soon mice settled down to gnawing at electric wiring, letting the stuffing out of cushions, burrowing through mattresses, chomping away on clothes in the wardrobes and drawers, eating rugs and mats, nibbling through wood and plaster, upholstery and wickerwork, cardboard and cloth. All over the House, new holes began to appear and old holes were rediscovered. In the bathroom, the cork tiles were devastated. In the living-room the tablecloth was eaten into strips of rag. In the bedrooms, the curtains were gnawed from their hooks.

There were extraordinary feats of bravery and sacrifice. A female Deathshead went on a suicide mission, climbing up a waste-pipe to stick there and block it. Her body was her contribution to the cause: her reward presumably obtained in Deathshead heaven. Straighteyes, an Invisible, got trapped in the springs of a mattress and had to remain there a whole eight hours, while a nudnik slept and did unspeakable things (unspoken of, that is, by everyone except Phart and Flegm) above him. When he finally got free, he needed another eight hours to recover the full use of his lungs.

A warrior of the Savage Tribe attempted to lure Eyeball into the boiler fire, an incredible act of courage inspired by an order from Gorm-the-old, and which succeeded in getting Eyeball's fur singed.

On the second night of the Drive, Cadwallon of the library mice met his death. He was the fourth victim of the Great Nudnik Drive. Cadwallon had fine, strong teeth, honed to penetrating sharpness by many nights of eating books. He was the first of the mice to bite through an electric cable and actually sever it completely.

Onlookers spoke of vivid blue flashes and raining sparks, of Cadwallon's limbs stiffening to twigs, of his fur crackling and smoking and, finally, of a charred smell which reeked through the rafters for hours afterwards. A new mousehole was gnawed in his honour.

No-one knew who actually started the fire, but it began in one of the bedrooms, and destroyed both that room and one of the bathrooms, as well as part of the landing. Some

274

said it was Hywel-the-bad, chewing through an electrical flex, but Iago claimed to have been biting holes in a bed sheet at the time and it was his contention that he was nibbling so fast the friction was responsible for the ignition of the fire.

Whoever it was, the blaze was both terrifying and magnificent. The flames ate away like mad crackling monsters at everything in their path. It was all red heat and smoke and stink. Mice had to admit to each other that they were absolutely scared stiff.

The smell of the smoke triggered some deeply ingrained terror within them. There were racial memory-caches of fires throughout the history of the mouse, from the first great plains fires which destroyed vast areas of grasslands full of mice, to the later forest fires and the more recent infernos that had enveloped and laid waste to whole cities of houses – houses from a time when the giant snails fashioned their shells of wood.

These memory-caches were opened up and their contents poured forth into the minds of mice. What came out were horrors: of running madly in no particular direction, of eyes blinded by smoke, of nostrils and lungs burning with the hot air, of smouldering fur and flesh, of being devoured by pain.

But *this* fire, the House fire, was started by the mice themselves, getting their own back on the nudniks.

The nudniks were all of a twitter about it, of course. They turned on the taps to get buckets of water and after a while a kind of smelly, green sludge oozed out. Kellog's work. It stank the House out from top to bottom.

Yet more nudniks came, this time in shiny metal hats. They hosed the fire to a standstill, causing a great deal of damage. The bedroom was first blackened and charred, and then had water and foam sloshed into it. Since there were no mouse nests in the bedrooms the mice suffered relatively little harm. The stairs became flooded and water poured into the cupboard-under; the living-room directly below the fire was also drenched and plaster fell from its ceiling. Apart from a few between-floors passageways being flooded, none of this affected the mice a great deal either and they were quite satisfied.

Pedlar went about the sabotage as enthusiastically as others. He was in part responsible for the devastation to the aspidistra in the parlour, its leaves gnawed through and the roots urinated on and left for dead. There was a wonderful feeling of mice pride throughout the whole House. For the first time in living memory the tribes were at peace with each other, bonded together by a common cause. Brother nodded to brother and sister to sister. Cousins met and rubbed noses.

Even the Stinkhorns were treated with a modicum of respect, especially when they managed to gnaw through a seal on one of the wine barrels and flood the cellar.

'Front-line stuff, eh yer honour?' said Phart to Gorm. 'You'll be invitin' me to join the Savage Tribe soon, I expect?'

'Over my dead body,' growled Gorm, which Phart took to be an encouraging statement from someone who could not hope to live a great deal longer.

'Thanks chief,' he said, humbly. 'Knew I'd done good.'

All in all, everyone seemed to be performing his or her part, with the 13-K the most enthusiastic of all, happy that they were accepted dissidents and could join in the guerrilla warfare.

Pedlar went flying across the floor, landing painfully on his back. He lay there stunned for a moment, his heart banging in his chest, then he managed to regain his feet. There was dust everywhere. The attic was choked with clouds of it. Mice were emerging from their nests and holes, from the places where they had been quietly gnawing on household supports, their whiskers twitching in fright, their tails swishing.

'What's happening?' one cried.

'I don't know, I don't know,' cried another. 'Is anyone hurt? Where are my young ones?'

Pedlar's ears were still ringing, but once his head had cleared, he went looking for Treadlightly. The Invisible had become his nest-mate and they'd tailor-built their own quarters in a nice little cavity below the roof slates. He found her lying near the water tank. For a moment he thought she was dead, but then he saw her stir. He nudged her with his nose and she opened her eyes.

'Where am I?' she asked.

'You were stunned,' he said. 'Any bones broken?'

She rolled over on to her front and lay trembling. 'I don't think so,' she murmured.

'No-one seems to know what's happened. Maybe it's something to do with the Drive? I find it hard to imagine that Gorm would have such power at his command though. That was some bang! You stay here and rest for a while. I'm going to have a look.'

Pedlar left her then, running towards an attic exit hole. He went along various tunnels until he felt a strong draught. When he emerged through the Gwenllian Hole into the hallway, he saw a scene of devastation. The hallway was full of dirt and debris – chunks of splintered wood and other rubbish. A nudnik was standing, pale-faced, staring at the gap that used to be the cupboard under the stairs.

The triangular door was missing from the cupboard-under. No doubt what was left of it was lying around the hallway in small pieces. There was a strong smell of coal gas in the air and some nudnik had opened the front door to let it waft out into the garden. It seemed that the gas meter had exploded.

The house nudniks stared at the mouse nerve-centre and twittered to each other. A short time later more outsider nudniks arrived and made straight for the cupboard. They carried metal things in their hands. Pedlar listened to them making a noise inside the cupboard for a while, fixing the damaged pipe, and returned to the attic.

When he arrived back at the place where he had left Treadlightly, he found her fully recovered. He began explaining to her what he had seen downstairs and soon found he was surrounded by other interested mice. Kellog, too, was sitting on the other side of his water tank, staring across as Pedlar talked. Merciful had flown out of the attic the instant the explosion occurred and everyone kept a wary eye on her doorway to the outside world, in case she suddenly returned. The crowd listened to Pedlar's description of the scene below, then all went off to their nests to discuss it.

For the next few hours the whole House was quivering with excitement. Messengers ran back and forth between tribes, with news of what was happening below the stairs, Gorm was predicting an early victory for the mice.

During the Great Nudnik Drive, the Headhunter and his cannibal pet had been having a high old time with mouse corpses. The silky tones of Little Prince could often be heard coming from the middle bedroom, with his, 'De*lic*ious mousey-meat, oh lovely, lovely! Cook it up nice and soft, nice and sweet.' And various other nauseating phrases. Pedlar wondered whether it was all going to be worth it: the vanquishing of the nudniks against the loss of life amongst the mouse population.

Still, the electric wiring had suffered great damage; the water system had been penetrated in several places causing floods and chaos; the gas had done its work all right – and the furnishings had suffered a great deal. One of the old nudniks had already left the House – taken away in a big white boxy vehicle. The other nudniks had gone into overdrive with snap-wire traps and poison, but the mice weren't that stupid. They were used to the traps and the poison, well, sometimes you could eat it and only feel a bit sick. It rarely killed.

Several times Kellog had called across the waters of the tank to the effect that he thought the plan was going well.

'You might just do it, you crazy mice,' he growled.

One visiting Bookeater, standing on the corner of a trunk stared across at Kellog and said, 'Crazy? That's rich, coming from a brooding paranoid psychotic with sociopathic tendencies.'

Kellog liked the way things were going. He had always got enough to eat, but that didn't mean he didn't want more. And he knew that once the nudniks had gone, taking their rat-responsive spaniel with them, he would reign supreme over the whole House. He could come and go as he pleased, eat mouse babies without worrying about tribute, kill one or two if there was a need, without cutting off his food supply. The dark lord could come down from his castle and lay waste to the territory of the poor, damned peasants. There would be no nudniks around to check him.

And Merciful? Well, who knew what Merciful thought about it all? The mind of an owl is a strange and surreal thing and quite out of reach of the understanding of mice. Who could comprehend what vast icy wastes lay behind the inscrutable eyes of such as Merciful? Who could understand the inner meaning behind swiftness of hooked beak and needle claw, that came out of nowhere and brought instant death?

So, Merciful's opinion of the Great Nudnik Drive was not given and certainly not sought. Whether she realized what was going on at all was a mystery. She simply went about her business as usual, resting and killing, asking for no one's views, seeking no information.

Pedlar was in the middle of his contemplations. He had just decided that if his present role was anything to go by, then he quite enjoyed being 'the One', when a messenger came into the attic from below.

'Something's happening!' cried Goingdownfast excitedly. 'The nudniks have all left the House, but they haven't gone further than the bottom of the garden. They've got all their pets with them. There's another nudnik coming down the path, towards the House. It looks *evil*.'

Pedlar began to catch a trace of fear in Goingdownfast's manner. A chill went through him. What did the other mouse mean by *evil*?

Goingdownfast was continuing in an agitated tone. 'You see, the nudnik is dressed in black and carries a sort of cylinder thing on its back. There's a tube coming from the cylinder with a blunt snout on the end of it. Then there's the nudnik's face – eyes—'

'What about them?' cried Treadlightly, obviously catching some of the fear herself.

280

'They're covered in these glass circles. I mean, the nudnik has got some sort of rubber mask on, with these glass covers, and a sort of thing to help it breathe.'

'Just a minute, just a minute,' said Pedlar. 'I'm a Hedge-row mouse. I don't know what all this means. You're obviously scared about something. Have you seen this kind of creature before? Are there any legends?'

Treadlightly looked at him with a stricken face. '*Are there any legends?* Yes, there are! What Goingdownfast is describing is one of our worst nightmares. The Gas-maker. The mask is to stop the nudnik from dying of the gas he makes with his machine. We're going to be gassed to death!'

At that moment Pedlar heard the cry going up all around the attic, throughout the House, as the racial memory of the Gas-maker rose bubbling to the conscious minds of mice.

'Gas! The gas is coming!'

'Quickly,' said Pedlar, as if he had been programmed all his life for this very emergency. 'We must all go down into Tunneller's maze, below the House. It's the one time she won't attack us for being there.'

'Yes!' replied Treadlightly. 'As quickly as possible.'

Mice streamed through, in and out of holes, in a sort of controlled panic. They flowed past the rooms, along attic rafters, across floors, behind skirting-boards. Kellog too had caught the general hue and cry and was making his silent way down to the labyrinth below the House. Everyone was heading for the nearest tunnel which connected with the maze. Every tribe had access to at least one passageway which led directly to Tunneller's dominion and, depending on where they stood, each mouse knew the closest exit point.

Pedlar and Treadlightly were two of the last down the

hallway hole and they witnessed the terrible Gas-maker entering the House through the front door, slamming it behind him. Pedlar paused for a moment in the hallway, looking up at the giant figure with its monstrous face of rubber and glass. The discs of glass glinted in the hallway light. The sound of heavy breathing was heard from inside the mask as the Gas-maker stood and surveyed the scene around him. Pedlar couldn't take his eyes off the ugly tank of death on the nudnik's back and the black-snouted nozzle through which the gas would come. The horrible apparition turned Pedlar's head for a moment and he froze. Treadlightly nipped him out of his trance and he quickly followed her down to the cellar.

To say it was an orderly evacuation would be a lie, but it wasn't an unrestrained hysterical retreat. There was fear in the air, urging mice to attempt the hole while someone else was halfway through, and occasionally there would be a clash of bodies, a few nips exchanged, but nothing serious enough to hamper the exodus as a whole.

Finally they were all through the hole and occupied the tunnels. Once inside there was a general murmuring rush to get to the middle of the maze. The exit hole into the garden had already been blocked by the Gas-maker, who had made a complete tour of the House before entering it. The Gas-maker knew its job. The plug it had left could be gnawed through, eventually, and old routes restored, but not in time for the mice to get out into the garden and reach *complete* safety while the gassing was in progress.

In the central chamber of the labyrinth was Tunneller, just as afraid of the gas as the mice were. She sat there, very still, while the mice milled around her. Normally of course she would be screaming at them, telling them if they didn't get out she'd tear their skins from their backs, but not today. Today she simply lay as if stupefied, waiting with the rest of them for the gassing to begin.

Kellog, too, had retreated somewhere down one of the many branches of the maze. He lay in a space on his own.

A general peace settled over the whole scene, in which few mice spoke. They simply lay like Tunneller, waiting for death to pass over, waiting to see if it was to be a holocaust, or whether the luck of Megator-Megator would be with them on this occasion. Mostly the mice were gathered in tribes: the Bookeaters clustered around Frych-the-freckled; the 13-K around Ulf and Drenchie; the Savages close to Gorm-the-old; the Invisibles next to Whispersoft; the Deathshead and Stinkhorns on their own in a corner.

When the silence was at its deepest, Gorm muttered to Tunneller, 'I'm told that the Outsider, the yellow-neck Pedlar, beat you to a standstill in a fair fight.'

'That's true,' murmured Tunneller.

Gorm grunted.

Apart from this one quiet exchange, nothing was said.

Everyone knew when the Gas-maker was in the cellar. They felt it, instinctively. Everyone could picture the pig-snout nozzle stalking through the cellar, belching gas in a thick cloud. Each one of them imagined the gas creeping through the maze, finding its way through the round and oval passages, seeking out the mice. Survival depended on the strength of the backdraught. Despite the plugged exit hole, air came in through other areas, through tiny cracks and nail-holes from the outside world. This cool air wafted through the labyrinth, forming into a draught. If it was powerful enough, it could keep the gas from reaching the middle of the maze.

They waited.

They waited.

There came a moment when those on the outer edge could smell the gas, faintly, and knew it was very close. There was a general shuffling movement, which was probably caused by Phart and Flegm trying to edge their way towards the middle, but it soon settled.

They waited.

They waited.

Then came the time when they knew the danger must be over, and a great soughing went through the maze. The gas had not reached them. It still lingered in the passageways of the labyrinth, but by now the Gas-maker must have passed on. There would be no more gas coming down the tunnels. The backdraught had been strong enough to prevent a massacre.

Treadlightly nuzzled into Pedlar's neck and all around there was a general murmur as mice began to speak to their neighbours, some from rival tribes, in quiet whispers pregnant with relief. There was a feeling of joy and triumph in the air. Even Gorm did not growl or snarl when he spoke to those around him, saying that deliverance had been theirs.

It was necessary to remain where they were for some quite considerable time. When the mice heard the nudniks banging about in the House above them, they gave it another two or three good long hours to allow the gas in the corners to disperse. During that time, Ulf and Drenchie gnawed away at the plug in the garden hole and though they didn't widen it enough to allow passage for a mouse, they did produce a small hole through which a wind whistled down the tunnels and blew away the remnants of the deadly gas.

Finally, they all filed away, back through the hole into the cellar, with Phart shouting, 'This way, this way through Stinkhorn territory – we don't mind you usin' our cellar at times like this, do we Flegm? Just think of it as our gift to the mouse nation as a whole . . .'

'Shut your gob,' snarled Gorm as he passed the cellar mouse.

The mice were not all able to pour through the hallway and up the stairs and along the landing, as they had done on their way down, because the House was once more full of nudniks. Not to mention the fact that Eyeball and Spitz were around somewhere. So they had to make their way back in ones and twos, dashing from shadow to shadow, until they were safely in a hole leading to the interior of the walls.

Once back in their nest, Pedlar said to Treadlightly, 'I'm glad that's over. Do they ever do it twice in a row?'

'Not to anyone's knowledge.'

Each knew that they had just taken part in an incident that would go down in the long annals of mouse memory, to be passed on from one generation to the next: no doubt receiving with each new telling more and more embellishments, until heroes and heroines arose out of the dust of mouse minds, doing what had never been done before, turning facts into fiction, and history into mythology.

SAGE DERBY

THE ALLTHING WAS HELD LIKE ALL INTER-TRIBAL ALL-things in the nerve centre of the House, the cupboard-under. It was of course conducted by Gorm-the-old. Every tribe was represented by at least three members. Pedlar the Outsider felt that the Revolution was in crisis and he had come resolved to assess any next step. Gorm opened proceedings in his usual gruff way.

'We seem to be getting nowhere fast,' he said. 'The fire should have got rid of them, but it didn't. And whilst the attempted gassing was turned into a great mouse victory, it didn't advance our cause. I therefore welcome any suggestions—' he paused to give the Stinkhorns a look, '—any *sensible* suggestions – for proceeding with the Revolution. We've tried gas explosions, fires, floods and various organized gnawings. Nothing has been bad enough to drive the nudniks from the House permanently. What next?'

'Magic,' said Frych-the-freckled. 'Necromancy,' she continued. 'Hocus-pocus, voodoo – all the more intense divisions of wizardry. Gruffydd Greentooth is an excellent practitioner of the more dubious forms of sorcery, and no doubt could conjure a vast array of wizard-weaponry with which to subdue the nudnik population of the House.'

'Interpreter?' growled Gorm.

'Things that go bump in the night,' explained Skrang.

Gorm nodded. 'Well, we can try that, though I've never had much time for all that mystical gobbledegook. What else? Whispersoft – what about a contribution from the Invisibles?'

'We've been doing the best we can,' said Whispersoft in his booming voice. 'We could try another flood by gnawing through the plug to the water tank, but Kellog won't like it very much. That tank is his personal lake and he takes exception to us messing around with it. He's already sworn to get Goingdownfast.'

Gorm grunted. 'So we're left with the magic stuff, are we? So be it. But if magic should fail, we'll have to bring in Ulug Beg. Is Fallingoffthings willing to go along the clothesline and fetch the sage to us on her back?'

Fallingoffthings was at the meeting and spoke for herself. 'It's a dangerous operation, piggy-backing along a clothesline, but if I have to do it, I will.'

'Has anyone else got anything to offer?' asked Gorm.

Astrid went high-nose and Gorm groaned.

Astrid said, 'You probably know what I'm going to tell you, because I've said it all before, but I feel it's my duty to keep warning you. If you persist with trying to drive the nudniks out, there'll be terror in the mouse nation. I see – see terrible times ahead. Bleak times. I hear pathetic screams of mice in great distress, and no-one to come to their aid. I see the gaunt faces, the wispy tails, the hollow eyes. I hear mothers weeping for their young. I see mouse turning against mouse. There will be pestilence and poverty, fear and hatred, starvation and death. There will be wailing in the nests of mice. There will be anguish and grief.'

'Fine,' said Gorm, yawning. 'Anybody else? Good. In that case, we try the magic first and if that fails, we bring in Ulug Beg.'

The meeting broke up and mice went their various ways back to their tribes.

Interested in what the Bookeaters were going to do, with their magic, Pedlar told Treadlightly that he was going to visit the library on his way back to the attics.

She was less interested in magic than he was.

'I'll see you back at the nest,' she said. 'Don't forget where you live.'

'I won't.'

Pedlar took the Gwenllian Hole and made his way through the floors and walls to the library. Since the truce, security had relaxed in the library and the guards no longer stopped people going in and out. In fact the hole that Pedlar entered was unguarded, the sentry having wandered off somewhere in search of a good book to eat.

Pedlar was always impressed by his first sight of the library after being away for a long while. All around him were thousands of books, of all sizes, all colours, and many odours.

But it was walking beneath them that made Pedlar feel insignificant, humble, for they were like great pillars, holding up the universe. Some of them were so massive that if they fell they would squash a hundred mice. Yet because he had once lived among them, Pedlar was also able to see them as food and sustenance.

The tensions of living under Revolution had not allowed for much in the way of a normal life and Pedlar was glad to meet up and exchange news with some of the mice he knew: Rhodri, Nesta and Ethil. Others he called to in passing: Owain and Mefyn. Cadwallon was now a martyr of course, his bones revered, but Marredud was around, and Hywel-the-bad. There were mice from other tribes there as well. Gytha Finewhiskers from the Savages, Phart from the Stinkhorns. Even Gunhild had crept in at the back and stood quietly watching, one eye on the Savages present. Many had come to watch the great magic show.

Gruffydd Greentooth was sitting high-nose on the shelf containing the black leather-covered books. He had already eaten some pages out of a tome which he said was all about magic. He had ruminated on the paper cud in order to digest the spells which would now be regurgitated.

'How does he know which book to choose?' whispered Pedlar to Nesta, as they formed a circle around the magician.

'Certain pictures. If you get nudniks in pointy hats, that's a magic book. Or nudnik skulls. Things like that. You can tell.'

'Oh.'

Gruffydd Greentooth's eyes glazed over and he began chanting in a monotonous voice.

'*Spell for pain in the bowels and in the fatty part of the abdomen* – when you see a dung beetle on the ground throwing up the earth, seize him and the heap with both hands and say three times *ipso, skipso, facto, frum*. Then throw away the beetle, but keep any dung you may find, put it in a tobacco pouch, and sleep with it under your pillow at night.'

Pedlar was very impressed by this show of magic, because he hardly understood a word Gruffydd was saying. Before he had much time to think about it further, Gruffydd came out with another equally impressive chant.

'*To cure the gout and make better a terrible flatulence* – take the blood of a snail, tie it up in a linen cloth, and make of it a wick for a lamp; give it to any sufferer and tell them to light the wick. Thereafter will they be able to walk without pain and will cease to break wind.'

Pedlar felt a vibration go through him on hearing the words of this chant. He could feel the magic in the air. It was a gruesome, weird, unearthly spell that Gruffydd Greentooth had regurgitated. If this did not drive the nudniks from the House, nothing would. Certainly, Pedlar reflected, if he had been on the sharp end of that spell, he would have fled back to his Hedgerow in no time flat.

To help Gruffydd with his formidable task of driving out the nudniks with magic spells, several young mice (under the tuition of Frych-the-freckled) danced around the shelves, flailing each other with their tails and singing in high voices about the coming of winter. Some of them overdid it and fell over, gibbering in a strange tongue. This was a show Pedlar had seen several times during his stay in the library. It was an infectious profession, that of sorcery, and seemed to grip all in the vicinity of the magicians and their helpers.

'*Achtung!*' shrieked one young mouse, who had obviously been chewing on the wrong book. '*Marschieren!*'

Gunhild, standing a little way away from Pedlar, seemed most impressed by this young mouse. '*Achtung!*' she muttered to herself. She liked the crisp sound of this word. It was smart and precise: a word which made one stiffen to attention.

Pedlar watched her do a self-conscious little trot beside the young revolutionary, who was now shouting, 'March or die, march or die. The French Foreign Legion for ever!'

'Any more?' asked Gunhild of the youngster.

'CHARGE!' screamed the mouse, encouraged by his audience of one.

Pedlar watched as Gunhild followed the fellow all the way to the end of the shelf, where he suddenly fell over and began foaming at the mouth. Pedlar shook his head and made his way to an exit hole.

Once back at the nest, he was questioned by Treadlightly about the magicking and whether it would work or not.

'I don't know,' said Pedlar, 'but it was most impressive. I'm always amazed by these long words the library mice come out with. I just wish we knew what they meant.' And as he pondered the matter he began to feel drowsy.

In a moment he was fast asleep.

While Treadlightly and Pedlar were curled into each other like two little furry commas, their tails draped over one another, a mouse crept by the opening to their nest. He glanced in and saw the pair and was envious of their contentment. Then he hurried on, towards the water tank.

It was Timorous, on his way to another assignation with Kellog among the rafters.

Kellog had just been to collect his daily tribute from the kitchen mice. His massive bulk was lying outside his mighty nest: a dark beast, gorging, melding with the shadows. He was the dark lord of the attics and soon he would be free to roam the whole House, pillaging and destroying as he pleased. First on his agenda was the death of Goingdownfast.

Timorous remained on the far shore. Even so he was quaking in fear. The only thing between death and himself was a stretch of water. Kellog needed the expanse of water to protect himself from his imaginary enemies, but at the same time he could not swim across it swiftly enough to catch a mouse on the far side.

'When are you going to give me Goingdownfast?' growled Kellog.

'Soon,' said Timorous. 'I'll have him for you soon. You must understand I have to get his trust back. We were enemies once and I have to wheedle my way back into his good graces, before he'll trust me enough to come with me. It takes time and patience . . .'

'I'm not a patient rodent,' grumbled Kellog. 'I want his eyes and liver. Why don't you just show me where his nest is hidden? I can do the rest.'

'He — he moves. Even I don't know from one moment to the next where he'll be. My plan is best, I assure you, Kellog. We'll get him out in the open, away from all bolt holes, and then you can pounce. If you can just hang on, I'm getting closer to him every hour.'

'Good. Well, it had better be soon, or I may have to settle for *your* eyes and liver instead.'

Timorous hurried away, glad to be out of range of the sight and smell of the great rat whose sheer malevolence was enough to clog the air around the water tank, even without the musty odour of his unkempt coat.

Timorous made his way to the nest of Goingdownfast and Nonsensical. It was cleverly hidden in the wedge between two rafters, camouflaged on the outside with wood shavings that had been aged, so that it looked like a piece of timber itself. Timorous called in a low voice.

'Goingdownfast — it's me — Timorous. I've come to say

how sorry I am for all those times I've caused you upset
. . . are you there, Goingdownfast?'

'What do you really want?' called Goingdownfast, in
a not too friendly voice.

Then Nonsensical's voice cut in with, 'Oh, come on,
let's hear what he has to say. It can't do any harm, can
it?'

'Why's he keep coming around here?' grumbled Goingdownfast.

'Because he's sorry, I suppose. Come on in Timorous,'
called Nonsensical. 'Come inside.'

Timorous did as he was invited.

While Timorous was busy apologizing to Goingdownfast
for all the times he had been nasty to him, another mouse
hurried by the entrance to the nest. She did not glance in
because she did not see through the nest's disguise and
being deaf she was unable to hear them talking. Her name
was in fact Hearallthings and she was on her way to the
Clock in the hall.

Hearallthings was the only mouse in the House who
enjoyed being inside the Clock. She had in fact been born in
there, when her very pregnant mother had used the Clock
as a bolt hole to escape Eyeball one night. The shadow-
coloured blue had been waiting in the corner-darkness of
the cupboard-under and had ambushed three mice on their
way along the hall. Hearallthings' mother had been the only
one to get away and she subsequently gave birth on the
last stroke of midnight to seven little ones. Unfortunately,
when she eventually ferried them out of the Clock, to the
attics, she forgot Hearallthings, and left her behind. When
mother eventually counted her young and realized to her
horror that one was missing, Hearallthings was by that time
as deaf as a post, from being left next to the Clock's chimer.

293

Now, Hearallthings needed her regular visits to the Clock. She got in the back and climbed up the chains, into the works, where the smell of oil was like perfume to her. There, amongst the ratchets and wheels, the cogs and levers and springs, she lay on the chimer shelf waiting for noon to happen. When it did, of course, she heard nothing, but the tremblings went through her as the whole case of the Clock vibrated. She loved those tremblings, was addicted to them, and would have risked worse than death to experience them when the need was upon her.

So far Hearallthings had played but a very minor role in the Drive. Since she was deaf, she lived in a different world from the rest of the mice. Her world was a place of silence, where reality was lightly shaded in. Although she could lip- and body-read, Hearallthings was mostly isolated by her condition: a lonely mouse whom few approached for any kind of contact. However, she was soon to play a big part in the Great Nudnik Drive and become the heroine of the hour.

GRUYÈRE

IMPRESSIVE AS THE DEMONSTRATION WAS, THE MAGIC DID not work. The nudniks' ears did not shrivel, their heads did not swivel on their necks and they continued with their bovine existence in the House without a pause.

The library mice found another book, one with pictures of nudniks travelling in containers over water, and they decided that this must be the magic book for sending nudniks on long voyages into an Unknown whence they could never return. So Iago ate some of the book and came up with this very awe-inspiring spell:

'The ability to establish a line of position by observation of a celestial body is based on the fundamental fact that, for any given instant of time, the altitude and azimuth of a celestial body in relation to the horizon of any assumed position of latitude can be calculated using formulas and tables made available to the mariner by the astronomer.'

After Iago had finished this wonderful piece of rhetoric the mice expected the nudniks to vanish over the said horizon. How could such complicated magic go unheeded? But, as with the magic of Gruffydd Greentooth, nothing untoward happened.

'Time to bring in Ulug Beg!' went up the cry.

Thus the great balancer, Fallingoffthings, was to be found at any moment of the hour limbering up and generally exercising her legs, making them supple, toning up her muscles. Other mice would stand and watch as Fallingoffthings turned her head, this way and that, getting out the cricks, making ready the shoulders that would carry Ulug Beg along the clothesline, high above the jungled garden.

Since Merciful's hole had to be used to reach the washing line which ran from the wall of the House to the abandoned treehouse where Ulug Beg had his monastic retreat, the mice had to wait until evening when the little owl would take to her wings and fly out into the purpling sky to hunt.

Once she was Outside they gave her a good length of time to get away from the House, for Fallingoffthings would be extremely vulnerable out on the washing line. Indeed, there was no guarantee of protection from other predators either. Who was to say that a barn or tawny owl would not fly past just as Fallingoffthings made her precarious passage along the tightrope?

Finally the time came for Fallingoffthings to nod briskly to those around her and set off. Once the mice had seen her go through Merciful's hole, they all rushed to the side of the attic on which the line ran. From there they could look through cracks in the weatherboarding, at their heroine crossing the quiet evening on nothing but a slim piece of rope. Some watched the mouse as she stepped out on to the swaying line, while other eyes searched the skies for signs of winged death.

Since the cracks in the weatherboarding were few and the mice were many, those with a view described what they saw to those without.

'She's on the line now – uh, uh, it's swaying, she's wobbling – no, she's all right – she's *running* now – yes, you should see her! Oh, and she's *there*!'

Fallingoffthings then disappeared into the ramshackle treehouse which some young nudnik had once used, but which had fallen into disrepair and neglect over the past several summers.

Fallingoffthings was in the treehouse for a very long time, before she emerged, *alone*. She began the journey back along the swaying line to the House. The speculation was rife.

'Ulug Beg is ill.'

'Ulug Beg is close to death.'

'Ulug Beg is dead and riddled with maggots.'

'He won't come,' said Fallingoffthings breathlessly to Gorm-the-old. 'Says he's too old to go traipsing along washing lines on the backs of whippersnappers.'

'What's a whippersnapper?' growled Gorm.

'Me, I think.'

There was an emergency Allthing called on the spot and it was decided that another mouse should go over with Fallingoffthings. Ideally, said Frych-the-freckled, it should be Gorm, who had met Ulug Beg in his younger nights before he was leader of the kitchen mice.

'If he's too old, I'm too damned old,' growled Gorm. 'And I'm too heavy to carry anyway.'

'Send Thorkils Threelegs,' yelled some joker outside the circle of leaders. 'He's got nimble feet.'

This suggestion was ignored by all except Thorkils himself, who wanted to root out the joker and sever his jugular. Instead, Gorm suggested that someone familiar with the outside world should go: someone more in tune with Ulug Beg's way of thinking. Someone who had recently been a Hedgerow mouse would be ideal, suggested Gorm casually.

'What's-his-name?' growled Gorm, as if searching his mind for the name. 'The vagrant.'

'Pedlar, you mean?' bellowed Whispersoft.

'Yes, I think so,' replied Gorm with an innocent expression on his face. 'Yes, that fellow Pedlar. Good at charming other mice, isn't he? So I've heard, anyway. Good at wheedling himself into their good books. Surely he's the right mouse for the job? He should be able to persuade Ulug Beg to come over here, if anyone can. I've heard that this Pedlar can con most mice to do anything – especially females.'

'Ulug Beg's a buck,' replied Frych.

'Yes, well, same principle,' growled Gorm in a satisfied tone. 'Same principle. Let's see if this Pedlar is as good at balancing as he is at smarming.'

'And if he falls off?' asked Frych.

'Nothing really lost,' said Gorm, cleaning between his incisor teeth with his nail. 'We'll get someone else to go. I mean, it'll be a great shame of course, and we'll all be devastated, but the good of the cause comes first, you know. Patriotic duty and all that. Should think the fellow will jump at the chance.'

Pedlar did not exactly *jump* at the chance to cross the washing line. He stared out through one of the cracks in the weatherboard and his eyes grew large and round. Still, he was a mouse – a Hedgerow mouse – and as such had done his share of balancing in his time. Usually there had been a network of twigs or corn stalks to stop him from falling too far and it had to be admitted the washing line was a *long* way up. But, he told himself, it didn't matter whether the line was ten or twenty or a hundred-thousand lengths high. If you fell, you fell, and you might as well say goodbye world.

'All right, I'm ready,' he told Fallingoffthings. 'You lead the way.'

The sun had now gone down and the moon was out. Fallingoffthings went through Merciful's hole and scrambled into the gutter. Pedlar did the same. The pair of them scuttled through the dead leaves gathering there, their tails sliding over the damp mush.

When they reached the washing line tied to the drainpipe, Pedlar's heart was knocking on his ribs.

'This is it then,' he said.

'Now, don't panic,' said his companion. 'Simply think of something else, something pleasant, and forget the drop. It's all in the tip of the tail, Pedlar. That's my secret. I'm really no better at balancing than any other mouse. The tip of the tail.'

She waved her tail like a magic balancing whip.

'I haven't *got* a tip to my tail,' groaned Pedlar.

'*Everyone*'s got a tip to their tail, even creatures without tails – even nudniks – it's not to do with the body, it's to do with the mind.'

'Right,' Pedlar said, unconvinced. 'Remember the tip of my tail and forget the drop.'

'Forget everything to do with balancing. Just think of Treadlightly. Picture her beautiful face with its long silky whiskers.'

'But if I don't concentrate, I'll fall.'

'You won't fall. Just do as I say.'

Fallingoffthings went out on to the line first. Pedlar hesitated just a moment and then stepped out after her. There was a suppressed gasp from inside the House, behind the weatherboard, as the line began to sway dangerously.

'Don't look up or down,' said Fallingoffthings calmly. 'Don't look at anything except the treehouse. Now tell me, where did you first meet Treadlightly?'

They were moving along the line now and Pedlar's limbs were beginning to tremble.

'What?' he asked. 'What did you say?'

'Keep moving, don't stop – I said, where did you first meet Treadlightly? Did you fall – er – that is, were you attracted to each other straightaway?'

'No – no, well, yes I suppose we did. She was with yooouuu . . .'

The line was obviously slacker in the middle than at the ends and the swaying was quite dramatic now that they had reached the midway point.

'Keep moving!' said Fallingoffthings sharply. 'Now, would you say Treadlightly threw herself at you?'

'Certainly not,' said Pedlar indignantly, almost unaware that his feet were still moving. 'She was attracted to me, naturally – well, not naturally,' he corrected, aware that this sounded very immodest, 'I mean, we were naturally suited to one another. I was just as keen on her. I simply didn't know it until we managed to be alone together.'

The moon was a big round ball in the branches of the tree, caught there after rolling up the sky. Pedlar marvelled at how little it had changed since he'd last seen it. When he had been in the Hedgerow he had often stared up at the benign mellow object, wondering how it changed shape, *why* it changed shape. The moon was an old friend. It refused to be disentangled by the breeze that was trying

300

to blow it out of the network of branches in the semi-bare autumn tree. Around him, the rest of the night was full of sounds — of foxes, birds and hedgehogs, of stoats and weasels, of mice and nudniks.

'We're there!' said Fallingoffthings. 'Well done.'

Pedlar looked at his feet and found he was standing on the edge of a piece of wood. He was on the platform which held the house in the tree. The wood was rotten, there was the smell of decay about it, but it was certainly strong enough to hold a mouse.

The treehouse in close-up did not inspire Pedlar with confidence. It was dark and gloomy and had a malevolent air about it. Normally he would not come within a double ditch of such a place.

Fallingoffthings had gone inside, entering through one of the many holes in the clapboard wall.

Pedlar followed her.

If the outside of the structure was worrying, the inside was even worse. The autumn leaves had collected in great heaps on the rotten planks of the platform floor. There were spiders' webs running in vast shrouds throughout the interior, and a multitude of bugs crawled and scampered over the twigs and other debris that had fallen through holes in the roof.

Pedlar stood for a while and allowed his eyes to become used to the gloom. He could see Fallingoffthings standing high-nose near a corner of the room. After a while, when the splash of moonbeams on the floor was no longer so distracting, Pedlar could discern a huddled shape in the corner.

If he had been alone, Pedlar would probably have run from the place, thinking he had encountered some hellish creature from the Otherworld. What he saw was hardly recognizable as a mouse. It was a shrivelled, wrinkled thing, with skin that rolled in creases the whole short length of its body: a sort of dark-dirty-grey colour. The eyes were rheumy around the rims, though bright and intense enough in the centre. The whiskers hung lank and almost seemed to form a straggly beard, such as the one Pedlar had seen on the face of the old nudnik who used the library so much. There was a tail, such as it was: a knobbly thread of a thing that trailed in the dirt behind the old mouse.

'This is Ulug Beg,' said Fallingoffthings. 'One of the oldest mice in existence.'

'*The* oldest mouse in existence,' rumbled a husky voice. 'If you know of another one, say so.'

'I – I don't think I've ever seen *any* creature as old as you,' confessed Pedlar. 'Even a nudnik.'

'Oh, there are no nudniks older than me,' corrected the heap of bones and fur in the corner.

'You must know a lot of things,' gulped Pedlar. 'You must have seen a great deal in your life.'

'I know everything,' remarked the old mouse. 'Everything *worth* knowing that is. If there's something I don't know, you can forget it, give it a miss. There's knowledge and then there's trivia. I don't need to concern myself with trivia.'

'No, I'm sure you don't,' said Pedlar.

'Now,' rumbled Ulug Beg, 'this is very nice and all that – a visit from the outside world – but as you will have gathered I'm a recluse, an eremite, a hermit. And I want to stay that way. This fellow told me something about chasing nudniks out of the House, but I'm much too old to go traipsing over washing lines now.'

'Excuse me, Ulug Beg,' said Pedlar, 'but I don't think

you realize the seriousness of the problem. You see, the mice were always at war . . .'

'Always have been in that House,' grumbled Ulug Beg.

'Yes, well we've put a stop to it. What we want to do next is drive out the nudniks and their pets – they eat such vast quantities of food – and having done that there should be enough food for all, without having to fight for it. Now I'm not really one of the House mice – I'm from the Hedgerow and have only recently come among them – but I can see the sense in what they're doing.'

'Can you now. Can you now. Well, there seems to be something wrong to me – some part of the equation which has got a little disjointed. However, I'll grant you on the surface it seems a good plan. Who devised it?'

'Gorm-the-old.'

'That *young* whippersnapper? There's bound to be something wrong with it then. I'll put my mind to that problem. However, you seem extremely anxious to get rid of the nudniks, or you wouldn't have bothered me. I like to be left alone, you know.'

Pedlar said, 'I can understand that. When I lived in the Hedgerow I was content enough, but since I moved into the House I find that sometimes – well, it just stifles me. There are mice *everywhere*.'

The two visiting mice waited for a short time, while Ulug Beg stared into space, then Fallingoffthings said, 'Well, sir, will you come with us now?'

Ulug Beg seemed to come out of a trance.

'Wha . . . what? Come with you? Certainly not! I can't be piggybacked across that line any more. Look at me – I'm a bag of skin and bones. Touch me and I'll fall to bits. I only survive by staying exactly where I am and eating acorns that drop through the holes in the roof.'

'But how can you address the Allthing from here?' said Fallingoffthings helplessly.

'Shan't,' snapped the old mouse.

Pedlar stared at Ulug Beg. It did seem entirely likely that he would crumble to tiny fragments the moment he was moved from where he sat.

'I'll tell you what,' said the sensible Hedgerow yellowneck. 'We'll explain the details of the problem and then you can pass your ideas for a solution to the Allthing *through us*. What about that? We'll be your messengers to Gorm and the leaders of the other tribes.'

'I've never done that before,' replied Ulug Beg simply.

Pedlar blinked and swished his tail. 'Never done what before?'

'Never used messengers. Don't intend to start now.'

Pedlar looked at Fallingoffthings, who shrugged, as if to say, I've done my best, now it's up to someone else.

Pedlar ground his teeth in frustration. What could *he* do? He could go back and tell Gorm to do the tightrope himself. It would serve the old beggar right: he'd either have to walk the rope or lose face in front of his tribe. However, Pedlar had his pride too, and he did not like to return to the House having failed to bring Ulug Beg or his solution with him. So he wasn't going to give up without trying his best.

Like anyone else, Pedlar had found that very old mice, however intelligent, liked to recall the past and the glorious hours of their youth. In fact they became very impatient with the present and had absolutely no time for the future. It was the past in which they wanted to bask: in the brilliant rays of their golden hours. Perhaps this characteristic could now be played on to save the day.

304

'Well, sir,' he said, nodding politely at Ulug Beg's concertinaed body, like a bag of skin collapsed on itself, 'we'll be going now. It was nice to meet you.' Fallingoffthings was giving Pedlar a funny look but Pedlar ignored his companion. 'I have wanted to speak with you ever since I heard you ate the Book of Knowledge.'

'True, true,' ruminated Ulug Beg. 'I nibbled and gnawed and now know all things. If there's something I don't know . . .'

'. . . it's not worth knowing. I heartily agree. How old are you, sir?'

'Older than the House,' nodded Ulug Beg. 'I'm the oldest living thing on the planet – almost.'

'Really? How extraordinary,' cried Pedlar, while Fallingoffthings appeared to be dropping off to sleep. 'You must have seen some things in your time. Tell me, were you born here in the treehouse . . .?'

. . . Several reminiscences later, by which time Pedlar felt he knew all there was to know about the creased figure in front of him, Ulug Beg was saying, 'Do you know, I think I'm going to break my rule! I *will* use you as a messenger after all. You strike me as a very competent fellow – so few about these nights you know. You'll do, you'll do. Tell me the problem and I'll give you the answer. I've never failed yet, so let's have them then – the facts – let's hear what you've got to say!'

PONT L'ÉVÊQUE

'THE GREAT NUDNIK DRIVE? YES, IT HAS PANACHE,' murmured Ulug Beg as Fallingoffthings snored quietly in the corner, just as she'd done while Pedlar had related the events of the Great Nudnik Drive to their host. 'Of course, I can see why you're not winning.'

'You can?'

'Well, it's only as plain as the whiskers on your face. You're trying to engage the nudniks in a physical battle – that's a battle you can never win. You won't get them out of the House that way. No!'

Pedlar stared at the pool of skin before him, wondering whether Ulug Beg was high-nose or low-nose. 'What do we do then?'

'The *supernatural*,' nodded the old sage, his little eyes shining in the moonlight. 'You have to make them think the House is haunted. Be gone in a flash.'

Pedlar sounded dubious, 'I suppose we could get the library mice to raise the ghost of Megator-Megator.'

Ulug Beg dismissed this. 'There's no such thing as Megator-Megator.'

'How do you know that?'

'Because I invented him. I'm always inventing stories that people take to be the gospel truth. Megator-Megator is a figment of my vast imagination.'

If Pedlar was dismayed at the loss of such a mouse icon, he managed not to show it, concerning himself only with the business in hand. 'Then how do we conjure up a ghost? I don't see how we can trick the nudniks into thinking one of *us* is a ghost. We're too small to bother about in their eyes. If one of the kitchen mice dipped himself in flour and went wailing through the House, they'd just tread on him – or put him in with Little Prince, thinking they'd found a mate for that nasty little beast.'

Ulug Beg sighed. It sounded like the wind soughing through the branches of the tree. It was a deep and impatient sigh.

'You mice these nights – and I thought I'd found a mouse in you that I'd been looking for, Pedlar. Why do you always think of the obvious? Visual tricks! We do have other senses besides sight. Let me tell you this – *show* them the ghost, and they'll no longer be afraid of it. You have to make them believe there's a ghost there, and *never* let them see it.'

'Noises!' Pedlar said quickly.

'Exactly – and touches, if you can get away with them.'

'Noises and touches. Not smells?'

Ulug Beg shook his head. 'What does a ghost smell like? Rotten cabbage? They'll just go looking for a rotten cabbage. Cat's poo? They'll blame the cats. No, sound is the big persuader. You give them a few unexplained noises and you'll drive them crazy.'

Pedlar realized he had at last got the answer to the nudnik problem.

'Thank you very much, Ulug Beg. It has been a very great honour to meet you, sir. I never thought I'd be talking to the creator of Megator-Megator.'

The rheumy old sage rose a little out the pool of his flesh. 'You can be a bit slow but you've got the makings of a very astute yellow-neck, Pedlar.'

Pedlar regarded the strange pile of mottled fur with its squinty eyes and wondered about something. Yellow-neck, house mouse, pet mouse, harvest mouse, wood mouse? Eventually he found the courage to ask.

'Er – what – what kind of mouse did you – er – start out as?'

'Same as I am now – can't you tell?'

Pedlar didn't even want to hazard a guess and indicated his bemusement.

'A *moon-star mouse* of course,' said Ulug Beg matter of factly.

'Of course, of course! How silly of me. Well, we must be going . . .' Pedlar gave Fallingoffthings a flick with his tail, to sting her awake.

'What?' cried Fallingoffthings, rolling to a low-nose position, her eyes wide open.

'Time to go,' said Pedlar.

'Oh, fine – but what about our mission?'

'Accomplished,' said Pedlar in a satisfied tone.

'Really?' said Fallingoffthings. 'Oh, excellent! Well done. Goodbye, Ulug Beg.'

'Yes, goodbye,' Pedlar repeated.

'Don't come back again,' grumbled Ulug Beg. 'I'll be dead.'

'You look dead already,' said Fallingoffthings, before she could stop herself.

'Exactly,' Ulug Beg murmured. 'Tell them I'm already dead and you talked to my ghost, ha, ha!'

He gave them a final wink and then they crossed the rotten floorboards and damp leaves and went through the doorway on to the moonlit platform to which the washing line was attached. They both stared about them, up into the branches of the tree and out into the night, both thinking of owls, both remaining silent on the subject. You never saw the owl that hit you.

'What was he on about, back there?' asked Fallingoffthings. 'Is he off his head?'

'No, it was a kind of joke, I think,' said Pedlar. 'Anyway, let's get back. I'm not looking forward to crossing this line again.'

Out in the garden's night there were doings and killings and eatings going on. Hedgehogs were munching unlucky worms, a fox was prowling near the privy wondering if that really was a dormousey scent mingling with the stink of old sewage. And above all this the scattered owls were cruising silently, their eyes sharp and unfailing. Outside the House, Nature was carrying on as normal as if there were no life-and-death struggle going on within, no mouse history being carved.

This time Pedlar went out on the line first, his confidence a little stronger since his earlier successful crossing. At that moment the moon went behind a cloud and darkness rushed in.

Fallingoffthings said, 'Get out into the middle. I want to dash across.'

309

Pedlar knew what the other mouse meant. The sky was dangerous. Fallingoffthings didn't want to expose herself to risk any longer than she need. This thought made Pedlar act in a hasty fashion. He tried to trot. The moon came out of the other side of the cloud, suddenly. Shadows leapt across Pedlar's line of sight. Was that an owl? He put more speed into his legs, slipped, turned upside down.

For a moment he dangled on two legs, then he could no longer hold on, and dropped downwards.

Despite the fact that he landed in springy grasses and old leaves, it knocked all the wind out of him. He turned over and lay on his stomach for a moment, staring upwards, getting his breath back. His heart was beating wildly. Above him, he saw Fallingoffthings make her dash across the line. The other mouse managed to reach the House in safety so quickly that Pedlar wondered whether they were both subject to the same laws of time. His own time on the rope had seemed like for ever!

The scents in the grasses came to him as he lay there. Many trails, many creatures. The night was full of them. A garden is a populous country, having much to offer, even a neglected one. Pedlar's thoughts turned on what to do next. He had to get back into the House of course and carry his message to the other mice. Tunneller's entrance hole was round the other side of the building. To travel all that way at night, with all the nocturnal predators around, might prove fatal. There would be cats from the neighbourhood, if not from the House itself. There would be foxes, stoats, weasels and owls. There might even be badgers around, who were not averse to a mouse or two, if the mice were foolish enough to be out and about.

There was a rustle in the grass ahead!

Pedlar stiffened then hunched up, ready for flight. Freeze first, run at the last resort. That was the golden rule.

Then a familiar smell assailed his nostrils. It was the scent of a dormouse: a nose poked through the grass and some eyes blinked at him. A creature in a sandy coat and wearing a bushy tail confronted Pedlar.

'Ah, a new mouse to the region,' said the dormouse. 'Out hunting foxes are we?'

'Hunting foxes?' said Pedlar.

'Little joke,' chuckled the dormouse. 'But you know, it would be better to be tucked up somewhere in a hole. There *are* foxes around. You must go and find a safe nest.'

'I must? What about you?'

'Oh, I'm on my way home now. The privy helps to hide the smells of my nest from predators. It confuses them. Good, eh?'

'So you're Stone! I've heard of you. My name's Pedlar – I live in the House – now.'

'Ah, the famous Pedlar. I've heard of you too. What on earth made you leave the lovely hedgerows and fields to enter that abomination?'

'Abomination?'

'The House. Mice don't need such dwellings. We are at one with Nature and at our best in natural surroundings. You must come out of there, back into the fresh air, back amongst the grasses and the mushrooms! What glorious vegetation we have out here, all for the asking. Daisies, dandelions, campion, stitchwort – thousands, millions of plants. Not at the moment of course, for the weather has turned, but spring will come again. You must definitely leave the House for good. One hour, the House will return to Nature too, you know.'

311

Pedlar explained, 'I'm here because my destiny lies within the House – for the moment anyway – and I must get back inside. What's the best way to get back in?'

'Through the maze or up a drainpipe. You take your choice.'

There was a sound like a peacock calling not far from where the two mice were talking. Both knew it to be a fox.

'Which is the *nearest* entrance?' said Pedlar quickly.

'Drainpipe,' said the dormouse. 'Goodbye.'

They parted and Pedlar ran to the wall of the House, he went along the edge of the cliff face until he came to a drainpipe. Up into this dark hole he disappeared. There was moss and lichen lining the inside, which Pedlar used to grip and climb, making steady progress.

It was a long haul but he eventually reached the gutter. Once out into the channel, he ran quickly around the corner, to find Merciful's hole. A quick check of the night sky, for silhouettes of owls and then into the tribal area of the Invisibles.

Once inside, Pedlar let out a huge sigh of relief. He began to make his way along the beams. But before he had achieved much headway, someone stepped out and barred his way.

'Who's there?' he shouted. 'Who's that?'

'Astrid,' answered the figure.

Pedlar stared. Astrid had struck a dramatic pose, half in, half out of the shadows. She seemed to be talking to someone.

'Who's with you?' asked Pedlar.

Astrid replied, 'No one. I was talking with my friends and informants the Shadows. Do you have news for the Allthing? Fallingoffthings said you had lost your balance on the line. Everyone's out looking for you, wondering whether you were hurt.'

'No, I'm not hurt. I think Ulug Beg's given me the answer to our problems.'

'The end of one problem may be the beginning of a vast new set.'

'What do you mean by that?'

'I mean answers become questions again, very soon. If we drive out the nudniks, we'll be sorry. That much I know from the cryptic warnings my Shadows give me. I say to you now, turn around and leave, take your news with you, return to the distant Hedgerow.'

A vision of his former home came into Pedlar's head. Suddenly, he could smell the hedge garlic and stitchwort. He could hear the voices of the many birds, passing up and down the Hedgerow. But it was another world, another time. The House had claimed him since then.

Pedlar shook his head and swished his tail. 'I can't do that,' he said solemnly.

'Well, carry your great tidings to the Allthing, then. But let it be noted: I've tried to stop you.' Astrid stood high-nose before Pedlar and raised her forelimbs in a dramatic gesture, as if pleading with the gods above. 'I've done my best to try to prevent the world from being destroyed.'

Pedlar said kindly, 'You always do your best, Astrid. I'm sorry, but I can't run away now. We're so close to reaching our goal. Besides, you could be wrong, you know. The Shadows could be trying to control us.'

With this, Pedlar made his escape quickly, before Astrid had time to make any more pronouncements. Whilst from deep within the attic, the Invisibles began to come out, their perfect camouflage fooling Pedlar up to the last moment.

'Call the Allthing,' he cried. 'There is news from Ulug Beg!'

'Call the Allthing! Call the Allthing!' went up the cry.

Pedlar saw Treadlightly and gave his mate an affectionate nip in passing. She nuzzled him back and then followed behind him, whispering that she was relieved to see him safe and well, and that she would hear what happened to him later. For the moment he was the important mouse, the messenger from Ulug Beg, and all were waiting to hear him speak.

Gorm-the-old was wakened from a doze. The Allthing was hastily assembled. Pedlar gave out his news.

'We are to create some noisy ghosts,' he told the ring of faces. 'We must frighten the nudniks from the House.'

'Ghosts!' the cry went up. 'We must put the fear of phantoms into the nudniks! Ulug Beg has done it again!'

There was a quick, excited discussion amongst the leaders of the tribes. The general consensus was that the idea was brilliant. Especially when Pedlar explained that it wasn't necessary to emulate ghosts visually, but simply to produce noises which might be made by ghosts. It all seemed so simple, now that it had been laid before them.

'Well done,' Gorm growled, reluctantly. 'Good work, what's-his-name.'

'Pedlar,' said Pedlar.

'As you wish,' said Gorm. 'Now, we must decide how to go about this noisy ghost business. Knock a few plates off the Welsh dresser – that sort of thing, eh? Scratch around some bedposts in the late night. Good, good. We'll soon have it operating . . .'

EMMENTHAL

In his room, the Headhunter was polishing his collection of mouse skulls, baring his teeth as he did so. Little Prince was running about restlessly in his cage. Little Prince was desperately trying to communicate with his master.

'They're up to something, I know they are. I can hear the whispers. They're doing something very, very bad – oh, yes – I can feel it in my precious fur. Nasty little house mice, nasty little sweetmeats. They're plotting plans, hatching schemes, I know they are . . .'

The Headhunter stopped polishing the skulls and with his stubby, dirty fingers, shook the cage roughly. Little Prince shuddered and rattled, falling on the floor. It was his master's way of telling him to shut up.

'You silly creature!' shouted Little Prince. 'I'm trying to warn you of those horrible mice . . .'

The cage was shaken again, this time more roughly. Little Prince wisely shut up this time. His master was trying to concentrate on cleaning his collection and did not want to be disturbed. There were about three dozen intact skulls and several more that had cracks or chips out of them. Presumably the latter was the result of a snapwire trap coming down on the head of the victim. The Headhunter did not like it when a mouse had its skull caved in. He preferred his skeletons to be perfect: just the spinal cord broken. Little Prince knew this because of the rages which occurred when a skull was damaged.

Little Prince could see out of the window from his cage. He stared down into the garden, observing the comings and goings of the creatures who inhabited it. Last night he had seen two mice tightrope-walking along the washing line.

They were obviously visiting the abandoned treehouse. Little Prince knew the ancient mouse called Ulug Beg lived in the treehouse – it was amazing the amount of information tortured mice spewed out – and Ulug Beg was an old sage who had eaten the Book of Knowledge and knew everything.

Ulug Beg was something else to Little Prince, too, something of which the rest of the mice in the House were completely unaware. It was a secret between Little Prince and the gods, and Little Prince wondered if even the gods still remembered it.

The important thing was, however, that mice only visited Ulug Beg when they had something serious to ask of the ancient creature.

'What we need to do,' murmured Little Prince, 'is get a mouse *now*, so that we can torture the sweet thing.'

What usually happened was that his master started doing things to the mouse, with needles and boiling water and bunsen-burner flames, and the mouse would puke in terror before shouting everything it had ever learned in an effort to save its life. In their agony the victims somehow got the mistaken idea that if they gave Little Prince the information he wanted, Little Prince could stop the torture. Little Prince encouraged this idea, for he learned all their secrets this way.

'The difficulty, once the secret is learned, is imparting what I know to this stupid nudnik,' murmured Little Prince to himself. 'He has the brain of a cow.'

Little Prince, like most mice, believed that the larger the creature, the smaller its brain. An ant was one of the most intelligent creatures on the planet, though it was despised for its obsessive nature and its manic work ethic. Mice were happy with their allocation of brains and considered all larger creatures to be dunces of varying degrees.

'Then the sweet little sugars came back again,' mused Little Prince, staring at the washing line. 'Then they came back again but *without* the Ulug Beg creature with its nasty smelly crinkled coat. Perhaps Ulug Beg is dead? All mice have to die some time. Perhaps she's just a pile of dust by now.'

Little Prince had seen Ulug Beg in the past, crossing the washing line with a mouse that had obviously been sent to fetch him. Previous to last night, there had always been only *one* mouse acting as messenger and guide to the antique sage. Yet last night there were two mice. Little Prince had recognized one of them. *It was the one who got away!* Never had a mouse escaped the Headhunter before that yellow-neck, Pedlar, had slipped out of his clutches. Master had been plenty mad. He had almost cooked Little Prince in the steaming broth in his rage. Little Prince had almost been boiled alive because of that Pedlar creature!

Now the yellow-neck was into some intrigue, some conspiracy, which involved all the mice in the household.

'I *hate* that yellow-neck with his sweet-honey face,' said Little Prince in a pleasant tone. 'I want his eyes to melt in my mouth. I want to lick his liver. I want to crack his gonads between my teeth. He will be my confectionery . . .'

The cage was rattled again and Little Prince realized he was talking too loud. It was that yellow-neck which did it to him. Pedlar was always getting Little Prince into trouble. Pedlar was a thorn in Little Prince's paw. Pedlar kept Little Prince awake at night, having to plot and scheme uselessly.

'I bet his tears taste like nectar,' murmured Little Prince. 'I bet his blood is molten sugar. I'll make him weep before me. I'll make him *bleed*.'

Little Prince worked this refrain up into a tune which he hummed to himself until he saw the Headhunter give him one of those looks.

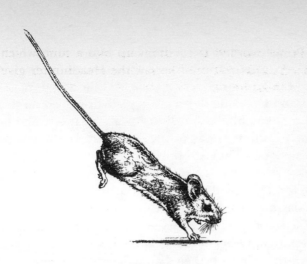

CAMBOZOLA

'WE MUST CONJURE PHANTOMS, APPARITIONS, spectres and wraiths from the very extremities of the supernatural world,' cried Frych-the-freckled. This ghost business was right up her alley. 'I personally will endeavour to devour any volume in the library which has the appearance of being a work containing information on ectoplasmic radiances or phantasmic disturbances. The very walls of the House must reek with hauntings.'

At times she would get so excited by the prospect of calling forth the spirits of the night, that she would leap to her feet and rush to a book with her young still clinging and dangling from her teats.

Gorm's lot saw the thing happening in a very practical way, with mice making ghostly noises, but keeping out of sight. They were going for what Frych would have

319

called 'the poltergeist effect'. The first of these efforts was extremely successful and involved a mouse running the full length of the Welsh dresser's top shelf, while a nudnik was close by, and knocking down every plate displayed on that particular shelf. Since the dishes were balanced on the slant, their bottom edges resting in a groove, they were easily dislodged. They dropped and shattered, bounced and broke, all around the dismayed nudnik.

It was evident to the hidden mice watching that the nudnik was puzzled as to the reason for the phenomena, because it stood there and scratched its head, staring at the devastation. Other nudniks arrived and chittered and chattered, throwing up their hands, walking amongst the broken crockery. While this was going on, a saucepan was pushed from another shelf, behind the nudniks, and fell to the tiles with a loud clatter. Again, the chittering in alarm and the walking around. A broom was then sent toppling over like a felled tree, to crash on the floor behind the nudniks, and cause them further consternation.

After this, the mice retreated, in case one of them was seen and the cause of the disturbance identified. Nudniks were stupid creatures, but they still had *some* brains.

In the library, the Bookeater Tribe had great success with Witless, the senile spaniel. They rushed out, nipped him on the tail, and rushed back to a cranny again. Witless then started shouting obscenities at the corner of the library, where unseen mice were sniggering, causing the old nudnik with Witless to stare at the empty space at which its dog was barking. Once or twice, the nudnik unfolded itself and got up from the desk, to walk to an area of the room and peer with a puzzled expression at . . . nothing.

Finally, the white-haired old creature unfolded itself for the last time and left the library, throwing a worried glance around the room. As it did so, several mice heaved a book off the shelf, sending it crashing to the floor. On the cover of the book was a picture of a nudnik skeleton, grinning skull and all. Witless lolloped across the room, grabbed the book in his teeth, and with wagging tail presented it to his master. The old nudnik's eyes started from its head when it removed the book from the dog's jaws. It took the volume with it and quickly closed the door.

The heroine of the hour, amongst the Invisibles, was Hearallthings, who had the idea of making the Clock strike a peculiar number of times at the wrong hours. Thus when three o'clock arrived, Hearallthings flicked a ratchet twice with her claw and the Great Clock struck five.

At midnight one night when the nudniks were still up, she even got it to strike thirteen, by leaping on the clapper once the regular chimes were over, and producing an extra very loud DOOOOOOOOOONG that reverberated throughout the House. This had the nudniks rushing from the living-room and staring at the Clock with wide and frightened eyes. While they were standing there, Hearallthings stepped on a rachet and made the hands go whizzing round on the face. Then she trod again on the chimer lever and the Clock chimed another five times. Finally, for good measure, she jumped on the release mechanism and the Clock unwound itself with a rattling groan and then was still.

There was great unease amongst the nudniks after that. Lights were left on, on the landing and in the hallway. The Headhunter had his light on all night. The mice were particularly pleased to find that the Headhunter was scared of ghosts. It was the cause of much satisfaction amongst them. Thus encouraged, during the night Fallingoffthings swung on the chain that hung from the cistern in the second toilet, making it rattle and clang against the metal pipes for at least an hour.

The mice considered it significant that no nudnik came to investigate the cause.

SHROPSHIRE BLUE

As the hours passed, the mice became more and more inventive at producing strange noises. Since most of the nudniks in the House were hard of hearing, the noises had to be reasonably loud. Scratching and scraping within the wainscot proved to be a useless exercise. It had to be a full-blown bang or clump, or a series of startling sounds, to grab nudnik attention. The Headhunter of course heard everything, but the Headhunter had little power amongst the nudniks. Terrifying as he was to the mice, he was all but ignored by his own kind.

Hywel-the-bad found that if he clung to the knob on the wireless set, and swayed around enough, the device would switch itself on. He was delighted to find that if it sent forth its incomprehensible blather when no nudnik was in the parlour, the great beasts would come running and stare at the gadget as if it were alive. It was especially rewarding when he managed to switch it back on again immediately after they had turned it off. They shrank from the apparatus with pale faces, sometimes making whimpering noises to each other.

Thorkils Threelegs had not earned a reputation for high intellectual powers during his time in the world, but it was he who discovered that visual arrangements could be just as frightening as strange sounds to the nudniks. One morning there were four letters delivered to the House. Before the nudniks discovered these missives Thorkils had arranged them in a neat row of white rectangles on the hall mat. Gripping each letter by a corner with his teeth, Thorkils dragged the envelopes around until they were as straight as a line of cups on a kitchen shelf. The old nudnik who found them stared first at the letters, then at the letter box, then back at the letters again. Finally it let out a piercing shriek.

Apparently the nudniks didn't like untidy piles sorting themselves out into orderly rows.

'It seems we're winning,' Pedlar said to Treadlightly, in their nest in the attic one hour. 'The nudniks are nervous and ready to bolt. You can tell. The air is full of tension and worry. We'll soon have the House to ourselves.'

'I sometimes wonder if that's going to be a good thing,' said Treadlightly, with a little frown.

Pedlar, who had never experienced anything as exciting as the Great Nudnik Drive, wanted Treadlightly to be as enthusiastic as he was about the whole thing.

'Whatever do you mean?' he asked.

'Well, I'm concerned about Astrid's warning.'

Pedlar nodded. 'No-one has greater respect for Astrid than I have,' said Pedlar, 'despite what they're saying about her and Iban, but even oracles are wrong sometimes . . .'

'What?' cried Treadlightly, suddenly fully awake. 'What about Astrid and Iban?'

Treadlightly had instantly gone high-nose and had knocked her head on the beam that formed the roof of their nest. She seemed not to mind this. Incredibly it was the gossip she was interested in, rather than discussions about the Great Nudnik Drive.

Pedlar looked at his mate quizzically. She was an adorable

mouse and quite irreplaceable in his life, but sometimes he wondered about her level of gravity. He was a bit of a snob about such things. He liked to think they were both a bit above tittle-tattle. In the Hedgerow there had been no time for such decadence as unfounded rumours and he found it difficult to accept the readiness with which mice in the House received idle talk and passed it on. They seemed genuinely excited about such things and his own dear Treadlightly was no exception.

'Tell me, tell me, *tell me*!' his mate was squealing.

Pedlar saw there was no possibility of keeping the information to himself.

'Well, as you know, Iban and Astrid have been, well, seeing each other for some time now, behind Gorm's back . . .'

'Oh, go on, go *on*,' urged Treadlightly.

Pedlar sighed. 'Some does amongst the library mice discovered what was going on and threatened Iban with exposure if he didn't . . .'

'Didn't what?'

'Didn't do the same for them.'

Treadlightly's eyes went wide and round.

'You mean to say that Iban has been with all those frustrated old biddies from the dusty book shelves?'

Pedlar went a little stiff and starchy. 'If you wish to put it that way, yes.'

'Good heavens,' cried Treadlightly. 'The poor mouse! And poor Astrid. Does she know?'

'I, er, I don't think so – she faintly suspects something is wrong but doesn't actually know – and let me add, I don't think we ought to tell her.'

'He's a silly old fool!' snorted Treadlightly. 'If he had any sense he would renounce his celibate Deathshead

324

status, face up to Gorm, and take Astrid into his nest. That's what any sensible buck would do, isn't it?'

'But they're not like ordinary mice, those two,' explained Pedlar. 'I mean, one talks to Shadows and sees visions, and the other follows a god of Darkness and Ignorance, and fails in his faith with every small step he takes. They're just not commonplace rodents, like you and me.'

She nuzzled up to him and licked his whiskers. 'You're not commonplace. You're an extraordinary mouse,' she whispered into his mousey ear.

The practical Pedlar, not at all displeased by her show of fondness, protested, 'Actually, I'm pretty ordinary you know.'

She nuzzled into his warm coat once again. 'Not at all *ordinary*,' she whispered, nipping the furry bit behind his cheek.

LEICESTER

It was while Pedlar and Treadlightly were snuggling up together that the main heroine of the Great Nudnik Drive emerged. Quite by accident she discovered the instrument that was to effect the final retreat of the useless creatures from the House. The Great Clock in the hall had just struck 3 a.m. Hearallthings had been resting inside it, waiting for the chimes that gave her so much pleasure with their vibrations. She stretched and then made her way out of the rosewood clockcase, to the hall below. There she paused and drank in the atmosphere of the small hours. All the nudniks were in bed, asleep, and most mice were up and about.

Hearallthings was of course an Invisible, despite the fact that she spent much of her time in the hall Clock, and so she began to make her way towards the Gwenllian Hole, intending to use the mouse passageways to reach the attic. However, before she could enter the safety of the hole, Spitz appeared on the stairs. She smelled him and turned to run. He either saw or heard her and instantly gave chase.

Hearallthings dashed along the hallway to the parlour door, which was slightly ajar. She ran through the gap as fast as her legs could carry her and then searched frantically with her eyes for a good hiding place. All the cupboards were shut. Spitz entered the room, the blood-lust evident in his eyes. Hearallthings shot across the centre carpet and under the piano stool. Spitz leapt, hitting the stool and sending it skating across the floor. Hearallthings dashed to the piano pedals and by a miracle managed to squeeze between the left pedal and the frame, finding herself inside the instrument.

She scrambled up the innards of the piano, until she found herself amongst the felt-covered hammers. There in her agitation, she ran up and down, causing the hammers to strike the wires. Gradually the vibrations they caused had a calming effect on the mouse and she slowed her pace along the hammers. She could not hear the sounds she was making of course, but she *felt* them, and they were almost as good as the chimes in the Clock.

When she had regained her composure, Hearallthings scampered up to peep over the edge of the piano at the point where its lid was raised. She wanted to see if she could catch a glimpse of Spitz. Like all mice, her eyesight was not good, but she hoped she might be able to notice movement in the moonlit room.

What she saw astounded her.

The room outside the piano was bathed in light. Standing in a semicircle around the piano were all the nudniks, their mouths agape, their eyes starting from their heads. They clutched each other, looking absolutely terrified. They stared at the piano as if it were a live thing, ready to jump on them and swallow them all whole. The piano appeared to be a monster which threatened their existence.

It was then she realized what she had done.

She had created sound without a nudnik sitting at the piano keys. The mice in the House all knew that the piano sent forth sounds – sometimes excruciating sounds, especially when the Headhunter was sitting on the stool and smashing his chubby fingers down on the keyboard – but only ever with a nudnik plonking the white and black oblongs.

Now Hearallthings had found a way of producing those sounds without a nudnik. No wonder they were scared. Perhaps they thought the piano was playing itself? Or even, that a *ghost* was pressing the keys? Hearallthings was delighted. She ran back to the hammers and bounced along them, full of glee. She leapt from minor heights, down on to the deep vibrant notes. She trickled her feet up and down the tinkly ones. She plonked along the middle in Treadlightly style. The tremors went through her body, filling her with a feeling of well-being. This was her great contribution to the cause – greater even than the thirteen chimes on the midnight hour – and she was going to enjoy it, safe from the cats in her piano fortress.

The other mice in the House all heard the piano playing itself, and though the sound was not a tune, it was not discordant either. There was a faint melodic touch in the way the notes ran together. It was as if someone were *searching*

327

for a song, but couldn't quite find it. When they learned it was a mouse who had produced the running sequences of notes, they were all most impressed. Gorm was heard to remark that Hearallthings was superior even to him in her ability to create pleasant sounds, which caused one or two whiskers to twitch. No one had ever heard Gorm utter praise of this kind, especially when it was to the detriment of his own skills.

All that week, at various hours, Hearallthings played the piano from within. On the second night a noticeboard appeared in the garden, with thick red symbols on it. On the fifth night there was feverish packing. On the seventh night the nudniks in the House went out with their suit-cases and climbed into their vehicle. They drove away for good.

The Headhunter was with them.

So were the cats and the dog.

The Great Nudnik Drive was a success.

The House had been left to the mice.

JARLSBERG

'THE VERMIN HAVE BEEN DRIVEN OUT!' WENT UP THE cry, 'The bounteous larder is *ours!*'

Immediately the nudniks had gone there was a great scampering and running, as the cry rang out and mice headed towards the magnificent larder in a body. They tumbled down the stairs, they flowed from holes in the skirting-board, they came in rivers from behind the wainscot. They poured into the kitchen from all directions, through the doors, through holes, out of the lean-to woodshed. Into the glorious larder they went, squeezing under the door, finding the secret passages bored by the kitchen mice when they had owned it.

There was great joy and feasting in the House. Mice scrambled over food cramming themselves, calling to one another in high voices, congratulating everyone, especially themselves, especially Gorm, especially Hearallthings.

Phart and Flegm became so gorged on honey they got drunk on vinegar afterwards, mistaking it for wine.

Gorm-the-old stuffed himself on cold mashed potato, until his eyes rolled in his head, and he flopped over and fell asleep in the dish, grumbling away to himself.

Frych-the-freckled swilled down blancmange by the mouthful, her young ones huddled around her, licking the drips that fell from her matronly whiskers.

Iban and Astrid rolled in some butter, covering their fur, then ate their way furiously into a great towering blackcurrant jelly which collapsed and almost drowned them.

Whispersoft yelled to everyone he saw that the biscuits were terrific and managed to spray crumbs over half his tribe in the process. And Goingdownfast, deciding to give any onlookers a demonstration of his swimming ability in the jug of milk, almost drowned.

Ulf ate a whole garlic clove and wilted anyone who came within breathing distance thereafter.

There were clouds of mustard powder, pepper and salt, flour and bran, filling the atmosphere, causing the tribes to sneeze and gasp for breath. Cornflakes were crunched, underfoot as well as in mouth. Apples were gnawed. Bread was ignored.

However, there were those who ate sparingly, remaining aloof from the general debauched banqueting. I-kucheng and his faithful follower Skrang were among them: they were not the kind to wassail. Nor was Treadlightly. She even cached some of the food near her nest. Iago, the book gourmet, also looked on in disgust, telling his fellow tribesmen that there were nice new magazines and newspapers to be had, in the now catless living-room, and to stop glutting themselves on rich food which would lay them low for eons afterwards.

330

Pedlar was not fashioned of the same stoic material as his mate. To his eternal shame he flung himself on to a desert of sugar and devoured the crunchy sweet sand until he had reduced it to a beach. Thereafter he moaned for an hour as the stuff passed through his system and gave rise to much pain, many words of regret.

There was food for all, of every description, to be eaten in vast quantities, but there was one fare which was still treated with great reverence, eaten only after I-kucheng had blessed and purified the eaters in a small impromptu ceremony, and then only tasted in small amounts.

It was the ambrosia of mice, the provender of the rodent gods, the stuff of dreams: delicious, delightful, delicate CHEESE.

Finally, Kellog arrived, emerging through one of the large holes from the kitchen which had its exit under the meat tray. Mice immediately cleared a space for him. Without a word he strode through the middle of the food, stepping in custard and cake, potato and sausage meat, leaving large clawmarks in his wake. When he came to a huge chunk of cheese and a bowl of cream, he settled down on his fours to eat through both of them. Not a mouse dared ask to share even a morsel of either with him. Goingdownfast, who had been drying off behind a loaf, was hastily smuggled out through a secret passage.

The only words Kellog spoke, with his mouth full at the time, were these:

'When I find you-know-who, I'll break his nasty little neck.'

Thereafter the banquet was conducted in a hushed and not altogether pleasant atmosphere.

331

TORTA SAN GAUDENZIO

Over the hours and nights, Kellog had come to accept Merciful's presence in the attics as inevitable. He had hoped in the beginning that she would find another roost and leave him king of the roof, but when it became evident that this was never going to happen he ceased to be concerned.

Kellog was of course even more wary of Merciful than he was of rhymers, as well he might be, for her kind was the nemesis of all rodents. Her natural prey was mainly insects, with some voles and mice, but Kellog knew she would kill a rat if that opportunity presented itself. In size there was little difference between the two of them: their body lengths were about the same. In ferocity and weapons however, she was the undoubted superior. If it came to a battle between them, there was no question that she would be the winner.

Thus, when she came to the water tank to wash, he stayed deep in his nest, and trembled. He hated being afraid of her, just as he hated not being lord of the attics: she had taken over that position. Once upon a time he had been the only creature to be feared amongst the attic mice. Since she had arrived, he had become the secondary fear, and she the primary.

If he heard the water being used, he would peer out cautiously, just once. Then, if he saw her facial disk, with its piercing eyes, he would duck back inside his nest with his heart beating at twice its normal speed.

The reason he had to look out was because, though he knew the difference between the sound of a mouse drinking and the sound of Merciful washing, Goingdownfast had once or twice simulated the owl's bathing sounds to frighten Kellog. Kellog now risked death looking out of his nest, to make sure it wasn't Goingdownfast tricking him. Even being rhymed to death was preferable to being fooled by that wood mouse he hated so much.

That very morning, Merciful had been to the water tank for a bathe. Kellog had looked out, seen her feathered form, with its vast array of terrible hooks, and then cowered in the back of his nest for the rest of the washing period. He had prayed of course, as he usually did, for the owl to get caught on some projection and drown. It had been known. Owls did like to bathe and they sometimes drowned in attic water-tanks. Kellog wasn't quite sure how this happened, but he wasn't above wishing for it. The Grand Nudnik Drive had seen off the humans and if only something could do the same for Merciful, it would certainly be the cherry on the cake.

While she washed, Merciful made funny chirruping sounds, which might have endeared her to any listening nudniks, but Kellog found them chillingly evil.

Later on, Kellog had another visit, this time from Timorous, to finalize their plans for killing Goingdownfast. The place where the deed was to be carried out had already been agreed upon: it was simply a matter of setting the date and time. Three nights hence, when the dusk was three-quarters grey, Timorous told his accomplice in murder, this would be the time to strike. Agreed, replied Kellog, anxious to have it over and done with, once and for all.

Then Timorous left him to dream: of delicious rotten cheeses full of meaty little maggots; of sacks of flour crawling with weevils; of apples covered in sweet brown bruises.

KÜMMEL

SINCE THE NUDNIKS HAD GONE IT WAS NOT JUST PHART
and Flegm who were carousing. There were drunken
mice all over the House, bickering over trivial things,
being generally foul and obnoxious, and sleeping in the
wrong nests. Some mice, it was true, remained sensible and
level-headed, while a few – here and there – actually wanted
the nudniks back again.

The latter were not organized into any strong body,
but formed twos or threes in corners, who spoke critically
about the judiciousness of driving out the nudniks. They
feared the anarchy that they now saw as its result.

'How *could* we get them back?' one mouse said to Astrid,
who was naturally the most outspoken of those desiring a
return to the old order. 'We can't just go out and say we've
made a mistake and herd them back in again.'

'I don't know what we can do,' she replied, 'but I

know that if they do return, we should settle back down to the way we were, and never again try to interfere with the forces of Nature.'

The forces of Nature. This phrase had a telling effect on the old guard. It encapsulated everything they felt about the situation. The nudniks were *meant* to own the House and the mice were not. It was as simple as that. Mice were not fashioned in the mould of owners. Nudniks were vermin, but they were necessary pests to a stable household.

Even Pedlar was beginning to suspect that the freedom the mice had obtained was not being well handled. Out in the distant Hedgerow they were used to freedom and over the centuries of nights, boundaries had been established, order maintained, by certain sensitivities. There was a tolerance, a forebearance, in the Hedgerow which seemed to be missing in the mouse-run House. Nothing so definite as 'this is my area, that's yours, and if you cross the line you die' existed in the Hedgerow. It was more by tacit agreement, unstated but understood, that harmony was regulated.

Here in the House, where absolutes had ruled and had been wiped out overnight, no new customs and practices had arisen to replace those which had gone.

Now that the nudniks had been driven out and there was food for all, tribal boundaries had all but disappeared. The kitchen was no longer regarded as the territory of the Savage Tribe, nor the library that of the Bookeaters. Mice were beginning to build nests where they pleased, some of them in the living-room and parlour. It was a free-for-all and there were fights for the best nesting places – in the sofa for instance, in the beds – and no-one quite knew what were his or her rights. There was, it seemed, a general breakdown of order.

Pedlar saw in this a potentially very dangerous situation, but he didn't know what to do about it. He didn't think, like Astrid, that the vanquished vermin should be persuaded to return, but he did believe that something should be done about the wilder elements of the house mice.

'Come and see what I've found! Come and see what I've found!' cried an excited young mouse.

The older, mature group of mice were sort of slobbing around the kitchen floor at the time, letting the food digest, allowing the god of lethargy to rule the body for a while. Bellies were propped, skin taut across tummies, their owners feeling bilious and bellicose. The mice were paying a price for overeating. Heads turned towards the unwelcome herald, but clearly they were all far too relaxed to want to move.

'What is it,' growled a truculent Gorm-the-old.

'Come and see!' cried the youngster, too excited to notice that the tribal elders were virtually incapacitated.

'I'll go,' said Pedlar.

'I'll come with you,' Treadlightly said.

Ferocious added, 'Me too.'

No one else seemed inclined to move, so the three of them ambled after the youngster as it led them out of the kitchen and up the stairs.

Pedlar found it strange, being able to wander throughout the House without fearing attack. He half expected to see Eyeball lurking in the shadows, her grey-blue fur melding with the dimness of dark corners. It was going to be a while before any of the mice would be able to go on walkabout without compulsively looking over their shoulders.

Certainly there were still dangers present. Merciful still ruled the rafters and the mice could not afford to underestimate her. Only hours ago a young Invisible, his brain dulled by too much food and drink, had disappeared on his way back to his nest. Whispersoft believed that Merciful was responsible: that the youngster had exposed himself at the wrong time.

There were signs too, that the mighty Kellog was beginning to realize his ambition of being Lord of the House. He swaggered from place to place, bullied anyone he found in his way, and was beginning to attract one or two of the more rebellious youngsters of the 13-K. They saw in Kellog the new master of the universe and, while they were terrified of him, they also recognized in him a chance to make themselves mice to be reckoned with, by becoming his disciples. There were already one or two small gangs beginning to make a nuisance of themselves. One such gang, calling itself the Wreckers, flattered Kellog in his hearing. They jeered at the old and defenceless, seeking his approval.

And now that the House was empty, what was to prevent feral cats from coming into it at will? At the moment it was all securely locked up, but there would come a time when the windows would be broken, or the door rotted, and then Outsiders would enter. Already the place was very cold and damp, the heating having gone off once the nudniks had left.

These thoughts ran through Pedlar's mind as the youngster scampered along the landing to the Headhunter's bedroom.

All the adult mice paused before entering the dreaded room. This place had been a death chamber for so long it still had the ambient stink of a slaughterhouse. Mice had been tortured, maimed and abused in this room, before being murdered and their remains fed to Little Prince. Their yawning skulls still decorated the shelves. Their

337

bleached bones remained scattered over the dressing-table top. Some impaled pelts still decked the cork display board. It was not easy to go boldly marching into a place which still retained an atmosphere of death.

The youngster, who was barely old enough to know what it was all about, scampered inside without hesitation.

Pedlar followed once he had subdued his terror of the place and the others were close on his tail.

They stared at what the youngster had found.

On the floor was the cage of Little Prince, the door left open, with Little Prince still inside. It seemed that the Headhunter had left his pet behind, abandoned him to the tribes, although he had allowed Little Prince a means of escape.

'They left you behind,' said Pedlar, going up to the open cage door. 'They left you to die.'

Little Prince cowered in the back of his cage, not looking at his visitors, but talking to the bars instead.

'No, well, you see, it's best not to go out there. I haven't had my nails clipped for one thing and I look such a sight tonight. Oh dear, how *fat* I've grown lately – look at my big fat tum. I can't seem to get enough sleep these hours, not since I ate all those horrid things that master gave me. Dear, dear, dear, what a dreadful state to get in . . .'

It was pitiful and immediately Pedlar's natural compassion became stronger than his desire for revenge.

'Little Prince?' he said.

'Of course, if master had brushed my pure and lovely white coat with that toothbrush before he left, I would look my best, wouldn't I, and then mice would have to say "Hello, Little Prince, you look nicely groomed tonight. You look as white and clean as cherry-plum blossom. You look as chaste as the first fall of snow." But he didn't, did he?'

338

Little Prince had perpetrated some terrible acts and Pedlar couldn't deny that, but there was something about the white mouse which fortified Pedlar's inherent empathy for all creatures, great and small. It wasn't something which Pedlar could put a name to – possibly just a spark of a feeling – but he sensed something more in the pathetic animal than just cruelty and a barbaric lust for mouse flesh. As much as Little Prince had abused, he had also been abused, reflected the sensitive yellow-neck.

'You've done some bad things, Little Prince,' said Pedlar. 'Some very bad things. You *look* so virtuous and innocent, yet you've been a perfect monster in this House.'

The white mouse stared at him. His gaze was long and steady. His face was devoid of expression.

'I did what I did then,' said Little Prince, suddenly rational. 'There's nothing more to be said, is there?'

With a strong feeling that more than Little Prince's fate was resting on his decision, Pedlar quickly turned to the other two, glad that he was accompanied by Treadlightly and Ferocious.

'What are we going to do with him? We can't hand him over to the tribes. They'll tear him to pieces. It won't be good for them either. Things are already getting way out of hand, without allowing blood-lust to run wild. It might trigger off all sorts of revenge killings. Mice settling old scores and feuds – there'll be things done that mice will regret later.'

'We should tell Gorm about this,' stated the young mouse who had found Little Prince. 'Gorm will know what to do with him.'

'Oh dear,' cried Little Prince, reverting to his little-mouse-lost demeanour. 'I'm sure my whiskers are not in the best condition. Shall I be executed, do you think, for

339

not keeping my whiskers neat and silky? Oh dear, oh dear! Shall I lick them, to make them pretty? What if it were to rain tonight? My poor whiskers would get wet.'

'You're more likely to have them pulled out by the roots,' said the youngster.

Treadlightly, picking up on Pedlar's attitude, went to the youngster and said, 'I don't think we should tell Gorm about this – or anyone else either.'

The youngster blinked and stared up at this doe with the kindly face. 'Why not?' he asked.

'Do you want to see a mouse torn to shreds before your eyes?'

'I don't care,' said the youngster. *He*'s killed lots of mice. *He*'s eaten them. He deserves it!'

'Well, in the first place, I don't think Little Prince has killed a single mouse, though as you say, he's eaten their flesh because he doesn't know any better. It was his master who killed and fed the mice to him. It's possible the Headhunter starved Little Prince in the beginning, so that he would *have* to eat whatever was offered him.'

She pointed to Little Prince, who was still chattering to the bars of his cage, very softly.

She said, 'What I asked you, however, is whether you actually want to see a mouse ripped apart before your eyes.'

The youngster shifted uncomfortably.

Ferocious said, 'Well, that's what will happen. They'll come up here and do it. You'll have to witness it – it will be your doing. I hope you can stand the sight of blood? The cage will be dripping with gore within seconds – guts hanging from the bars, loose eyeballs rolling around the floor, joints torn from sockets . . . you want to see that happen, do you? You want to be responsible for such a scene?'

340

The youngster started to look a little sick. 'Well – no,' he murmured. 'But what will we do with him then?'

'What will we do with the poor little mousie?' echoed Little Prince. 'Shut his cage door then? Or send him into the garden to play? Oh, what will we do with Little Prince? Such a delicate mouse, such a loving son to his mother, such a fragile little fellow – cultured, clean and considerate to his father. Has he a home to go to? Has he a friend in the world? Poor little creature with such a *tragic* past.'

'Shut up, while I try to think,' said Pedlar. 'Look, you, what's your name?'

'Elisedd,' said the young house mouse.

'A Bookeater, eh? Well, Elisedd, I think we're going to have to keep this very, very secret. You look to us to be a responsible mouse, mature for your age. We'll take care of Little Prince and if we're caught we won't implicate you, all right? There's been bloodshed enough in this House – without adding to it. So far as we're concerned, you were never here, all right? We'll have a strict code of silence . . .' he drew a cross over his mouth with his claw, 'and we'll honour it to the death.

'I personally think we *can* trust you. You know what that means? It means I have faith in your loyalty, not to me or to Little Prince, but to yourself. Because I can see in you a deeper kind of mouse beneath the surface: a mouse that believes in a higher justice, to be administered by a higher authority than the living.'

Elisedd gulped and looked up, from face to face.

'I understand,' he said. 'I – I promise to keep this a secret.'

'Good,' said Pedlar, quietly. 'We appreciate this and we won't forget it. I think you're doing the right thing, Elisedd, and if ever you want to talk about this to anyone, if anything worries you, you come and speak to me. All right?'

'All right,' replied Elisedd. 'I'd better go now.'

'Remember,' said Treadlightly. 'Not a word.'

Elisedd left them.

'Now,' said Pedlar, turning to Little Prince. 'What do we do with this white mouse? Smuggle him out into the garden and let him go? He'd be spotted a mile off by any hawk or weasel, wouldn't he? He might as well stand on a hill with his forelimbs wide and shout, "Come and get me." '

'Gardens are beautiful places,' said Little Prince, to the bars of his cage, 'lovely, lovely places, full of nice flowers to eat, nice soft petals to chew. Come with me into the garden, my little friends, and I will show you the green, green grasses . . .'

They ignored him. Treadlightly said, 'You're right. If we turn him loose in the garden, he'll die. He can't survive in the wild. He's a tame mouse. If he doesn't eat something poisonous within a day, something will eat *him*. No matter what he's done, we can't do that. We might as well cast him down the cesspit and leave him to drown.'

'Well, what's our alternative?'

'He'll have to come into our nest for a while,' she said, 'until we can decide what's best.'

'Into our nest?' cried Pedlar. 'Oh, come on Treadlightly!'

'I think that's a very good idea,' intervened Ferocious quickly.

'That's because she didn't say *your* nest,' retorted Pedlar. 'Come to think of it, you live alone—'

'Well, that's settled then,' said Ferocious. 'I'll be off then. Let me know what happens.' And he was gone, through the doorway, along the hall, and down the stairs.

'Oh well,' sighed Pedlar, 'I suppose I'd better make the best of it. Come on then, let's smuggle him up there before the feasting stops in the sublime larder. *You* – are you coming, or not? We're not dragging you, you know, but if you stay here, sooner or later other mice are going to find you, and then it will just be a matter of picking up the pieces.'

Little Prince hopped across his cage, paused at the doorway, and then jumped out. His red-rimmed eyes looked around him in a frightened fashion and then he hopped back inside again, his legs trembling.

'What's the matter with him?' asked Pedlar.

'I think he's been in the cage so long he's afraid of open spaces,' replied Treadlightly.

'Open spaces!' cried Pedlar, who had always regarded the House's rooms as tight, enclosed boxes. 'He should come out to the fields. I'll show him some open spaces.'

'Little Prince doesn't like it,' whispered the white mouse. 'Little Prince wants to stay here.'

Pedlar went into the cage, shot behind Little Prince, and nipped his rump until he ran out of the open door. In this way he drove the tame mouse out on to the landing and into the Skelldulgan Hole at the end of the landing. Once inside the narrow tunnels which led up through the walls to the attics, the white mouse was not so reluctant to be out of his cage. He followed Pedlar meekly, with Treadlightly close behind him. Just before they entered the water-tank attic, Pedlar stopped to view the scene ahead.

'He's going to stand out like a nudnik without its clothes,' grumbled Pedlar, indicating Little Prince's white coat. 'This is the land of the Invisibles and we have a mouse that you can see from ten fields away. What are we going to do with him? Kellog will spot him, if no-one else does, and he won't keep something as strange as this to himself.'

'Let's roll him in the dirt and cobwebs,' replied Tread-lightly. 'If we spit on his coat beforehand, and pee on him, the dirt will stick to him that much easier.'

Little Prince looked horrified and shuddered. '*Dirt?* I'd rather die.'

'All right,' said Pedlar, walking away, 'Die. Merciful will fly in, in a moment, and she'll make very short work of you. You'll be a bit of white fluff catching in her throat before you can say—'

'I'm rolling, look at me, I'm rolling!' cried Little Prince.

They wet his fur as he rolled, and when they had finished a dark thing with two reddish eyes peered back at them. They felt they stood a better chance with him, now.

'I *smell*,' whined Little Prince.

Pedlar grunted. 'A good job too. Kellog would have scented your perfumed fur right across the attic. Tread-lightly's odour he knows – he won't take any notice of that. Nor mine either. I've been here a good time now, and he knows my mark too.'

'You'll never make an Invisible,' said Treadlightly, 'but it's the best we can do for now.'

It was she who led the way out on to the rafters, telling Little Prince to move only when she moved. The way to the nest was fraught with danger of discovery because one or two of the Invisibles had started coming back to their nests. Neither Pedlar nor Treadlightly were sure what Whispersoft would do, if he found Little Prince on his domain, but they had a good idea. Little Prince's reputation had gone before him and he was not loved by the attic mice, any more than he was by the kitchen or the library mice. Whispersoft was a fine leader but he was not above sacrificing a deadly enemy to appease the wrath of his tribe. Little Prince had eaten some of their ancestors, their close relatives, and most of them would not hesitate to tear his throat open.

Finally, they managed to get him inside their nest, and Treadlightly fell into her body-shaped bed of wood shavings and shredded cardboard with relief.

Pedlar went down beside her, leaving Little Prince to find a place somewhere at the back of the nest.

'Why are you doing this?' asked Pedlar of his mate. 'Oh, I know Little Prince would have eaten me, if the Headhunter had managed to cook me, and he ridiculed and taunted me, but I suffered no serious harm. But you – surely he's devoured some of your family – your brothers and sisters, your cousins?'

'I don't like to think about things like that,' answered Treadlightly, 'but anyway, I don't believe it's all Little Prince's fault. He's been turned into a monster by the Headhunter.' She looked grave. 'It was awful the way he seemed to *enjoy* it so much; he took such a delight in taunting other mice. But, well, what would you be like, cooped up in a cage? It would be enough to drive any mouse mad.'

'I know, I know,' sighed Pedlar. 'I've told myself all that too. So, I suppose we'll have to keep him here until we can think of something else. We'll have to smuggle food to him from the ever-full larder. Fortunately that belongs to us mice now . . .'

MÜNSTER

TIMOROUS WAS TREMBLING AS HE MADE HIS WAY across the attic towards Kellog's nest. He slipped in and out of thin shafts of light, keeping down low behind the beams, using the secret paths in the junk jungle: over a pile of rags here, through a rusty pair of bicycle handlebars, under a toy-train bridge. He was wondering why he had decided to do this thing: almost regretting his decision to have a fellow creature assassinated.

There was a great deal of danger involved in the plot and while Timorous presented a careless, violent front to the world, he now felt just as vulnerable as any other wood mouse inside. He had discovered something in himself which he always despised in others: fear.

It was twilight. The attic was particularly silent and devoid of life at this time of the evening, when the sun was going down. It was coming to the time when Merciful woke, shook herself, and went out to hunt. Although the Invisibles were adept at avoiding the flying killer, it was sensible not to be around when she was alert, hungry and restless, her bright yellow eyes burning. She was like some lamp that automatically lit with the going down of the sun and the intensity of her light was awesome to behold.

It was, however, a good time for an assassination, for obvious reasons: there were no witnesses around and the shadows were at their trickiest.

Timorous had asked Goingdownfast to meet him at a certain place in the attic. Now Timorous was on his way to the dreaded Kellog. This was a delicate affair, to be handled with extreme skill, and Timorous was not sure he himself was up to it. His whole body was shaking with fright.

Finally he came to the water tank and slipped into the water. He was not such a good swimmer as Goingdownfast, but like all mice he could hold himself up long enough to get across the lake. As he swam across he could smell the deep musty odour of Kellog, wafting over the surface of the water from the other side. The great roof rat was in his nest, waiting, having heard the small splash of Timorous entering the tank.

Timorous crawled out on the other side, shook the water from his coat, and said softly, 'Are you in there, Kellog?'

Something inside the darkness of the huge nest moved in response.

Timorous trembled anew. Kellog's nest was awe-inspiring to the mice in the attic, standing like a massive keep on the shores of the water tank. It was the home of a giant – a despotic giant – who stole babies and killed wantonly for pleasure. A raven's feather had been woven into the outer framework of the nest and this, to the Invisibles, seemed to symbolize the black heart of the occupant within.

A fresh wave of odour hit Timorous as Kellog appeared at the entrance to his nest. The hard eyes stared. The great whiskers quivered. The large, bare tail flicked.

Timorous regarded the long yellow incisors.

'Well?' said the enormous rat. 'What?'

Timorous's heart sank. 'It's *time* – you remember? – I promised to give you Goingdownfast.'

'Of course I remember,' replied Kellog. 'I wonder that *you* have, you miserable little wretch, what with all this feasting going on in the exalted larder. I must pay it another visit myself soon, after we've disposed of Goingdownfast. It's time to make my stand. Time that I was treated with the respect I deserve from you miserable mice. I shall make my nest in the splendid larder. How would that be? You'd need to gain my favour for a crumb. All that food – but Kellog in the way. You'll need to worship me then, won't you? You'll have to crawl on your bellies before me, whimpering for food, crying out my name. "Kellog! Kellog!" I shall become a deity amongst rodents, a living legend, to be revered and loved – or else.'

'I'm sure – everyone would agree to that,' murmured Timorous.

'I'm sure they'd damn well have to, wouldn't they?' snarled Kellog, 'or I'd bite their damn heads off, wouldn't I?'

'Yes, yes, you would.'

'Lord of the House, eh? No Merciful to interfere with my rule down there, is there? Just you mice, saying, "Yes sir, no sir, bite my rump sir." ' Kellog nodded his great head slowly. 'Speaking of Merciful,' he said. 'Is this a wise time to be going out after that piece of rubbish, Goingdownfast? It's coming on dark.'

'I've chosen this time specially for that reason,' explained Timorous. 'There's no one about. It won't take long, will it? Just a few quick bites and you can be on your way back to this nest. So long as there's no undue noise to attract Merciful's attention. Can you do it without any fuss?'

'You show me the mouse and I'll kill him within a moment,' said Kellog. 'He won't even know what's severed his jugular.'

Timorous shuddered, but then pulled himself together.

'Let's go then, before Goingdownfast gets tired of waiting for me and goes back to his nest. I've arranged to meet him in the agreed spot in order to settle our differences. At least, that's what I've told him, and he believes me. I said I didn't want anyone else around because I was embarrassed by having to apologize to him – something I didn't want to do in public – so that will explain the timing.'

'You're *sure* he'll be there?'

'Certain of it. His mate, Nonsensical, has been urging him to make it up with me. She'll make sure he goes.'

'I hope so – for your sake,' said Kellog, sliding his massive body into the water. 'I'm going to kill a mouse tonight. I want its name to be Goingdownfast, but if I'm disappointed in that, I'll take another. You understand?'

'Yes,' whispered Timorous. 'I understand.' And he dropped into the water and began swimming alongside the roof rat, to the far shore.

They travelled together, the pair of them, across the country of the attics, through the junk jungle. Finally, Timorous indicated he was going to stop. He pointed with his nose at a distant shadow, under a beam, and whispered, 'He's over there, waiting for me. If you crawl

349

along the other side of the beam, he won't see or smell you coming. You'll have to be quiet though.'

'I intend to be,' murmured Kellog, checking the attic air for signs of the owl. 'I shall be as silent as death.'

With these final words, Kellog fixed the position of Goingdownfast with a stare, then dropped down on the far side of the rafter and began crawling along in the triangle of darkness created by the beam. When he got close, he slowed to a painstaking pace, moving by fractions.

The light began to flow rapidly out of the air. Outside, the sun was almost down. Shadows participated in the transformation which would lead to their disappearance. Finally, Kellog settled in the dust. On the other side of the beam was his enemy, Goingdownfast. Kellog could scent the wood mouse now. Goingdownfast would also be able to smell the roof rat and Kellog knew this: he listened for any sounds of escape, knowing also that he could outrun the mouse within a few moments. He imagined Goingdownfast was shaking in terror, now that the odour of rat was in the air and escape impossible.

He's lying there quivering, Kellog told himself, *and wondering why he ever agreed to meet with Timorous.*

There was pure silence in the attic. Nothing seemed to be stirring. It was as if the whole world were waiting for the rat to pounce, to end this blood feud. Every ear listening for the sounds of strangulated cries. Every nose anticipating the smell of death. The moments fled.

Suddenly, there was movement!

'Hi! Over here, owl. Come and get me! Come and get me! I'm waiting for you, owl . . .'

Incredibly, Goingdownfast had leapt on to the top of the beam and was shrieking at the top of his voice.

What was the mad creature doing? Courting death by owl to avoid death by rat?

Kellog felt panic surging through him. He was confused: torn between running away and killing his enemy. There was great peril in remaining – but the wood mouse was only a lunge away. That wood mouse he hated so much. A quick, agonized decision – *he had to kill Goingdownfast himself!* Kellog hunched, tensed himself for a leap, to end this thing now. There was the wood mouse, dancing and yelling shrilly. Kellog glanced once, swiftly, over his shoulder, before springing.

Candlepower! Bright yellow eyes were already travelling through the gloom. Eyes a hundred times more powerful than Kellog's own: eyes that could mark an insect in poor light. Hooks with razor edges, fine needle-fine points – talons and beak – spread and gaped. They flew through the gloaming at lightning-bolt speed.

Kellog's teeth grazed the mouse's skin, drawing blood. But Goingdownfast had been dropping away, down behind the beam, as Kellog struck. The rat's teeth obtained no hold. They failed to sink deeply enough to keep a grip.

Goingdownfast fell into the shadows, Kellog a fraction of a second behind him. The rat's weight soared over the timber. He was exposed in mid-air, a large plump target, halfway through his pounce. There was a soft feathery hiss above him. Kellog felt the claws strike, ripping open his back, laying the flesh bare to his spinal cord.

Kellog suddenly realized exactly what had happened.

'Betrayed!' he screamed, as he spun through the rafters, his body gushing blood.

He lay on his side, his twisted body draining life into the dust, knowing he was going to die, knowing he was the victim of an elaborate plot. They had set him up for the kill, those two damned wood mice, knowing the depth of his hate, knowing he would risk all for the chance to kill his mortal enemy. Kellog's eyes were dimming, his heart pumping fast, his hate still raw. He choked on bile as he waited for the killing stroke.

Merciful hovered, dropped, struck again. This time Kellog's throat was opened. The rat's red thoughts mingled with his pain, until both drifted rapidly away, into oblivion.

The last words he thought he heard were, '*Fie, rat, fie – die, rat, die . . .*' but whether they came from a mouse's tongue, or were merely formed in the mists of his fading brain he never knew.

From his hiding place Goingdownfast could see that Kellog's grip on the world was gone. The eyes stared, glassily. Merciful jabbed rapidly with her beak, opening Kellog's underside to get at the soft lights. A rat was an unusually large kill and cause for triumph. She feasted for a while, the air reeking with the smell of warm gore. Goingdownfast remained part of the shadow, still, unseen. He was after all, an Invisible. When the owl had finished, the corpse was left, torn and bloody, for the maggots to colonize. Merciful flew out, through her hole, into the evening.

Goingdownfast met with Timorous.

'So much for the rat,' said Goingdownfast. 'Whispersoft's plan worked well.'

'The timing was delicate, but as you say, it worked.'

The two mice spoke politely, but coldly to one another. They were not friends. They never could be friends. Their thinking was too much apart. Also, Goingdownfast had the mate Timorous had wanted. This was enough to make them enemies.

The rat had made a mistake, however, in thinking that mice could betray one another. One mouse might hate another, but he would never side with a rat against that mouse. A mouse was a mouse, and a rat an outsider. *I am against my cousin, but my cousin and I are against the stranger*. Goingdownfast and Timorous had been brought together, after the death of Goingdownfast's brother at the jaws of Kellog, in order to assassinate the rat. It was Whispersoft who had laid the plan before them. Gorm had been in on it too. They had each followed the scheme carefully and carried it out efficiently.

Now the pact was at an end. When they left the corpse of Kellog, they went their different ways. Before he went back to his nest, Goingdownfast retrieved the red silk ribbon he had brought with him on his mission and ceremonially draped it over the rat's corpse. It was difficult to see where the scarlet blood left off and the crimson ribbon began. 'Red on red,' whispered Goingdownfast to the lengthening shadows. 'Blood on blood.'

The avenger of Miserable returned to his mate who was waiting anxiously in their nest. Nonsensical came to him as soon as he entered the nest, now built in the bedroom of a doll's house.

'Well?' she said, obviously relieved to see him.

'It's done,' replied her mate.

She saw the blood on his flank. 'You're hurt,' she cried. 'Here, let me lick it.'

'It's nothing,' said Goingdownfast, allowing her to minister to him. 'You should see Kellog's wounds.'

'Is he dead then?'

'Dead as a lump of wood.'

There was no more said of the matter after that.

It was over.

353

FRIESCHE KAAS

After seven nights had passed some male nudniks emerged from an enormous vehicle and came up the path. They were large and muscular-looking. The mice watched them march up to the House, enter, and begin to remove the furniture from the rooms. The forest of wooden legs went from the parlour and the living-room. The carpets were taken up. The lamps disappeared. The pictures came down from the walls. The attics were emptied. The Headhunter's jars containing mice floating in liquid, were shattered on the garden path at the back, their contents left to rot in the weather.

A revered and familiar landmark disappeared when the Great Clock in the hall went too, and the mice lost all sense of time: the rhythms of their existence were turned upside down, inside out. They could be seen rushing to the window to find out if it was light or dark Outside, whether sun or moon. Having no sense of time put them out of sorts, made them moody and irritable, and changed individual personalities overnight.

Not only was the House stripped of furniture, but most of what was left of the food was taken too. Some of it was cast into the dustbin, but a lot went inside the big vehicle. When the nudniks finally left, at the end of the day, the whole House was like the giant snail shell it had once been.

The mice were stunned, but rallied very quickly, knowing that the munificent larder would never allow itself to remain empty for long.

They didn't care so much about the furniture, though they preferred things to run over and burrow through. In the attics, many nests had gone with the departed junk, but nests could be rebuilt. The bleakness of the atticscape, transformed from mountains to flatlands in a day, was a little difficult on the soul, gave mice a frightening feeling of vast emptiness, but that might be overcome with time. Even the departing of the Great Clock was a calamity that could be conquered with strength of will. The loss of the food would have been a catastrophe, if the copious larder were to remain bare, but of course that was not possible.

Some secretly doubted the *immediate* renewal of contents: they believed in a waiting period.

It was possible, they whispered, that the seven fat days might be followed by seven lean days.

Astrid informed everyone openly that the days of plenty were over *for ever* and the days of want were nigh.

'You watch,' said Gorm, optimistically. 'It won't be long before the shelves fill up again.'

They sat and mooched around the kitchen, watching the empty larder, waiting for the food to appear. There were knots of mice around the larder door. There were rings of mice on the shelves, staring at the emptiness, waiting for the miracle to happen. There were lone mice, who sent up prayers to the gods of cornucopia, or to the one great Creator, for the marvellous resurrection of the one true larder.

GLUX

Yellow-necks, being the largest mice in the House, needed more food than the wood or house mice. However, yellow-necks tend to be less demanding on the whole: they have a

355

pleasant and amiable disposition. They are a species who have come to terms with life and its vagaries, and when things take a bad turn, they twitch their whiskers, flick their tails and set about making the best of it. This is probably why yellow-necks were more suited to a Deathshead existence. They had a sound philosophy to begin with, which could be built upon during their wandering priesthood hours.

I-kucheng was a mouse respected by several other mice, here and there. Skrang, for one, and the odd one or two mice who were satisfied with the judgements he had handed out when they had taken their disputes to him. These tended to be few in number.

However, amongst the Deathshead, he was revered. It was he who had refined the martial art of Ik-to, to pure, defensive combat. If Deathshead mice followed the techniques developed by I-kucheng, then no permanent injuries resulted. He was known also to practise the art of self-obliteration, the removal of *self*. His greatest sorrow was that his pupil, Iban, had decided to follow Yo, the god of Darkness and Ignorance, and the obliteration of *memory*, rather than self.

Now I-kucheng was on his deathbed in the Rajang Hole; his faithful warrior-priestess and Deathshead in her own right, Skrang, sat by him and watched and regretted his fading from the world. Outside the hole, now no longer secret in a House without furniture to hide it, many mice kept vigil. Most of them were there to make sure he actually *went*.

'Skrang,' croaked I-kucheng, lying on his back in his last moments and staring at the ceiling. 'This is a triumph, you understand. Death is a triumph, not a failure.'

'Yes,' she whispered. 'I know. Do you have anything to

356

confess. Some sin perhaps, from your youth? You should get it out of the way now, before you begin the journey.'

She herself could not think of anything: not since she had known him and become his guardian.

'I hate the wallpaper in this room.'

'Pardon?' said Skrang, caught unawares.

'The wallpaper – fussy little roses. I hate it,' admitted I-kucheng. 'There, I've made my deathbed confession.'

'Is that it?' said Skrang.

'Isn't that terrible enough? To hate something that nudniks consider a work of art? I saw it go up, with nudniks all busy-busy, using brushes and paste – tasted *awful* that paste, and I'm allowed to say that because I wasn't a Deathshead then. I've hated the wallpaper all this time, but I suppressed the feeling until now.'

'Unn will forgive you your transgressions . . .' droned Skrang.

At that moment there was a cry from within the crowd around the hole, *'Hurry up and get on with it!'* someone yelled.

'What was that?' whispered I-kucheng. 'One of the faith-ful?'

'Nothing,' replied Skrang. 'Someone – er – someone heard you say death was a triumph – and they yelled encouragement.'

I-kucheng frowned. 'Not a *bawdy* triumph – a solemn one . . .'

'Right – I'll stop any further cheers.'

But, as it happened, she had no need to do so for I-kucheng had breathed his last and the last true Deathshead was gone.

When Skrang duly informed the crowd there was a quick file-past the body, but little emotion except from

357

a perceptive few who knew the end of an era when they saw one.

Skrang herself was comforted by the thought that the dead mouse lived on through others, through the influences he or she had left behind in living mice. She believed that a bit of us rubs off on to everyone we come into contact with, even if it is just a single brief meeting, perhaps to ask the way to the nearest piece of cheese. That indefinable smudge of our personality, on each individual, is what is left behind of us when we go to the Otherworld. Sometimes the smudge is great, where the living mouse is a good friend or relative, sometimes it is minuscule. It doesn't matter. The dead live on in the living: still part of the great, sprawling mass of mice that inhabit the world.

VESTGÖTAÖST

THERE WAS A GREAT FAMINE IN THE HOUSE.
These were the worst hours in the history of the
tribes. In fact the word 'tribe' meant nothing any
more. There was no sense of unity, of brother and sister-
hood: no sense of *belonging* to a particular group. There
were still some couples who watched out for each other,
but in most cases it was every mouse for him- or herself
and starvation get the hindmost.

Certainly no-one could remember a more desperate
time from their own yesterhours. Not only was there not
unlimited cheese, there was no cheese at all. Almost every
mouse was on the edge of starvation and madness.

The rhythms of the House had fallen into discord.
The mice were out of tune with the House and the
House had never been regulated by the Earth, so the
spiral of disharmony became a vortex from which it

seemed nothing could extract them.

Astrid's prediction had come true, but no-one felt much like congratulating her, and to her credit she never said 'I told you so'.

Even the larder had fallen from grace. It was no longer celestial, no longer divine, no longer bounteous: it was a neglected place, with no hallowed platters of meat, no breadbin choc-a-bloc with crusts, no full marble slabs, no crammed cooling slate. It was so empty it echoed. It was so empty that even the ants had gone. It was a failed temple, where miracles no longer happened.

The mice slipped into a period of misery. There were fights for scraps. Some went out into the garden (much to the delight of Stone) and foraged for food there. However, they were in competition with the harvest mice, voles, shrews and other wildlife, and didn't fare much better than those that remained in the House.

Iago, who all his life had advocated the eating of books, was caught chewing electrical flex, not for sabotage because of course the Revolution was over, but for *food*.

'You'll kill yourself,' remarked Whispersoft. 'That rubber will clog your bowels and you'll die in agony.'

'I'm addicted to it,' confessed Iago hollowly. 'I gnawed so much of it during the Great Nudnik Drive, I got a taste for it. I can't help it. All the books are gone. If there was some food in the larder I could probably break the habit, but . . .'

Two hours later Iago was in a dreadful state, rolling on the floorboards in great pain. He managed by some miracle to survive the next twenty-four hours, however, and vowed he would never again touch electrical flex. Some time after that he was back at it, nibbling tiny pieces of rubber, making himself marginally ill every few hours.

Thereafter he became a mouse who haunted dark corners, growing more sullen, ignoring attempts to steer him back to being the affable mouse he once was.

Ferocious, always that fair-minded and most honest of fellows, found a hoard of nuts near the opening to Tunneller's maze. Some squirrel had obviously cached and forgotten them. He told no-one of his discovery and it was only when Tunneller herself, after receiving his toll in nuts, revealed her suspicions to others in the House, that he was found out. Immediately there was a general descent and free-for-all which spread to the harvest mice in the garden and finally resulted in the complete sacking and pillaging of the nut store. Ferocious was savagely bitten, and savagely retaliated, in the scrummage.

These incidents, and many others, were typical of the anarchy that had spread as a result of the Great Nudnik Drive.

The House was like a great tomb, its larder an empty vault, echoing with the cries of hungry mice. They gnawed at the floorboards, they ate their own nests, and if they were fast eaters and finished first – they ate the nests of others too. There were stories of unspeakable acts, to do with the Headhunter's shattered bottles and their preserved remains of mouse ancestors, which were too terrible even to enter the annals of mouse history. The tribes became drifting ghosts, their frames thin and wasted, their ribs prominent. The House seemed uncaring of their plight. It was a cold, dead thing.

There was a sudden revival of the greeting, 'Eight', no longer used only by pretentious library mice. This was since whiskers (along with fur) had begun to fall out due to malnutrition. Proud mice wished others to know that they had their full set of whiskers and that even in their

361

poverty they were still respectable creatures.

Surprisingly, and suspiciously, Phart and Flegm still remained round-bellied. It was not just their corpulence that aroused suspicion however, but their lack of complaint. When challenged by Thorkils Threelegs, Phart cried, 'We've distended stomicks, ain't we? I mean, we're as hungry as everyone else. Worse, in fact. 'Cept me and Flegm 'ere take things in our stride. We don't sweat and whine. Stokes, that's what we are . . .'

'Stokes?' growled Thorkils. 'What the devil is that?'

'We're stoke-ical,' explained Flegm. 'Ain't you never heard of that? Means we put up with things, don't it?'

'Is that a fact?' snarled Thorkils. 'Well, since you haven't got two crumbs to rub together, we'll just pay you a little visit in that cellar of yours, to see if we can help you out. I hate to think of two of our fellow mice on the verge of death.'

'No, that's not necessary,' said Phart quickly, 'we'll just bear our burden, stoke-ically, and not bother you other mice with our troubles, eh?'

'No trouble,' promised Thorkils Threelegs. 'No trouble at all.'

The Savages and the 13-K searched the cellar systematically and discovered the sack of potatoes in an empty wine barrel. When Gorm and his wrecking crew found it, they approached Phart and Flegm who denied all knowledge.

'Spuds in our very own cellar, and 'ere we are, starvin' our guts out!'

Pedlar was dispirited by such disintegration among mice. He contemplated abandoning the House and spoke to Treadlightly about it, but though she said she was tempted,

362

she foresaw the winter coming on.

'I've never lived out in the cold,' she said. 'I haven't known a winter because I was born in the spring, but I can feel the coldness in the air. Even though the heating isn't on any longer, the House is still warmer than Outside. I'm sorry, I know I sound a softy.'

Pedlar said that was all right, he preferred to stay in the House anyway, which wasn't true. In fact he yearned to be in his Hedgerow. He was now 290 nights old – middle-aged – and he felt he wanted to get back to his roots. Having survived most of one winter in the Hedgerow, he knew he could get through another, especially since he was now worldly-wise. However, the idea of parting from Treadlightly at this time, leaving her to an unpleasant fate, was unthinkable. There were many mice who would have sneered at this, not being especially faithful to one mate, but one or two bucks like Pedlar preferred to stay with one doe. It was not a life-long commitment for mice are not pigeons, faithful to one partner unto death, but some did prefer a little steadiness.

So Pedlar remained in the House, going hungry along with the rest of them, and was respected for it. He was an Outsider, yes, and would always be one, but he was an acceptable Outsider, one who was willing to go through thick and thin with the rest of the residents.

During this period of darkness, Pedlar and Treadlightly did not only have themselves to feed – difficult enough – but also the creature they were hiding. Little Prince was not especially grateful for any food they brought him either, and in fact complained bitterly that he was having to put up with inferior nourishment and little of it. Neither Pedlar nor Treadlightly felt inclined to argue. They hadn't the energy for it. Treadlightly was of the opinion that Little

363

Prince would never change, though Pedlar hoped otherwise. For now, though, it seemed Little Prince had used up any reserves of finer feeling with one or two thank yous in the beginning. As time went on, he just became obstinate, sulky and completely thoughtless.

There were times when discovery seemed to be unavoidable.

One hour Treadlightly, Pedlar and Little Prince were gnawing on a piece of crab apple. Little Prince was grumbling as usual.

'This tastes like wet cardboard. Horrible! After that lovely food Little Prince used to get. Not the *flesh* – Little Prince isn't trying to upset anybody – but the nice titbits and sweeties I used to be given. Why did you save me? I'd have been better off being killed by the tribes.'

'That can still be arranged,' said Pedlar. 'I'll go and fetch Whispersoft.'

He pretended to go to the exit hole, but Little Prince cried, 'Yes, you would, wouldn't you? You've always hated me!' He whined, 'Nobody knows how unhappy I am . . .'

'You'll be *dead* unhappy, in a moment,' muttered Treadlightly. 'Come here, Pedlar. Eat some more of the apple before this greedy-guts scoffs the lot.'

But at that moment there was a caller at the door. It was a lean and haggard-looking Ulf, son-of-Gorm. The leader of the youthful rebels did not even pause in the entrance, but just blundered in. He sat high-nose on the threshold, making the light within dim.

'Hope I'm not interrupting?' he said, his voice sounding shallow and wasted.

Little Prince melted into the shadows at the back of the nest. He was still in the same filthy state he had acquired when they first entered the attic. His little red-rimmed eyes

364

were possibly the only feature which might give him away. Certainly he was thinner, his cheeks hollow, his ribs like the ripples on the surface of the water tank.

'No, no,' replied Pedlar, his heart racing a little. 'Not at all, Ulf. What can I do for you?'

'I just wondered if you might tell me where you found the apple, on the off chance there might be another one. I've searched high and low for food tonight and Drenchie's done the same. We haven't a crumb between us.'

'Sure – look, if you take a northerly direction from the privy, you'll come to the garden wall. There's a crab-apple tree overhanging the wall, from the spinney beyond. If you sort of scrabble around at the base of the wall—'

'Hello,' cried Ulf. 'Who's that in the back of your nest – I don't know you, do I?'

Little Prince crouched low-nose in the shadows and was silent. Treadlightly said nothing. Pedlar *wanted* to say something, but the words stuck in his throat. Ulf remained speechless too, apparently waiting for the mouse at the back of the nest to say something. Time dragged on for several long moments. Finally when the quiet became unbearable Little Prince edged forward a fraction, went half high-nose. Pedlar swallowed hard and closed his eyes.

Then he heard Little Prince say incomprehensibly, '*Kon-nichi wa! Goschiso-sama deshta, totemo oish kat-ta dess. Chiz-keki, mmmmmmm!*'

'Pardon?' said Ulf, blinking.

'*Hajime-mashte, dozo yoroshku!*' cried Little Prince, and added a little chuckle at the end, as if he was appreciating some joke that Ulf had just told him.

Ulf frowned and turned to Pedlar.

'Who *is* this? What's he saying? That's *Canidae* language,

365

isn't it? The language of the dogs and foxes?'

'Ah, yeeees,' murmured Pedlar. 'He appeared to be lost, so we took him in. I – er – found him in the garden. From what I can gather he was – ah – trapped in one of those crates the furniture was packed in, when the nudniks came to collect it all. Must have been a crate from a far-off place! Doesn't speak a word of *Rondentae*, poor fellow. Reason being, near as I can fathom, he was – er – he ate some strange books.'

Ulf was peering into the dimness at the back of the nest. 'Must have been strange to make him forget his mother tongue!'

'Yes,' said Pedlar, warming to his subject. 'He's even got a canid name. Eh-he, he calls himself.'

Ulf turned to Little Prince. 'Er – *sugoi*!' He turned back to Pedlar, 'Only dog word I know,' he confessed. 'It means welcome or good, or something.'

'*At-chi e it-te, Shukurim,*' cried Little Prince, as if delighted.

Ulf continued to stare at the mouse in the back. 'Funny-looking fellow, isn't he? What's the matter with his coat?'

'He's got – er – scurvy,' said Pedlar. 'Lack of vegetables and fruit while he was in the crate. It discolours one's pelt, you know.'

Ulf seemed reluctant to leave. 'Well, I suppose I'd better get off. See if I can find one of those crab apples, before I get *scurvy* too. I'll see you later.'

'*Sayonara!*' sang Little Prince.

Once he had gone, Treadlightly turned to the two males.

'Between you, you've managed to make up a story that will have every mouse in the House around here within the hour! Are you bonkers, or what? Couldn't you at least have made up a plain tale which would bore the skin off everyone? Instead, we have the most exotic episode since a water vole wandered in here from the well outside and told everyone she was a pygmy coypu.'

Little Prince said, 'Don't be angry with Little Prince – he panicked.'

'What did all that mean anyway?' asked Pedlar. 'All that mumbo jumbo? Was it really *Canidae*?'

'I learned it from Witless,' said Little Prince proudly, 'before he went doolally in his old age. When Ulf said, "Welcome", I said, "Get lost, cream puff!" '

'You didn't?' cried Pedlar, delighted.

'Yes, I did,' crowed Little Prince.

Treadlightly interrupted them, 'You say you knew Witless when he wasn't senile. How old are you then?'

'Little Prince is one thousand and twenty-five nights old next birthnight.'

'Over a thousand nights old?' cried Pedlar. 'Surely that's not possible, mice only live for five hundred nights – six hundred at the most. You don't look even that.'

'Tame mice live longer than wild ones,' said Little Prince proudly. 'You rough wild creatures all die like mayflies. Tame mice have been known to live two and a half thousand nights. Why, look at Ulug Beg . . .'

'Ulug Beg is a tame mouse?' cried Treadlightly, amazed at these revelations.

'Ulug Beg is my mother,' murmured Little Prince.

There was stunned silence in the nest for a moment, before Treadlightly and Pedlar recovered.

'I thought he – she – I thought Ulug Beg was a buck?' said Pedlar.

'She likes a little mystery,' replied Little Prince. 'My mother escaped some one and half thousand nights ago.'

Pedlar said, 'But he's – she's not *white* like you. She's a sort of dark-dirty-grey mottled colour.'

'So am I at the moment,' murmured Little Prince.

This took only a few moments to sink in and then Pedlar twitched his whiskers and flicked his tail.

'I see what you mean. She's become permanently filthy and stained from being out in the open, amongst the dirty leaves, for so long. This is some eye-opener, Little Prince, I hope you're not lying.'

Little Prince looked shocked.

Treadlightly said, 'I suggest we keep this to ourselves. Gorm would have a fit if he knew he had taken advice from a tame female mouse!'

'I agree,' said Pedlar. 'Ulug Beg – herself – wouldn't want it spread around the House. She prefers to be thought of as some mythical creature older than the Ancient of Days. I suggest we honour her desire to leave the truth undisclosed.'

'Lovely speech,' murmured Little Prince, returning to the back of the nest where he curled up and fell asleep.

Pedlar felt that ever since they had discovered Little Prince abandoned in his cage, something or someone had been nagging at him to keep the white mouse alive. He wondered if it was his ancestral voices trying to reach him again? Trying to convince him that Little Prince had some use, and that use would be needed by the mice one hour? All Pedlar knew was that he had to keep Little Prince from falling into the claws of others.

Treadlightly, however, warned Pedlar that there would be trouble ahead.

True enough, within the hour there were half a dozen mice around the nest, enquiring about the 'stranger' of whom they had heard. They wanted to meet him but

368

Treadlightly told them there was nothing doing. 'He's very ill,' she told them, 'with – er – scurvy. We're not sure that it isn't catching. We don't want to start a plague, do we?'

The crowd's curiosity seemed to wither after this remark and they hastily shrank away from the entrance to the nest.

Later, Treadlightly regretted starting the story about the plague, because the leaders of the tribes called an inter-tribal Allthing and announced that if the stranger had a catching illness, he ought to be cast out, into the wilderness, and probably Pedlar and Treadlightly with him, because they would be bound to have caught it by now. It took all of Pedlar's oratorical skills to convince the leaders that he and Treadlightly were only being *extra* cautious, that they were sure the stranger *hadn't* got the plague, but it was better to be over-safe than very-sorry.

This was accepted after a lot of argument, but with reservations. Gorm-the-old ordered that Treadlightly, Pedlar and the stranger Eh-he were not to go anywhere near the young of other mice, until the stranger's condition had improved.

'And you can keep him away from me too,' growled Gorm.

Pedlar confidently assured Gorm that Eh-he would come nowhere near him.

After the Allthing, tribal curiosity in the stranger died a natural death. Pedlar and Treadlightly's nest was no longer besieged. They were able to get on with life in peace.

And a miserable life it was throughout the House. Mice were now reduced to eating chalk and plaster from the walls, glue from the fittings, pieces of matting, sacking and lino, and – when they could find it – old bits of soap from the bathrooms. Food became an obsession, giving rise to strange dreams of animated vegetables, walking chunks of cheese, slithering sausages. There were several deaths, especially amongst the young. It was a time of nightmares, a terrible holocaust. Mice began to lay blame for the catastrophe, but never at the right door. They picked on unpopular mice, rather than Gorm and the other leaders, to berate and attack.

In the search for scapegoats, there were many instances when even members of the same tribe would accuse one another.

'Why didn't you stop me,' roared Gorm to Ketil. 'Why didn't you tell me the plan was stupid?'

'It's all Astrid's fault,' Ketil cried in defence. 'She's the one who should have stopped you – *she knew*. We didn't.'

Mice were frightened to walk the boards of the House alone, for fear of being attacked by fellow mice.

Happinessandlight, of the old Invisibles, was scrabbling around Merciful's hole one night when he was pushed by an unknown assailant. He fell to the ground outside and fortunately landed in a rose bush, escaping serious injury.

Mefyn and Nesta of the Bookeaters were accused of being cat-worshippers by some of the old Savages.

'We caught them in a corner,' cried Elfwin, '*meowing*.'

Gytha Finewhiskers said, 'It was probably their black magic that caused the larder to become empty. We ought to bite them to death. We ought to—'

'Yes,' shrieked Highstander, of the old 13-K. 'They've been conjuring up cats disguised as *beetles*. Have you noticed how the numbers of beetles have increased? That's because they're not beetles at all, but cats! Kill the dirty cat-worshippers. Smash them dead!'

'We were only discussing where next to search for food,' complained Nesta. 'We weren't meowing at all.'

370

'Liars!' cried the gathered rabble, moving in on them as one.

'Stop!' pleaded Pedlar, trying to get some order back into the scene. 'The beetles have increased because there're no nudniks to keep them down—'

'Hurt him too!' cried some of the crowd. 'Hurt the interfering Outsider!'

It was, surprisingly, the filthy mouse Eh-he, from the nest of Pedlar and Treadlightly, who saved Nesta and Mefyn from being slaughtered by the mob.

'Let those who have never wished to be a cat themselves, take the first bite,' he called in sweet, clear tones.

This stopped them. There was not a mouse amongst them who had not, at one time, dreamed of being a cat and ruling the world. All had, in their secret moments, wanted to be big and immensely strong, armed with long fangs and crescent claws.

'I thought you only spoke dog,' accused Ulf, pointing to Little Prince.

'He does – normally,' Treadlightly said, stepping in 'He has these – these bouts of lucidity when he can remember the rodent language.'

They all stared at the dirty creature.

Little Prince stepped forward.

'I have never wished to be a cat,' he said, 'so I shall take the first bite.'

He nipped the two offenders smartly on their rumps. Mefyn and Nesta howled. The mob roared in approval.

'You've really never wanted to be a cat?' cried Ulf, to the mouse he knew as Eh-he.

'Well,' said Little Prince, cocking his head coyly to one side, 'only a *little* cat.'

There was another roar and mouse began talking to

mouse about this strange newcomer and his clever remarks. While this was going on Mefyn and Nesta were encouraged to creep away by Pedlar. Shortly afterwards, Little Prince was hustled back to the half-eaten nest in the attic.

'That was a *good* thing you did back there,' said Pedlar to him. 'You put yourself at risk for others.'

'I must have been crazy,' Little Prince replied. 'I was just repeating something from an old parable told to me by my mother Ulug Beg.'

'Crazy – but good,' said Pedlar, nodding.

The troubles however, continued. Even leaders did not escape completely. On the night of the full moon there was a riot. It started somewhere in the lean-to woodshed and spread quickly throughout the kitchen and library, then up into the attics. Hollow-eyed mice went on the rampage, destroying nests, attacking anyone who would not join them. Gorm-the-old and Skuli were caught in the open kitchen and had to fight for their lives. Each gave an excellent account of himself, despite vastly superior numbers, and sent one or two rioters away with bleeding wounds.

Property damage was enormous, there were one or two more deaths, and many mice fled the House for good, including Gorm's one remaining brother-double, Tostig. Pedlar, Treadlightly and Little Prince were fortunately not in the House at the time of the riot, but searching for crab apples at the end of the garden. They heard about it when they returned to the attic, to find what remained of their nest in tatters. There had been looting and a few bits of their nest material had been stolen. Some sawdust, found in an old stuffed toy and used to cover the floor of the nest, had been eaten in mistake for cereals. Somewhere in the House a mouse was doubled-up with stomach cramps and Pedlar thought it served it right.

Principal offenders amongst the rioters were the cellar mice, Phart and Flegm, who quickly became the chief inciters to violence and wanton destruction. Their ranting and raving had initially stirred to action the youngsters in the lean-to, and then they had headed the great surge of mice that rolled like a wave throughout the ground floor.

'Kill, maim, torture!' Phart had screamed. 'Destroy, loot, rape!'

Later, Phart was to deny these chants, saying it was someone in the crowd imitating his voice. So the two reprobates got away with it once more.

The riot had frightened everyone, including the rioters themselves. It showed how normally disciplined ordinary mice could go out of their heads and on the rampage simply because they were starving. When things had cooled down, the majority of the rioters were ashamed of themselves. They viewed the mess they had caused – which included a lot of their own nests too – and were contrite.

It'll never happen again, they told each other.

Pedlar, Treadlightly and Little Prince set about rebuilding their attic nest, with Little Prince moaning about how his muscles ached and how he needed more fuel for his energy banks if he was going to do hard labour for the rest of his natural life.

The mice thought if they were *good* the larder would once more be favoured by the gods of cornucopia and their prayers for food answered.

This was not to be.

WALNUT CRÉDIOUX

THE GARDEN REMAINED WHERE IT WAS ONLY BECAUSE winter was approaching. Astrid informed the tribes that once the spring came again, the garden would enter the House. Since her credibility had returned, with the ever-empty larder testifying to her old claims of being a visionary, mice listened to her.

'Nature wishes to reclaim this House, and the House wishes to go back to Nature,' she said. 'The process is inevitable. The bricks will crumble, the concrete will crack apart under the terrible force of weeds, and vines will crush the rotting wood. The inside will become the outside, and once the roof blows away in the gales, fieldmice will enter the House and occupy our holes. We are no longer welcome here . . .'

'No longer welcome?' said Phart to Flegm. 'Who would want to be? I need a nice comfy warm House, I do – nudniks and all if it has to be that way. Naychur? You can keep it! We're civilized house mice, we are – not ruddy primitives.'

One night Gorm-the-old called an inter-tribal Allthing in the cupboard-under and every mouse was invited, from the smallest and most insignificant, to important mice like Frych-the-freckled, Whispersoft and Gorm-the-old himself. Pedlar was there at Gorm's express wish; tribal survival was at stake and Gorm was prepared to acknowledge anyone or anything that could save the hour.

Even Little Prince was there, in his disguise as the mouse Eh-he. No-one was turned away. This concerned the whole future of the House-mouse nation.

Despite the fact that the tribes had been trimmed, there was still quite a crowd in the cupboard-under. They jostled against one another and trod on each other's tails until Gorm opened the meeting.

'You all know why we're here,' he rumbled. 'It's time to make a decision and we'd better make it quick. A feral cat's been spotted prowling around the House. Where there's one, more will follow. I repeat, we've got to do something and we've got to do it now. I'll hand you over to Gunhild.'

Gunhild went to the centre of the circle.

'Listen up, chaps,' she said briskly. 'As Gorm said, it's time to make a decision. I like decisions – nice clean things, decisions. No faffing about, just a sharp yes or no—'

'Get on with it then,' groaned someone in the crowd.

'Right. Understood. Need a quick decision.'

She began pacing up and down, her tail swishing just one centimetre to the left, then one centimetre to the right. Her whiskers, all trimmed to the same length, were starched stiff as needles having been dipped purposely in wallpaper paste. Her hind legs kept exact pace with her forelegs – she was like two small nudniks in marching order.

'Thing is this, chaps,' she said. 'I've been ordered – requested that is – to get you into shape for a long march. *The* long march. We have to find new quarters – our old barracks have been transformed into a pigsty. You can't even hold a decent parade without skidding on some polished surface. So we have to smarten ourselves up, get a bit of discipline into our lines, and tackle the organized retreat. I don't want a shambles. We have to leave in good order. Is that understood? Speak up, chaps.'

There was complete silence for a few moments, then someone, it must have been a library mouse, shouted, 'Will someone please tell us what in Dickens' name she's talking about?'

Skrang stepped into the circle. 'We have to leave the House,' she said, 'is everyone ready to do so?'

'Why didn't she say so?' grumbled the same voice. 'Well I'm ready. The sooner the better.'

Gorm cried, 'Understand this. It's coming on winter out there. We've got to find another house, which won't be easy. There'll be hostile tribes to encounter. Mice will die. But I promise you we'll find some unoccupied territory, somewhere – a house where we can settle down once more and get some good old-fashioned wars going—' he smirked. 'A few raids on each other, just like the old days. I can't remember when I last yelled "Assundoon" down the hallway.'

'I can remember when you last sank your teeth into my butt,' yelled someone at the back. 'I haven't forgotten that – I owe you one.'

'If that's you, Ulf,' growled Gorm, 'you'll get your chance, son, don't worry. There's still some fight left in the old mouse yet.'

'Who's going to lead us?' cried Rhodri. 'Who's going to be the pathfinder?'

'I am of course,' rumbled Gorm. 'Who else?'

There was silence again, before Astrid stepped forward.

'Not you Gorm, I'm sorry. You might be a fine old warrior – no-one would dispute that – but you're no navigator of the wilderness. You know nothing about the Outside world. We need someone with knowledge if we're to make the journey to the promised house safely.'

'If I say I'm leading, I am, you worn-out harlot!' snarled Gorm. 'What's a strumpet like you telling *me* what to do?'

'Won't wash, Gorm,' said the loud voice of Whispersoft. 'She's right.'

Frych said, 'The female's status is thus – she may have exceeded the bounds of propriety recently, with her liaisons in dark corners – but she is still the high priestess. Her prophecies have always come true. She has the special favours of the Shadows and the gods, and her utterances have to be taken as genuinely serious prognostications. We require a leader who can guide us through perilous straits to an unknown destination – I myself propose Pedlar, the yellow-necked Outsider.'

Astrid closed her eyes then opened them.

'Pedlar is the chosen one!' she cried. 'I have seen it!'

'Damn Shadow-talking trollop,' cried Gorm. 'Will I be thrust aside like this? Like hell!'

Ulf stepped forward. 'This involves the whole mouse nation, not just the Savages. For once you'll do as you're told Father Gorm. Pedlar is the right mouse to lead us – if he agrees. I can't think of a better one. He's honest and straightforward. He has courage and resourcefulness. And most important of all – he knows what it's like out there.'

377

'I tell you—' snarled Gorm, making the nearest mice to him back away rapidly.

'You want to fight the whole nation?' said Ulf.

'If need be!' cried the old warrior, vehemently regretting his invitation to Pedlar to join the meeting.

'Step down,' shouted several mice in the crowd. 'You're making yourself look a fool.'

'AM I, BY DAMN!' roared Gorm. 'I'll—'

He was immediately ringed by a dozen tough mice from all tribes, including his own.

One of them was, astoundingly, Phart.

'Look,' cried Phart. 'You ain't goin' to ruin this for us, Gorm, with all yer bluster. We've gotta get out of this place. It's killin' us – and you ain't the mouse to do it. Pedlar is. I hate the self-righteous bleeder as much as you do, but he's the one Gorm, like it or lump it.'

Gorm stared around him, seeing Gytha Finewhiskers and Elfwin, members of his very own tribe threatening him, and knew he had no chance.

'I won't forget this,' he snarled. 'Once the march is over – I'll have that Pedlar for breakfast.'

Pedlar came forward to acknowledge his destiny. *You are the One who will walk with the many*.

But just as he did so, there was an almighty shriek from Gorm. 'ASSUNDOON!'

The leader of the Savages then launched himself at Pedlar, who quickly leapt out of the way.

The crowd scattered, forming a huge space for the two combatants.

Gorm was clearly angry that his first pounce should have missed. He began by hunching his back to make himself look bigger. Then he drummed his tail on the ground and stamped his hind feet. He followed up this threatening

378

body language with more high-piercing shrieks, designed to intimidate his opponent.

Instead of just standing watching this show, Pedlar was carrying out the same rituals, trying to menace his adversary before the actual fighting began. Now that he'd found his status as Pedlar the Pathfinder, his whole destiny made sense and he did not intend to be deprived of it.

It was Pedlar who made the first bite. He rushed forward as soon as Gorm's aggressive display was over and bit the chieftain on the back. Gorm tried a counter-bite during Pedlar's retreat, but failed to connect. This set the pattern for the combat, because clearly Gorm's reflexes were not as fast as those of Pedlar. Some said it was to do with the fact that the Savage leader was getting old. Others said that Pedlar's time in the wild accounted for his sharpness.

Not that Gorm failed to get a bite in the whole match. Indeed, he sank several incisors into that yellow-necked creature he hated so much. In fact, they were nastier bites than those which Pedlar inflicted on his opponent, for unlike battles to protect territory the idea of single combat is not to wound or draw blood, but to inflict as many bites as possible. There are very few fatalities in single combat.

Eventually, Pedlar began to wear Gorm down. Gorm's attacks became fewer and less vigorous than Pedlar's. The Outsider inflicted bite after bite on the older mouse, until Gorm became weary and was spending the whole time defending himself. He became slower and slower, his eyes blinking in pain, his legs weak. His tongue lolled, he gasped for breath. Some of the spectators turned away, unable to watch the demise of a great and terrible mouse in this way. Gunhild sobbed openly. Ulf swallowed and hid his face.

Astrid looked very, very sad. Finally, Gorm was tottering and wheezing, not even bothering to return the bites he was receiving.

Still Pedlar did not let up. He was now Pedlar the One. But he knew if he stopped attacking, Gorm would regain his strength and perhaps counter-attack and win. So the Hedgerow mouse continued the assault, even when Gorm rolled on his back in an effort to avoid the onslaught.

Inevitably, Gorm had to make the noises that meant he accepted defeat. Already he had passed the point where any normal mouse would have given in. He was a tough old brute, but he had met his match at last. His was now a hopeless cause and to continue would be to court death, for the biting would not end with Pedlar. The mighty had fallen and those whom the mighty had oppressed would want to get their own back.

Once the necessary and now expected display of humility was forthcoming from Gorm, Pedlar ceased his attacks. He had won the single combat. For the first time in his life, Gorm had lost in a one-to-one fight.

As soon as Pedlar stopped attacking, dozens of mice rushed forward and began to bite the helpless Gorm. He lay on the floor, completely submissive, while the bites rained down on his back, head and flanks. This was the loser's punishment, to be relegated to the lowest rank of the social order. Chieftainship was a position he would have to regain by forcing the other members of his tribe to submit to him again, one after the other, climbing back up the ladder. If he failed in any one confrontation he would lose his rank permanently.

'All right,' cried Pedlar, 'that's enough. Leave him alone now.'

A few more bites and Gorm was left to himself, a

pathetic heap on the floor of the cupboard-under, covered in saliva from the mouths of his fellow mice. There was very little blood visible – where the incisors had pierced the skin they had done so cleanly – but the pain from the bruises and the humiliation must have been terrible to bear.

It was Astrid who went over to him.

'Gorm, are you all right?'

'Leave me alone,' he hissed. 'Just leave me alone.'

'You did the best you could,' she said. 'He was too strong for you.'

Gorm-the-old was silent for a while, then he turned his great head towards his erstwhile concubine.

'That's not what I want to hear,' he said softly. 'It doesn't help in the least. Tell me he's collapsed and died. Tell me he's shrivelled into something that can be packed into a walnut shell and dropped down the well. Tell me his eyes have fallen out and he's blind.'

'I don't think any of those things have happened,' replied Astrid.

'Then there are no gods and my prayers go unanswered, but don't tell me he's *strong*. Did you think that would cheer me up, strumpet?'

Astrid shook her head sadly and left Gorm lying there. She rejoined the Allthing. Pedlar was just being elected leader of the expedition to find what he called the 'Promised House'. He said he would take his duties seriously, would elect others to help him, would do his utmost to fulfil his task honourably.

Astrid knew he would do all he undertook. He was the reliable one, the trustworthy one. He had charisma too. And perhaps he had something to prove. But he wasn't the great Gorm. He didn't have Gorm's thunder, Gorm's balls, Gorm's utter disregard for anything fearful. There would never be another like Gorm. Gorm was the lion and the eagle rolled into one.

Astrid hoped this would not affect the expedition. They would need all the resilience they could muster. They could not afford to doubt.

Unfortunately, when the mighty fell it left a big hole in the confidence of the mouse nation.

PART THREE
Journey to the Promised House

TRAPPISTES

A GREAT EXPEDITION HAS TO BE PREPARED FOR, mentally, before the embarking.

The mice used the term *expedition*, rather than the more correct *exodus*, because they could not bear to think they were never coming back. Everyone but Pedlar had been born in the House, their parents, their grandparents, their great-grandparents had been born and had died there. The House was their soul country, where their spirits resided. It was the land of their fathers and mothers, their temples, their gods. To leave the House without the faint hope that they might return was too heavy a load to carry. So they kidded themselves with the word *expedition*, which implied a homecoming, if not for them personally, for their offspring or their offspring's offspring.

Astrid was to be Pedlar's second-in-command, while

Gunhild had promised to organize the walkers into manageable groups each with a mouse at their head. Since it was winter and there had been few new births for some time, the young were all old enough to walk for themselves, and needed no adult mouse to carry them.

They spent a whole night and day, a whole twenty-four hours, preparing themselves spiritually and mentally, for the leaving. To the House it must have seemed that the mice had gone already, for they simply lay quietly in their favourite places and contemplated the past, seeing old ghosts romping through the rafters, down the hallway, over the landing. They were saying goodbye to their ancestors. There were certain corners to bid farewell to, there were nooks and crannies to mark before leaving, secret places to fix in the memory.

If there was any doubt about going, it was dispelled one hour of a day when the mice were awakened from sleep by terrible sounds. There was smashing and crashing, thunder down the hall and along the landing. Some nudnik youths had entered the House and were breaking windows, running with hobnail boots through passageways and rooms.

Apart from the noise, which frightened the whole mouse nation, the intruders created a tremendous amount of damage. Floorboards were kicked until they broke; doors were torn off their hinges; a small fire was lit on one of the bedroom floors; the banister rails were ripped out; light bulbs were used as bombs. For two hours it was bedlam in the House, then the roaring nudnik youths left, riding away on bicycles down the lane.

Winter now came into the House through the holes in the windows, and through the open back doorway. Jack Frost came in and nipped the mice painfully as they lay in their nests. Old leaves filled the House as they were blown through the gaps. It became a damper and more depressing place for those used to comfort, dryness and warmth. The House was indeed submitting itself to the forces of Nature.

Astrid bid adieu to her Shadows and they wept to see her go. She was the only living thing that had taken notice of them, had made a connection with them, and there was great sorrow amongst them. They told her they would be less black without her, less eerie of a moonlit night, less inclined to inhabit those corners where she had been most likely to be found.

Look after yourself, Astrid, they said.

'You too,' she replied, sadly.

We expect you'll find some new Shadows to talk to – you'll soon forget us.

'I'll never forget my old Shadows,' she murmured. 'I'll see you in every change of light.'

In another part of the House, Phart and Flegm were trying to bolster each other's courage.

'You'll be all right, mate – it won't be as garsly as you fink, you wait an' see.'

'Oh, I'm not worried for me, pal. It's you what worries me. You're a bit of a homebody, you know.'

'Still, so long as we're together, it don't matter do it? There's nuffink that can defeat the two of us together . . .'

Thus did the two cellar mice encourage one another and build their confidence for the great ordeal ahead.

Frych-the-freckled called her whole tribe together.

'Tome-devourers,' she cried. 'One has assembled this solemn congregation in order to apprise the multitude of what one must expect on the Great Highway. There will be vast deserts to circumnavigate; there will be great lakes

387

to traverse; there will be mountain ranges, dense jungles, hedgerows and wide ditches. This will be no minor excursion. One must gird one's loins!'

The congregation knew where their loins were. They might not understand much else Frych said, but they certainly knew where to find their loins. Every member of the audience snatched at this sentence eagerly. Each mouse bent its head and looked through the tunnel of its legs and stared at its loins, wondering how to gird this vital area of the anatomy. What were the advantages of the suggested girding? What were the consequences of *failing* to gird? Obviously it helped one cross deserts, seas, mountains, jungles and ditches, but no-one, except presumably Frych, knew exactly how it accomplished this aid. Nonetheless, this was exactly the sort of practical instruction the mice felt they needed at this point.

'One expects,' cried Frych, looking down and finding every head stuck between each set of front legs, 'attention when one delivers lectures on survival. Now is not the time to contemplate one's navel . . .'

In the attic a very similar talk was being given by Whispersoft, who praised his tribe for being the best in the House and said he knew they wouldn't let him down.

'We are a tribe to be proud of,' he boomed. 'Our members have defeated roof rats, defied owls and successfully defended the attics against attacks from other tribes. Now we are called upon to leave our homes and find new attics where we can settle in peace, away from these helmeted hills, these peacock-feathered valleys. One of our very own has been chosen to lead us in this enterprise – Pedlar, whom some call an Outsider, but who came among us and chose an Invisible for his mate—'

Pedlar, at the back of the crowd, nodded to acquaintances

388

and friends who turned to acknowledge him. Treadlightly snuggled up closer to him, possessively. She knew he was feeling the weight of responsibility that he carried and she was going to have to support him a great deal in the time ahead.

In the cupboard-under – for the kitchen had become far too draughty a place – the Savage Army were listening to their new chieftain (or general, as she preferred to be called) Gunhild. They had been arranged in neat rows by Gunhild herself, each mouse exactly one whisker's length from the mouse at his side, all sitting high-nose. They formed, so Gunhild thought, a beautiful square of mice. She had made sure those with the darker coats were on the four corners of the square, fading to the lightest coats in the centre. Symmetry, she told them, was what it was all about. No-one, she said, respects a sloppy army. Neatness was at the core of every successful expedition into the wilderness.

'March or die,' she snapped, 'that is our watch phrase. March or die! I want no slackers. Smart, disciplined soldiers is what I expect. I'm going to assign ranks before we leave; there'll be corporals, sergeants, lieutenants, captains, majors, colonels, brigadiers – enough for everyone to have one. But you have to *earn* your rank in my army, so I'll be watching each of you closely, gauging your worth, assessing your capabilities. Pedlar is to be our field marshal on this march and I shall take my orders from him. These orders will be filtered down through the ranks, from the brigadiers, to the colonels, to the majors, and so on. It is essential that each and every one of you keeps themselves posted of any such order. You'll put the rest of the troop out of step otherwise . . .'

They listened, stupefied, to this briefing. Most of them

had no desire to become soldiers, but had little choice. They were wishing they had chosen someone like Gytha Finewhiskers as their temporary leader. He might be a bit of a ponce, but he wasn't full of this army crap. Plots were hatched there and then, to get rid of this maniac general whom Gorm-the-old had suggested as his replacement.

Gorm himself, on the end of the last row because his coat was a shade of charcoal grey, listened with satisfaction. It would not be long before he would be offered his old place as chieftain of the tribe, he was sure of that. He could still beat most of them in single combat, but he didn't want to have to fight his way back to the top. It would leave him scarred and bruised. Better to give them a dose of General Gunhild and then head a revolt against her at some later stage. In the meantime he needed to rest and recuperate from his wounds.

All over the House, among the Deathshead, among the 13-K, tribal preparations and pep talks were taking place.

'At least,' said Ulf to his band in the lean-to woodshed, 'my old pa isn't going to be in charge for once. He's just a ranker now in Gunhild's storm-troopers. Serve the old devil right!'

He said this, but running through Ulf's real feelings was a deep vein of chagrin. Mice like Ulf are always able to do political U-turns and justify them. Now his father was disgraced, Ulf felt a burning desire to punish those who had been responsible for the old chieftain's downfall. Gorm was *family*, after all.

But ahead of them all lay the Great Trek. So that when their various meetings broke up, mice wandered through the House widdling on everything they could find, leaving their mark behind them. Some took comfort in the fact that they had, after all, fooled the nudniks. They might have got themselves into trouble doing so, but the nudniks had been duped. The nudniks were thick. They had always been thick and they would always remain thick. Only their hugeness made them worth a mention at all. They were *big* and *thick*.

Now mice were quite different. Mice were normal size and very, very smart, the most daring mammals that walked on four legs.

Those that only walked on *two*, well, 'nuff said.

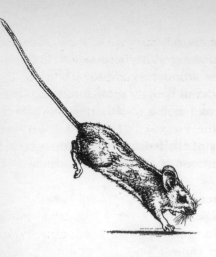

HALOUMI

THE MICE SPENT THE LAST FEW MINUTES OF THEIR TIME in the House, yelling from the attic to the treehouse, telling Ulug Beg they were on their way to a new land. Whether she heard them, no-one knew. Perhaps the ancient crabbed mouse was no longer alive? If so, most mice preferred not to know. Ulug Beg was one of their shrines and if the antique creature was gone it would serve to make them more depressed. Only the scruffy new mouse who spoke dog and went by the strange name of Eh-he seemed anxious that Fallingoffthings should attempt the high-wire journey, but the balancing attic mouse wasn't going to make the trip just for a stranger.

The mice decided to use the maze exit to leave the House for the last time, rather than just walk out of the door. This was pure cussedness on their part. They wanted to tromp through Tunneller's labyrinth and put her in her place. Pedlar did not entirely approve of the motive behind this exit, but he went along with it because he wanted to say goodbye to the shrew whom he had fought to a standstill.

So, with an Outsider at their head, the mice bid farewell to their birthplace and home of their ancestors, and set forth in search of the Promised House. The shrew, who had heard the news of their departing on the grapevine, lay low-nose on the floor of the maze and watched them approach.

Pedlar spoke to her.

'Goodbye, Tunneller – we – er – we came this way to pay tribute to your generosity for lending us the maze when the Gas-maker came.'

'Codswallop,' she said shortly.

'Yes, well,' Pedlar said, uncomfortably. 'I particularly wanted to say goodbye to you. We fought a hard match, until the sun was blood, and I shan't forget you.'

'Goodbye,' she said, only a little less shortly.

Pedlar nodded and then led the others towards the moonlight. The mice filed past the bad-tempered Tunneller one by one, some of them smirking, but none of them daring to make a remark. Even the Deathshead were wary of the unpredictable and vicious nature of shrews. Finally, Gorm-the-old brought up the rear. He was the last in the line.

As he passed, Tunneller said quietly, 'And good blasted riddance.'

'Same to you,' said Gorm, not even looking at her, 'with knobs on.'

Thus the last connection with the House was broken.

Once out in the garden, Pedlar led his nation towards the roadway. It was cold outside, with a sky swirling with faint stars. The breath of the mice came out in sprigs of steam and they hunched inside their pelts, hoping that Pedlar would find them warm holes for their rest periods. There was a crisp frost on the earth and the whitened grass stood stiff and keen. The animal highways through the grasses were clearly defined.

They had to pass Stone's privy on the way and were amazed when they got there to find it was gone. The young nudniks had torn it down and scattered the bits around the orchard. Stone was still there, looking a little bewildered. He should have been hibernating by this time, but the shock had kept him awake.

'They took my hideaway,' he said in a bemused voice to Pedlar. 'They just came and smashed it down.'

Pedlar surveyed the bare spot which had once held the monument in whose shadow Stone had long dwelt. The great edifice had been part of the scenery and the world looked quite different without it. The stink had gone too. Stone's place wasn't quite the same without the stink. The dormouse looked as if he had been picked up and transplanted to a foreign land.

'You could come with us,' said Pedlar. 'On our journey to a better place.'

Stone shook his head. 'No, no. This is my place, here in the garden; anyway, I have to sleep the winter away.' He seemed to buck up a little, and added, 'I'm glad to see you've all come to your senses at last. Going back to Nature, eh? Jolly good! Nothing like fresh air. Out on the open road, eh?' His eyes scanned the line of mice. 'Good lord, just about everyone here. Everyone. Even grizzly old Gorm.'

'Not so much of the grizzly if you don't mind,' growled Gorm.

'And Little Prince,' said Stone, shaking his head. 'Little

394

Prince here, and my privy gone – I don't know what the world's coming to . . .'

The mice were taken aback and all started looking along the line, going, 'Little Prince, what's he talking about? Where? Where's Little Prince?' Little Prince himself followed suit, staring back and forth along the line with a puzzled expression on his dirty face, repeating over and over, *'Never mind Little Prince – oteari wa doko dess ka?'* which, in the language of foxes, dogs and wolves, roughly translated means, *Forget Little Prince – where's Stone's dunny box gone?*

Finally, everyone shrugged and Phart said, 'Silly old sausage is goin' senile.'

Indeed it seemed this was true, for Stone had forgotten about the mice and was crooning, 'Hello flowers, hello trees, hello grass . . . hail to thee happy phantoms.'

So the line moved on, leaving the old dormouse to commune with Nature.

They reached the roadway and crossed without incident, it being in the early hours of the morning. They entered the ditch and travelled along its iced-over bottom for quite a while, until Pedlar struck north over the barren fields. They kept to a furrow, in order to avoid being seen by owls. Progress was slow because there were frozen grains of corn on the ground and mice kept stopping to pick-eat. Finally, they reached the far side of the field and stopped for a rest.

The world was very still, but they knew that out there on moonlit ways were foxes and stoats, weasels and badgers, all with hollow stomachs, prowling the Earth. These were the lean nights, when animals and birds were constantly hungry. Predators' eyes were sharper, their ears keener, their noses whetted. The mice had to trust to luck and the gods to stay clear of roaming killers, or they could be taken in one bunch.

A jack hare came by and eyed them curiously, probably wondering why so many mice were gathered in one place. The mice in turn envied the hare its legs. *He* would be all right if he saw a fox. Hares could leave foxes standing. In fact they often stood up on their hind legs on seeing a fox in the distance and stared at the predator to let it know that they had seen it. *Hi foxy, this is to let you know I know you're there, so it's not worth coming any closer*. What the mice would have given to be able to run like the hare!

Astrid curled up close with Iban, their reserve gone now that the hours of adversity were on them. No-one commented on their open togetherness, not even Skrang. Iban was secretly glad that he had come out of the closet. It meant that the blackmailing library does no longer had a hold over him. He just wanted to spend what last nights he had with his Astrid.

'Come on, snuggle up,' Astrid was urging him. 'This frosty ground is damp and cold. Let's have a quick nap. We're neither of us sprightly youngsters any more. We're not exactly eligible for the 13-K.'

He did as he was told saying, 'The 13-K are not exactly the youthful rebels they once were either. They're shooting towards middle age now. In a while one of the sons of Ulf will decide his father is too conservative in his views and will go off and start a rebel gang in direct confrontation with his father's rebel gang.'

She twitched her whiskers in amusement.

'You're probably right. Funny old world, isn't it?'

'It's just that nothing's new,' he said.

'Right,' called Pedlar after no time at all, 'on your feet

396

everyone. There's a wood in front of us which we need to reach the centre of before daybreak. Woods mean foxes, stoats and badgers – owls too, probably. But not many hawks. Most hawks don't like to fly amongst trees.'

'Oh well, that's fine, isn't it?' snarled Gorm sarcastically. 'We don't have to worry then. Just a few dozen savage predators – but we don't need to concern ourselves about hawks. That's wonderful!'

In another corner of the group, Phart was climbing wearily to his feet. He had walked more in the last two hours than he had done in his whole life. He was out of condition and sore in several places. His muscles ached, his bones felt deeply rheumatoid, and his chest heaved when he started walking again. It was not so much himself that he worried about however, but his companion.

Flegm remained on the ground when the others had got to their feet and had begun shambling off after Pedlar.

'Come on,' cried Phart, 'we'll get left behind.'

'I can't go on,' wheezed Flegm. 'S'been too many nights of booze, Phart.' A tear squeezed out of the corner of Flegm's eye. 'I can't make it.'

'Course you can, you oaf,' exhorted Phart, feeling scared.

Gorm-the-old, taking up the rear of the column, shouted. 'Come on, you motley cellar mice, catch up! I'm not going to be responsible for you.'

'All right, all right,' shouted Phart, glad to have someone to be angry with. 'Keep your pelt on – we're comin'.'

He turned again to his companion, stretched out on the frosty turf. Please, Flegm,' he pleaded. 'You got to.' As he spoke he looked over his shoulder in desperation at the disappearing column of mice.

'I ain't got to do nuffink but lay here till me bones freezes solid,' came the response.

'Look you!' shouted Phart, in a final bid to get his companion on his feet. 'You get up or I'll go an' get Iban to Ik-to bite you.'

This had the effect of Flegm heaving himself to his feet. Flegm hated pain. He was in a sorry state, Phart could see that. When he eventually got his legs moving, they wobbled precariously, as if they were about to collapse at any moment. It brought a lump to Phart's throat.

'You'll be all right, mate. You see. I'll get Pedlar to stop again in a bit, to give you some more rest. Come on, we got to catch up now . . .'

He looked ahead at the dark, forbidding wood.

Gorm actually came back and growled at them, then rushed off back to the line. Phart encouraged his tribe to hurry themselves, to get those four paws going, to set their eyes on the distant horizon and push forward.

'Push forward,' grumbled Flegm as they approached the first tree. 'Push forward? I couldn't push a spr—'

'A what?' asked Phart, turning.

He was never to learn what *spr*— meant and puzzled over it for hours afterwards. It was the one thing that kept him busy and helped him through his grief in those lonely hours without his friend Flegm. Sprocket? Spring? Sprout? Sprinkler?

For Flegm had vanished from the Earth.

'What?' cried Phart again, this time instinctively looking up.

Across the face of the moon a ragged-winged owl was moving in silent flight. In its talons was something small and pathetic, with a dangling tail, and dangling legs. The irony of it was that the predator looked a lot like Merciful.

Phart panicked and ran towards the front of the column, passing astonished mice labouring up steep

398

banks where the wild thyme grew.

'Pedlar!' he called, gasping for breath. 'Pedlar, Pedlar, we gotta stop, we gotta stop. An owl's gone and took Flegm. We got to go back . . .'

The column halted as Pedlar came back down the line to meet the stricken Phart.

'Stop?' he said. 'But what can we do, Phart? If an owl has truly taken Flegm, I'm very sorry for it, but we must go on. It won't do any good to turn back now.'

'But . . .?' cried Phart, wildly. 'It's gone an' took Flegm. We got to . . .'

He stopped and looked at Pedlar beseechingly.

'We've got to what, Phart?' asked Pedlar kindly.

'We – got – to – *help* – him,' cried Phart, breaking down in front of everyone.

Gorm came up from the rear. 'What's up?' he snarled.

'Flegm's been took by an owl,' bawled Phart.

'Give the bleeder gut-ache, I shouldn't wonder,' said Gorm. 'Anyway, so what are we stopped for? Can't do anything about it now, can we? Let's get moving. This place is dangerous enough without standing out here waiting to be picked off by owls. Come on you lot, get these lines going. You're supposed to be the leader of this lot, Pedlar, whatever your name is. Let's have a bit of leadership.'

Thus the first member of the expedition was lost to the predators of the wild. Phart stumbled along with the rest of the column once it started moving, but he was never quite the same again. His bombast had been quashed, his bluster had been quelled. The only friend he had in the world was now making slow progress through the belly of an owl. There would be a final burp, a cough, and then what remained of the Great and Honourable Flegm would come shooting out of the owl's throat in the form of a pellet of fur and bones.

Pedlar felt a sense of loss too. It was not that he had been over-fond of Flegm, but every member of the expedition was his responsibility. He was the pathfinder. He felt he should in some way have prevented the tragedy. Still, he told himself, there would be more deaths before the end was in sight. You couldn't take a few dozen mice through the wilderness without losing one or two before the end of the journey. Pedlar posted four scouts after this, two ahead and on either side of the column, and two in similar positions at the rear.

Inside the wood the terrain was much easier to travel. It was mossy and bouncy underfoot, there were a few nibbles in the way of old seeds and nuts lying around. There were also the remains of autumn fungi and some crab apples. You could dash for holes under the roots and in the trunks of trees if you felt threatened at all. Pedlar quite liked woods in a way, though in his old Hedgerow he had had the best of both worlds. It had been like living in a long narrow wood with a cool ditch and water on one side and open fields full of food on the other.

'Scatter!' yelled one of the scouts. 'Fox!'

Fortunately they were crossing the roots of a big oak at the time. Its massive roots were exposed and there were holes underneath them. The mice dashed down these, only to find wild mice already there. Since there was plenty of room, it did not seem unreasonable that the wild wood mice should allow the travellers to stay until the danger had gone. The residents however appeared to object quite strongly. Their conversation was conducted in the dark.

'What the hell do you lot want? Get out!' cried a large wood mouse.

Pedlar said, 'We're sheltering from a fox – a vixen I think. We'll leave just as soon as she does.'

'You'll leave *now* or there'll be trouble,' said the brash wood mouse. Pedlar could almost hear his whiskers bristling.

'Listen,' shouted Treadlightly, 'we outnumber you five to one at least. I should think the Savage Tribe could settle your hash on their own.'

'The Savage Tribe?' repeated the wood mouse, as if he didn't quite like the sound of that name. 'Who the hell are they?'

Gunhild snarled, '*We're* the Savage Tribe, and we'll rip you from whiskers to tail if you mess with us.'

'Oh, will you?' shouted another resident, but in a voice which showed she was none too sure of herself.

'Yes,' boomed Whispersoft, 'and when the Savages have finished with you, the Invisibles will eat what's left of you.'

'That's if the Deathshead don't Ik-to bite you first,' called Skrang.

'And afterwards,' shouted Ulf, 'the 13 K Gang will use your pelts to line their nests.'

'If the Bookeaters don't require them for use in their magic spells,' cried Frych-the-freckled.

'Quite unnecessary,' growled Gorm. 'Why, me and Phart will take the lot of them on, just the two of us, and stamp them into the turf, won't we Phart?'

'Too right, mate,' Phart confirmed. 'Fink you're a load of hard nuts? I've seen tougher things come out of me nose than you lot.'

Phart was almost his old self again, siding with the strong, taking advantage of the weak, being thoroughly obnoxious.

After this tirade had ended there was silence in the

401

network of holes. It seemed the residents no longer wished to complain about their temporary visitors. All there was to worry about now was the fox.

The vixen had seen the mice disappearing down the holes and she came sniffing around the entrances. She was massive. A great red giantess with a mouthful of sharp teeth, each one probably itching to impale a mouse. The stink of her filled the labyrinth of tunnels and every mouse trembled, even Gorm-the-old. None of the House mice had encountered a canid before, other than their dear old Witless, and this monster was nothing like him. It was sharp and lively, with bright burning eyes that peered into the holes, and it had claws with which it could dig.

'Now you've done for us,' whispered one of the resident mice. 'It won't leave without it gets *someone*.'

The vixen began scratching at the entrance to one of the holes and the moss came away easily. She poked her nose down the widened gap and sniffed loudly. Phart was about two body lengths from that black snorting snout.

'Crikey,' moaned Phart. 'I wisht I was with old Flegm now – at least we would've gone together.'

'I can smell rabbit on her breath,' whispered one of the residents. 'She can't be *that* hungry.'

'I suppose she's thinking,' moaned Frych, 'that a few extra titbits won't go amiss.'

The fox began digging with more enthusiasm now that she knew her prey was only a short bite away.

Suddenly one of the mice shouted up to the fox.

'Donata o oyobi dess ka?'

The fox stopped digging, seemingly shocked that someone should be addressing her in her own tongue from under the ground.

She said, *'Donata-sama dess ka?'*

402

The resident mice, too, were stunned that one of these newcomers should be conversing with a fox. After all, who could have got close enough to one of the terrible creatures long enough to learn its language? They were beginning to feel relieved they hadn't attacked these invaders of their nests, or they might have been shredded by now.

'What did you say to it?' whispered Pedlar, to Little Prince.

'I asked who she would like to speak to.'

'And what did she reply?'

'She wants to know who's talking to her in *Canidae*.'

Pedlar said, 'Ask her again who she wants to speak to.'

Little Prince repeated his earlier question and the fox, now getting in on the game, said the name of one of her friends.

'Sorry,' Little Prince went to the entrance of the main hole and, putting himself in danger, showed himself to the vixen. 'Your friend isn't here at the moment,' he offered. '*Moshi-wake gozai-asen ga gai-shuts chu dess. Ashta mo ichido odenwas itadake-masen ka.* Come back tomorrow.'

The fox let out a long series of coughing barks, and seemed to know a little rodent tongue herself, probably learned from a river coypu by her accent, for she said, 'You very funny mouse. Very funny! I think I let you live, OK? Good job I no very hungry. I call again tomorrow. I like taste of mouse.'

'I did once too,' murmured Little Prince, before he could stop himself, 'but now I've repented.'

With that, incredibly, the vixen sauntered off.

A huge sigh of relief swept through the labyrinth. Pedlar could feel the tenseness dissipate. Evidently the fox had suddenly decided she'd eaten enough for her not to be bothered with scrabbling around to get at a few mouthfuls of mouse.

Pedlar said to the residents, 'I suggest that by the morning you change your address, because I think she intends to pay you another visit.'

'Oh great, thanks very much!' grumbled a sarcastic host. 'So nice of you to lead her here. Come again, won't you?'

Pedlar said that he was sorry and led his column out of the holes again, anxious to be out of the wood. On the way out he spoke quietly to Little Prince.

'I heard what you said back there, about repenting. Do you mean that? Are you truly contrite.'

Little Prince said, 'I hope no-one else heard, but *yes*, I feel good, and I like feeling good. You've shown me another side to myself, Pedlar. I'm sick of what I once was. It disgusts me. I know I can't ever hope to be as good a mouse as you, but I want to try now, I really do.'

Pedlar glanced at Little Prince, wondering if he was speaking the truth, and believed he saw before him the face of a penitent mouse. There was genuine remorse in Little Prince's eyes, as well as his words.

'I don't think I'm a *good* mouse either, but I'm glad you feel as you do,' said Pedlar. 'That's more comforting to me at the moment than having a whole bunch of do-gooders at my side.'

They reached the edge of the trees an hour later and began the descent of a slope on the far side. Pedlar could see a hedgerow at the bottom of the meadow and he instinctively decided they would camp there. They needed somewhere to get some proper sleep. These were mice that were not used to walking and they were exhausted by their march. There was still a long way to go to the Promised House. Pedlar did not know exactly where it was: now that he was doing their bidding his ancestral voices were in touch again, urging him on, and providing him with his only sense of direction.

Luckily the meadow had been mown in the autumn and the grasses were short, with many animal paths travelling through them. The mice walked on: they knew they were out in the glorious open, but they were too tired to appreciate it or care. They could almost hear their old dormouse-friend Stone, Nature-lover extraordinaire, berating them. But one paw in front of the other: that was as much as they could think about. Muscles were aching to the point of numbness; legs were leaden and unstable; tails were like metal chains being dragged behind. Some mice could hardly keep their eyes open, but relied on the one in front to guide the way and the one behind to nudge them forward. Their whiskers felt heavy and pulled their faces towards the Earth. There were murmurs amongst them that perhaps the Great Nudnik Drive had all been a dream and that if they returned to the House, they would find it as vermin-ridden as before.

The sky clouded over, the stars disappeared. Halfway across the field, it began to rain. It was a cold sleeting rain which hammered into the fur. The drops were compact and almost ice. They struck the body like nails. When the raindrops are as big as your nose, they are bound to hurt.

Although Pedlar did not want to stop in the middle of a meadow, a very exposed and dangerous landscape, he knew his mice needed shelter.

'Find what cover you can,' he said, 'and we'll start off again as soon as it stops.'

They found docks and other flat broadleafed plants to protect them from the rain. Some of them wondered if there might be some rhubarb around, with its nice thick,

405

wide canopy, but Pedlar told them you didn't get rhubarb on meadowland.

'Why not?' asked Gruffydd Greentooth. 'There was rhubarb outside the House.'

'I've only seen it growing in a house garden,' replied Pedlar. 'But if you can find some hart's-tongue or figwort you'll find that pretty effective.'

'Since I don't know what either of those look like,' grumbled Gruffydd, 'I'm not likely to be able to find them, am I? I wish I'd eaten a book on broadleafed plants before I left the library, then I'd be an expert.'

Once, they had known only the rain which had thundered on the rooftop. They knew it was wet, but the slates on the roof protected them from its force. It had been almost a comforting sound in those hours. Now they'd just experienced real contact. With what curiosity they had left, as they sheltered they marvelled at the thunderous roar the rain created while battering on the leaves above, driving them down upon their bodies, flattening the wet rough undersides against their backs. Some of these undersides had little spikes, hooks or hairs, which irritated the skin. If they stepped back out in the rain again, however, the force of it stung their bodies.

The downpour lasted half an hour, an incredibly long time to the homeless mice.

Pedlar immediately called them to order again. 'March!' he cried.

'Or die!' yelled Grunhild grimly.

The long walk continued. But suddenly there was a yell from Thorkils Threelegs.

'Little Prince! We've got Little Prince with us! He's been hiding under the name of Eh-he!'

The whole column stopped, broke up, and gathered

406

around the gibbering form of Little Prince.

'It was the rain, you see, my dears. It washed away the dirt from your sweet Little Prince. Don't worry, I won't hurt you. I'm a *nice* mousey now, aren't I, Pedlar? Pedlar? Pedlar, where are you?'

Pedlar was anxiously trying to get to the spot before Little Prince was overwhelmed and bitten to death.

Gorm-the-old cried, 'You're not going to hurt *us*? I should say you're not! I've got dibs on first bite of this creature.'

'Bags me second!' cried Phart.

'Oh dear, how nasty,' whispered Little Prince. 'What must be, must be, however. Here's my throat. Tear it open.'

Gorm stepped forward, accepting the invitation.

'Wait a bit! Stop!' cried Pedlar, forcing his way through the crowd around Little Prince.

On reaching Little Prince's side, Pedlar spoke these words, 'This mouse has just saved our skins. Without him we would have been eaten by the fox. Or some of us would. Do you want to kill someone who's just saved your life? Is that a good act?'

'Yes,' growled Gorm, without hesitation.

LIMBURGER

THE MICE CLOSED THE RING AROUND LITTLE PRINCE, their faces set and grim. A lot of them had waited a long time to get their teeth into the hated pet of the nudniks. His cannibalism had revolted the tribes of the House for generations. It did not seem fair that he had already lived many more nights than proper mice in any case. They wanted to end his hours here, on the turf of a foreign field.

'What a lovely hour of the night, isn't it sweeties?' cried Little Prince, in a shrill nervous voice, as they pressed in on him. 'Just imagine being back in your nice kitchen, or the attic with its lovely old junk, or the library books . . . Careful, don't come too close to me; I'm very highly strung, you know.'

'Stop!' cried Pedlar, shielding Little Prince. 'I will not have this expedition deliberately besmirched by the blood of one of our own.'

'One of our own?' shouted Phart. 'He's a nudnik puppet, that's what he is!'

'He is a *mouse*,' said Pedlar.

'And he's going to be a dead mouse, very shortly,' snarled Thorkils Threelegs.

What Pedlar did next, he did entirely of his own accord. With no prompting from his ancestral voices.

'You'll have to take me first,' he said. 'But I'm not going to resist you.' He made a submissive gesture. 'Kill me instead. Let the white mouse live, and kill me.'

'No!' cried Treadlightly.

'You're bloomin' barmy,' said Phart.

'Daft,' said Goingdownfast.

'Completely unbalanced,' added Whispersoft.

'Utterly insane,' confirmed Marredud.

Jarl Forkwhiskers murmured, 'It was the best of times, it was the worst of times . . .'

'Hey!' cried Owain, turning on the last speaker, 'that's book talk that is. You've been stealing into the library and eating our books!'

'*Your* books!' roared Jarl. 'I like that.'

It was Gorm-the-old who stopped this argument with just a look. Then he surprised everyone with his next speech.

'Look around you,' he growled. 'Just look around you everyone.'

The mice did as they were told. They stared at the great black bowl of the sky above them, immense and unyielding. They went high-nose, their eyes just above the short grass, and stared at the fields which seemed to stretch out for ever. An ocean of blackness above, a sea of grass all around. Tiny distant lights like stars on the landscape, too far away to be of any comfort. Tight clumps of trees here and there, on the horizon, where the dark Earth met the dark sky. It made them shiver with apprehension.

'Agoraphobia,' murmured Mefyn.

'Never mind that,' snarled Gorm, 'it's ruddy weird. And damn frightening, I don't mind admitting. Not a house in sight – nothing. Just open space. I don't know where we are, do you? I can't find my way back. No doubt one of you pretentious library mice has eaten a map at some time, but is it the right one . . .?'

'Mongolia,' murmured Frych-the-freckled. 'Or Sarawak?'

'There, you see?' cried Gorm. 'Whoever heard of a house with names like that? I'm afraid we can't kill Pedlar, we need him too much. And I suppose it follows that we can't kill Little Prince either, if Pedlar is determined to protect him.'

'I just don't want any more deaths on this walk than necessary,' said Pedlar. 'There'll be enough of them as it is. We've already lost Flegm—'

Phart gave out a little sob.

Gorm grunted, as if to say, *no great loss*.

'—Little Prince has proved himself once and I have a feeling we'll be needing him again. Forget his revolting past, which I deplore as much as anyone. He's clever – he's cleverer than me or anyone else here – and he's not without courage either. Those are the qualities we're going to *need* if we're going to survive. We're not on the whole a brainy bunch, us mice. Cunning and crafty, but not especially brainy.

'Little Prince has assured me that he's turned over a new leaf. I believe him. But listen to this. My ancestral voices tell me that a "white mouse" is to do great things, become revered among us. I know of no other white mouse but Little Prince.'

410

Little Prince rose to the moment and said, 'Yea verily, I say unto you, if ever I do a mouse wrong again I shall chastise me and smite mine own self as dead as a dodo, and that is the truth. And if any mouse is in dire straits, I shall be there to give him succour. And if any mouse be sorely tried, I shall be there to comfort him. And if any mouse have need of food, I shall go hungry to fill his belly. I lay down myself for mousedom.'

'What's that?' growled Gorm.

'He says he'll be as good as his coat is white,' replied Frych.

'He'd better be,' grunted the old Savage.

Pedlar struck a note of leadership.

'Now, let's get to that hedgerow before dawn, or we're in trouble. Move!'

So the march began again and though Jarl Forkwhiskers nudged Little Prince hard in the back, saying, 'We'll get you later,' the white pet of the nudniks was allowed to live. He owed his life to Pedlar.

They reached the hedgerow just before dawn. There Treadlightly gave birth to a litter of five young. She had not even told Pedlar she was pregnant, and he had been too busy over the preceding nights to notice the swelling of her tummy.

'Why didn't you say something?' he accused her.

'I knew it would distract you,' she murmured. 'There was all that anarchy at the House, then the expedition to plan. It's been a hectic time. I didn't want your mind on me, when it should be on the whole nation of the House.'

'But – why have you had a litter *now*? I mean, winter of all times.'

'Mice who live in houses,' she said, 'don't take very much note of the seasons.'

411

'Well, they should,' Pedlar replied.

And he was probably right, because all but one of the litter died that night, of the cold. Even under normal circumstances, not all the litter would have lived: mice were used to a high infant-mortality rate. Eighty per cent of the litter was indeed high, but Pedlar and Treadlightly were grateful that even one managed to live, given that the mother had been starved for much of the pregnancy, and had then taken up hiking with a vengeance.

The one that lived was a female whom they called Gypsy. The parents had decided to follow Pedlar's name-line rather than Treadlightly's, because the only name they could think of which would suit an attic mouse was Arrived-attherighttime, and that seemed too much of a mouthful even for an Invisible. Treadlightly said she would be able to carry Gypsy in her mouth, given a few hours rest.

The rest of the nation were so tired they slept for several hours anyway, giving time for Treadlightly to get her strength back. Frych-the-freckled, so many times a mother it was almost a profession with her, came and fussed over Gypsy. Frych looked wistful as she helped Treadlightly lick the young one and later went off and suggested to Hywel-the-bad that the two of them might set up nest again as soon as they reached a house.

Secretly, Pedlar was glad that Gypsy had been born in a hedgerow. The Hedgerow was his ancestral home and even if his daughter went off to live in a house, as well she might, she would have had at least a brush with Hedgelore. Pedlar himself was happy to be back, in *any* part of the Hedgerow, even though it was not his own.

He knew none of the other creatures in this hawthorn hedge, neither bird nor beast, but the old familiar smells

412

came to his nostrils, of lords-and-ladies, great black slugs, burying beetles, primroses, rabbit's droppings, snail trails and a host of other plant and animal scents, both active and dormant. When he closed his eyes he was back with Tinker and Diddycoy again – the latter now most probably passed away – sitting in the hazel fork under the thrush's nest, feeling a part of every twig and leaf.

Yet he knew he would have to open his eyes sooner or later and lead his multitude forth, into the wilderness again, on the wearying search for a new house that would restore to the tribes the society they had lost.

TROÔ

They travelled for many, many more hours, with shorter and shorter rest periods between. Over hump and down ditch, across the bare hard fields, into regions where the ice grew thick and there was little to eat. Pedlar spurned the nudnik roads and followed his own path. Or so it seemed to the other mice who could not hear the ancestral voices that guided their leader.

The trek became more and more arduous. Until on the third night they came to a vast expanse of very short grass surrounded by a high fence. The fence was no problem, for the mice just slipped through. Beyond the short grass was a giant building, the like of which not even the Bookeaters had seen before. It was so massive as to take up half the sky and in truth its great size frightened the mice.

'What is it?' cried Phart. 'Can't be a house, can it? S'too big.'

'I don't know,' replied Pedlar truthfully, 'but I don't

like the look of it. There are no windows and only those two huge doors. It doesn't look very welcoming.'

Iban said, 'I'm so exhausted I'm willing to try anything. Why don't we wait until morning, then see it in the day-light? Maybe it'll look more inviting?'

They followed Iban's suggestion and huddled close to the fence, to protect themselves from owls.

When they woke, they were amazed to see a great oval grey shape floating outside the big hangar, tethered to the ground by various ropes and chains. Fixed to the bottom of this floating giant was something which looked as if it might be a house *of sorts*. Though it was a funny shape, it had windows all along it and a doorway.

Fallingoffthings was sent to investigate this weird-looking house, and she went scuttling up one of the guy ropes with her usual skill, to enter the object. Not long afterwards she reappeared again, came running down the guy to the ground and reported.

'There's lots of chairs in there, and beds fixed to the wall, and a kitchen with lots of food.'

'Any nudniks?' asked Pedlar.

'Quite a few,' was the reply, 'but I didn't smell any cats there. Just a load of stupid nudniks, all stuffing their faces as usual. Food galore! I caught the scent of cheese.'

'Sounds like the house for me,' growled Gorm. 'I'm willing to risk it. I'm fed up with this marching business.'

'Wait a bit,' said Pedlar. 'There's too much we don't know yet. Where was this floating house last night, when we arrived?'

'Who cares,' snarled Thorkils Threelegs who was suffer-ing more than most from sore feet and aching limbs, even though he had less of them. 'Let's damn well get in there.'

Pedlar asked Fallingoffthings, 'Were there any other mice? Or rats? How about a dog?'

'None of those, as far as I could smell,' said Fallingoffthings. 'I had a good sniff round too. No droppings, no urine markings, nothing like that. It was very very – *clean*.'

'Clean, eh?' Pedlar said. 'Well I, for one, mistrust clean places.'

'I call an Allthing,' shouted Gorm-the-old.

'You've got no say,' cried Gunhild. 'I'm leader of the tribe now.'

Gorm stepped forward a pace, thinking that now was the time for him to raise a rebellion.

'Well, here I stand,' he snarled, 'and those who wish to stand with me, do so. I've had enough of taking orders from a jumped-up corporal and a hedgerow yellow-neck. Come on, who stands with Gorm-the-old?'

There was an embarrassing silence amongst the other mice for a few moments, then Thorkils Threelegs slipped over to Gorm's side, followed by Jarl Forkwhiskers. These three stood strong and defiant, staring down the rest of the expedition members. Finally, young Elisedd, the library mouse who had discovered the abandoned Little Prince, rushed over to join them.

'Right,' snarled Gorm, 'that's it then, is it? What about you, Elfwin – or you, Ulf? Are you going to continue to be browbeaten by this upstart?'

Elfwin nodded her head. 'If you mean Pedlar, I think he's doing the best he can for us.'

'I'm torn,' said Ulf, 'but I still think we have to trust the leader we started out with.'

'I might join you, sweetie – I'm exhausted,' cried Little Prince.

'We don't want *you*,' shouted Thorkils. 'You can go to hell with the rest of them.'

'Huh! – suit yourself,' replied Little Prince petulantly. 'I was only teasing anyway.'

'That's it then,' said Gorm. 'Come on, you three. This is the house for us. There'll be cheeses! Beloved cheeses of inestimable worth! I can smell their fragrance from here!'

The four rebels had started for one of the guy ropes, when Astrid screamed after them, 'Don't do it! I see another terrible holocaust! A great whiteness lighting up the dark. A whiteness that devours! Come back!'

Elisedd looked frightened on hearing this prophecy from the high priestess of the Savages. He wavered. One way lay cheese-and-fear, and the other way lay no-cheese-but-no-fear, and finally the negatives won and he ran back to the main group again.

'Coward,' snarled Gorm. 'If you believe that old harlot, you'll believe anyone.'

'She's always been right before,' cried Pedlar. 'You ignored her last time and that's why we're here.'

'She's a fake,' shouted Gorm. 'Just got lucky last time, that's all.'

With that he turned his back and led the precarious climb up the guy rope to the floating house above. Pedlar and the others watched the three ascend. They climbed until they were three dots on a thin black curving line. There was a heart-stopping moment when Thorkils Threelegs lost his grip and clung on by one claw, but through sheer tenacity he managed to find two more holds and remain on the mooring line.

Finally, all three reached the top and disappeared into the floating house. It was the last the mice on the ground ever saw of them.

Pedlar and his expedition set off along the edge of the fence, to avoid crossing that vast expanse of short grass. As he led them towards a corner there was a loud shout from the rear. Pedlar turned his head, to see that all his mice were now looking upwards. When he did so himself he was amazed to see the floating house. The mooring ropes and tethering chains had been cast off and the great grey structure, buffeted gently by the winds, was drifting skywards.

Nudniks were rushing around on the ground, turning huge winches, securing the cast-off lines. They obviously expected the house to float away, for there was no smell of panic in the air, no jerky movements denoting terror. Instead some of them were waving farewell handkerchiefs and hats, and making excited yipping sounds.

Gorm, Thorkils and Jarl were obviously on their way to a great adventure in the clouds. Pedlar *almost* envied them, thinking of what great adventures they might have. They were moving amongst the birds in their great and wonderful floating house.

'I wonder how they feel?' he said, wistfully.

'Like gods I imagine!' Elisedd cried, probably thinking how close to going with them he had been himself.

But Little Prince muttered, 'Sick, I should think, with all that rolling and swaying.'

The great grey movable gradually turned its nose in the direction in which Pedlar and his mice were themselves heading. It came forward slowly, propelled by some unseen force. It passed high over the wandering tribes, and then entered the high country of the clouds, to be lost to their sight.

BLEU DE BRESSE

IT WAS A WHOLE NIGHT LATER THAT THE TRAVELLERS came across a nudnik hamlet of four or five houses. A vanguard of the best fighters was formed out of Gunhild, Highstander, Ulf, Drenchie, Whispersoft, Skuli, Gruffydd Greentooth and Rhodri. These intrepid eight went into the houses first, using any entrance they could find. In one after another, they met with stiff resistance from local tribes.

'You in there,' cried Gunhild, not wasting words, 'won't you welcome new comrades?'

'Get lost!' yelled them in there.

'We're strong and healthy,' shouted Gunhild. 'I'm good at drill.'

'So? Go and find your own house . . .'

As soon as Pedlar was told about the hostile tribes already in occupation, he knew that they had yet to find the Promised House, yet he also knew that it lay within reach.

He called an Allthing just outside the hamlet to advise his mice accordingly. And so it was that the remnants of the House of tribes gathered together their strength and moved off into the wasteland again, leaving the hamlet behind. Before they had gone too far however, Gunhild and the rest of the Savage Tribe (all except Astrid) announced their intention of turning back.

'I'm sure we can integrate if we declare ourselves fewer in number. You go on Pedlar, with the rest of them, and good luck to you!'

So the 13-K, Bookeaters, Deathshead and Invisibles continued the march without the Savages. It took seven hours, and there it was. The Promised House.

It stood on the far side of an uneven roadway: a ramshackle place with strange towers, tall windows and ramparts. Red ivy grew over the blue-slate roof. There was a rusted weather vane on one of the towers, bearing a cockerel with bent wattle. The grounds were extensive and reasonably well kept, without too many fussy little flowerbeds. There was a massive greenhouse, two sheds, a gazebo and many box-hedged walks.

The mice surveyed this building, which looked very promising. Astrid commented favourably on it.

'I have spoken with one or two local Shadows,' she announced, 'and they say the house has just been occupied by nudniks after a long period of being empty.'

'That does sound promising,' said Pedlar of the Promised House. 'That would mean there probably aren't any tribes in there yet.'

Whispersoft was sent to investigate the new house and he came back an hour later.

'Not bad,' he said. 'Not much in the way of furniture or

carpets, but a *huge* kitchen, big enough for us all. Smells as though it's been cooked in recently too. Caught a definite whiff of blue-vein . . .'

'Any hostile tribes?' asked Pedlar.

'There's a small bunch in there, but my guess is they've wandered in as individuals. They don't seem to be at all organized and their territory markings are a bit haphazard, to say the least. I reckon we could absorb them, without too much trouble, into our own tribes.'

'Is there a library?' asked Frych-the-freckled, now pregnant for the umpteenth time by Hywel-the-bad.

'Massive one – gift from the gods.'

'Well,' she said, 'the prognosis for the future is indeed favourable . . .'

'Attics?' asked Timorous.

'Dozens of 'em – every tower has one for a start.'

'It seems ideal.'

'Cellar?' croaked Phart.

'Full of wine racks as far as the eye can see,' announced Whispersoft. 'You'll be dead of liver failure in a week, Phart.'

'What are we waiting for?' cried Treadlightly. 'Let's get our Gypsy in out of the cold!'

'Yes,' said Pedlar, 'go on. However, for myself, now that I've seen the Promised House, I shan't enter. I've led you here, my duty as pathfinder is done. You'll have to go in without me. One of you is a leader yet to emerge. I know who it is and I think the mouse in question knows who it is, but it may take a little time for the rest of you to accept it.'

The mice looked at him with stunned expressions.

'What are you saying?' cried Treadlightly.

Little Prince murmured, 'You can't mean that – you have to come with us – we need you.'

'My time with you is over, Little Prince, you know that better than anyone. You and I, we're the only ones ever to spend time behind bars. My own time was relatively short, yours was almost an eternity. However, that time spent close to the nudniks has given you a keen insight into their ways. It gave you time to think, develop a brain. You, of all the mice, have the knowledge which will enable these lost ones from the old tribes to survive . . .'

One or two mice, Treadlightly among them, understood by these words that Pedlar's chosen successor was Little Prince. If they baulked at such a transition, from Fiend to Leader, they did not say so there. They respected Pedlar's choice and there would be time enough for Little Prince to prove his worth.

'Good luck to you all,' said Pedlar. 'Whispersoft, Frych, Ulf, everyone . . .'

'Are you sure about this?' said Ulf. 'I mean, you know you're welcome.'

'Yes,' replied Pedlar. 'I'm sure, but I don't want to explain it – except to Treadlightly . . .'

Treadlightly was standing nearby looking sad.

'. . . I'm sure you understand that.'

'Of course,' replied Ulf.

'Comprehended,' Frych said.

Skrang nodded thoughtfully.

Iban said, 'An honour to have known you.'

'What?' cried Hearallthings.

Whispersoft, Nonsensical, Goingdownfast, Fallingoffthings, Ferocious, Timorous, Nesta, Mefyn and various others murmured their goodbyes. They might have been sad except that they were excited about the House of Promise.

'Doesn't seem bleedin' right,' sniffed Phart, staring at the House, 'goin' in without you.'

'I'm very touched, Phart,' replied Pedlar.

Phart turned round and wrinkled his nose, making his ugly whiskers twitch.

'Not *you* – I was talkin' to Flegm, wasn't I? Poor ole bleeder's probably just an owl's droppin' by now, but I still talk to him sometimes, like he was here.'

'Oh, I'm sorry.'

'Think nothing of it, squire,' said Phart, relenting. 'Have one on me, when you next find a keg.'

'I will,' replied Pedlar.

One by one the mice filed past Pedlar and crossed the neat lawns to the House. Finally, only Treadlightly, carrying Gypsy in her mouth, was left. She put the infant down and stared at Pedlar without saying anything at first.

Pedlar was firm. 'I must go back to the Hedgerow.'

'I know,' she said.

'I would like to have seen Gypsy grow a little, but they're soon off, aren't they? They don't need us for long, not young mice.'

'That's true,' Treadlightly replied.

'I don't think she'll miss me – not with so many other mice around.'

'No, probably not.'

'And she'll have you – you're the most important one,' Pedlar nodded.

'Yes.'

'I'll come back, some hour.'

Treadlightly shook her head. 'No you won't.'

He sighed. 'You're right – I probably won't. I'd ask you to come with me but you know, you wouldn't last a month in the Hedgerow.'

'I know,' she said.

'I'm sorry.'

'It doesn't matter – at least, what I mean is, we've had the best time. You look after yourself in the Hedgerow. Don't take any chances with those foxes.'

'No, I won't – goodbye Treadlightly.'

'Goodbye Pedlar.'

With that she took Gypsy in her mouth and scampered across the lawn, turning to look back once, before entering the Promised House. Pedlar gave a deep sigh and set his face to the North, in which direction he believed his old Hedgerow to be. He wasn't *absolutely* sure that was the right way, but there were certain signs, the sun and the moon, the prevailing wind, which might lead him to his home.

It was sad about Treadlightly and him, but he could not go into another house. He had been born a rustic and he needed to get back to his roots. The hawthorn and the blackthorn were calling him. He wanted to wake up smelling hawkweed and hedge garlic. He wanted to see next spring in with the red-tailed bumblebee, the mason wasp and the burying beetle. He wanted to make his nest under the broad-leaved dock, next to the cockchafer larva and the gatekeeper's pupa.

He would miss Treadlightly, for a few hours, just as she would miss him, but one mouse was rarely linked to another for life. They might never forget each other, but they would soon be busy with new tasks: life was too interesting to be mooning about with a head full of sentiment. Treadlightly was part of him and he was part of her. This was a fact that would go with him to the end of his hours.

The moon came out from behind a cloud and Pedlar found a ditch to use as his path.

QUARK

THE NIGHT WAS NEARING ITS END. THE OLD MOUSE named Tinker was busying himself collecting bits of fresh hay for his nest. There had been a storm in the early hours and some water had got into the burrow – nothing serious but the nest lining was damp and had to be removed. Tinker hated the extra work, but saw the need for it. His rheumatism would not let him sleep in a damp bed.

He fussed over which strands to take and which to leave, making sure there were no spiky thistle leaves in amongst the dried grass. There was nothing worse than waking up with a stabbing feeling in your back. Tinker liked his comfort in his old age. As a youngster he would have rolled over and dozed off again, but these hours once he woke it was hard to get back to sleep.

His eyes were getting a little dim now, but he found a suitable stalk and nipped it neatly at the base. Then he dragged the piece to the nest. He believed it might be his imagination, but hay stalks were getting heavier by the night.

'Where do you think *you're* going, oldster?' jeered a big yellow-neck, lounging at the entrance to the burrow.

Tinker stopped and sighed. The burrow had become overrun by a gang of young bullies. These burly micesters had rejected Hedgelore and decided they were entitled to idle away their hours, taking what they pleased from the burrow without giving anything in return. They stole food, and took the best nests, and generally made a nuisance of themselves.

'Just making my bed,' said Tinker.

'Well make it nice and comfy,' sneered the mouse, now joined by the worst of the bullies, 'we might feel inclined towards a nap soon.'

'Once we've had a good look at the daylight hours,' scoffed his companion.

It was true that they caroused well into the day, these young thugs, careless both of the noise they made and whether they were disturbing others at slumber. Just as they slept all night, when most decent mice were out foraging and nest-building. Their activities threw the burrow into disharmony and unhappiness.

Tinker returned to the surface again after depositing his piece of straw and suffered more insults while he collected another.

Halfway back to his nest, he looked along the ditch to see a lone figure stumbling under the giant nettles. The mouse, for it was definitely a mouse, seemed vaguely familiar. Tinker could have sworn it looked like his cousin, who had left the Hedgerow over 250 nights ago, to visit a distant house.

The other mouse, getting on a bit in nights by his gait, suddenly looked up and stared at Tinker.

'Is that you?' said the other mouse. 'Is that my country cousin, Tinker?'

'*Pedlar?*' said Tinker, astonished. 'I thought you were either lost or dead.'

'I think I've been one and the other's not *that* far behind.'

'Well, after me, if you don't mind,' said Tinker. 'I'm quite a bit older than you, after all.'

'You're welcome,' said Pedlar. He looked around him with weary eyes. 'Am I glad to be home!'

Tinker said excitedly, 'Did you ever get to the House? Where have you been? What's happened to you? There are stories and rumours of course – news travels along the Hedgerow – but who can believe them? I mean, they may have been spread by weasels. Come on, tell . . .'

'Oh, I got to the House of tribes all right, and that's a long story in itself. But the most astounding part was getting home, here to the Hedgerow, after I found the Promised House.'

'The Promised House? Oh, Pedlar!'

'It seems like another world now,' said Pedlar. 'You wouldn't believe the encounters I've had. I'm lucky to be alive, lucky to be in one piece. I *am* in one piece, aren't I?' He looked down at himself.

Staring at his cousin, Tinker said, 'You seem to be whole. A couple of bent whiskers. Can't see any bits missing, except maybe the tip of your tail. What happened to that? You must tell me everything – *every* little detail. Start with the House of tribes – what was it like? Full of greasy nudniks?'

'Let me get settled in. Let's go down to my old nest . . .'

Tinker laughed. 'Your old nest? That went long ago!

A doe moved in, then a buck after her. Good grief, did you think we were going to leave your chamber empty, on the off chance that you might appear on the horizon one night?'

'No,' said Pedlar, a little put out, 'no I suppose not. Well, let's go to *your* nest then. You can put me up for a few hours until I get sorted out. But first I have a ritual to perform.'

Tinker waited by the burrow while Pedlar took a mouthful of water from the ditch and went looking for the wild rosehip he had buried many nights ago on his departure. At first he couldn't find it, but then he remembered where the primrose marker-beacon was and found the spot.

To his great joy there was a shoot growing out of the Earth from the seed he had planted. This was a sure sign that he was welcome back. It was new life and meant that he, Pedlar, was responsible for one more strand in the immortal Hedgerow. He had added to the world in which he lived and one day that wild rose might be a stalwart part of the Hedge, necessary to its survival and eternal there-ness.

He deposited his mouthful of water on the new plant and then returned to Tinker.

Tinker was standing by the entrance hole, below the curlie-wurlie. There were two fat young mice lying near him, staring insolently at Pedlar. No doubt they had watched him water his wild rose shoot.

'Where d'you think you're off to, mouth-waterer?' growled the bigger of the two yellow-necks. 'Y'know, I might just go and nip off that succulent shoot for my supper. How about that?'

Pedlar looked at Tinker, whose expression told the

wandering mouse that all was not well with the burrow.

'I think,' said Pedlar pointedly, while still staring at Tinker, 'that would make me very upset.'

'Oh yeah?' said the big mouse's companion. 'And another thing. Think you can just walk into *our* burrow without so much as a by your leave—?'

Pedlar leapt swiftly, and extremely agilely for his age, and gripped the bigger mouse by the throat. The attack was so sudden the two bullies didn't realize what was happening until it was too late for them. The attacked mouse immediately rolled on his back, submissively, his eyes full of terror. Pedlar then let him go and grabbed his companion by the base of the tail, a very sensitive part of the anatomy. The mouse squealed in pain. Satisfied, Pedlar jumped back beside Tinker and surveyed the shaken bullies through narrowed eyes.

Two or three more hefty young yellow-necks had emerged from the burrow's exit hole, having caught the action, but they just stood high-nose and stared.

'The name's *Pedlar*,' said the returned hero. 'See that you remember it. I don't answer to any other. If I hear you calling me anything else you'll find I can become very upset. And I don't like being upset. Being upset upsets me even more. I'm sure you understand me.

'Another thing, that wild rose shoot is a sacred plant – we all know what happens to mice who eat sacred plants, don't we?' growled Pedlar. 'They suffer horrible dreams about what might occur if they come across the owner of that sacred plant.'

It could have been Gorm-the-old speaking.

The two shaken bullies, knowing they had escaped death or serious injury by a whisker, said nothing. They saw that this mouse Pedlar was totally unafraid of them, and since they ran the burrow on fear that meant they were upstaged. Here was a mouse to be taken at his word.

'You,' said Pedlar to the main bully, 'find another burrow. If I smell your scent round here again, I'll know you've got tired of living.'

Pedlar then shrugged his broad shoulders and turned his back saying, 'Now, we *were* going to your nest, Tinker . . .'

'How do you know they won't attack you?' whispered Tinker, 'while you're not looking.'

'Because I've scared the tails off them,' muttered Pedlar, 'and they're confused. They don't know who I am or where I come from and that's my advantage. It's nothing to do with strength and everything to do with the mystery of strangers. The big one will either leave or come to beg my pardon – in any case he's lost credibility with his gang.'

'He might decide to fight you, one to one.'

'Then he'd lose,' said Pedlar emphatically. 'And he knows it. Or at least, he thinks there's a chance he might lose, which is the same thing.'

'I'm very impressed,' said the happy Tinker. 'Very impressed.'

'Don't be, bullies are just a wearisome fact of life, Tinker. Now, the House was one thing, and the Promised House was another thing, but as for the journey back? An odyssey! Let me tell you . . . no wait, I've got to get something to eat, then some fresh straw for my side of the nest, settle in a bit – *then* I'll tell you . . .'